The Chains of Fate

Pamela Belle was born and bred in Suffolk, the daughter of a local prep school headmaster. She went to the University of Sussex, and is now teaching in Hertfordshire. *The Chains of Fate* is her second book and the sequel to her first, *The Moon in the Water*, also published by Pan.

Also by Pamela Belle
in Pan Books

The Moon in the Water

Pamela Belle

The Chains of Fate

Pan Original Pan Books London and Sydney

First published 1984 by Pan Books Ltd,
Cavaye Place, London SW10 9PG
© Pamela Belle 1984
ISBN 0 330 28208 5 (paperback)
ISBN 0 330 28472 X (hardcover)
Phototypeset by Input Typesetting Ltd, London
Printed and bound in Great Britain by
Collins, Glasgow

For the Lion, with love

Historical note

Like its predecessor *The Moon in the Water*, *The Chains of Fate* is based on fact, and save for the parts played by my fictional characters, the Herons, Sewells, Grahams and their closest connections, all the events described actually happened, including the events leading up to Montrose's invasion of Scotland, the rebellions in Essex and Suffolk in 1648, and the part played therein by the Jermyn family. Some idea of the social life in West Suffolk at the time may be glimpsed in the letters of Tom Hervey to Isabella May, and my portrayal of local characters (including the formidable Lady Penelope Gage and her dreaded bowls matches) owes much to these.

I would like to take this opportunity to thank all those people, friends and family, who helped me both with this book and its predecessor, especially the late Lt-Col. J. M. Langley, and my uncle, Noel Wilkinson, who read the typescripts and made many helpful comments and suggestions; all the library staff in Oxford, Hawick, Bury, Ipswich and Hertfordshire who found obscure books for me, some of them dangerously weighty; and last, but definitely not least, my mother, who introduced me to the Jermyns and Rushbrooke, where she had lived as a child, and who has read and re-read both books *ad nauseam* searching for blunders major and minor. Without her practical mind there would have been many more: and so all the mistakes remaining are my own.

P.D.A.B.

Contents

Synopsis of *The Moon in the Water*   11

part one

The last hero

1 The unfortunate travellers   21
2 A candle in the dark   86
3 The last good-night   115
4 Annus mirabilis   172

part two

The cruel mother

5 Returnings   219
6 Kit   275
7 Stones against the wind   305
8 Bounden duty   351

part three

A loyal sacrifice

9   Beleaguered   391
10 Homing flight   411
11 The worm in the bud   461
12 The trumpets of Heaven   488

Sir Henry (Hal) Heron (1550–1612), great-grandson of the builder of Goldhayes

married

(i) his cousin, Isobel Drakelon (1552–1570) in 1569

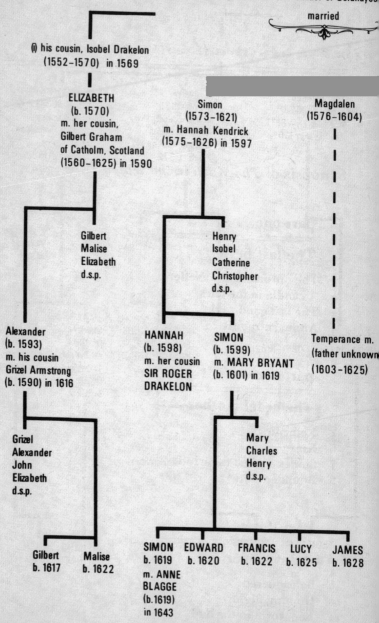

ELIZABETH
(b. 1570)
m. her cousin,
Gilbert Graham
of Catholm, Scotland
(1560–1625) in 1590

Simon
(1573–1621)
m. Hannah Kendrick
(1575–1626) in 1597

Magdalen
(1576–1604)

Gilbert
Malise
Elizabeth
d.s.p.

Henry
Isobel
Catherine
Christopher
d.s.p.

Alexander
(b. 1593)
m. his cousin
Grizel Armstrong
(b. 1590) in 1616

HANNAH
(b. 1598)
m. her cousin
SIR ROGER
DRAKELON

SIMON
(b. 1599)
m. MARY BRYANT
(b. 1601) in 1619

Temperance m.
(father unknown)
(1603–1625)

Grizel
Alexander
John
Elizabeth
d.s.p.

Mary
Charles
Henry
d.s.p.

Gilbert
b. 1617

Malise
b. 1622

SIMON
b. 1619
m. ANNE
BLAGGE
(b.1619)
in 1643

EDWARD
b. 1620

FRANCIS
b. 1622

LUCY
b. 1625

JAMES
b. 1628

Sir Christopher Heron: trader, privateer and courtier to Queen Elizabeth:

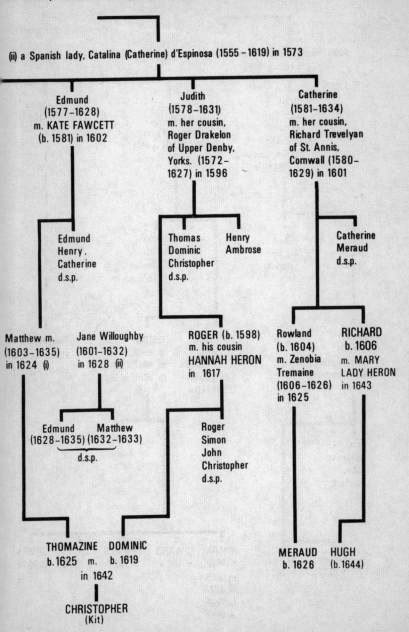

(ii) a Spanish lady, Catalina (Catherine) d'Espinosa (1555 – 1619) in 1573

Edmund
(1577 –1628)
m. KATE FAWCETT
(b. 1581) in 1602

Judith
(1578 –1631)
m. her cousin,
Roger Drakelon
of Upper Denby,
Yorks. (1572 –
1627) in 1596

Catherine
(1581 –1634)
m. her cousin,
Richard Trevelyan
of St. Annis,
Cornwall (1580 –
1629) in 1601

Edmund
Henry.
Catherine
d.s.p.

Thomas
Dominic
Christopher
d.s.p.

Henry
Ambrose

Catherine
Meraud
d.s.p.

Matthew m.
(1603 –1635)
in 1624 (i)

Jane Willoughby
(1601 –1632)
in 1628 (ii)

ROGER (b. 1598)
m. his cousin
HANNAH HERON
in 1617

Rowland
(b. 1604)
m. Zenobia
Tremaine
(1606 –1626)
in 1625

RICHARD
b. 1606
m. MARY
LADY HERON
in 1643

Edmund   Matthew
(1628 –1635) (1632 –1633)
        d.s.p.

Roger
Simon
John
Christopher
d.s.p.

THOMAZINE DOMINIC
b. 1625 m. b. 1619
        in 1642

MERAUD
b. 1626

HUGH
(b. 1644)

CHRISTOPHER
(Kit)

Synopsis of *The Moon in the Water*, the first book featuring the Herons of Goldhayes.

At the age of ten, in the year 1635, Thomazine Heron recovered from smallpox which had just killed her father and her younger brother. She was now the ward of a cousin she had never seen, Sir Simon Heron. He summoned her to his Suffolk mansion, Goldhayes, to be brought up with his five children: Simon, Edward, Francis, Lucy and Jamie. Thomazine, an independent and self-willed child, at first bitterly resented this abrupt and enforced change in her life, and was very unhappy at the prospect of leaving her stern grandmother, the only remaining close member of her family, and Ashcott, her father's Oxfordshire house to which she was now sole heiress. But the size, luxury and splendour of Goldhayes proved overwhelming after the small shabby house where she had been brought up, and her Heron cousins, although intimidating at first, soon became her friends. Two of them in particular attracted her: Lucy Heron, who was her own age and, although Thomazine's complete opposite, being a romantic dreamy little girl with her head stuffed full of stage plays, grew to be a generous and warm-hearted companion: and Lucy's brother Francis, at that time thirteen. Thomazine managed to win his admiration and friendship by her unladylike skills of acrobatics and tree-climbing: she in her turn was drawn to his difference from his brothers and sister, a rebellious, enigmatic, poetic child who longed to be free of constraints and convention. Together they dreamed of magic unicorns, a symbol of the power of imagination against the forces of cold reality, personified by Francis's upright, pedantic, self-righteous eldest brother Simon: or by the slightly disturbing, sinister presence of Dominic Drakelon, first cousin to Francis, who was staying at Goldhayes with his parents, and to whom Thomazine had found herself reluctantly betrothed by order of her guardian, Sir Simon Heron.

But almost before this friendship with Francis had begun, it was abruptly terminated. He fell foul of his father, a strict and forbidding cripple who disliked his wayward third son: and as a punishment, Francis's troublesome dog Drake was threatened with death. Fortunately, his great-aunt, Elizabeth Graham, who was visiting Goldhayes with the Drakelons, had taken a liking to boy and dog, and suggested that she take them both back to live for a time at Catholm, her son's house in Liddesdale on the Scottish Borders. Sir Simon readily agreed, and even Thomazine, although upset at this sudden separation from Francis when their friendship had scarcely begun, realized the wisdom of her Great-Aunt's decision. So Francis left Goldhayes, eager for the chance of a different, freer life: and Thomazine would not see him again for two years.

In those two years she was drawn deeper into the life of Goldhayes, and despite Francis's absence, lived very happily with her cousins and their friends, the Sewell family, from the Home Farm. The father, John Sewell, was Sir Simon's friend and ran the Goldhayes estate, and his elder son, Henry, went to Holland with Edward Heron to fight in the war there against the Spanish. There were other families whom Thomazine came to know well, but she still missed Francis and the unicorns. At last he returned, under something of a cloud, and Thomazine's delight was slightly muted when she accidentally discovered that he had been sent away from Catholm because of his dalliance with a servant girl. But although he was now a mature fifteen, and Thomazine only twelve, their friendship continued until Francis was sent away to Oxford to join his eldest brother Simon. The hardworking, priggish Simon bitterly resented his wild younger brother's success at the University, and the seeds of his obsessive hatred of Francis were sown. Thomazine, distressed, tried to mend matters. She was helped by the return of Henry Sewell and Edward Heron after two years on the Continent, the former bringing with him his pregnant young Irish wife, Grainne (pronounced Grarnya), who became Thomazine's great friend.

The next few years saw changes at Goldhayes. The ill-feeling between Francis and Simon smouldered on, fuelled by the former's taunts and the latter's jealousy. Grainne had her baby, a boy named Jasper, and another was soon expected. Sir Simon Heron died, after a long illness that had done nothing to lessen the tension between his first and third sons, and his deathbed was the occasion for yet another quarrel between them. Shortly afterwards, a distant cousin died in Cornwall, willing the guardianship of his only daughter, Meraud Trevelyan, to Simon.

Meraud duly arrived at Goldhayes, in the spring of 1641. She was at that time fifteen, a year younger than Lucy and Thomazine, and so bewitchingly lovely with her fair hair and angelic blue eyes that almost everyone was enchanted, particularly young Jamie Heron, who at the age of thirteen discovered calf-love. But her beauty did not impress Thomazine, nor her apparent sweetness and piety: and Francis shared her mistrust, although he appeared to assume that her motive was jealousy. Thomazine's bewilderment at the complex emotions around her and within her was at last resolved by a riding accident in the park at Goldhayes, and Francis, in his concern for her, revealed at last that he loved her. His declaration brought Thomazine to the realization that she loved him too, and all her doubts and fears were melted away in her happiness. But problems remained: although Francis, for her sake, apologized to Simon for his unpleasantness towards him, their instinctive feeling was to keep their love secret for the moment, more particularly since Thomazine was still bound by her six-year betrothal to her cousin Dominic Drakelon.

Their precarious secret was kept from Simon, though not from his romantic sister Lucy, nor from Edward and Grainne. That summer, 1641, was a very happy one, although Meraud's uncle, Richard Trevelyan, who had up until then been a Puritan dissident, arrived at Goldhayes with tidings of probable civil war: he had been intimately concerned with the King's opponents in London, but now dissociated himself from them. Thomazine and Francis distrusted his motives, but Simon welcomed him with open arms, and he stayed at Goldhayes until war actually broke out in the summer of 1642. By this time, Simon placed so much confidence in Richard that he made him one of the trustees to look after Goldhayes while he and the troop of horse he had raised went off to fight for the King. Amongst the officers of the troop were Edward and Francis Heron, and Henry Sewell. Grainne, now encumbered with her two children, Jasper and the baby Hester, insisted on accompanying her husband Henry, and Thomazine suggested that she, Meraud, Lucy, Jamie, Grainne and the children should be placed for safety at Ashcott, her childhood home, which was a fortified manor-house and far more defensible than gracious Goldhayes. The troop eventually arrived at Ashcott, finding it decrepit and neglected: Henry Sewell broke a leg in a riding accident and had to be left there to recover: and Thomazine's intimate farewell to Francis on the hillside above the house was disturbed by Meraud, who seemed to be storing her knowledge of their love for further use.

Simon, Francis, Edward and the troop rode away to join the King, and Henry, despite his injury, ensured that the house and the tiny garrison left by Simon were put in order. However, he was killed two months later, helping Royalists to storm the nearby town of Banbury, leaving Grainne a widow with two orphaned children and a third expected in January. His death removed the only competent soldier in their garrison and, seriously worried about their safety, Thomazine went to seek help from the approaching Royalist army. She and young Jamie, who insisted on going with her, found it eventually, just after the battle of Edgehill had been fought. They located Simon's troop only to find that both Edward and Francis were missing. Shortly afterwards, Francis rode up, wounded, and bearing the unconscious body of Holofernes Greenwood, one of the Suffolk troopers, whose sister Heppy was Thomazine's and Lucy's maid. He announced that he had left Edward's body on the battlefield, and in his rage and grief Simon accused Francis of looting and drunkenness, despite the fact that his condition was due rather to loss of blood. Although deep down his resentment remained, he was brought at last to see reason by Francis's collapse. Thomazine achieved her wish, and five lightly-wounded men were assigned to Ashcott's garrison, amongst them Francis, who made a temporary recovery, and was placed in command.

They had hardly returned to Ashcott when it was attacked by Parliament forces from Banbury. A siege followed: the gun which Henry had mounted on the ramparts blew up, killing three men, but a greater tragedy happened when a petard was placed on the gate and its explosion killed Grainne's little daughter Hester, who had strayed into the courtyard. Grainne and Thomazine were too late to save her, and were stranded between the Parliament men and the defenders of Ashcott: only Francis's timely surrender snatched them from certain death in the crossfire. The house was now in the hands of the leader of the Roundhead forces, Captain Daniel Ashley, a kind and honourable man who let them all go free. Thomazine led her friends and the remaining soldiers to her house at Pennyfarthing Street in Oxford, presided over by the Widow Gooch. Once there, Francis collapsed with a high fever, his life despaired of: while he was ill Simon came to the house, enraged by his brother's 'cowardly' surrender of Ashcott. Unsatisfied by Thomazine's explanation of the facts behind Francis's capitulation, he left, promising a final reckoning.

Francis recovered slowly, nursed by the Widow, and he and Thomazine at last made no secret of their love for one another. At the end of November 1642, one of the Ashcott garrison, Charles Lawrence, held a birthday party at Pennyfarthing Street, and Thomazine and

Francis announced that they would be married as soon as possible. The celebrations were rudely interrupted by Simon, inflamed with disgust and fury at what he considered to be his brother's licentious behaviour. Meraud 'accidentally' let slip that Thomazine and Francis were, as she thought, lovers. The prudish Simon then attacked Francis, who managed to escape him and fled into the night. Recognizing that Simon's insane hatred would not permit him to marry Thomazine, Francis sent her a secret message, arranging to meet one night and run away to Catholm, where they would be safe from pursuit and free to marry. But the note was found by Meraud, who betrayed the plan to Simon. He was waiting for them at the arranged place: Francis was captured and flung into prison to await trial for his surrender of Ashcott, and Thomazine was forced to receive the attentions of of her betrothed cousin, Dominic Drakelon, who had come to Oxford with the King's army. In desperation Francis attempted to escape from his prison in Oxford Castle: he was shot by a sentry, fell into the river, and in a dream Thomazine, so she believed, shared his death.

The tragedy brought Simon to his senses. He repented bitterly of the mad rage and jealousy that had been the cause of his brother's death, but it would not bring Francis back to life. Dazed with grief, Thomazine married Dominic, and was soon expecting a child: but she could not bring herself to love or even to like her overwhelming husband, who was jealous of her friends and even of Francis's old dog, Drake, who had attached himself to her. During one of Dominic's petulant absences, Lucy recognized Captain Daniel Ashley amongst prisoners brought to Oxford, and insisted on bringing the sick Roundhead back to Pennyfarthing Street to nurse him back to health. She and Dan fell in love, although their opposing politics would have seemed to doom the affair from the start. Lucy was heartbroken when he was exchanged and returned to London.

Then Mistress Gooch, who had long had her suspicions, received confirmation that Francis was not in fact dead: he had escaped drowning, and recovered in secret at the house of an acquaintance of the Widow's, on the river bank. Thomazine learned to her horror that her husband had traced him there, and had told him that she had renounced his love and had agreed to marry Dominic for his lands, wealth and title. Francis at last had been compelled to believe Dominic when he showed him the marriage-licence, and in bitterness and anger had left Oxford. Thomazine, although overjoyed to find he was alive, felt nothing but loathing for her husband and bitterly regretted her marriage and the coming child. In an attempt to find out where Francis had gone, she wrote to her Great-Aunt Elizabeth Graham at Catholm, where they had once planned to elope, asking if he was there. While she waited for the reply, news came that Lady Heron, his mother, was to marry Richard Trevelyan at Goldhayes, and Simon announced that he was also to be married. His intended bride was to be Nan Blagge, the daughter of a Suffolk neighbour and one of the Queen's waiting-women in Oxford: although this had long been expected, Meraud was most upset by the news and revealed to Thomazine, in an unguarded moment, that she loved Simon and that her betrayals of Thomazine and Francis had been intended to put herself in his favour. Thomazine could only feel that she had received her just deserts.

Then, early in August 1643, the Earl of Montrose brought her a letter from Great-Aunt Elizabeth Graham, who was his distant kin by marriage. It contained the news that Francis was indeed at Catholm, uncommunicative but obviously unhappy. Great-Aunt had also copied out a poem which displayed in full measure his anger and bitterness at Thomazine's supposed betrayal. The emotional shock of the letter brought on the premature birth of her baby, a boy whom she named Christopher. In the aftermath of the birth she tried to decide whether she could abandon her husband and child and friends, her home, wealth and inheritance to go north to Francis. For some weeks she was caught on the horns of dilemma, unable to bring herself to desert her baby: for she knew that if she were to take him with her, Dominic would never rest until he had regained posession of his longed-for son and heir. The balance was finally tipped by her discovery of another poem on the back of her Great-Aunt's letter, a sonnet remembering the magic of the unicorns. At last, she made her decision, and together with Grainne and her children, Jasper and the baby Henrietta, and Holly Greenwood for their protection, and Francis's beloved horse Hobgoblin and his dog Drake, set out from Oxford on the long and perilous journey to the north, Catholm, and Francis.

part one

The last hero

He either fears his fates too much,
Or his deserts are small,
That puts it not unto the touch
To win or lose it all.
                (The Marquis of Montrose)

Chapter 1

The unfortunate travellers

Oh Western Wind, when wilt thou blow,
That the small rain down can rain?
Oh, Christ, that my true love were in my arms,
And I in my own bed again.

                                        (Traditional)

I had thought my true love to be dead; and so I had married a man I hated.

So close were my cousin and my lover Francis Heron and I, that I had known of his death before I was told of it; in my dreams that terrible night in December 1642, I had shared the moment when, a sentry's bullet in his body, he had been flung into the chill winter waters of the river round Oxford Castle, and was lost.

As I was also lost, for his attempted escape from the Castle had been a desperate, hopeless bid to reach me, to spirit me away north to a haven where we could be free to marry, to fulfil at last the powerful desires and passions which had held us enchanted for two years of peace and civil war. I was bereft of Francis, my soul's companion, and of the love that bound us; and therefore as incomplete as one half of a map, a song without music, a traveller struck dumb in a land full of strangers. Believing him dead, numb and uncaring of my future, dazed with grief, I married Sir Dominic Drakelon, my vivid, dashing, compelling cousin who had been my betrothed for seven years, since I was ten. And thus, without really thinking of the consequences, gave up my old, independent, self-willed identity, Thomazine Heron, heiress to the house called Ashcott in Oxfordshire and many lands besides: to become Lady Drakelon, the chattel and possession of a man I did not even like very much.

Soon after my marriage I came to loathe him; for too late, tied to him by the chains of matrimony and, more significantly, our unborn child, I was told the truth. Dominic had concealed from me the fact that Francis was not dead, but alive, and in Scotland. He had also told Francis with triumphant glee of my marriage, and so my lover believed me false and fickle, ready to cast away my feelings for a poverty-stricken third son with no prospects in favour of Dominic's wealth and title. And I deserted my husband and my baby son Kit, and began the long journey north, through an England ravaged by a year of civil war, to bring him the truth.

As my dreams had once carried his death to me, so much were our minds in tune, so now, on that long, arduous and terrible journey, my thoughts fled northwards each night, and each night I dreamed the same dream: our reunion.

I had never seen Catholm, the grim Scots Border tower that belonged to our Graham cousins: but Francis knew it well, for he had spent two very happy years of his childhood there, and Malise Graham was his great friend. So in my dream the house was indistinct, a grey bleak blur amongst threatening bare hills: and although my travelling companions were with me, they had no place in my dream. All my being, my eyes, ears, every sense of brain and heart were focussed on the road ahead, and the man standing there.

He was tall, slender, with an unconscious, casual grace that touched every movement that he made, and would have marked him out to me in the furthest corner of the earth. His pale, ash-fair hair had distinguished him always as different amongst his three dark brothers and his sister Lucy: as apart from them in his looks as in his temperament. Francis, with his complicated, quicksilver nature, his love of music and laughter and freedom, could not have resembled his self-righteous, humourless, dutiful elder brother Simon less, save, fatally, in one respect: their stubbornness. Francis would not bend his neck to his brother and meekly submit to being the sober, godly lawyer it was intended he should become; and neither would Simon allow him to live his own life, to follow his own rules and heart and desires – to marry me.

He could not marry me now, for I was tied to Dominic Drakelon until death should part us: but Francis's thoughts had always been firmly rooted in the earthly present rather than in nebulous future threats or promises of the hereafter, and I doubted that he would be much inhibited by the sin of adultery. Such was my love and desire for him that I had at last defied the pressures upon me to be a good, conventional, dutiful wife to my despised, treacherous, deceitful husband Dominic, and was willing likewise to risk the flames of Hell and torment for my love's sake.

In my dream, I came nearer, so that I could see his face at last, the face I had last seen so many months ago, bruised and unconscious, on the night Simon had had him flung into the Castle for trying to elope with me. How well I remembered that thin pale face, cast in the long Heron mould, with the far-spaced eyes and flexible, humorous mouth, an expression misleadingly, mockingly perfect, like a mischievous and anarchic fallen angel. He did not smile, but his eyes, that familiar, strange, shadowy green, coloured and changeable like the sea, seemed to have a life of their own in his still, clear face, and burned with delight into my soul. And suddenly I could not move any further: my bones turned to water by my love and desire, and my joy that at last we were together again, and for ever more.

'Hello,' he said, always, and the gentle, loving mockery in his voice barely disguised the depth of feeling beneath. 'What in God's name are you doing here, owd gal?'

At his use of the Suffolk endearment, I knew that all must be well, and yet I could not project my overwhelming love into my words. 'I came to find you,' I said each time, hesitantly. 'I thought you were dead, and they persuaded me to marry Dominic; and I grieved so much for you that I did not care whom I married, until too late.'

'But you care now,' Francis said. 'You cared enough to leave him, and go through danger and hardship to find me again; and so you are forgiven.'

'And here, despite everything, I am,' I said foolishly, each time: never daring to mention the baby I had left behind in Oxford, little Kit Drakelon, a month-old infant I had tried not to love, for I had feared from his birth that I would have to abandon him. I knew full well that Dominic would never have allowed me to remove his longed-for, most precious son and heir, and would undoubtedly have pursued me to the ends of the earth had I done so. I would not mention Kit now: there would be time for that later, when I was certain. Nor would I mention the poem that Great-Aunt Elizabeth Graham had copied and sent to me, the bitter, cruel poem that Francis had written, revealing all too clearly the extent of the hurt I had unwittingly, unwillingly done him. But there had been another poem in her letter, a sonnet possessed of such truth and beauty that the balance was tipped and I had realized, reading it, that whatever the perils of the journey, however great the risk of humiliation and rejection at the end of it all, I must leave husband, child, friends, wealth, safety in Oxford, burn all my bridges behind me for the sake of this self-contained, enigmatic, strange young man who stood before me now in my dream, on the road to Catholm. And because of that sonnet, I added softly, breathing life into our stiff and stilted talk, 'Remember the Unicorns – do you still remember the Unicorns that we created in our minds when we were children, the summer I came to Goldhayes and met you all for the first time? The Unicorns all made of "water and light and ice and fire", you said? Do you carry them still, in your heart?'

'For ever,' he said simply: and I knew that the memory of that day still held us both enchanted, far away and long ago at Goldhayes, the jewel-like, lovely Suffolk house that was home and heart and lodestar to every Heron. The remembered magic prompted me to quote his own words to him, part of that sonnet which I knew by heart. ' "The moon, that in the darken'd water dwells, Is't that which danceth in the sky by night? And does the Unicorn exist?" '

'Oh, it exists,' said Francis, 'how could you doubt it? And one day, my dear brave lady, one day I shall bring you a Unicorn's horn for our chamber, when we are wed.' And for the first time he smiled, vivid and loving and real: and held out his hands. 'Welcome to Catholm, my own dear love: and may we never more be parted.'

And each time I dreamed that I walked forward to reach him, to feel again the light deft touch of his hands, and the kiss that would melt my soul and blot out the sun: and yet somehow, no matter how fast I moved, my feet stood still and I could not touch him: his slight, smiling, mocking figure vanishing back down the road beyond my reach, still with his hands outstretched, forever welcoming but never, ever to be caught and held close.

It was then, always, that I woke, weeping with the most terrible and desperate sense of loss; for although I had set out on the long journey with high heart and hopes, knowing that Francis was worth more to me than all the other people I valued, yet secretly I dreaded my arrival at Catholm. I feared above all else that the poem, which warned me that 'should we chance to meet, some bitter day, My heart, beware', would prove a truer mirror of his feelings towards me than the sonnet. I had been admitted, long ago, to his private world, a dazzling enchanted place inhabited by dragons and Unicorns and other fantastical creatures of his strange imagination, and all coloured and surrounded by the music we both loved, lute and flageolet, virginals and viol, the dances of Dowland and the songs of the people: and now, I knew, I could not bear the pain, should I come to Catholm, riding up to the gates like some long-lost lover in an old ballad, and find them barred to me, and his love turned to the kind of malicious cruelty I knew he could employ towards those who had betrayed him, as my dream had betrayed me.

So I could not hide my tears on waking and, inevitably, Grainne soon realized what happened each night at the beginning of our journey. Not only was she by nature blessed with an uncanny perception into the thoughts and feelings of others, she had also been my dear and close friend and confidante since the day, five years before, when she had come into our lives and hearts as the young Irish bride of Henry Sewell, the friend of Francis's elder brother Edward who had been so tragically, uselessly cut down by a Parliamentary bullet at Edgehill Fight. Her calm, smiling strength and wisdom had supported all of the Herons through grief and stress, though she herself had lost husband and baby daughter in the war. Unasked, she had insisted on accompanying me on my journey to Francis, despite the danger to herself and to her two surviving children, four-year-old Jasper and the posthumous baby Henrietta, and I had never felt I truly deserved such unthinking, unselfish friendship. So, on the first two nights of the journey, I succeeded in concealing my tears from her; but on the third occasion, as I tried desperately to muffle my sobs in the pillow, I felt her gentle hand on my shoulder, and her soft Irish voice, whispering so as not to wake the children: 'Thomazine! Oh, Thomazine, what is it? Did you have a nightmare?'

When I had first known the power Francis held even over my dreams, when my nightmare had contained not his mockery of welcome, but his death, it had been his sister Lucy, who was also like a sister to me, who had woken me, whose curious, insistent, overwhelming sympathy had failed entirely to penetrate my grief. Now, I was glad of Grainne's unseen company, her understanding and intelligence very different from Lucy's romantic, impetuous nature: and felt no doubts about unburdening myself to her, as so often before. For

Grainne, too, had lost the man she loved, and had known sorrow and despair.

So I said, shakily, trying to control my voice, 'No, not a nightmare . . . except at the end, perhaps. I dreamed of Francis, I've dreamed of him every night since we left Oxford . . . I dream we meet again but . . . but we can never touch . . . and oh, Grainne, I am so afraid it will all come to nothing, and he will not want me any more!'

In the dark, her fingers found my face and proffered a kerchief, doubtless used earlier to mop Henrietta's infant tears. I scrubbed furiously at my eyes and nose, glad of her presence and yet also ashamed that I should need her yet again. Grainne said, her voice invisibly encouraging in the thick darkness behind the bed-curtains, 'What was that poem by Shakespeare, that you always quoted to each other? "Let me not to the marriage of true minds Admit impediments"? You have had to contend with Simon's hatred, with the misfortunes of war, with death and betrayal: and above all with Meraud, though precious little good did all her treachery do her, she should have known that Simon would always be honour and duty bound to marry Nan Blagge, for all Meraud's charm and beauty.'

The charm and beauty of a viper, I thought. Meraud Trevelyan, a cousin of the Herons, was a little younger than I, and like me was Simon's ward. Unlike me, however, she was enchantingly, delicately lovely, a fair and fragile blonde whose sleek silver-gilt curls concealed a selfish, ruthless and scheming brain. She had long and secretly harboured an unrequited passion for Simon (or for Goldhayes, which was his), and in an attempt to creep into his favour, had betrayed to him my plans to elope with Francis. From that treachery had followed directly Francis's imprisonment in Oxford Castle, his supposed death, and my marriage with Dominic. All my woes could, with justification, be laid at her door: and I was very glad to know that she was behind me, in Oxford, and that I was free of her prying, cold, assessing blue eyes.

'You no longer have any of those in your way,' said Grainne softly, consideringly. 'Your love has been strong enough to overcome all these obstacles; you have sacrificed your husband, your son, your home, all your friends save me, and I don't doubt you would have left me behind in Oxford too if I hadn't offered freely to come with you.'

'I didn't want to put anyone else in hazard,' I muttered. 'And besides, there was Holly.' Holofernes Greenwood, a staunch young Suffolk farmer, was our groom and escort. 'You had no need to come – not with the children.'

'But *you* had the need for me to come with you,' Grainne pointed out equably: and although I could not see her face, I could tell that she was smiling. 'And since I am now, to my grief, a lone woman once more, I can do as I please – and it did not please me to contemplate a picture of you, on your own or with Holly, setting off for Scotland. So I am here – are you glad of it?'

'You don't need to ask that – of course I am, more than glad – and I have a feeling that I shall need you a great deal over the next few weeks. Especially . . . I might . . . at Catholm.'

'Your love is strong enough, that's what I was trying to tell you – why should you think that his love has changed?'

I swallowed painfully, reluctant even now to bring out into the open my secret terror. In the end, I muttered, 'That letter that Great-Aunt sent to me, telling me that he was at Catholm . . . it said he was angry, and bitter, and spent all his time drinking and whoring in Carlisle . . . he hadn't told her anything of what had happened in Oxford, it wasn't until she had my letter that she understood *why* he was behaving so strangely . . . and also, she sent me a poem. She sent me *two* poems; one was about the Unicorns, and beautiful . . . and the other showed what he thought about me.'

I had no need to elaborate. Somehow – she seemed able to see like a cat in the dark – Grainne's hand found mine, and squeezed it gently. 'But when he hears the truth from you, discovers what you have given up for his sake, *then*, I am sure, he will find that nothing has really altered, nothing in you, or in him.'

'In the dream, he forgives me, it all seems so easy and natural and *right* that he does so, and I believe in the truth and reality of it, it all seems so plain . . . but if I believe that part of the dream, with all my hopes fulfilled, then I have to believe in the bad part too, the moment when I realize that I will never ever catch him, and it seems as if he's betrayed me, just as I once betrayed him.'

'Think of the first part of your dream coming true, the meeting and the welcome and the love . . . the second part belongs to nightmare, and is no part of reality. Hold to that thought,' said Grainne, 'and you will win through in the end.'

'Yes,' I whispered, sliding down beside her in the luxurious nest of the feather bed we shared, and closing my eyes. Part of my dream was reality, perhaps . . . and after the nightmare when I had known Francis's supposed death, I believed implicitly in the power and truth of dreams. But which would come true in the end, the welcome or the rejection? Which face of my many-sided, complicated Francis would I see, the cruel jester or the gentle, passionate lover? Only when I reached Catholm would I know; and Catholm was a long way distant, and would prove much further than I imagined.

It happened a few days later, near a tiny town in Staffordshire called Stone. We had now been a week or so in travelling and our progress, though slow because of the children carried on our horses, the bad weather and my uncertain state of health so soon after Kit's birth, had up until now been steady. Our little procession – Grainne on her sway-backed old mare, Holly riding a huge feather-heeled brute and leading the old white cob that carried our baggage, myself on Francis's lovely black Arabian mare Hobgoblin with his disreputable dog Drake in eager attendance, and Henrietta in a basket slung from her mother's saddle and Jasper riding with each of us in turn – plodded on northwards through rain and mist and, occasionally, sunshine, and I day-dreamed of Francis, vivid and bright in my mind, and was glad that after my talk with Grainne, his living ghost no longer disturbed my nights and overturned my reality. Waking, I could guide my mind into sunnier paths, and avoid the dark shadows of foreboding which seemed to lurk at the end of every train of thought.

Then we lost our way, in fog so thick we could not discern the edges of the road, and blundered on through the eerie diminished landscape in the hope of coming upon some habitation and finding out where we were. But it was not until the fog was clearing, to give way to beautiful autumn sunshine, that we could find someone to tell us what road we were on: and it was the road to Nantwich, meaning that very soon after leaving Stone we had taken a left fork rather than carry straight on towards Newcastle-under-Lyme. It was too late now to make for Newcastle that day, so we thanked our amused informant and pressed on, in the still afternoon sunlight, with a tang to the air that promised more fog that night. To keep up our spirits Grainne proposed a song: it was one we all knew well, a soldiering ditty often bawled in Oxford alehouses, and we sang with gusto:

> Of all the brave birds that ever I see,
> The owl is the fairest in her degree:
> For all day long she sits in a tree,
> And when the night comes away flies she.

'Too whit, too whoo, too whit, too whoo,' Jasper hooted loudly to my instruction. Holly continued, his voice somewhere between a croak and a shout, with the second verse, one not at all suitable for female singers:

> This song is well-sung, I make you a vow,
> And he is a knave that drinketh now.
> Nose, nose, nose, nose,

And who gave thee that jolly red nose?
Cinnamon and ginger, nutmeg and cloves,
That's what gave me this jolly red nose!

His voice died away on the last note. We had rounded a bend in the road and there, coming at a brisk trot towards us, was a substantial body of soldiers. There was no room for us both to pass, so we took the course of prudence and reined our horses in to the side of the road. The troop, however, halted raggedly in obedience to their leader's shout, and gradually and ominously their horses sidled towards us, blocking our way. I stared at them, seeing greedy, rapacious, assessing eyes, lingering on the packs slung over the Widow Gooch's white cob, on our horses, on Grainne's remote and lovely face and on my slender neat figure and cloudy dark hair: and on my mount Hobgoblin, small and black and beautiful, a horse for any cavalry captain to covet.

There were perhaps twenty or more troopers, all well-armed. I clenched my hands on the reins. Jasper's white tense face stared at them: despite his love of all things military, some childish intuition had informed him that those soldiers were to be feared. Their leader's eyes were small and glistening. He swept off his hat. 'Good day to you, ladies! May I ask where you are going?'

It had to be me to give the answers, for Grainne's Irish-accented voice was, as we had found more than once on our journey, the signal for hostility from many ordinary people, let alone possible soldiers of the Parliament, to whom Irish was synonymous with Papist. My mouth had gone suddenly dry, and l swallowed convulsively. On my wits, I suspected with horror, and none of the bravado that had once buoyed me up at Ashcott when faced by unfriendly soldiers, depended our possessions and quite possibly the safety of us all. 'We make for Nantwich, sir,' I said in a croak I hardly recognized, 'and we're anxious to reach it before dark.'

'You live in Nantwich, Mistress?'

There was a Parliament garrison there: best to tell the

truth, I realized, or as near to it as prudent. 'No, sir, it is but a stop on our journey to Carlisle. We had not expected to be on this road, but in the fog this morning we lost our way.'

'To Carlisle? For what purpose do you visit Carlisle?' the captain asked softly, and his hand played gently with the fine-wrought hilt of his sword. The troopers' horses shifted a little bit closer, and Jasper suddenly found one of my hands with his own and clutched as much of it as he could reach.

'We go to visit a cousin of mine, sir,' I improvised hastily. 'She has been recently widowed and has now fallen grievously sick. I and my friend Mistress Sewell, who is also a widow, will give her aid and comfort, and help to care for her poor fatherless children. Is there any harm in that, sir?' I asked ingenuously, eyes open and shining with what I hoped was innocence.

'Carlisle, Mistress, happens to be a hotbed of malignancy! And I have heard it said that the Cavaliers are in the habit of employing ladies to spy for them and take messages across the country without suspicion. How am I to know, madam, that you have not some Royal command hidden on your person?'

A low lascivious snigger arose from some of his men. I said, trying to be as reasonable as I could, 'I can assure you, sir, that I have not, nor have my friends. And I beg you, sir, to let us past and into Nantwich without further hindrance. The children are sorely tired from their long journey today.'

'I have only your word for it, madam,' said the captain. He urged his horse closer to us, and his hand shot out suddenly to stab at Jasper. 'You, brat! What place did you lie last night?'

Jasper started almost imperceptibly to shake – I could feel the tremors running through his small stiff body, pressed close to mine. I could also sense his unthinking defiance, and gave him a little pat. 'Go on, Jasper, you know where it was.'

It seemed an age before his small voice said flatly, 'Stone.'

'Where are your manners, brat? You should address your elders in the proper way. "Sir", you will call me, understand?'

Jasper's shaking grew worse; his mouth shut tight in a thin line, he stared defiantly at the captain. 'For God's sake, sir,' I said indignantly, 'he's but a child not five years old! Have you no thought for him?'

The captain ignored me. He reached out and with a flick of the loop of his reins whipped the small boy lightly across the face. 'Where did you live, brat? Where have you ridden from?'

Jasper did not move at all, though I could feel the tension building up in him as the horrible ordeal went on. Nor, beyond a sudden intake of breath, did he flinch from the blow. And before I could stop him, he said, very stiff and clear in a voice loaded with fear and hatred, 'I won't tell you!'

'Then your mother can tell me, or I'll mark your face for life,' said the captain, and carelessly began to draw his sword from the scabbard. Feeling sick and faint with my anger, I said, 'That's not necessary. We have ridden from Coventry, and I can assure you that when we do finally reach Nantwich I shall waste no time in letting your colonel know all about this outrageous assault.'

'You'll get no joy from him, madam, I can promise you. Coventry, eh? A fine godly place, by all accounts, and so if you are inclined to our way of thinking you will not object should we relieve you of that fine horse you have. It's wasted as a lady's ride, believe me, and Sir William Brereton might even be persuaded to offer you a small sum as recompense for your generous gift to his forces. Would you be so kind as to dismount, madam?' The words were courteous enough, but his voice held a sly, insolent menace that finally shattered my temper. Hardly able to believe what he was so blatantly demanding, I said furiously, 'You must be out of your mind to think I'd meekly hand over my horse to you and your pack of villains! By God, this is nothing better than highway robbery, and even footpads don't usually have the bare-faced audacity to try it in broad daylight not two miles out of town!'

'You had better dismount, madam, I warn you, or it will be the worse for you and your friends. You would not wish the children hurt, would you? I can assure you, you are being most unwise to defy us.'

I gently reined the restive Hobgoblin backwards. There was somewhere behind me a ditch, a low bank and then an open field, soggy with the spoiled half-rotten harvest. My blood was up now, and not for anyone would I have given away Francis's beloved Arabian mare to a captain who was no more than a horse-thief. As I was nerving myself to escape, thinking foolishly that it might draw them away from the others, Holly entered the fray. His normally placid face reddened with anger, he kicked his big bay gelding into the space between me and the captain. 'I reckon as we've had enough of your bullying, *Captain*, and we in't a-going to give in to you that easy!' And before my horrified gaze, dragged out one of the heavy horse-pistols in the saddle-holsters and levelled it at my tormentor.

The world erupted. Something exploded with a roar and a bullet sang past Hobgoblin's nose. Someone cried out, and Henrietta screamed. My mare reared up in fright as another pistol went off. All was a confusion of kicking, heaving, jostling men and horses as I clung desperately to my seat and to Jasper. The captain made a lunge for Goblin's bridle and Holly, roaring curses, hurled his horse to block him. Another shot crashed nearby, and Goblin plunged wildly: I heard Grainne's voice shrieking 'Jasper!' as he clutched frantically at my sleeve, and then he was gone, slid kicking and sobbing with terror underneath the mare's lashing hooves. I did not even stop to think: I freed my legs of pommel and stirrup and dived after him. He was curled up in a tight ball on the ground, between Goblin's trampling legs, and I snatched him from under the horse and pulled him back with me, desperately trying to get as far away as possible from the danger. Suddenly the ground fell away from beneath me and I landed with a soggy splash on my back in the stagnant water and rank nettles of the ditch, Jasper on top of me. A second later, a horse's bulk darkened the sky, a rhythmic thudding assaulted my ears and I had a brief glimpse of black belly and brown girth-strap and shining hooves, as Hobgoblin, riderless, leapt the bank and galloped away to freedom across the field.

I lay there on my back in the ditch, dazed and dizzy with shock, still clutching Jasper tightly to my breast. Suddenly, I realized that what I had taken to be the sound of Hobgoblin's retreating hooves was in actual fact the noise made by a much larger body. With difficulty, I struggled to a sitting position, whispering incoherently to Jasper, who was still whimpering and rigid with fright, and stared straight into Grainne's white distraught face. 'Thomazine! Oh, thank God, I thought you were dead.'

'It takes more than that to kill me,' I told her weakly. Jasper, hearing his mother's voice, turned his head and saw her. All at once his self-control, so long and bravely held, shattered like brittle glass: he gave a muffled sob and hurled himself into her arms. Above his weeping head, Grainne said, 'They've gone. Holly – Holly's hurt, go to Holly.'

I struggled out of the ditch, soaking and smelling highly. The road was empty. Five horses stood aimlessly about, nosing at grass or bushes: three of ours, and two cavalry mounts. On the ground, sprawled in the mud, lay the casualties of Holly's rash action – the captain of the troop, one of his men, and Holly himself. He was the only one to show any sign of life, though groaning would have been inaudible in the thick of Henrietta's frantic howls. My first thought to stop the noise, I ran over to Grainne's horse and lifted her out of the basket. She was wet, dribbling in the extravagance of her grief, and quite scarlet in the face. When I held her close, philosophically ignoring her unsavoury state, her screams died away into convulsive hiccups.

'I'll take her,' said Grainne. She came up to me, her poise recovered, and relieved me of the baby. 'You look after her for me, sweeting?'

Jasper took his thumb out of his mouth and gave her a watery smile. 'Yes, mamma, I'll look after her.'

We left the children in a tear-stained huddle by the roadside, and went to Holly. He was attempting to sit up, but weakness got the better of him. The other two men were either dead or unconscious, and I did not intend to waste much sympathy on them. With a sudden sinking feeling of despair and anger and horror, I saw that Holly's old russet doublet was soaked and darkly stained all over his right shoulder, and that his hand clutching the wound with cramped stiff fingers was running, dripping scarlet.

'We must stop the blood,' Grainne said, 'quick, your petticoats and mine should do it.' She pulled up the heavy voluminous folds of her riding-habit skirts, and untied the petticoats beneath without a thought for modesty. I did likewise: then we somehow got Holly out of the mud, on to a patch of grass and unlaced his doublet. A bullet had gone clean through his shoulder, and blood was pouring out. Grainne made pad after pad of tightly-folded lawn and holland, pressing each against the wound and holding it there until it grew soaked and rank and red with Holly's blood. His breath came in shallow ragged gasps, his face was chalk-white and his skin cold and clammy to the touch. I found myself whispering, 'Oh, Holly, don't die, please don't die.'

'I don't fare to be a-dying jest yet,' Holly whispered with untypical optimism. At the same instant Grainne said, 'Thank God, it's slowing.'

I had not thought one body could squander so much blood and still live. The grass around was soaked with it, little trickles and pools leaking into the earth. Grainne made a final pad, pressed it in place, tore up the last petticoat into strips, and bound it tight. 'There, that should do until we can find a surgeon.'

'And a bonesetter,' Holly muttered, his eyes closed. 'I reckon as my arm's broke. I fell off that horse awkward-like, and that hurt like merry hell.'

'How are we going to get him on to a horse?' I whispered, drawing back. 'For Christ's sake, what are we going to do? Where did the rest of the troop go? What happens if they come back?'

'They went back to Nantwich,' Grainne said. 'They turned and fled when the captain fell. I don't think Holly shot him, he was hit by one of his own men by mistake. The other one fell off his horse, I think, and the rest took fright at what they'd done. Or else they've gone for reinforcements.'

'Against us? Two women and two tiny children and a wounded man?' I laughed weakly. Grainne said slowly, 'Or they've gone to put about some tale of being set upon by wicked Cavaliers to cover their shame, and give the lie to any story we could put about.' She knelt by the captain and turned him over on to his back. He was dead, no doubt about it, the small greedy cruel eyes glaring blankly at the sky, and a neat bullet-hole marring his forehead. The trooper had been luckier: he appeared to be merely stunned by his fall, with a big blood-stained lump on the back of his head. Neither of the men had been wearing pot-helmets, luckily for us.

'Be this your horse, Mistress?'

We whipped round. Standing at the edge of the field was Hobgoblin, sidling and restless, and holding her bridle a small, barefoot girl of about nine or ten years old. She gave us a broad grin, and added, 'Be they Brereton's men?'

'Yes, it's my horse, and they are Brereton's – or were,' I said. The child's sharp grey eyes took in the scene, the bloodstains and the children and loose horses and sprawled bodies, and then said, 'Tryin' to steal your horse, was they, Mistress?'

'They were indeed,' I said, 'and thank you for bringing her back.'

'She be a nice horse,' said the child. 'Nice an' gentle. What's wrong wi' him?' A jerk of the head indicated Holly.

'He tried to protect us when the soldiers threatened us,' said Grainne. 'And got a broken arm and a bullet through his shoulder for it. Can you tell us of a place where we can take him before those villains come back?'

The girl frowned. 'Tain't no good takin' him into Nantwich. There's a mort o' soldiers there, makin' trouble, fightin' an' thievin' things. They'd string him up for murder most like. But me Mam'd have you.'

'Your mother . . .' I said dubiously. The girl went on enthusiastically. 'Our farm's over there, behind those trees. She'd have you, and look after him, she's good wi' simples and bonesetting and that, is me Mam. And since me Da's bin away to the War we've bin terrible shorthanded, there's only me and me brother Robin and me Mam and Old Harry.' Her eyes grew bright as her idea took hold. 'We could hide you from the soldiers if they came looking, we've got a fine big barn . . . Come on, Mistress, afore they come back!'

Somehow the three of us got Holly, white-lipped with pain and loss of blood, on to his horse. We caught Grainne's mare and the white cob, and replaced Henrietta in her basket, and collected Drake from the hedgerow whence he had ignominiously fled, and then, leaving the dead captain and the unconscious trooper with their horses in the road, set out across the fields towards the child's farm. She told us, in her blunt cheerful chatter, that she was eleven years old, and her name was Jennet Morrison. Her brother Robin was fifteen, and attempting just as Holly had once done to run the farm in the absence of his father, save that Jennet's Da was not dead but away at the wars, a sergeant in Sir Edward Fitton's Foot. I was not at all sure that Mistress Morrison would be so hospitable in these uncertain times, despite Jennet's confidence in her generosity:

especially as harbouring this particular party of refugees might well incur the wrath of Sir William Brereton's Horse. But I need not have worried. At first sight of the tall, stout smiling woman at the door of her farmhouse, my forebodings eased, and when Jennet had poured out the whole story in her enthusiastic staccato sentences, she at once took competent charge. Holly was helped down from his mountain of a horse, and managed to get inside the house before succumbing finally to pain and loss of blood and fainting clean away. The four of us somehow, puffing, carried him up the narrow stairs of the stone-built farmhouse and into a spare bedchamber. Mistress Morrison had her daughter fetch dressings and bowls and water and a pair of stout stakes and twine, and while Robin, a tall shy boy with his sister's fair hair and his mother's warm brown eyes, stabled and unsaddled and fed our horses, and looked after the children, we worked quickly to set Holly's arm and change the makeshift dressings before he came to himself.

'He'll live,' said Mistress Morrison at last, binding the splints firmly to the broken arm. It had been a clean simple break, relatively easy to mend, and even the strain and effort of getting on to and off his horse had not seriously started the shoulder bleeding afresh. 'But it'll take a couple of months before he'll be able to ride, I'd say.' She looked kindly at Grainne and me, standing relieved and suddenly exhausted by the bed, and added, 'I daresay Jennet's bespoke a bed for you already, Mistress Heron, Mistress Sewell, but I'll welcome you on me own account. Those men of Brereton's be a right menace, especially to them who don't favour the Roundheads. They're always here, levying this and that, taking our crops and cutting our timber and thieving our cattle without so much as a by-your-leave and making us buy 'em back at market, and all because my John's a soldier for the King. That's the trouble, o' course, so many round here, gentry and all, have gone away to fight there's none left for our protection and Brereton's band of robbers can do what they please, and none to gainsay them. Before they came, we used to go into Nantwich market every Saturday, with things to buy and sell, and now we ain't got the money to buy nor the corn and cheese to sell; the bastards even took the unripe green cheeses, and I pray nightly it gives 'em gut-rot! So we're not as rich as we were, but we're not poor neither, and you're welcome to share it for as long as you need.'

We could not possibly travel on until Holly's arm and shoulder were mended and so, despite my impatience at the delay, I had perforce to accept it. And in truth, during that autumn, I came to enjoy our sojourn at the Morrison farm; a strange and almost idyllic interlude in my restless life. While Holly recuperated under the watchful eye of Agnes Morrison, feeding resentfully upon nourishing broths and egg custards, Grainne and I assisted Jennet and Robin in the farm and the dairy, helping to milk those cows still yielding, to make butter and cream and the sweet crumbly cheeses for which Nantwich was so justly famous: and Drake was confined to the farmyard as unofficial watch-dog. Our fears about being sought out by the soldiers who had threatened us proved groundless, for although troopers came every week to the farm to demand levy, or excise, or whatever was currently the polite euphemism for their extortions, there was no search, no hue-and-cry, and we saw no one who would have been able to recognize us. Mistress Morrison discovered during her next visit to Nantwich that it had been put about that the dead captain, whose name was Pritchard, had been foully murdered by a company of wicked malignant Cavaliers, doubtless Irish in origin, who were said to be terrorizing parts of Cheshire: this tale presumably was felt to have a more heroic ring to it than the truth.

In this quiet backwater, news of the country at large filtered through fitfully and much delayed. We heard of the lifting of the siege of Gloucester, and of the battle at Newbury, which saw the death of so many brave men on either side, Lord Falkland in particular: and I prayed that none of those I knew had suffered the same fate, for as Prince Rupert had been present at the battle, so also must have been Simon and his Suffolk troop. Away from the main armies there was a fight at Winceby, My Lord of Newcastle's siege of Parliamentarian Hull was abandoned, Sir William Brereton captured Wrexham: and Sir John Byron, veteran of Newbury, Edgehill and the man who had made himself so unpopular at Oxford in the first days of the war by pulling down Botley Bridge, was sent north to assume command of the depressed Cheshire Royalists. With men from regiments who had recently landed in Chester after the truce in Ireland, he was to form a new army.

Brereton's men had been disliked enough in Nantwich and round about: but Byron and the Irish were a different matter. They outnumbered Brereton, were more experienced, and as a rule more ruthless. Unpleasant stories began to circulate as Byron's men started to clear the county of Parliamentary soldiers, and Grainne and I began to realize that a farm two miles outside Nantwich was not, after all, the quiet isolated little backwater it had promised to be.

But we could not go without Holly, and Holly's injuries were slow to mend. He was weak from loss of blood, and feverish, for two or three weeks after our brush with the soldiers, and just as we thought him on the way to recovery, an infection developed in his shoulder. The Nantwich surgeon was brought out, and re-opened the wound to recover shreds of cloth that he said had caused the trouble. It was not enough, however, to prevent Holly from suffering a relapse, with a high fever which lasted almost a week. By the time he was well enough to be escorted downstairs to Agnes's comfortable parlour, it lacked two weeks to Christmas, and the weather was turning bitterly cold. The cows were huddled together in the fields, frost blighted the last vegetables in Agnes Morrison's garden, poor cold Drake was allowed into the house at nights for shelter, and Grainne and I discovered that the garments we had brought with us were inadequate against the winter – especially as we only had left two under-petticoats each to our name. Jasper, too, was fast growing out of his baby skirts, and in early December we went into Nantwich, well cloaked and hooded against recognition, and managed to purchase three bolts of humble russets, a deep dark green, a warm brown and the other of mulberry. The long dark evenings by the cheery fire in the parlour, with smoky tallow candles that made my eyes smart until I grew used to them, were then spent in making ourselves warm winter dresses, with a proper boy's suit, breeches and doublet, for Jasper out of the brown. And each night we lay, Grainne and I, in the bed that had been Jennet's (she shared now with her mother), with Jasper in the little truckle bed at its foot, and Hen in her cradle, and listened to the chill north wind singing evilly around the chimneys, promising frost and snow and further delay. And each night, as the pigeon returns to its home, so also did my thoughts fly ever to Francis, though I never dreamed that bitter-sweet dream of welcome again: to wonder whether he was safe, and if he thought at all of me. Again and again my vivid memory summoned scenes from our past lives to cheer and to hearten me: the lovely high swooping sound of his little flageolet, or an image of his long, sensitive fingers playing so exactly, yet with such fire, upon his lute, and the dark tuneful notes of his voice singing the songs we both loved, songs by Byrd or Dowland, and humbler airs which owned no known composer but tradition; quoting the words of Shakespeare to me, in love and mockery – 'My mistress's eyes are nothing like the sun' – or, in utter seriousness, speaking the lines of the sonnet that was a true reflection of our feelings for each other, and which had come to seem so tragically apposite over the years of our separation: 'Let me not to the marriage of true minds Admit impediments'.

But true though our minds were, joined heart and

body and soul like two halves of a book, or a painting, there had been too many impediments. My memory avoided those, in my sleeping and waking reveries recalling only the many moments of happiness, with no reality to intrude upon our dreaming: and sometimes also presented to me a vision of the future, bright and vivid and perfect in the darkness behind my eyes, a picture of the reunion we might have. I imagined the joy and delight I would bring him, and his face when he discovered that I was after all true to him, and had rejected my false husband, and the child I had tried not to love, and braved the dangers of wartorn England to be with him. I could not let myself approach the abyss of any less delightful meeting: that way, as Lear had said, lay madness.

It was those dreams that kept me from impatience, and depression, and futile raging against the fate that imprisoned us here. Not once did I dare to consider any other possibility, my face was turned resolutely from the thought that he might even be dead or, the nightmare that had haunted me in Oxford, so estranged from me by my supposed treachery that he would reject me, and retreat within that armour of cynical indifference I knew of old, which few shafts could penetrate. I could not bear to contemplate any such eventuality again: for I had paid my price for him, I had given away my child, and my husband, and my home and friends to have him, and without him I would be nothing, my life would hold no purpose, no meaning, no direction. As Meraud had once said to me, with a truth that, much as I disliked her, I had to admit, a lover dead but true was preferable to one living who had spurned all advances.

I had thought, if the weather did not break, that we might be able to leave before Christmas: but I was proved wrong. Although Holly mended well, and the days though bitter cold withheld the threatened snow, it was the war which intruded to prevent our going. Sir John, now Lord Byron, and his newly-formed Irish army had since early November made great progress against the Parliament men in Cheshire. Gradually, Brereton's forces were pushed in towards Nantwich as their garrisons were overcome one by one: until by the second week in December, only Nantwich was left. Brereton himself was elsewhere, trying to organize help from Yorkshire, and his troops, under the command of Colonel Sir George Booth, poured into the town and commenced to fortify it as best they could. There were some rudimentary earthworks already thrown up: more were constructed, barricades erected, and provisions brought in for the expected siege. The Morrison farm was one of the many visited by a detachment of urgent troopers who threatened to fire the roof over our heads if they were not instantly supplied with almost all the food we had. Fortunately, a large part of the winter supplies, the casks of salt meat, the tuns of beer, the butter and cheese and honey and hams and sacks of grain and barrels of flour, had been well hidden in a cunningly partitioned-off portion of the cellar. But they took away a dozen fine fat geese, their cackling and hissing stilled for ever by wrung necks, some fodder and whatever was in the larder, all in Agnes's prized light cart. The horses, the dairy cattle and goats, had been hidden in the nearby copse with Jennet, who had instructions to send them galloping to all points of the compass if soldiers approached. When they had gone with their booty, we sat back in relief, grateful that we appeared to have escaped so lightly, and even managed a joke or two about the animals and provisions moved so abruptly and hastily in and out of hiding.

The next day, Lord Byron's men came. We had no warning this time: the first we knew of their arrival was Drake's hysterical barking outside, and we tumbled out of barn and stable and dairy to face a menacing group of Byron's horses filling the farmyard.

'Are you the tenant of this farm?' demanded their captain of Agnes: and with a deferential curtsey she told him that her husband was, but he was absent, fighting for the King. At this news their manner became a trifle less intimidating: the villainous-looking captain, with a scar across his face to rival Byron's own, even smiled a fraction. 'Then you will understand our necessity, Mistress. We are by the orders of Lord Byron, the general of our forces, to besiege the Roundheads in Nantwich, and we shall require quarters for our troops in all the farms and villages around until the town can be taken. You have a fine barn and stabling, which could be put to good use aiding the King's cause in Cheshire, and doubtless you will not object to quartering a dozen of our fine fellows until Nantwich is reduced?' He smiled again, showing discoloured teeth: and despite his seeming geniality, and the courtesy of his words, it was very obvious that to protest would be most unwise. Agnes curtseyed again, and lying in her teeth said that no, of course, she had no objection.

So twelve of Byron's 'Irish' soldiers were foisted on us, great uncouth men for the most part, though the young corporal in charge of them was at first pleasant enough. They were in actual fact no more Irish than I was, hailing from the Midland Shires, and objected strongly to that epithet. The character of the Irish war had brutalized them; though Agnes laboured long and unwillingly to feed them with what she had, things were forever being pilfered, hens disappeared with monotonous regularity, and they cheerfully chopped down several of her precious apple trees for firewood. Their eyes, greedily assessing in the same manner as Brereton's captain on the road outside Nantwich, followed us everywhere: and after it became obvious that they had recognized Grainne's Irish accent, so that shouts of 'Irish bitch' or worse, and obscene suggestions, greeted her whenever she went out of doors, Mistress Morrison and I made sure that she was never left alone. But I was less careful of myself, and the outcome of that omission was far from pleasant.

I had gone, one cold December day a week or so from Christmas, to the stables with apples for the horses: a luxury we could ill spare, though these fruits lay shrivelled and brown in my apron, the worst of a poor season's crop. But I was glad of a chance to escape the chilly comfortless farmhouse with its poor apology for a kitchen fire, Grainne's white strained face and Jennet's chilblained fingers struggling with spindle or churn, and even Mistress Morrison's false cheerfulness as she prepared the scanty meal: and to take refuge for a while in the warm stables, sharply aromatic with the smell of horse.

The Widow Gooch's old white cob slobbered up his apple with ungrateful greed and returned to searching his manger in a desultory way for the oats we no longer had: Grainne's ugly mare took her meagre morsel with enthusiasm, and Holly's feather-legged unwieldy animal nearly had my thumb as well for good measure. The two big farm horses snatched their apples from my hand almost before I had raised it to their noses: and then I wiped my slimy wet palm on a hank of clean straw and turned to the beautiful Hobgoblin, kept in the furthest, darkest corner of the stables out of the notice of Byron's acquisitive and ruthless men. Francis loved her as he loved Drake, and so both horse and dog were my charge: but I would have loved her too in any case, for her sweet black head with the small enquiring ears and wise dark eyes and fine ridges of bone sweeping down to the flared nostrils, soft and smooth as ebony velvet, her fine close-coupled neat body and swift strong supple legs and feet and proudly carried plumed tail. She and Francis had had an understanding uncanny to anyone not used to the close companionship of an intelligent horse or dog: and now, rubbing her nose as she took the mouldering apple as if it were a gift of rare delicacy, I felt a similar empathy between us. 'Not long now, my lady,' I whispered to those neat attentive ears that flicked and turned to catch the sound of my voice, 'wait till the cold goes and the soldiers go and then we'll leave for Catholm and you'll see Francis again.'

Under my hand the warm nose ducked and pushed up as if in agreement, and I laughed softly and wryly, remembering how lightly and cheerfully I had set out on this journey from Oxford to attain my heart's desire; a journey only meant to last a month that had already taken three times that long, and we were not a fifth of the way there. All my energy had been turned towards reaching that momentous decision to leave Oxford in the first place: I had not given a thought to the dangers that we might encounter on the way, nor considered that I might put my companions in great hazard, for my sake and for Francis. Yet, despite the war, and the hardships and terrors and trials we had faced and, I suspected, had yet to face before we finally reached Catholm; despite these, had I been able to look into the future on the morning I made my choice to leave all my safe security and venture into the unknown, I would still have ridden away: for the sake of a dream, a hope, a vision of future happiness that was far more real to me than my everyday, workaday, briar-full world.

And so I stood there, resting my cold weary body against Goblin's smooth dark warmth in the dim stables, absently stroking her neck and running my fingers through the long silky strands of her mane, and dreaming of what I longed for most, which was Francis: riding Goblin with that characteristic, casual, cat-like grace, flinging a hawk from his fist in the gentle, green Suffolk countryside around Goldhayes and watching its pursuit of pigeon or partridge with the same sharp vivid eagerness as the bird; or discussing politics or warfare or horses with his brother Edward, reliable, solid and knowledgeable, two brothers quite dissimilar in looks and temperament, and yet with a remarkably deep, unadmitted friendship. And that friendship surely, had Ned survived Edgehill, would have prevented that final disastrous rift between Francis and Simon. I clenched my hands on Hobgoblin's mane and squeezed the tears behind my tight-closed eyes, as my desperate longing for Francis, for his warmth and humour and the knowledge that he loved and wanted and needed me, and no other, threatened to overwhelm me completely.

Goblin flung up her head and turned abruptly, almost knocking me over. Suddenly snatched from my reverie, my eyes snapped open in the gloom and, staring, beheld one of Byron's men, a lean and ill-favoured youth I had previously noted to be one of the rottenmost apples in a particularly unpleasant barrel, standing not two or three yards from me.

His eyes lingered on me in a way which lifted the hairs on my neck: and I became suddenly very frightened indeed. Were I to scream with all the breath in my lungs, no one likely to help me would be within earshot, and it was all too likely that the soldiers summoned by my cries would want to participate, too, in the rape I saw writ plain on that pocked and leering face.

'Hello,' said the soldier, in a soft insinuating lecherous whine. 'Look what I've found here, all alone and no one to hear . . . come here, my pretty sweetheart, and let's have a bit o' fun while no one's about, eh?'

He was blocking my route to the stable door and safety. I said nothing, my eyes and mind frantically searching, desperately seeking escape. 'Come on,' said the horrible, sneering slimy voice, 'there's no call to be so uppish, I know the likes of you, all hoity toity to them what's lower and a whore once you get them on their backs, you fine ladies are all the same . . . Come on, if you don't struggle I won't hurt you, and I ain't had no complaints yet.'

'Probably because they've never known any better, poor things,' I snapped back, a flash of temper overcoming my fear. I had seen something that gave me a sliver of hope, a pitchfork stabbed into a pile of filthy straw a yard or so behind my tormentor: but I was allowed no chance to snatch at it. The man's slow brain had worked out the implications of my foolish taunt, and before I could move he pounced. With terror I felt his arms lock about me and gasped as his hot stinking breath assailed my nostrils before his wet loose mouth came down upon mine: and then fury gripped me, cold and calculating. My mouth shut tight against his assault,

I relaxed for a second and then, with all my strength, kicked him hard upon the shin with my stoutly-shod foot.

It must have hurt not a little: he swore, staggered back, and slackened his hold. I followed that blow with another, to a far more tender and vulnerable part of his anatomy, and as he released me and doubled up, retching, I whipped the pitchfork from its pile of straw and held it firmly braced in front of me like a pike, the narrow vicious tines pointed steadily at his stomach. 'Try that again and I swear I'll kill you!'

Gasping, scarlet, his sweating face raised itself suddenly into view, contorted with frustration and rage. 'You filthy little bitch, I'll get you for this, I'll cut you to ribbons, we'll all have you one after the other and when we've finished with you – ah!'

Sick with disgust and fury, I could tolerate his obscenities no longer, and jabbed him savagely with the tines. 'And I'll tell your corporal every word of what you've just said, you foul-mouthed rapist, and since my cousin is a good friend to Lord Byron, you'll not hear the last of it, I can tell you. Go on, back – get back!'

Blustering, he slunk backwards, and at every step I prodded him with the pitchfork, not particularly caring how hard I did it. Brought up short by the wall, he stood glaring balefully at me. Then the anger all drained abruptly out of him as he read the intention in my face. With a vicious and overwhelming sense of satisfaction, I let him see that I was enjoying his fear: and then, choosing my spot carefully, stabbed the pitchfork savagely so that the prongs entered the wooden wall of the stable, one each side of his dirty scrofulous neck. One tine slashed his skin, I was glad to see: and then I left pitchfork and tormentor quivering alike against the wall, and fled from the stables.

I was sick into the midden, and sick again by the kitchen door: I staggered in through it, shut it with a desperate force as if all the Furies were outside, and, leaning against it, burst helplessly into tears: all my fury vanished in the shock and weakness of reaction. Fear also made me weep, for I knew how dreadfully close I had been, in my loathing and rage and terror, to killing him.

Grainne and Mistress Morrison offered their bewildered comfort, and when I had mastered myself and explained what had happened to overturn me thus, they were united in their outrage and indignation.

'I'd not have had your delicacy, Thomazine,' said Agnes grimly, 'I'd have pinned him to the wall *through* his gullet instead of either side of it. And now I reckon we'd best go and tell your tale to the corporal before he hears t'other side of it.'

And so we made an aggrieved and purposeful delegation to the young corporal, fortunately finding him dicing in the barn before my assailant could track him down: and the thinly-disguised sneer on his face when I began my tale vanished, I was pleased to see, when I made mention of Lord Byron, and my cousin's acquaintance with him. Whether complaints to his Lordship would ever have had any result, I doubted very much, but the mere threat of it was sufficient to ensure that we remained comparatively unmolested, so much was their general feared. And my tormentor was punished by a vigorous flogging.

But even if my waking self attempted, with some success, to push my unpleasant experience to the furthest corners of my mind, my dreams all too often reminded me of how horrifyingly narrow had been my escape, and I would wake sweating and shaking with my terror at the fates which had almost befallen me, the one only a little worse than the other: to be raped, or in self-defence to resort to murder. I too had learned my lesson, and from thence none of us, from 'Old Harry', a slow old man in his late sixties, down to the scampering Jasper, ever ventured out-of-doors unaccompanied. It was plain that without our support and help, and the solid presence of the convalescent Holly, it would go ill with Agnes and her little family: and that in itself was an excellent reason for further delaying our departure, had it not been made quite clear to us that, friends in high places or no, we were all virtually prisoners within the bounds of the farm, lest we in any way aid the besieged garrison or attempt to convey intelligence to any attacking force. By Christmas I was frantic to be gone, to continue this journey that I had undertaken so casually: never thinking once of the dangers of war that had overtaken us, never thinking of the peril and anguish caused to Grainne because she was Irish, or the responsibilities placed upon Holly as our protector, or the risks to the health and happiness of the children. I felt guilty now, on my companions' behalf, and knew, none better, how we were balanced on the slenderest of knife-edges. One false move, one rash deed, and we would find ourselves ravished or plundered or with our throats cut, as had so dreadfully happened to a group of hostile civilians, some no more than children, in Bartholmey church at Christmas. If Byron's men could stoop thus low, they were quite capable of inflicting harm on us: and though they fought for the King, I was beginning to hate them.

The siege dragged on. The weather turned colder still, and the River Weaver froze over. Our Christmas was chill and cheerless, with a scanty fire and precious little feasting, although we sang and made merry for the children's sake, and turned Jasper's breeching into an extra celebration. The soldiers had consumed far more than their share of our food, without the slightest intention of reimbursement, and with besieged Nantwich and its market closed to us, times were lean. Every day the cows and horses had to be tended and fed, food prepared, and wool spun and carded with our blue chilblained fingers. Snow fell thickly, and for a week nothing moved anywhere save for the frozen cattle in the field nearest the farmhouse, subsisting on hay and straw and what they could dig from under the snow. Lying packed in the one bed for warmth with Grainne and the children, and shivering despite the blankets and quilts piled on top of us, I began to realize what it was like to be poor, and cold, and hungry; to understand the insecurity and terror visited upon anyone without an assured, regular supply of food during such a winter as this; and to know that if matters went on as they did, there would come a point next week, or next month, when there would be no bread, nothing to give the children, and we would all starve.

Despite the weather, an attack on Nantwich was launched on the eighteenth of January, and repulsed by the stalwart defenders. Byron's men suffered some losses: only seven of our twelve uninvited guests returned the next day, my attacker happily not amongst them, and for the sake of the fretful, hungry children we were grateful. But further deliverance was at hand, for Sir Thomas Fairfax, Black Tom, was said to be marching to the relief of Nantwich: and for the first time in my life, I prayed for the success of the Parliament men, almost as hard as I prayed for our deliverance from any involvement in the fighting.

An abrupt thaw on the night of the twenty-fourth of January heralded the arrival of Fairfax's army. Our soldiers were hastily summoned to join their regiment in the small hours: they marched out in the softening, damp air through snow that clung wetly and soggily to their shoes, and clogged the horses' hooves, and we were free at last. It was as if a black shroud had been lifted from our lives: we listened keenly all day for the sounds of battle, and were rewarded in the afternoon by the flat distant thuds of gunfire.

It was not until the next day that we discovered what had happened, how in the thaw the River Weaver had flooded, hurling down bridges and cutting off Byron's cavalry on the east bank from his Foot on the west. Fairfax was thus able to concentrate on attacking the Royalist Foot, with the help of Brereton's men who had sallied forth from Nantwich to take their enemies in the rear, whilst holding off Byron's Horse with a small detachment. By dusk it was all over, the Royalist Foot dead or prisoners, and the Horse fled with Byron to Chester. Good generalship on the Parliament side, despite Fairfax's rag-tag-and-bobtail army collected from all over the North, had triumphed over bad luck and tactical error.

With a strange mixture of eagerness and reluctance, we began to make our plans for departure. Reluctance on my part at least, because despite my overwhelming need to be with Francis again, to salve my bruised, exhausted mind and body in the balm of his need and love and laughter, leaving Nantwich to continue our journey to Catholm was the final commitment, after my three-month's respite, to the sin of adultery and the crime of abandoning my child.

I would not admit then, even to myself, that I was afraid of what might be waiting for me, at the end of our long road to Catholm.

There were tears on both sides as we said our farewells one chilly damp dawn in late February – for the sudden thaw had brought heavy rain and flooding that had delayed our departure two weeks past the day we had originally intended. I had earlier tried to press upon Agnes some payment for our stay, but she indignantly waved it aside. 'Money? No, Thomazine, I don't want no money. The way you helped us all, and kept those villains from our throats, that's payment if it was needed.' I was touched and, despite her strong feelings, left on the clothes-press in the chamber Grainne and I had shared, the ring that Dominic had given me on our marriage. The dark heavy gold glinted sullenly against the black-stained oak, the menacing dragon's head crest of the Drakelons delineated only fitfully by the dim early morning light, and I reminded myself of what Dominic had done, and went out of the room with no sense of betrayal.

As on the first half of our journey in September, everything now seemed to conspire against us to slow us down, so that a Puritan would instantly have seen obvious signs of God's displeasure at the sinful purpose of my travels. Rain fell frequently, the roads were thick glutinous mud well-nigh impassable even for a horse, and floods were commonplace. Drake ran on ahead of us, as was his habit, and once, out of sight, fell into a water-filled pothole that must have been four foot deep, and nearly drowned before we reached him. It became obvious that, despite his long convalescence, Holly was by no means fully restored to health: probably the lack of nourishing food and sufficient warmth and rest at the farm had delayed his recovery. Typically, he plodded stoically on, ignoring the warning signs of returning illness, and after five days' travel in appalling weather, collapsed with a fever. Fortunately, we were able to get him to a reputable inn not too far away, and after a week's nursing he appeared to be returned to his normal robust health. With weary thankfulness we resumed our journey, so slow and so much beset by misfortunes. I had thought that nothing could be worse now than the disasters we had already endured, but still bad luck and inclement weather bedevilled our progress, so that we made on average barely seven or eight miles in any one day. Grainne's mare developed an inability to keep her shoes, and cast four on successive days, so that most of them were spent hunting for blacksmiths. We were accosted by soldiers in Lancashire, who fortunately were deceived by Hobgoblin's bedraggled ungroomed appearance and demanded only to know our business and destination before letting us continue, and by footpads in the Kent valley, a half-dozen miles before we entered Kendal. Holly drove these off easily enough, for they were armed only with cudgels and were obviously not expecting to face pistols, but we were further delayed by the necessity of finding a Justice in Kendal, to whom we had to deliver a groaning footpad with Holly's bullet in his arm. It would have been easier to have left the man on the ground by the roadside, but the day was ending and he would not have survived the frozen night: and I did not want anything else to weigh down my burdened conscience. So we spent two days in Kendal, a bustling wool town amidst the grim fells, and then continued on our way.

By now the road was no more than a rough, stony, treacherous track worn by the packhorses that were the only means of transport in these parts. It wound between the huge endless bulks of the great fells: bisected by rushing chilly streams, frequently obliterated by piles of rocks and boulders that had fallen in the winter's frosts and gales, or vanishing in a sudden slough of green moss or mud like a young lake, formed from rain and melted snow. Frequently we had to dismount and lead our exhausted stumbling mounts through or around such obstacles: our pathetic little procession, three adults, two children, four horses and a dog, toiling wearily up and round and down and along the endless road. We seemed utterly dwarfed by the enormous rocky hills, the highest mountains I had yet seen, incomparably grander and more threatening, with their heather and scree and boulders and streaked patches of old snow, than the green gentle hills of Oxfordshire or Suffolk. Those twenty-odd miles between Kendal and Penrith were the longest and most wearisome that ever I had travelled: expecting a village, a farm, a friendly face around each corner of the road, and seeing only more of this apparently endless, dreary desolation. Three days we spent on that dreadful track, and just as, at long last, we toiled gratefully into Penrith by the last light of the sinking sun, I discovered that Hobgoblin had gone lame.

It was to be expected, given the nature of the appalling conditions we had endured, but it was nevertheless a most bitter blow. Had it been one of the other horses thus afflicted, we could perhaps have sold it and purchased another, but not Hobgoblin. As we bespoke rooms in one of the town's inns, I wondered in despair whether we were ever going to reach Catholm. In two weeks' time, impossible though it seemed, it would be April, though as spring came late to this chill bleak inhospitable country there were few signs of it other than frail shy snowdrops and catkins, and daffodil spikes in sheltered places.

The only cure for Goblin's strained off-fore was rest, and we had perforce to stay in Penrith until she was sound again. It was the largest town in those parts, situated in a valley between wooded hills, and beside Oxford seemed little more than a sizeable village. There was nothing to do save sit in our chamber and stare out of the window: for throughout our stay, or so it seemed, it poured with rain. Worry about our dwindling store of coin, hidden in a money-belt I wore round my waist beneath my petticoats, added to our other anxieties, and I, depressed and exhausted by the rigours of our journey, became shamefully bad-tempered and impossible. Grainne did her best to cheer me, and the children and Drake were a great help. It was here that Henrietta decided to heave herself off all fours and stood and took steps for the first time; and here that Jasper made his greatest strides in learning to read, using a crudely-printed chap-book Grainne had bought from a pedlar. But despite these diversions, and the walks we took around the town and along the river when the rain cleared, the days crawled past. At long last, however, after the slowest fortnight I have ever experienced, Hobgoblin was pronounced sound and fully recovered by the ostler of our inn, who had been tending her daily with poultices and liniments, and had lovingly restored her to her former spectacular glossy beauty. And so on the third day of April, seven months after we had left Oxford, we set out on the last lap of our journey.

As we rode out of the town, a ruffianly band of soldiers were gathered in the Market Square, their young officer addressing a motley crowd of Penrith folk: and my interest quickened at once, for we had been hearing vague reports for the last week that Montrose was in Cumberland, raising the militia for an invasion of Scotland. But the officer was not Montrose, of course, though his voice as he read My Lord Newcastle's Commission of Array held the same Scots intonation. Reluctantly, as though the soldiers were in some way a link with Francis, I tore myself away and we took the road for Carlisle.

We reached the city the following afternoon, and rode in under the huge twin-towered citadel known as the English Gate, passing by the soldiers on guard-duty without question: and enquired of the first respectable passer-by we saw, where a decent bed might be had for the night.

The reply was almost unintelligible. Grainne and I looked at each other, and Jasper said in his penetrating voice, '*What* did that man say, Mamma?' Fortunately, the worthy citizen had a sense of humour: amidst his chuckles he told us of the best inn in Carlisle, 'But it's verra dear, Mistress,' and of one slightly cheaper and not nearly so palatial. We decided without thought on the more expensive one, for surely by this time tomorrow we would be at Catholm?

So close it was now, and I looked at small, grim, decaying Carlisle with fresh eyes. For certain, Francis knew these narrow, cobbled dirty streets, had ridden and walked them, had (bearing in mind the unwelcome information given to me in the letter I had received in Oxford from my Great-Aunt Elizabeth at Catholm) visited the squalid alehouses and taverns which seemed to proliferate here. There was of course a garrison, Royalist, and I wondered if My Lord of Montrose, who had brought Elizabeth Graham's letter to me, was within the town, or elsewhere in Cumberland raising his army. And I began to look at every young man with fair hair, with a mixture of hope and fear, in case I should see Francis.

But I did not, and we duly arrived, desperately tired but elated at being so near to our goal, at the recommended hostelry and ordered two chambers, one for us and one for Holly, stabling for our horses, a hearty supper and provisions for the next day's journey. The landlady herself brought our food up to the low-ceilinged, comfortable little bedchamber, and displayed a friendly interest in us. When she heard of our destination, her round sleepy brown eyes grew larger still. 'Liddesdale! Are you *sure* that's the place you want, Mistress?'

'It is,' I said, 'we're visiting cousins there.'

'Well, I don't know,' said the landlady. 'Yon place has a very bad name. Fifty years ago you'd have dared enter it only with an army at your back; infested from end to end with thieves and murderers of the worst sort it was. Of course, they hanged a lot of them after the Union, and it's peaceable enough now, but there's still thieves and robbers about, Mistress, and I wouldn't have thought it wise to go there without a guide at least.'

'Oh, no!' I said, despairingly, for this seemed like yet another intolerable and frustrating delay in our apparently never-to-be-ended journey. 'Are you sure? We were told it was quite safe . . .'

'Begging your pardon, Mistress, but that may have been true a half-dozen years ago, not now. Times are bad, the gentry go off to fight for King or Parliament, there's no one to keep order or check the robbers, and all the soldiers are cooped up in Carlisle waiting for My Lord of Montrose to lead them into Scotland, and God alone knows what trouble *that* will bring. The Scots Army is over the Tweed, they say, and the harvest was bad last year, and all in all folk have got to live, and more often than not in these parts they do what their fathers and grandfathers did, which is take to thieving. So you see, Mistress, it *isn't* safe, it's twenty miles or more from here, and after this rain we've had you won't be going fast, and there are mosses, floods, burns that can trap you if you don't know the road. Yes, Mistress, you need a guide.'

'Well, do you know of anybody?' Grainne asked, and the landlady said slowly, 'There's a gentleman downstairs from those parts, come in on business. I know him, he'll see you safely to your cousins as long as he's sober – I wouldn't trust him with his own mother, drunk. He's the only one I can think of who might be able to take you there tomorrow.'

It did not sound a very safe idea, to go with this unknown and distinctly unreliable-sounding 'gentleman', but my impatience was getting the better of my natural prudence. Despite Grainne's dubious look, I said instantly, 'Is he below? Might we talk with him about it?'

'He's in my back parlour with my Johnnie, they often play cards together,' said the landlady. 'If you would like to come down, I'll tell him you wish to speak with him.'

So Grainne and I stood at the door of the landlady's back parlour and waited while she ascertained that our prospective guide was in a fit state to receive us. Then she ushered us into a small, cosy room with a cheerful fire and a large table, covered with a red turkey carpet, at which two young men sat, with cards and a pile of money in front of each. 'Mistress Heron and Mistress Sewell wish to discuss the matter of a guide with you, sir,' she said, curtseyed, and went out.

The two young men rose and bowed, removing their hats. One was obviously the landlady's son Johnnie, sharing her brown eyes and large, clumsy build. The other was not so tall, and though as yet probably only in his mid-twenties, already inclined to stoutness. Despite this, he was a very good-looking man, with long curling hair of a most unusual shade of deep beech-red, a curved jutting nose and rather prominent blue-grey eyes. His high colour rather spoiled the effect: it owed something to an excess of wind and sun on a fair skin, and more I guessed to a surfeit of strong liquor; he appeared to be sober, however. With a gallant smile, he said, his voice strongly Scots, 'Gilbert Graham at your service, ladies. May I be of assistance to you?'

I stared in astonishment, for a Gilbert Graham was Great-Aunt Elizabeth's grandson, elder brother of Francis's boyhood friend Malise. Now the thought had been implanted, I could see the likeness to Elizabeth Graham, in the high-bridged imperious nose and peaked eyebrows, and most of all in the red hair which had once, judging by her portrait still at Goldhayes and made when she was young, been her greatest beauty. I glanced at Grainne, seeing her look of startled enquiry, and then, wondering if I was about to make a fool of myself, said, 'Yes, I believe you can, Cousin Gilbert.'

He stared at me in bewilderment. 'Cousin? Mistress, I canna say that I've ever seen you before, to my knowledge, though that's a sair loss indeed ... What were your names again, Mistress?'

'My friend is Mistress Sewell, and I am Thomazine Heron. Your grandmother and my grandfather were sister and brother, and to my mind that is kinship.'

'Heron!' said Gilbert Graham, enlightenment cracking across his face. 'So that's it ... Mistress, I crave your pardon, I hadna suspected ... well, well, I think this calls for something of a celebration, eh, Johnnie? Another long-lost cousin!'

'Another?' I said hopefully. Gilbert guided us into chairs and sat down himself, while Johnnie went in search of further liquid refreshment. 'Aye, your cousin Francis came back, oh, a year ago or more. Now, there's a lad after my own heart, no' like that sickly feeble brother o' mine, though when he was wi' us before I'd nae such hopes o' him – apart from that affair wi' that wee lass Kirsty, which was why Mam wanted him sent back tae ye. Aye, she's glad enough tae see him again, and Johnnie's sister Meg is sighing after him too, not tae mention half the whores in this Godforsaken town, begging your pardon, Cousin.'

Something had happened to my stomach, constricting it. I had long known of the existence of this Kirsty Armstrong, with whom Francis had dallied briefly, when he was fifteen. He had assured me later that it meant nothing, that it had been nothing more than youthful experimentation, but now Gilbert's information seemed to give the lie to that. I said carefully and casually, 'I was hoping I might see Francis, I haven't spoken with him for so long ... is he still at Catholm?'

'Well, he's there at the moment, though he's likely to

be awa' any time,' said Gilbert. 'He and my brother Malise were wi' Montrose down in the Fells, drumming up men for this invasion they're planning, and they came back tae Catholm for a wee rest. Wi' any luck they should still be there when we get back tomorrow, Cousin.'

At this moment Johnnie returned with a jug of wine and two extra cups, so that in the bustle of pouring I was able to control my excitement and keep it from my face. Grainne reached across and squeezed my hand briefly, and I gave her a hopeful smile in return. The wine was a strong dark claret, and I greatly appreciated its fortifying strength at that moment. Cousin Gilbert continued talking, a pastime he seemed to enjoy greatly, but it all flowed over me. I was overwhelmed by the one outstanding fact, that Francis would be at Catholm to greet my arrival: and after all the sacrifices, the delays and frustrations and ordeals of our journey, this seemed to be, at last, the justification for all we had endured, the culmination of all my hopes. I could have wept with delight: and only my utter exhaustion kept me from wishing, most desperately, that I could persuade Cousin Gilbert to ride with me now, to Catholm, so that I could see my dear and only love at last, after eighteen months or more of grief and despair and separation.

Despite our weariness, I was not prepared, so near now to my goal, to indulge in any unnecessary rest, and so we were up betimes the next morning, ready for the last day of our travels. Cousin Gilbert, however, was evidently not so eager, for we had broken our fast before he appeared, red-eyed and unshaven, to join us in the stable-yard. He had obviously celebrated our meeting lavishly after we had left him the previous night, for his breath still stank of stale wine. However, he was jovial enough, displaying something of the gallant charm to which Francis had once referred, and explaining his business in Carlisle. 'I bought a nice wee mare from a friend o' mine here, she's won a race or two in her time and I've a mind tae breed from her. But I need nae excuse tae come up tae Carlisle, it's a grand place for the lassies, ye ken, the Minister at Castleton's gey hot on fornication and drunkenness, and my Mam has the deil's own tongue in her heid. God rot all those self-righteous interfering busybodies that call themselves ministers o' the Kirk!' He recognized Drake and Hobgoblin, and extolled the latter's ability to win races, and was still waxing strong on what was evidently one of his favourite topics of conversation as we left the inn.

Grainne and I exchanged grins behind his back as we clattered through the stone-cobbled streets of Carlisle towards the Scotch Gate. Gib Graham certainly had an entertaining style of speech, unless you were the sort to be shocked by his bluntness: and I was glad we had Holly, purposeful and pessimistic, trotting gloomily at our back, for I would not have put it past Gib, escorting two attractive young ladies alone, to have attempted to force his unwanted gallantry on us. Certainly, he gave the impression of being, as well as easy-going and jovial, negligent, careless and thoroughly unscrupulous. He did not seem, in character at any rate, to bear the slightest resemblance to his formidable grandmother Elizabeth, save possibly in the last-mentioned quality.

For the first few miles, we rode through the flat, open country to the north of Carlisle, a bleak and featureless landscape that made little impression on my excitement. For the past eight months, ever since Great-Aunt Elizabeth had sent word that Francis was at Catholm, I had hoped and planned and dreamed of this day, of how I would ride up to the place like some long-lost lover in an old ballad, and fall into his welcoming arms: and now it had come at last. This was country he knew, his eyes had seen these moors and mosses, his horse's hooves had trodden the same cold muddy tracks. Suddenly I felt so close to him that it seemed almost as if I had only to turn round to see him riding up behind me, assured and mocking and eager, his long mouth curling in the wry ironic way I knew so well. But all I saw was Gib, fat and garrulous and good-natured, riding with all the grace of a sack of meal. Yet even that unfortunate picture did not seriously upset my fantasy, and I turned back to stare avidly at the approaching North, and the promise of Francis that drove me onwards.

As we neared the Border, the hills of Scotland reared up ahead of us, blue with distance, ominous on this grey, windy April day. We crossed the River Lyne and the road, or rather track, began to climb out of the low-lying scrub and moss and occasional bleak village or farmstead. Showers of rain swept over us from the west, out of a rushing magnificent sky, ragged and torn with shades of grey. The hills in the distance were blotted out periodically with rain or low cloud, and occasionally a great shaft of sunlight, like a huge moving finger, would sweep across the landscape, touching trees and hills with sudden vivid glory. Once a rainbow, graceful and soaring, balanced its ethereal colours in a broad arch in front of us, lending a faerie, multicoloured light to everything it touched: and seeing it reminded me acutely of the April day three years ago, very like this one, when Francis and I had first declared our love for each other. It seemed a good omen: my heart lifted still higher, despite the squalls and the discomfort of my cold wet cloak, and I peered eagerly between Goblin's ears as we reached the edge of a low hill and saw Liddesdale laid out below us.

Here, at its south-westerly extremity, not many miles from the sea at Solway, the River Liddel was wide and curved gracefully between the low hills on either side, well-wooded and seamed and troughed by little burns, or sikes, of clear frothing water. There were many signs of habitation, both the poverty-stricken hovels of grass and mud, with the smoke finding its way out through the roof, that Francis had once mentioned, and the more substantial stone-built towers or houses of the lairds. Several of the latter which we passed were in ruins, some no more now than a heap of rubble from which, evidently, a large proportion of the community obtained building stone for walls or byres. Sheep abounded, fine beasts with plentiful wool, but the cattle grazing near the homesteads were small, dark and distinctly under-nourished. Up here, too, it had obviously been a long hard winter.

As we rode upstream, along the side of the valley above the river to avoid the often marshy and flooded ground below, the high fells began to close in. On the other side, two or three miles away, a great range of hills emerged menacingly through the low cloud which shrouded their heights. They were, perhaps, less spectacular than the mountains through which we had passed in Cumberland, but somehow infinitely more bleak and terrible. The new grass had not yet begun to grow, nor had the bracken, and they presented their winter aspect – hunched, sullen shoulders ochre-yellow with dead grass, patched and dappled here and there by the rich russet of last year's bracken, and dotted with the faint greyish blobs of sheep. Their lamenting cries could be heard on the hills above us, wind-borne, eerie and full of loneliness. I am not a particularly fanciful person, but something about the place, the sinister bleakness under the thin veneer of green moss and the trees on the riverbank, made me shiver. It was easy to remember that only forty years ago, it had been the most evil, lawless dale in all the Borders.

After we crossed the Kershope Burn, and so entered Scotland, the hills drew inexorably closer, as did night-fall. Our progress was slow, guiding our horses along a narrow, stony, treacherous path, frequently pausing to dismount so that the horses could more safely negotiate the burns and gullies that crossed our path. Gib pointed out the places of note as we passed them: Whithaugh, the tower of one of the most notorious branches of the Armstrongs; Capshaws, a green park by the river almost in the English manner; the crouched bulky hills with their strange harsh uncouth names, Blinkbonny and Beddo, Blackgate Rig and Cooms Fell. A mile or so after Whithaugh, the river divided. From the right, below the homestead of Powis, flowed the Liddel, and running into it was Hermitage Water. We altered our course to follow the latter stream and now, Gib informed us, we were entering the Elliot part of the valley, for the Armstrongs had tended to dominate the western and lower half of Liddesdale, the Elliots the upper. The tower on our left, on a bluff or 'heugh' above the stream, was Redheugh, home with Larriston in upper Liddesdale of the chief of the Elliots, Robin of that name, who by virtue of having friends in high places had escaped the retribution meted out to some of his less fortunate kin at the scouring of the Borders forty years previously. Opposite was another Elliot stronghold, 'The Park'. We saw few people: occasionally a string of pack animals would straggle past, or a man ploughing his 'infield' would shout a greeting, but the rain which had now begun to fall more heavily obviously kept most within doors.

'How much further is it?' Jasper asked his mother, and Gib, overhearing, said, 'No' more than three miles left, laddie, no' long at a'.'

I was glad, being by now soaked, and stiff, and weary, and also very hungry, for the provisions we had eaten at dinner-time, on horseback, had been fairly inadequate. We followed Hermitage Water as it rushed down its valley, broad and fairly shallow, with flat marshy meadows and rank mosses, spiky with gorse, out of which rose gently the tawny hills, with the bracken scars on them like blotches of dried blood. Snaberlee Rig, Thiefsike Head, Arnton Fell, and behind the steep conical shape of the latter, the shallower rise of Ninestane Rig. 'And just below yon hill,' said Gib, pointing, 'is Catholm, between the Whitrope Burn and Roughley Burn. See yon trees, there, ahead?'

As we drew steadily nearer, the hooves splashing and squelching through the mud and puddles, I could discern something, a grim grey finger of rock, stabbing between the trees. 'There it is,' said Gib, and into his careless voice came a new note, strangely compounded of pride and dislike. 'Yon's Catholm.'

It stood by the side of a tiny burn, Catholm Sike, that trickled down Ninestane Rig to join Hermitage Water. The ground here rose gently from the valley floor, and the various streams were lined with alders and ash and crab-apples, gnarled and bent from their winter confrontation with the wind. On a tiny outcrop of rock some past Graham had built his tower, and flung round it a low stone wall, seven or so feet in height and some sixty feet in diameter, behind which he could shelter his stock in time of raid and war. In these slightly more peaceful days, the wall now supported barns and stables, as had the wall round Ashcott. But there the comparison with the other family houses which I knew, ended. Goldhayes was a gracious, civilized mansion, its moat for enhancement of its warm beauty, doubled by reflection, and not intended for defence. Ashcott, golden and sleepy, had flirted with warlike intentions, the battlements and towers and the pretty, impractical gatehouse no serious deterrents, rather like the coy protestations of some lovely lady to her not unwelcome seducer. But to the builder of Catholm, the impregnability of his tower, sixty feet of nearly solid stone, broken only by a few tiny windows and an iron-grilled door, had quite literally been a matter of life and death. Death, and threat, and grim purpose hung all about it like a shroud: and I could well imagine a tower like this being a suitable setting for shouts of the Heron motto: 'No surrender!'

Had the tower been all there was to Catholm, our lodging would, I suspected, have been comfortless indeed: but some recent owner, Elizabeth Graham's long-dead husband as I later discovered, had had some pretensions to civilization, for adjoining the tower, built on to it of the same hard rough-hewn dark grey stone, was a simple two-storeyed dwelling, with an arched door in its porch and fine large mullioned windows. The whole building, tower and extension, gave a curious impression of mismarriage, old and new, barbarity and comfort, ugliness and comeliness, like some hardened battered old soldier wed to a pretty, fresh young maid.

Our horses trod wearily in through the gate, dragging their feet. The yard around the house, though smaller, was very reminiscent of Ashcott: the same mud, the ubiquitous hens and richly aromatic midden, and the utilitarian buildings essential for farming. There was no one about, no sign of Francis met my eager, devouring gaze: and Gib, looking round annoyed, shouted, 'Hey there! Sim!'

After a long pause an elderly and most villainous-looking man appeared at the door of what must be the stables. His jaw was unshaven, his greying hair dirty and straggling round his face under the filthy bonnet that seemed to be obligatory wear for all farm workers in this region, and to complete the picture he was hideously scarred where some long-ago sword had tried, and just failed, to slice off his nose. 'Oh, aye, Maister Gib, I'm comin', I'm comin', lad,' he muttered, and shuffled through the mud and muck to take my cousin's mount and the mare he had bought in Carlisle: his eyes all the while, bloodshot and curious, never leaving Grainne and me.

'Tak' nae notice o' Sim,' Gib said to us, 'he's gey old and past it, aye, Sim?'

Sim muttered some curse. Gib dismounted with a flourish and tossed him the reins. 'And see she gets a good feed, mon, none o' your skimping, mind.' He watched Sim leading his rain-sodden bay mare into the stable, and turning back to us took the reins of our exhausted horses and led them over to the porch, where we could dismount dryshod. The door swung open as we slid painfully down, and a little maid-servant, scrawny and pock-marked, peered round it. 'Oh, it's yoursel', Maister Gib. Mistress Grizel said . . .' She saw Grainne, with a tired dozy Henrietta in her arms and Jasper by her side, and her jaw dropped. I could read her mind and was hard put to it to disguise my laughter. In that fading light the bright orange-red hair of the children, inherited from their dead father, looked very much like Gib's darker crimson, and I could see that she thought he had brought his mistress and bastards to the house. Gib had evidently had the same idea, for he said, chuckling, 'Now, Bessie, they're none o' mine, so put that notion out o' your heid. It's my cousin Mistress Heron, and her friend Mistress Sewell and her wee bairns come for a visit – I met them in Carlisle and brought them hame. Go and tell Mistress Grizel and Mistress Graham, lass, and be quick about it – and a bite tae eat and drink wouldna come amiss!'

With a terrified curtsey, the little girl – she could not have been more than ten or eleven – scuttled away into the dimness. Gib flung wide the door and stood aside for us to enter. I heard him bellowing back across the yard, 'And mak' sure you unsaddle the ladies' horses and bring the packs in, you thievin' old rogue.' Though with Holly to assist him, I did not think that Sim was in any danger of being slapdash.

The room in which we found ourselves was some sort of small hall or parlour, simply furnished, with an immaculate stone-flagged floor. In the gloom, for there were no candles lit, I could discern a sullen fire burning smokily in the huge stone hearth, and precious little else. Then illumination arrived abruptly: the door opposite us opened and a woman came in, the maid Bessie carrying two three-branched silver candlesticks behind her. The sudden flaring light brought the room into sharp vivid colour out of the greyness, the whitewashed plastered walls, the mellowed hangings that depicted, I saw with a start of shock, the painful demise of Absalom, the old-fashioned chest and stools and a more modern gate-legged table against one wall. But I took all this in with only a swift glance, for the woman held my attention. She was tall, as tall as Grainne, and as thin and angular as a winter branch. Her black dress hung on her figure in folds, relieved only by the spotless white of her apron and collar and cuffs and the plain coif which hid every scrap of hair. Her eyes, a pale, clear, cold greyish-blue, gazed inhospitably at us out of a bony, sour-tempered face. I remembered Francis's unfavourable description of Grizel Graham, the mother of Gib and Malise, and my heart sank.

She ignored us after that first hostile look, and addressed Gib. 'Well, what's a' this? I couldna get any sense out o' Bessie.' Her voice was loud, brusque and unfriendly.

'Mother,' said Gib, not a whit perturbed by this unpromising greeting, 'may I present my cousin and yours, Mistress Thomazine Heron, frae Suffolk? And her friend and journey-companion, Mistress Grainne Sewell, and her bairns.'

We all curtseyed, and Jasper bowed very correctly, hat in hand, with all the solemnity of his five years and two weeks. Mistress Grizel Graham made no move to welcome us: she went on talking querulously to Gib, as if we were not there. 'And where did ye find your *cousin*, Gilbert? In some alehouse, nae doot.' And I realized with a shock of indignation that she did not believe him, and had probably made the same mistake as Bessie.

Then Drake, mired to the shoulder, grunted, shook himself with a clap of wet ears and a shower of water, and trotted over to the fire, leaving a trail of damp paw-prints behind him. He turned round, stiff-legged, two or three times and subsided on to the warm stones with a deeply-satisfied groan of weariness. Grizel Graham's expression froze as she recognized him. She said slowly, 'That's Francis's dog ... Did ye bring it with ye, Mistress Heron?' The pebble-hard grey-blue eyes did not meet mine, but stared past my ear. Feeling suddenly awkward with this woman who should by rights have intimidated me, and did not, I said, 'Yes, Mistress Graham, I did. You see, er, Francis left Oxford very suddenly ... in fact, we all thought he was dead ... and when we heard he was here I resolved to see him, and bring Drake and Hobgoblin, that's his horse if you remember, back to him. I'm sorry we gave you no warning of our visit, but England is in some turmoil with the war, and we were sadly delayed on our journey.'

'I had some sma' knowledge of ye,' said Grizel.

'Mistress Graham said something of ye, and that ye might be coming here. She's been looking for ye these six months or more, I know – she'll be glad tae know ye're here safely, I dinna doot. Bessie! Gi'e Mistress Heron and Mistress Sewell the tower chambers, above Maister Malise. They're no' verra comfortable compared wi' what ye're used tae, I'm thinking, but they're the best we ha' free. Mak' sure the fires are lit, Bessie, and put fresh linen on the beds.'

'And dinna forget the food and wine!' Gib called as the poor child fled, with a muttered, 'Aye, Mistress!'

We shed our drenched cloaks and laid them at Gib's direction over the chest underneath the window. Grizel closed the shutters against the night and the draughts and turned to us once more, still appearing unfriendly and thoroughly ill-at-ease. She cleared her throat loudly, and at the sound Henrietta woke up and started to whimper. Grainne sat down on the tall carved chair by the hearth, and began to dry the damp russet hair with a fold of her skirt. Grizel stood by, silent, her narrow mouth shut in a disapproving line, while Jasper fidgeted, his eyes huge in his white exhausted face, evidently feeling the awkwardness and tension in the air. And then the same door opened again, to admit not Bessie but a tallish, upright, elderly lady with a laden tray in her hands. She put it down on the table and smiled at me. 'Well, Thomazine, against all the odds I see you've turned into a beauty.'

'Great-Aunt!' I cried. Such was my weariness, and sense of disappointment at our chilly welcome, that although I had not seen her for nearly ten years, I flung myself into her arms and all but broke into tears. 'Oh, Great-Aunt, how glad I am to see you!'

'Now, now, what's all this to-do?' said Elizabeth Graham, just as she had admonished me when I was ten. She pushed me gently away and held me at arm's length, looking at my face. 'Yes, a beauty, of sorts . . . Well, I'm right glad to see you again too, child, though you've taken your time to get here, I must say.'

'We couldn't help it,' I said, shaky still with pent-up emotion. 'We fell among thieves.' And I told her what had happened at Nantwich. 'It was that, and the weather, delayed us,' I finished. Great-Aunt shook her head with sad exasperation. 'And a pretty pass things have come to, if a peaceful party can't make their way through England without being waylaid and robbed by soldiers in some jumped-up general's army . . . almost like the bad old days on the Borders, when it was most unwise to go travelling without twenty armed men at one's back. Now, Thomazine, I haven't seen you for nigh on ten years, but I can still reckon you look exhausted. I trust Grizel has made you welcome?' Her shrewd glance at me and at her daughter-in-law revealed that she was very well aware of the quality of that welcome. Feeling distinctly uncomfortable, as if caught in an unseen crossfire, I said, 'Great-Aunt, may I present my very, very dear friend from Goldhayes, Mistress Grainne Sewell, who has given up a home and safety to come with me . . . and Jasper and Henrietta, her children.'

As Grainne, smiling, curtseyed, Elizabeth Graham said, 'Sewell, eh? I remember John Sewell most clearly, he lived at the Home Farm, did he not? But you're not wed to him, surely?'

'No, it was his elder son, Henry, who was my husband,' said Grainne, 'but he was killed at the beginning of the war.'

Despite my desperate urge to discover if Francis was indeed still at Catholm, I had then to tell my great-aunt of the death at Edgehill of Edward Heron, brother to Simon, Francis, Lucy and Jamie. She sighed wearily. 'Oh, not Ned . . . he was such a dear child, I recall, so cheerful and kind and reliable. And Henry I remember as well, the two of them were such good friends. I am so very sorry, Mistress Sewell, for you and your children; it's always the best seem to die in wars such as this one . . . Now, I have kept you both talking long enough. The little parlour is far more cosy than this, so we'll take the food and wine in with us, and you can tell me the rest of your news while you eat. Will you join us, Grizel, Gib?'

'I regret I ha' too much tae do just now,' said her daughter-in-law. 'Will you excuse me, Cousin?' With a brief, cold smile, she went out. Gib gave a wry shrug and grinned. 'What's soured her today, Grandam? Dinna mind my mither, Thomazine, she's aye like that, aye snappin' and findin' fault. Ye'll ken soon enough, she's no' to be minded, dinna let her worry you.'

'Gib!' said Great-Aunt, quite sharply. 'You forget yourself!' To my surprise Gib looked almost sheepish: he picked up the tray and went out without another word. Elizabeth Graham laughed drily. 'Poor Grizel is a much-tried woman, I fear, and you must be patient with her. Also, with my rogue of an elder grandson. The younger one, now, he's altogether different, but alas he's not here at the moment. Nor, I am afraid, is Francis, though you've only missed him by a matter of hours: he and Malise rode out this morning, and I do not know when they will return.'

Suddenly, in my exhaustion, it was all too much. Francis was not here, had left Catholm almost as though he were trying to avoid me, although he could have no way of knowing about my imminent arrival: and even though he had not gone for ever, it felt to me in my despair as though we were destined never to be reunited, and the terrible hardships and ordeals of our seven-month journey all for nothing. I dragged the back of my hand across my trembling mouth and whispered, 'Not here? I thought . . . Gib said . . . He *will* come back, won't he?'

Great-Aunt's ancient, lined, cragged face softened for a moment. 'I pray God he will, with my dear Malise to look to him. But do understand, your journey has not been a wasted one: I am very glad you made the decision to come here, and I pray it will succeed. He may not realize it, but he has been trying to destroy himself for the past year or more, and this lunatic invasion plan of

Jamie Graham's is the way he will do it – unless you can prevent it.'

'But have I come too late, do you think?' I said, feeling despair wash over me in my weariness. 'Oh God, don't say I'm too late – we couldn't help it, I couldn't leave until the baby was born . . .' To my horror, I found myself weeping in anguish, all control lost. Grainne was almost instantly at my side, and from somewhere below my sobs I heard Jasper's high distressed voice. 'Aunt Thomazine! Please don't, Aunt Thomazine, please don't.'

'A *baby*?' said Elizabeth Graham. 'You had a *baby*, and left it behind?'

'It was the only way she could come here,' said Grainne, quick in my defence. 'Her husband would never have rested if she had taken his son away from him.'

'A baby,' said Great-Aunt Elizabeth again, more quietly, 'you gave up your child for Francis, as well as everything else . . . I can only pray that your sacrifice is not in vain . . . and take my advice, tell no one else of this, least of all him, till you are sure of him.'

'You think it's hopeless, don't you,' I whispered through the veiling mass of my bedraggled, tangled hair. 'You think it *is* all in vain . . . what's wrong? How has he changed? He *can't* be indifferent to me, he *must* understand what happened, how it was. I can tell him what Dominic did and he'll know I couldn't have done anything else, won't he?'

Great-Aunt was silent. I turned my head and pushed back my hair to see her properly. Her face was full of compassion. 'Won't he?' I whispered.

'We'll see,' said Elizabeth Graham. 'If I remember you aright, Thomazine, you were ever a young lady of more than ordinary strength of will, and that will stand you in good stead. But I warn you, I do not think it will be easy – he has been too deeply hurt for that, and besides, I must tell you that you may well have a rival, for he has been keeping company with that slut Kirsty Armstrong, who you may or may not know was the reason he was sent from here back to Goldhayes seven years ago: so prepare yourself for that. Now, before we go into the other parlour, which we must do quickly for if I know Gib he'll have filched all the wine, let me give you some more advice. I have not told anyone else of your marriage, and I would advise you not to. Francis and I are the only ones who know, and up until now he has been singularly unforthcoming, even for him. But I tell you because I think that if Grizel knew that you had left your husband, whatever your justification, she could make things very unpleasant for you. She's what we English would call a Puritan, and has no room for compromise, and even here on the Borders the Kirk has more power than you dream of. So unless you want to find yourself on the penitents' stool at Castleton Kirk, say nothing to anyone. Understand?'

I nodded, dazed, not really absorbing the implications of her words. She gave me a friendly touch on the arm, and continued, 'I am glad you brought his dog, disreputable animal though it is: it has a corner of his heart, I suspect, though the sawny fule would die rather than admit it. Now, I do hope that your large and stalwart-looking groom is as true a Suffolker as he appears to be: to hear that speech again brings my childhood to me so strongly, and sometimes now, with Gil dead so long, I could wish I were back in a kinder country than this.'

We went through the little door into the smaller parlour, and found, if not an empty wine-jug, at least a much reduced one. Gib, cheerfully impenitent, bellowed for Bessie to fetch some more. We fell upon the food, which was strange to my eyes and taste, though palatable enough in our hungry state; flat oatcakes, a fifth of an inch thick, spread with honey, and wheaten bread and bowls of steaming barley and chicken broth that had been set in the hearth to keep hot. We ate our fill almost in silence, while Great-Aunt watched us with a benevolent eye: the awe-inspiring figure of my childhood revealed to be, as I had long suspected, as human and friendly as any of my younger friends.

At last we finished, replete, even the dry crumbly oatcakes all disappeared, though Hen was still licking off the honey smeared abundantly around her mouth. Drake had been given a mutton bone, still liberally covered in meat, and Gib had told us that Holly was being royally fed in the kitchen by Janet, the cook, who I guessed from Gib's nudging comments had taken a fancy to his pleasant face. I felt a great deal better for the meal, and could even achieve a semblance of cheerfulness despite my bitter disappointment at Francis's unexpected absence, and the disturbing news about his state of mind. Our tongues freed by the wine and hot spicy ale which followed it, Grainne and I related the full story of our journey, suitably edited for Gib's ear.

As we ended, the door from the outer parlour swung open and a tall, stout grey-haired man stamped cheerfully in, shaking water from his hat, and stopped when he saw us. 'Why, Mam, have we visitors then?'

This must be Great-Aunt's only surviving son, Sandy. He bowed, and we curtseyed, and Jasper, who had been visibly falling asleep, jerked to his feet and bowed also. Drake leapt up from his bone and went to sniff at the newcomer's muddy boots, and Sandy, bending to pat him, stopped with his hand outstretched. 'Yon's surely Francis's old dog?'

Elizabeth introduced us, and Sandy's face cracked into a beaming smile. 'Cousin Thomazine! I remember your mother, though I didna know her verra well. What brings you here, in these times?'

'Oh, just a friendly visit,' I said, too tired and full of food and ale to think of a better excuse. Sandy grinned. 'Oh, aye? Well, ye may yet wish ye'd stayed in Suffolk, it's a chilly country here, and bleak besides. Ye'll no' find it sae comfortable as Goldhayes. How did ye find us?'

'We found Gib in Carlisle, by chance,' I said. Gib

gave his typical, slightly crude chuckle. 'They asked me to guide them here, and with twa bonny lassies like yon, I couldna refuse!'

From his talk, Sandy Graham seemed to be an open, cheerful, even slightly naive man, curiously boy-like despite his age. How Elizabeth Graham had come to give birth to such a character, I could not imagine. Gib obviously accorded well with his father, to judge by the friendly banter about his business in Carlisle, equine and otherwise: and Great-Aunt, when she was not talking to me and Grainne, fixed them both with a benign eye. But it was evident, from her tone and expression earlier, that the absent Malise was her favourite grandson, and that Francis also held no small place in her affections.

At last, when I was ready to sleep where I sat, she noted our tiredness, and briskly escorted all of us to our chambers. We entered the tower by the door in the arras wall of the other parlour, and a curious doorway it was too, like a tunnel due to the thickness of the tower wall. The room at the base of the tower, which I learned later had once been used to stable cattle in time of raid, was given over to arms, various items of military equipment and stores, arranged round the walls and stacked in the corners. On perches at one side sat three hooded birds, a goshawk and two peregrines, and beside them the intricate and malodorous paraphernalia associated with hawking. We climbed the turnpike stairs which led up through a door at the far end, and lay hidden in the thickness of the wall. Great-Aunt led the way with her candle, tireless and tough, her forceful nose echoing the prominent curved beaks of the birds downstairs. 'The first floor was the parlour once, but when my Gil built the new house he divided it into two bedchambers. When they're here Francis has the one and Malise the other. The rest of us have chambers in the new house. The two rooms above this are yours, I believe, and should be comfortable enough with the fires lit and clean linen and warming-pan or two, and if you're not used to such stairs remember that they'll keep you hale and fit.'

'What's above our chambers?' I asked, and Great-Aunt, opening the stout wooden door, said, 'Some little attic chambers. Janet has one, and Bessie another. Sim sleeps in a little cubby-hole in the hay-loft, with the other groom, whose name is Jockie. All Grahams, of course, though there aren't many of them left, now – all gone, Richie of Brackenhill, Jock o' the Peartree, Richie's Will, all dead and gone, and not many to lament their passing.'

'What happened to them?' Grainne enquired, as we entered the first of the two chambers. Both were quite small, with one window apiece, shuttered and barred against the wind. Rain drummed on the panes, and I felt relief to know that the tower windows *had* got glass – in this barbaric, backward country anything seemed possible. But the rooms were cosy, each with a fire in the hearth and a pan in the simple oak half-tester beds. There was no truckle bed for Jasper, but a small pallet laid on the floor and covered most warmly with a thick, furry blanket made of sewn sheepskin. The little boy's eyes gleamed at the sight of it; he ran over and dived headfirst into the thick coarse wool, running his fingers through it, rubbing his face against it and rolling over and over. Drake, who had his own priorities, stalked over to the fire and stretched his length in front of it, still gnawing the mutton-bone.

'What happened to the Grahams?' said Great-Aunt Elizabeth, shutting the door behind us. 'Vengeance fell upon them, for all the havoc they wreaked. They were hanged, transported to Ireland, dispersed, sent to fight in the Low Countries. Some of them made their way back under other names, risking death and outlawry, but the Name was broken – save for us, and some in Eskdale. Gil, my dear Gil, had been an outlaw himself when I met him, but he came to see the error of his ways, and grew to love peace and to become sick of the feuds and killing and raiding. He helped Buccleugh to clear Liddesdale, until he saw how he was feathering his own nest. Robin Elliot at Redheugh suffered greatly from that greedy Scott: the two families had been at feud, you see.' She smiled. 'But enough of our bloodstained past, the present is mild enough. Good night, and may you sleep sound against all that wind!'

We did indeed sleep well, despite the strangeness of our surroundings, and on the morrow began the process of winning acceptance at Catholm. Great-Aunt, of course, welcomed our presence, as did Sandy and Gib: the latter was obviously delighted at the prospect of two unattached and comely young females joining the household for a long stay, and promptly began wooing us both. From Grainne, of course, he received a calm, smiling, amused indifference which did not seem to dampen his enthusiasm: and from me, obsessed with thoughts of Francis, scant encouragement. At first, I was sorely irritated by his ponderous conceited gallantries: then my sense of humour took over and, like Grainne, I could find amusement in the situation. Gib did not take his failure to heart, but treated it all, after it became obvious that he was getting nowhere, like an elaborate game from which we all derived some merriment. He and Sandy showed us round the rest of the house and the outbuildings, and took us riding along Hermitage Water to see the local sight, the grim fortress of that name, square and uncompromising behind the ditches and banks that circled its site on the edge of the stream. It was owned now by the ubiquitous Scotts of Buccleugh, and stood desolate and uninhabited, save by the uneasy and tormented ghosts of its past.

'There are some grand and terrible tales of yon,' Sandy told us, as we stared awestruck at the huge shape, so brutally incongruous amidst the round yellow hills and the fuzzy alders along the burn. 'But old Meg can tell you better than I.'

Meg Macdonald was the nurse, from the Western

Isles, who had looked after Gib and Malise in their childhood, and Sandy before them. Old now, almost bent double with the burden of her years, she spent most of her time in the chimney-corner in the kitchen. Without the Grahams' protection she would surely have been thought a witch – the Scots were very hot against witches – and burnt under the barbaric Scots laws, for she was hook-nosed with a habit of muttering to herself, and made an especial pet of Malkin, the black, sleek and sinister kitchen cat. But she was regarded with respect and affection by everyone, and took our sudden unheralded arrival in her stride. Indeed, Jasper quite won her heart, and on the second evening at Catholm we mislaid him, running him to earth in Meg's corner, listening with utter fascination to some ancient tale in her almost unintelligible dialect, Drake slumbering beside him.

'Och, no harm,' said Janet softly, seeing Grainne's dubious glance at her son, pressed against the old woman's unsavoury skirts. 'She's aye been pining for a bairn to tell her stories to, sin' Maister Malise grew too old. She'll keep him hushed for hours, Meg will.'

'I don't reckon as I've ever seed him so quiet,' Holly put in from the brew-house opening off the kitchen, where he was tapping a fresh barrel of ale. 'And thass a wonder, for that little mite.' I saw Janet's face as he spoke, her delighted involuntary laughter at the strangeness of his speech, and grinned to myself. Young Holly had best look to her, or he might well find himself snared by her neat pale rose-cheeked face and glossy brown hair.

So our little party settled in quickly at Catholm. Holly and Grainne and I, and even Jasper, learned new words for familiar things, and remembered to refer to the byre and barmkin instead of barn and yard, to talk about bigg and nolt and insight and pullyn rather than barley, cattle, furniture and poultry. We watched our cousins at work, for Sandy, although deriving a large part of his income from properties in Liddesdale and around

Hawick, a town in Teviotdale a few miles away over the northern hills, still farmed his land around Catholm himself, in the age-old manner: oats and barley, kale and a little wheat in the well-fertilized 'infield' around the tower, cattle and sheep on the 'outfield', which meant that they were more or less free to roam over the lower, southern slopes of Ninestane Rig, each animal being branded with the Graham mark, a tarry spot on the left shoulder. In a little while, the shepherds and their families would take most of the cattle and sheep, with the new calves and lambs, up into the hills for 'summering', building themselves the little makeshift turf and boulder huts known as shiels against the weather, and every so often Gib or Sandy would be riding up to check that all was well and that no beast had been thieved by the irrepressible descendants of more murderous Armstrongs and Elliots. 'It's grand up there on a warm night,' Gib said to us, his indolent bluish eyes kindling, 'when the aqua vitae goes round and old Archie Graham gets up tae sing. Ye maun come up wi' us, in the summer.' I determined to do so with Francis, when he came.

If he came. Two things only spoiled those first weeks at Catholm. One was my desperate desire to see him once more, coupled with my terror that I would not, that he would be somehow killed before we could meet again, struck down by a cruel and ironic blow, unknowing of my presence at Catholm. Every day I watched the hills, and the track to Liddesdale and thence to green and comfortable England, in the vain hope that I would see him. And every day there were only the sheep, and their guardians, and passing neighbours or farmworkers going about their business. And, too often for almost everyone's liking, Master Scott, the Minister at Castleton, the chief township (if such a name could dignify that small and primitive settlement) in Liddesdale, would come to visit Grizel.

And she was the other pebble in the bread. Her family and servants were quite accustomed to her bitterness, her lack of feeling and her sharp tongue. All of them easy-going and tolerant, or in the case of Meg stone-deaf, they had long ago discovered that the easiest way to live with her was to ignore her as much as they could. Besides, in the case of Sandy and the older servants, they were used to having Great-Aunt Elizabeth in authority, as indeed she was still. I might have sympathized with Grizel, for it evidently had not been easy to arrive at Catholm as Sandy's bride, to find his domineering mother firmly and immovably ensconced in charge. But Grizel's was not a character that readily inspired sympathy. She was in all respects a mean, ungenerous woman, sparse and pinched in her appearance as in her nature, sustained by her devotion to her Kirk. Once, to judge by what information others let fall, she had been an idealistic, enthusiastic, almost beautiful young girl, fired by notions of bringing God to a household thoroughly imbued with the humanist reasonableness of Elizabeth Graham and her reformed outlaw husband. She had had some support from the Minister, who had done wonders with what was, to all intents and purposes, virgin territory in Liddesdale. Master Scott had arrived triumphantly at a situation where, if the older inhabitants clung stubbornly to their irreligious ways, the younger ones, hauled to school in Castleton by persuasion, threats, bribery or blackmail – those time-honoured Border methods – were at least regular attenders at the Kirk. But Grizel's efforts at Catholm fell on stony ground, finding no comfort or support from any of the family, and so she turned at last to the Minister, now an elderly man but still zealous, for her spiritual comfort and guidance: and everyone at Catholm either ignored her outbursts of self-righteous anger or reproach, or belittled her behind her back. Gib found especial amusement in scurrilous and, to my mind, rather objectionable references to 'my Mam's second husband.'

Everyone save for old Meg, who was too aged and infirm to stir from the house, went to the Castleton Kirk when weather permitted. So did most other people in

Liddesdale and, given the far-flung isolated nature of the parish, I was surprised to see how many did make the often inconvenient, long and arduous journey in to the township on the Sabbath. And I was horrified by the penitents' stool, on which offenders had to sit: a girl who had produced a bastard baby, a woman accused of being a whore, a man caught fornicating with a neighbour's daughter. This busybodying, harsh interference by the Kirk and Session into the daily and private lives of their parishioners, with that humiliating exhibition in front of the congregation, and the overtones of self-righteous salaciousness, was an appalling revelation, and I fully appreciated Great-Aunt's warning. Grainne and Holly were also shocked, though fortunately Jasper was too young to understand. As we rode home after the first service, Great-Aunt, who sat her lively and spirited brown gelding like a young girl, turned to us. '*Now* do you understand why we have no love for the Kirk, nor for Minister Scott?'

'I do indeed,' said Grainne, and shuddered suddenly. I saw remembered fear in her face, as she added slowly, 'Tell me, Mistress Graham – do the people here recognize an Irish voice?'

'I pray not,' said Elizabeth shortly, with a warning glance at Grizel's poker-straight back fifteen yards in front of us. 'But to most here, you are no more than English, because to them any voice not Scottish must be English. If it became generally known, however . . . I do not know. But I do not think there is the same hatred against your people here as seems to be prevalent in England.'

Grainne smiled, and I saw some of the shadow lift from her eyes. To someone as tolerant and reasonable as was she, the shock of such blind savage prejudice as we had met on our journey had come as a disturbing revelation, not to be easily shrugged aside.

'But I cannot answer for Grizel,' Great-Aunt went on, 'so your Irishness, Grainne, must be for ourselves only. Fortunately, no one has yet questioned your name:

perhaps Holofernes sounds as outlandish to them, though of course he is mentioned in the Scriptures, albeit in a somewhat unfavourable light.'

'Thass all my mother's fault,' said Holly gloomily, 'she would have that name, no matter how my father and Parson went on. She thought that sounded grand, you see, Mistress, and I've cursed her for it ever since.'

'And so, I suppose, have the various other bearers of that name around Goldhayes,' I said drily. 'Holly's good mother unfortunately started a fashion.'

'Mind yew,' Holly added, thoughtfully irreverent, 'I'd rather be named for owd Holofernes than any of they self-righteous botty owd buggers elsewhere in the Book, begging your pardon, Mistress Graham.'

'Blasphemy,' said my Great-Aunt, 'is not yet a capital crime in Scotland, but I really would advise you to moderate your tongue, Holofernes Greenwood, or you may well find yourself decorating that misbegotten stool next Sunday.' And Holly's broad, snub-nosed face flushed a deep crimson.

I reflected often during those first weeks that it was just as well that Grizel had not yet in her desperate zeal stooped to reporting erring members of her family to the Castleton Kirk Session, or Gib at least would have sat on the stool of repentance nearly every week. But she was an impotent tyrant, taking refuge in prayer and fasting, and her pronouncements on religion and politics largely ignored.

Politics, however, came suddenly to the fore when Montrose marched into Scotland at the head of his motley army after we had been a week or two at Catholm. At the Kirk on Sunday, the fourteenth of April, the day after the invasion, everyone was full of the news, and the Minister neglected his usual tedious Biblical exposition to preach a most fiery sermon denouncing the Earl as Antichrist waging war on God's chosen people, the only truly godly Kirk in all Christendom. My head whirled as his flaming impassioned words thundered in the air around us, for this surely meant that Francis would come, that he was even now, perhaps, within a few miles of the bare cold stark little kirk where the congregation prayed for the vanquishing of their enemies and I, caught on the soaring wings of hope, prayed for quite another deliverance.

But it was not to be. Montrose and his draggle-tailed army marched away westwards, to Dumfries, and the raw Cumberland militia melted away like snow in summer. After two days they were gone, fled back to their homes at the first threat of opposition, and Montrose was left with three or four hundred men. They took Dumfries without a fight and then paused, while at Catholm we waited with desperate impatience for news, for surely this pathetic forlorn hope of an invasion would lead to disaster? And though the main Scottish army, under General Leslie, was fully occupied around Newcastle, there were other troops in Scotland which could be sent against Dumfries.

For a week we hung on a knife-edge between despondency and hope, not knowing what to expect. Every rider that came past the tower was enough to bring someone, be it Gib or Sim or Jockie, or even Jasper, to the barmkin gate to see who it was. I discovered that the window in Grainne's tower chamber gave an excellent view of the road: it was what Scots called a 'shot window', made with a stone embrasure ledge sufficiently large to sit in, and I spent a great deal of time there, reading or sewing or making soft, anguished music on Great-Aunt's cherished sweet-toned lute. It occasioned some comment, but I did not care. I wanted to watch for him, to be the first to see him, to look at him as he rode unknowing through the gate. I wanted to see the look on his face when he realized that I was here, and waiting for him.

Fortunately, Elizabeth Graham understood what I wanted, and why, and often she sat with me, working a tapestry pillow-cover, and making friendly conversation. She had a good mind, undimmed by her seventy-odd years, and our talk ranged widely: but somehow it always seemed to come back to the two places we had in common, Goldhayes and Catholm. I listened avidly, with half an eye on the road, to her tales of midnight raids, of the wild savage past when no cow nor sheep nor house for fifty miles around was safe from the reivers of Liddesdale, and when the boldness and daring of the Armstrongs and Elliots and Crosers and Grahams and all the others was only equalled by their insolence. 'There is a story,' said Great-Aunt, during one of our talks, a wicked smile curving her mouth as she sewed, 'that a churchman visited Liddesdale, a hundred years ago or more, and expressed horror that there was no church. "What," he cried, "are there no Christians here?" To which his companion replied, "Christians? We's a' Elliots and Armstrongs hereaboots!"'

I grinned at the thought of a heathen Liddesdale, and wondered whether Master Scott had heard the story. Great-Aunt added reflectively, 'There had been Kirks, there was one at Ellestoun down by the Park, and Wheen Kirk up at the head of the dale, as well as Castleton, but they fell into ruin long ago . . .' Her voice tailed away oddly, and I looked up from my own sewing to see her staring past my shoulder out of the window. 'My dear,' said Elizabeth Graham, her face at once hopeful and compassionate, 'I do believe he is coming.'

On the track up from Liddesdale two men were riding. There was one I did not recognize, mounted on a tall chestnut horse with four flashy white stockings, whom I guessed to be Malise. The other, with his relaxed way of riding, the pale hair pulled out behind him by the April wind, I would have known had he come riding through the gates of Hell, wreathed and shrouded and disguised in smoke.

At last, it was Francis.

Chapter 2

A candle in the dark

The miserable hath no other medicine
But only hope.
(Shakespeare, *Measure for Measure*)

Francis was coming at last, and I felt no great uprush of joy or happiness: instead, I felt suddenly sick, and faint. For a moment the bright image rocked and grew unreal, and I shut my eyes, seeing instead that other Francis, the haunter of my dreams, who had promised me my heart's desire and denied it to me the next moment. I could not bear the memory of that terrible betrayal, so vivid in my mind: I snapped my eyes open again and saw my real love, closer, close enough to see that he was talking to his companion, close enough to have a sudden, heart-stopping glimpse of his smile. Great-Aunt got to her feet and touched my arm. 'You stay here, Thomazine. I will send him up. Do you wish me to say that you are here?'

'No,' I said, feeling panic rise in me, 'no, don't say it's me, just say, just say, oh, I don't know, just that there's someone to see him.'

'I will,' said Elizabeth. She smiled suddenly, her aged, creased face made abruptly vivid and alive, as she must have looked in her captivating youth. 'In a strange way, he reminds me of my Gil, and I do not wish to see him hurt any more . . . good luck, my dear child, for your sake and for his.' She gripped my shoulder and went out. I walked back to the window, blinking back the stupid, weakling tears, and stared down into the barmkin, at the stream which rushed just beyond it, and the dun-coloured hill behind, growing faintly greener now with the new grass. The two horses, chestnut and bay, forded the Water and walked sedately up the rise to Catholm. Great-Aunt emerged suddenly, directly below me, white head surrounded by black skirts, and I saw her wave in greeting as her grandson and his friend rode in through the gate. I lurked furtively at the edge of the embrasure, peering round the shutters to see them dismount and greet her, Malise with a stooped kiss (he was as tall as Francis, but more broadly built) and Francis, I was interested to see, with a clasp of the hand as if she were a male comrade. I devoured him greedily with my gaze as they stood talking, looking for any signs of change in him: for, I remembered with a shock, I had last seen him sixteen months ago, on that dreadful night when Simon had had him thrown into the Castle at Oxford. All that while, I had held his image in my mind like a talisman, and now that I was faced with the reality, I was disconcerted. There was something about him, some alteration, which at this distance I could not identify. Sim led the steaming horses into the stables, and the three turned to walk across to the house. For an instant, Francis glanced up at it, almost as though he were seeking me: his face flashed vividly, and I saw the brown skin, bleached-straw hair and the impression he always gave of casual, unthinking grace and power. Then I ducked behind the window opening; when I looked out again he was gone from my sight.

Drake lifted his head from his muddy paws and surveyed me enquiringly, his tail drifting softly from side to side as if he knew that something was about to happen. I did not want anyone sharing our reunion: I snapped my fingers gently at him. 'Drake! Here, boy!'

He heaved himself up and came trotting over to me, keen and expectant, and I felt like the worst kind of traitor as I put my hand around his collar, pulled him into my empty inner chamber, and callously shut the door. For a moment, I heard his puzzled whines, followed by the sound of his heavy body flopping down in front of the fire. Then the enormity of what was about to happen overwhelmed me, and I stumbled to the window-seat and sat down before my legs could give way. I found that I felt sick, and my stomach was clenched, and a chill sweat made my hands and back clammy. I gazed at the faded, much-repaired hangings, and thought with fierce concentration of what I would do, and say, when he opened the door and found me . . .

There were footsteps ascending the stone stairs towards me. I heard them remotely, my whole self, heart, mind, body, fixed upon the thought of him, rigid and trembling with anticipation. The steps reached the top and paused on the other side of the door. There was a perfunctory knock, and the latch lifted . . .

I turned my face towards the door and saw Francis, poised under the lintel, staring at me in total astonishment. For a second I thought I saw in his face an unguarded delight, and leapt to my feet, and then, so swiftly that I wondered if I had been mistaken, it vanished, and his expression grew closed, and cold, and empty, the green changeable eyes as bleak and hostile as a winter sea. He said, his voice hard, 'What in Christ's name are you doing here?'

I stood, numb with shock, not daring to believe it: for if I did believe it, if I did acknowledge the bitterness and contempt plain in his face and voice, then I was lost for ever. I whispered, my throat suddenly dry and painful, 'I – I came to see you.'

'To see me?' Francis queried, frankly incredulous, and laughed. The noise echoed in my ears like a passing bell. He shut the door, and his eyes lingered over me, in a stranger's face, the face of a man I had never loved, never laughed with, never been friends with: not the boy who had built a bridge of Unicorns between us with the power of his imagination, or wakened in me the first flowering of desire and delight. Bewildered, utterly lost in this suddenly uncharted, threatening sea, I stammered, 'I h-had to come, to explain, you see . . .'

'Explain what? Has he tired of you then? Or have you wearied of him, so soon? Most likely,' said Francis, with a casual, calculated cruelty, 'he has expended all his money in the King's cause, and there is none left to keep you in the style you expect – and so you come crawling back to me.'

'No,' I said desperately, 'no, Francis, you don't understand, it wasn't like that . . . I hate him, I never want to see him again, I never loved him, ever, it was always you I wanted, no one else . . .'

'Why did you marry him, then?' Francis said, his eyebrows raised in enquiry. 'Though of course, now I come to think of it, he never mentioned love. There were other attractions entirely. What's he like in bed, your fine and handsome husband? Well, My Lady Drakelon?'

I could not answer. I had no words, no defences to ward off this sort of attack: protesting was as futile as the crash and foam and fury of the sea beating against an implacable cliff-face. I stared at his inhospitable figure, realizing suddenly and with a curious detachment what it was that had changed in him. We had parted as young lovers, and his cynicism then had been only on the surface: underneath had still been the eager, idealistic boy who had communicated to me his delight in so many things: words, ideas, music, laughter, love, friendship. Now, I saw as though looking through glass, it was all gone, burned away in those sixteen months as though the friend of my childhood had never been, leaving only the hardness and cruelty, and I wanted to weep, not for myself, but for him and for what he had lost. The silence stretched taut and desperate between us: then Francis said, 'You can go back to him now. There's nothing for you here, nothing at all.'

'No,' I whispered, and turned away so that he would not see my tears, the final humiliating degradation. 'No, I'm not going back, I can't.'

'It would be more pleasant for both of us in the end if you did,' said Francis, in a matter-of-fact way, as though he were discussing some banal everyday event. I heard the implied menace in his voice, and knew what it meant. That, and his manner, finally spurred my temper: I whipped round, heedless of the tears washing my face. 'God, you fool, you're worse than Simon! Will you not *see* what happened? I thought you were dead, and it didn't matter to me what I did any more, I married Dominic because I was sick of all their pestering, there was nothing left for me to do! Then the Widow found out what had really happened, and I was trapped. It was not my fault,' I said desperately. 'Can't you see, it was Dominic? He let me believe you were dead, and while he was trying to persuade me into marriage he was making sure that you wouldn't have anything to do with me in the future. You're doing just what Dominic wants,' I finished. 'You're choosing to believe him rather than me, well, you can ask Grainne for the truth of it, she'll tell you.'

'Grainne?' he said, and something approaching warmth touched his voice for the first time. 'Is she here too?'

'Yes, she is,' I told him, 'and you should be grateful, for we brought Drake with us, and Hobgoblin too, and if you think it was easy to come here, then I'll tell you, it took six months, and Holly nearly died protecting us from soldiers who wanted to steal Goblin, we've been cold and wet and gone hungry for your sake, and whatever you might think it wasn't easy to leave my friends and my baby . . .' I stopped, appalled both at my loose-running tongue, freed by grief and anger, and at the look on his face. 'You had Dominic's child?' Francis said, and his eyes showed me the depth and extent of the hurt I had done him. 'Then you are all I thought you to be, you whore.' With that, he turned and went out. The door slammed behind him, but I did not hear his footsteps on the stairs, descending, for the terrible nature of my situation overwhelmed me, and I abandoned myself to the anguish of my grief.

That evening, Malise came to see me. I was calm now, I had spent my desperate tears, and had listened to Grainne's and Great-Aunt's comments and advice as they comforted me. 'Why?' I had demanded of them both. 'Why? *Why* won't he believe me?' Great-Aunt had shaken her head, and said something about his perversity, and that she had feared all along that it would be like this. Grainne, with her usual precise insight into other minds, said at once, 'You have hurt him once, most terribly – oh, I know you didn't *mean* to, but you did nevertheless, and that's what counts. Just as a child, once burnt, will not pick up another hot ember, so will Francis be reluctant to accept you once more, in case you betray him again.'

'But I won't,' I cried, striking my fist into my palm in my anger and frustration. 'Why can't he understand that?' And Grainne answered, her bleak green eyes staring out at the dusk-shadowed hills, 'Because he can never trust you again – or so he thinks. You must stay here, try to win him round – don't give up, Thomazine, not now.'

'I wasn't going to give up,' I said savagely, getting up and resuming my restless walking around the floor. The candle burned, a gleam of hope in the shrouding dark, and I took it and lit others, heedless of the hot wax dripping over my fingers. 'I wasn't going to. I have nothing left now save him. My husband, my baby, all my friends but you, I have given them up for his sake, and I do not intend to be so easily thwarted. But Grainne, tell me, he seems so changed, so different, unreachable, a stranger to me, as if it was all a dream, what we had . . .' I paused, my eyes on her face, and she said quietly, 'Thomazine, do you think he is now worth the struggle?'

The silence was utter. The wind sighed mournfully round the walls of the tower chamber, out in the chilly blue April dusk. The fire smoked and smouldered gently amongst the dark earthy peats, and the candlelight flashed on the rhythmic movement of Elizabeth Graham's needle as it wove in and out of the fabric she held. I sat down softly on the windowseat. 'Yes,' I said, 'I still love him, more than I can ever say, and I cannot believe he does not still feel the same for me. He would not be so cruel and bitter, if he did not.' I remembered as I spoke what Francis had said once, surely on the afternoon we discovered our love, that he was tempted to hurt most cruelly those whom he loved the most. If that was true, then I had some reason for hope. I had to have it, to cling to it, for if I did not, I no longer had any reason to go on. 'I think I am right,' I added reflectively. 'I pray God I am ... it hurts my pride sore, to play the beseeching, begging supplicant to his indifference and hostility, but set in the balance my pride is such a small thing, beside the love we had once ... I thought in Oxford that I had lost him for ever, and against all hope I found him again. I am not going to lose him a second time.'

In the ensuing pause, we heard footsteps coming up, two pairs, one quick and eager and childish, the other heavier and adult. 'Henrietta's only a baby,' said Jasper's voice with some scorn. 'She can hardly walk yet, so she's no fun to play with. I *used* to have another sister but she was killed ages ago, I can't really 'member her at all. Will you *really* teach me to ride, Master Graham?'

A deep Scots voice, not Gib's, said just outside the door, 'I said I would, and I didna say it lightly. There's a nice wee horse out on the hills that I used to ride, old now but steady enough. He'll do you grand, Jasper.'

'Thank you, Master Graham!' Grainne's son said in an excited squeak, the door burst open and he galloped in. 'Mother, Mother, Master Graham says he'll teach me to ride!'

Behind his exuberance stood Malise Graham, a big man, as large-framed as his brother, but gaunt and wiry where Gib was flabbily fat. His face was very like his grandmother's, the same green eyes and crimson hair and fiercely-hooked nose, but for all the uncompromising qualities of his features and colouring, there was something oddly diffident and awkward and likeable in the way he stood in the door: and the smile with which he greeted us had, I could have sworn, something of shyness about it, an uncertainty of his welcome, which was very endearing.

'Jasper,' said Grainne, 'do you not remember your manners?' Her son, with a guilty grin, let go of her arm and turned. 'Master Graham, may I present my mother, Mistress Sewell, and Mistress Heron?'

True to the game of formalities, we rose and curtseyed, and Malise bowed, and Jasper said again on the same urgent note, 'Mother, Master Graham's going to teach me to *ride*.'

'I heard you the first time,' said Grainne, smiling. 'Has my child been importuning you, Master Graham? I'm afraid few find him resistable, and it's very bad for him.'

'On the contrary,' said my cousin, 'it was I who offered it. I found him in the stables, getting under Sim's feet, and I thought it best to bribe him away afore murder was done. Sim's a grand old lad, ye ken, but a wee thing hasty in his temper.'

'I thank you,' Grainne said, smiling more broadly, 'but you do that young ruffian too much honour, Master Graham. Will you not sit down?'

'Aye, that I will,' he said, and shut the door behind him. 'And no more of the "Master Graham" now; we're friends, I trust, as well as kin, and my name is Malise.'

'And mine is Grainne, and this is Thomazine. I think you already know Mistress Graham.'

'I do, for my sins,' said Malise, grinning at his grand-mother. He sat down on one of the fireside chairs, and all but struck his head open on the corner of the court-cupboard as he did so. 'I've heard Francis tell of you, when he was here years ago,' he added. 'Not so much of late, though.' I felt his grass-green eyes, so like Eliza-beth's, resting sharply on me: then he added, his voice lowered for Jasper's sake, 'Forgive me saying this, Thomazine, but is there anything between you and Francis? No, nobody's told me, but it's not verra difficult to guess when you know him as well as I do.'

'There is,' I said, recognizing that in Malise I might

well have an ally, 'or rather, there was. That's why we came here.' And briefly, softly, against the hissing whispers of the fire and wind, I told again all that had happened in the past two years. Occasionally I glanced at Jasper, whose attention had wandered, and who was practising his writing at the table, using a badly-cut and spluttering quill. Grainne sat calmly by Great-Aunt, her long slender hands folded in her lap, and the soft light deepening the fine contours of her face; more than once I saw Malise glance towards her. But he kept his attention for me and my story, and when I had finished, nodded slowly. 'Aye, it's a sorry tale, is yon, and no wonder he's changed, different, ye ken? As though . . .' he paused, searching for the words to explain, and I said, 'As though something had gone, and left him a stranger?'

Malise's eyes widened and met mine with sudden understanding. 'Aye, that's it. And . . . well, we were friends, before, Francis and me, and at the end of it we had few secrets from each other – save for that Armstrong girl, but that's another story. I *knew* him. It isna like that any more, there's something wrong. He's said nothing of why he came back, nothing of any of all this, that you've told me. And there's another thing, too. Before, we used to go with Gib sometimes into Carlisle, for the hell of it, but there was aye too much else for him to be doing for him to get verra interested in wine, women and song – save for Kirsty Armstrong, o' course, and I'm thinking you'll be wishing her to the Devil, Thomazine. But now, it's like he's interested in nothing else. With that, and the way he's taking no heed of what he does, volunteering for all the dangerous duties, well, I'm verra glad of your coming, Thomazine, even if he'll have none of you. Are you staying here, then, to fight off Kirsty Armstrong?'

'For as long as it takes to bring him back,' I said, with a stout certainty I did not feel at all. Malise smiled, a wide infectious smile that had nothing of shyness in it now. 'Then I wish you the best of luck, Cousin, and I'll

94

do all I can to help. But you may not have much time – have you heard yet why we've returned?'

We shook our heads.

'Well, you know how we went to Dumfries, after the Cumberland men deserted. That was a poor business, though they were a sorry enough lot when all's said and done. Two days, it took them to decide they'd had enough, and then they just turned round and went home again, leaving us in the lurch. So, we pushed on to Dumfries, and they opened the gate to us – and the men who did that will live to rue it. And we hadna been there more than two days when a messenger came in from the Lady Keir, who's a Napier and Montrose's niece, telling him to go straightway to Stirling, where he would find the garrison ready to change sides. But he had no help other than the soldiers from England – all those trimming Border men, Homes and Maxwells and the rest, and Roxburgh, never trust a Kerr, they're an unchancy race – none of them would take the King's commission. It would have been lunacy to try to cut across to Stirling, and Montrose may be daring and opportunist, but he isna stupid. When we heard that Callender – he's the general Leslie left behind to watch over Scotland – when we heard he was coming with five thousand men against us, there was no choice but to go back to England. But he told Francis and me to come here, and keep watch for him, send word when time is ripe to try again, and try to sound out some support from the lesser lairds along the Border. He's going to stay in the North of England, ye ken, and make Leslie's life a misery.'

'What's he like, the Earl of Montrose?' Grainne asked curiously, and Malise spread his hands, calloused with riding and lute-playing. 'I could tell you what he looks like, and sounds like, but for what he *is*, you'd have to meet him. He isna very tall, nor very broad, he has reddish hair and grey eyes . . . I could paint his picture in words, but you wouldna have the essence of him, his character, what makes men follow him . . .'

'I think I know what you mean,' I said slowly. 'I met him in Oxford, you see, he brought Great-Aunt's letter telling me that Francis was here. He was very quiet, and calm, and friendly, though I know he's been accused of overmuch pride, and he looked to me like a man who knew exactly where he was going, and what he had to do, and would do it regardless of cost to himself.'

'That describes him verra nicely,' Malise said. 'Add to that, that he perhaps sees a greater purpose in all this; he's like a man who follows a light, the light of his own destiny. I think all his life he has wanted to shine, like a candle in the dark, and now in this darkness is his chance. He risks his life in a venture many would call madness, and yet he is happier than I have ever seen him, because he knows it is what he has to do; to win Scotland for the King's cause. And because he has that quality about him, we follow him, though left to ourselves we might not care so deeply for a King who after all has cared very little for us.'

'Will he do it, do you think?' Grainne asked. 'Will he take Scotland?'

Malise smiled. 'If he were any other man, I'd say no, not a hope of it – the dream of a lunatic, or of a King three hundred miles away who doesna realize the situation, and likes to live on fanciful schemes and foolish hope. But James Graham believes he can do it, *knows* he can, or die in the attempting.' He paused, thoughtfully, and added, 'He showed me a poem in Dumfries. He'd written it, oh, two-three years ago, when he was up at Kincardine in disgrace. It wasna verra long, and most of it I canna remember, but one piece stuck in my mind, you might say, and if you're looking for the key to Jamie Graham, you couldna do better, I'm thinking. Listen:

He either fears his fates too much,
Or his deserts are small,
That puts it not unto the touch
To win or lose it all.

'He sees his destiny, as I said,' Malise finished, 'and

in the balance he has cast himself, and his wife and children, all his friends, the Grahams . . . to win, or lose them all. But I do know this. He alone has the will, and the ability, to conquer Scotland for the King: and when he does, I'd like nothing better than to be there to see him do it.'

Far away, spring thunder muttered unseasonably. I shivered suddenly and said hesitantly, 'What will Francis do? Will he go with you, to Montrose?'

'God knows,' said Malise. 'I think he will, if you don't convince him that you are sincere in what you offer him. If he persists in rejecting you, he isna going to stay here stonily eyeing you over the dinner table, he'll want to escape; and Montrose offers the best means of doing it. So you have until the next invasion, if there is one, to persuade him otherwise.'

'Don't you mean, "we"?' Grainne said, her beautiful eyes resting on Malise's eaglish face, and he laughed. 'Yes, I reckon I do. But we all know him well enough to realize it must be slowly and subtly done, for Francis can be as stubborn as an old mule if he knows he's being pushed.'

That did not stop Great-Aunt adding her forceful personality to the argument. The next morning, I went down to the stable to see Sim about which horse I could have for our foray up into the hills to find Jasper's new pony. As I slipped under the lintel, my eyes slow to adjust to the thick odorous gloom, I heard her sharp voice, still as young and positive as her attitude to life, saying, 'I never thought I'd live to have to tell you this, but you're a fool, Francis Heron!'

'Why?' He spoke softly and clearly, but there was an incipient hardness somewhere in his speech. I tiptoed inside the stable, and slunk into one of the stalls. It contained Malise's nervy chestnut mare, who eyed me and stamped a round hard pink forefoot in warning. I ignored her and stretched up to peer over the low wooden dividing wall. I could see Francis standing just by one of the two tiny windows: the light filtered through the cobwebs on to his face, lending his fine, delicately-drawn features a new, harder, more ruthless maturity. The same light gave Elizabeth Graham an almost witch-like appearance. She said, 'You know very well why. That girl has sacrificed a very great deal for you. She could have made something of her marriage, she had everything most young women would sell their souls for, particularly that flibbertigibbet sister of yours – a handsome, rich young husband, a title, a baby son . . . all those she has given up for your sake, and you throw them back in her face. Francis, she cannot go back, her boats are burned and she has no one else, no other place to go . . . why can you not admit it, and be reconciled?'

'Admit what?' Francis asked, his voice caressingly, deceptively gentle. In all his new strangeness, this was a landmark I did recognize, and I clenched my hands against the rough wood. 'And she did not sell her soul, she sold her body . . . Admit what, Great-Aunt?'

'Admit you still love her,' said Elizabeth Graham, straight and undaunted behind her eagle's beak nose. 'Admit that you still want her, and that lacking her your life has as much meaning as a day-fly's . . . Go on, Francis Heron, admit it! I dare you to!' She jutted her nose at him, and he smiled mockingly in return. 'Why should I admit it, madam, since it so patently is not true? Now if you will excuse me, I have much to do.' He turned and walked away from her, past the stalls towards the door. I instinctively crouched low, hunching into the damp straw by the mare's threatening feet, but it was no good: Drake was with him, as he had been since the previous day, forsaking me and Jasper entirely, and now he came sniffing in friendly welcome at my skirts. Feeling foolish in the extreme, I rose reluctantly to my feet, to meet Francis's unblinking, hostile eyes. 'Why don't you give over and go back to your unspeakable husband?' he enquired coldly. 'Instead of following me around like a mooning child in the throes of her first infatuation.'

'Francis!' said Great-Aunt's voice, reprovingly, and I looked at his dim-lit face and decided, with a calculation that astonished me, to lose my temper. 'If that's the only way I can come face to face with you, then I'll do it and be damned to your stupid hostility. Why can't we at least have a civilized conversation instead of glaring at each other? Or are you afraid of having a conversation with me? Can't we at least,' I added, unable despite all my efforts to keep the wobbly note of pleading out of my voice, 'go riding in the same group? I know Malise asked you to come with us today, and you refused. Why? Why did you?' I broke off, swallowing fiercely to contain my grief, and searched the blank, callous, bored face before me for any sign, any vestige, of the love and companionship we had once shared. And Great-Aunt snapped, 'I think I can tell you why, Thomazine – because he's afraid. He's never been in the habit of running away before, has Francis Heron, but he is now. He fled from Oxford, rather than find out the truth about your marriage, and he'll escape now, to Montrose, rather than admit to himself and to you that there's something left between you. You've built up a fine armour to cover your hurts, Francis, and to prevent anyone ever coming close enough to hurt you again, and now you can't summon the courage to fling it away. It's true, isn't it? It's not her lies you're fleeing, it's her truth.'

There was a brief, fraught silence in the gloomy stable, and then without a word Francis turned again and went out. The plank door banged behind him and his dog: and for the second time in two days, I found some comfort in weeping on to Great-Aunt's stiff black-clad shoulder, and being prickled by the starched gofferings of her old-fashioned ruff. 'Don't worry, child,' she said quietly, against my muffled desperate sobs. 'It will come right in the end, I'm sure of it. He will not hold out against us for very long, you'll see.'

But I had my doubts, recognizing in this new twist to his character a strong resemblance to his eldest brother

Simon, who had an infinite capacity for clinging to unreasonable beliefs, despite all proofs being offered to the contrary, for far longer than anyone who was not a Heron would do. Simon had been brought to his senses at last by Francis's supposed death: I hoped fervently that it would not take a similar disaster befalling me to make Francis see the error of his ways.

But he did come riding with us that morning. We gathered in the barmkin, Grainne and myself and a highly-excited, capering Jasper, to find him sitting the Goblin impassively beside Malise. He ignored me, but there was a slight twitch of his lips for Grainne, and a full-blown smile for Jasper, who rushed up shrieking a welcome, this being the first time the child had seen Francis since his arrival. 'Hullo, shrimp. You're a deal bigger than when I last saw you. No petticoats now!'

'I'm five,' said Jasper breathlessly, 'I've been five for a whole month, nearly. And I'm going to have a pony, Master Graham says I can have the pony he had when he was a little boy, that's where we're going, he's up on the rig with the sheep and we're going to catch him and then I can have him for my very own and Master Graham's going to teach me to ride!' He paused for a much-needed breath and added, 'Are you coming too? Where's Drake?'

'Drake's tied up to keep him from the sheep, and yes, I am coming too, for my sins,' said Francis. 'Do you want to ride with me, for a little?'

I watched as he bent to take Jasper's eager outstretched hands, and swung the little boy up to perch in front of him, and then turned away, biting my lip. That, I thought miserably, was the Francis I had known of old, who had delighted in Jasper's company even in the child's infancy, and the two had slipped back into their old happy unpatronizing friendship as though that terrible sixteen months had never intervened. Sim, eyeing me curiously, helped me up on to my horse's back: a smallish, furry, dapple-grey gelding with long legs and a deceptively sleepy appearance. He was known to all at Catholm as The Thunderflash, and unless kept on a very tight rein was apt to prove his name at the most awkward moments. After all those months with Hobgoblin, he seemed very homely and rustic, but I had ridden him a few days previously and asked Sandy if I could have him for my use. At least, I reasoned, keeping The Thunderflash in control would take my mind off the disturbing proximity of Francis.

He was riding through the gate now, talking to Grainne: I was left with Malise, who gave me an understanding, friendly grin. With Sim dour and silent on a brown garron behind us, we followed them out of the barmkin, along the wall, and turned left up a little muddy track which led between the fields near the tower towards the upland moors of Ninestane Rig. It was not warm, although the sun shone with the bright hard light of a spring morning, and the new crop of oats and bigg was showing fuzzily green in the infield. We climbed in leisurely fashion up the long, shallow hill, and shortly reached the head dyke, which separated infield from outfield. There was a gate here, low and roughly made between the banks of earth, and Francis passed Jasper to his mother and then put Goblin at it. She soared over the obstacle, ears pricked and the plume of her tail flying proudly behind her, and then galloped ahead of us through the brown and green grass and heather and swathes of bracken, her rider crouched low over her neck. We followed more sedately, though I had a job to keep The Thunderflash from flying in pursuit, and Malise's mare snorted and shuffled and sidestepped, flinging up her proud white-blazed head in her impatience to be free. I admired her, for though not with the Arabian breeding of Hobgoblin, she was a beautiful horse. Malise grinned. 'Yon's a terrible trial. An Englishman's horse, she is, or so Sim says – fine for racing at Carlisle on flat firm ground, but if you galloped her over some of these hills she'd break a leg inside five minutes. Too big, ye ken, and no' verra careful where she puts her fine white feet, eh, my lady Tanaquill?'

The mare flicked her russet ears in response, and dipped her head restively. 'Tanaquill?' I said. 'Isn't that from *The Faerie Queen*?' An irresistible memory of Lucy and her endless stream of horses with literary names rose to amuse me. Malise said, slightly sheepishly, 'Aye, from *The Faerie Queen* she is, one of Gloriana's names if I remember rightly. Ye ken Spenser, then?'

I said that I did, but did not like him so well as Shakespeare or Doctor Donne, and we fell to discussing poetry and plays with enthusiasm, Grainne joining in whenever she could get a word in between us and Jasper's chatter. Behind us, Sim whistled tunelessly through his remaining teeth, and above us was an infinity of sky, blue and cloud-crossed, and before us the wide rippling dun grassy moors, where the sheep roamed in their ceaseless search for new fodder, their bleak melancholy cries blown across to us by the wind. A long way ahead, Francis turned Goblin and sent her racing back to us, and a brown bird shot out of the grass with a ghastly echoing shriek of warning. 'A whaup,' said Malise, 'you'd call it a curlew, I'm thinking. Many's the reiver whose hiding-place has been discovered through yon bird. And he shouldna be galloping her over this ground, she isna used to it.'

Francis pulled Hobgoblin up in front of us with a flourish. The weeks of standing in the stables or being briefly exercised by Holly or myself had not diminished her fitness: she hardly sweated at all. 'Archie's up ahead, by the Stones,' he said, 'he'll know where the pony is.'

We rode on through grass and heather, whin and dead bracken, skirting the tempting greener areas of wet moss, where a horse could swiftly be stuck fast if it strayed too far. Staring ahead, trying not to be aware of Francis, I could discern what appeared to be an outcropping of rocks. However, as we drew nearer the shapeless grey mass revealed itself to be a circle of stones, man-high, on the right-hand edge of the long ridge where it started to fall away more steeply towards the Roughley Burn.

'There they are,' said Malise, pointing, 'the Stones of Ninestane Rig. God knows who raised them, whether it was men at all, or done by olden giants, or magic. Some say Merlin had a hand in it, as he seems to have had a hand in most strange things hereabouts – if it was not Thomas the Rhymer, of course. There's evil tales of yon, and not all of them fanciful, and when they come up here for the summering with the cattle, the shieling huts are a good way off.'

'What tales, Master Graham?' Jasper asked. 'Can you tell me some of them, please?'

'I doubt they're suitable for a wee lad,' Malise began, but Jasper interrupted. 'Oh, please! Mother tells me *horrible* stories about Ireland and Cuchulain and the Red Hand and I haven't had a single bad dream – oh, please!'

'It's true,' said Grainne, 'he's tougher than he looks, my Jasper, and he's long exhausted my stock of tales, and Thomazine's too – and anyhow it'll sound better up here in the wind and the daylight.'

'Well,' said Malise, 'the story tells of a certain wizard called Lord Soulis, who was the Lord of Hermitage in the bad old days, hundreds of years ago. Now Lord Soulis was evil, as evil a man as ever walked in Liddesdale, and that's saying a good deal. He killed a giant called the Cout of Kielder – Kielder's in Tyneside, just over the Border – by drowning him in Hermitage Water.'

'But he couldn't if he was a giant,' said the literal-minded Jasper, 'the water isn't deep enough, I can walk across it if I hop on the stones.'

'Aye, and the Cout had magic armour into the bargain. No usual way of killing him would work. But somehow, by magic or trickery, Lord Soulis got him to go down to the burn, and then he and his spearmen forced the Cout's head under the water until he was dead. There's a grave-mound by the old ruined chapel just upstream from the Castle and that's supposed to be where the Cout's buried.'

'And what happened to Lord Soulis?' asked Jasper. Malise grinned. 'Oh, you needna worry, he met his just deserts. There was a tale that he couldna die till he was bound with three ropes of sand, but of course you need magic for that, ye ken, Jasper? So when his wickedness grew too great for even his followers to stomach, they sent for Thomas the Rhymer, True Thomas of Ercildoune, and he helped them make the rope to bind Lord Soulis.'

Jasper's eyes were huge. 'And *then* what did they do?'

'They wrapped him in a cope of lead, and took him up here, to the Stones, and there they lit a great fire – just over there, perhaps, where it's a wee bit sheltered from the west winds – and over the fire, when it grew all hot and white and glowing, they put a brazen cauldron full of water, and in it they cast Lord Soulis, still bound with sand and lead, and they boiled him.'

I shivered. Jasper, quite unaffected, said cheerfully, 'And did he die, then?'

'Well, I dinna reckon even Lord Soulis would survive being boiled alive, once bound with ropes of sand,' Malise told him. 'They say that when he finally died, Hermitage sunk a little way into the ground because it was burdened with so many of his evils. And on winter nights you can still hear Lord Soulis shrieking in his last agonies, in the wind round the Stones.' He smiled wryly. 'Despite all the Minister's efforts to root out every vestige of superstition, Archie reckons he hasna lost one lamb nor sheep nor cow since he took to summering them on this side of the Rig.'

'But doesn't he fear the ghosts?' Grainne asked, and Malise said, 'There's nothing on earth Archie Graham fears. He's one of my grandfather's old companions in mischief, they went reiving together in the days before the Union, and he knows all the hills and fells and mosses like his own hand; which he'd not have had the chance to do if he'd been frightened of Lord Soulis's ghost.'

We were almost at the Stones now, and grim and strange they were, sprouting out of the grass like giants' bones. Oblivious to ghosts or eeriness, sheep grazed all around, and the new lambs skipped and bounced through the heather. Archie came to greet us, his dogs at his heels, a tiny, gnarled, wizened old man, bonneted and leather-jerkined like Sim, with a sheepskin cloak over his shoulders to shield him from the cold winds of April. As soon as the snow had gone from the hills he had taken his flocks up the Rig, with only a couple of boys and another shepherd to help him. Later, the Graham tenants and farmworkers would bring the cattle up, to take advantage of the new-sprouting grass and put some flesh back on their ribs after the long, hard winter spent surviving on scanty hay and straw, and even broom and gorse: but for now, Archie and his flocks had this side of the hill to themselves.

He greeted us in a stream of Scottish, from which I could make out barely one word in three. Malise introduced Grainne, myself and Jasper, and explained the errand, and at once Archie's face cracked into a grin. 'Aye, I ken where the wee garron is. Hobbie's got 'un to go after a coupla yowes, ower to Whitrope. He'll be back betimes.'

'Then we'll wait for him,' said Malise. 'We can have our dinner here by your sheep, Archie, and maybe you can sing the ladies one of your songs?'

So we found ourselves a sheltered spot by Archie's hut, a tiny primitive edifice built of stones and turves, with a bush for a door and a hole in the roof for the fire-smoke. Our alfresco dinner was plentiful, if rather plain fare: oatcakes and butter and the hard local cheese, that had to have the hairs removed from it before it was eaten, a venison pie and cold roast pieces of chicken. Archie disappeared with an earthenware jug almost as lined and cracked as his whiskery face, and returned some time later with his own contribution, two or three pints of frothy, warm, strange-tasting ewes' milk. I was not yet accustomed to the Scottish habit of drinking fresh milk, whether from cows, goats or sheep, in such quantity, and a few sips of the pale liquid was enough for me: the others in the party, however, drank deeply. Then Archie, with sly winks and a knowing cackle, produced from somewhere on his person a small flask. He uncorked this and passed it to Francis, who took a long draught and handed it on to Malise. 'A wee drappie o' uisquebaugh niver hurt nane,' Archie said, seeing my curious face; and Malise, who had no more than sipped it, added, 'Try some if you want to, though I'd advise you not to take too much in one swig.'

'Don't worry,' said Grainne. 'I know the Irish version of this, and no, Jasper, you can't have any – it would burn a hole in your throat.'

'Oh,' said Jasper, crestfallen. 'But if it'd burn a hole in my throat,' he added shrewdly, 'then why won't it burn a hole in yours?'

'Ah,' said Grainne, her eyes suddenly dancing with a mischief I had not seen in her since Henry died, 'but you are only little, and your throat is soft and tender. Mine, on the other hand, is all tough and leathery and no amount of uisquebaugh will make any impression on it: and so I reserve the right to have a sip.'

Jasper sat pondering this, his face wrinkled with the seriousness of his thought. Then, as his mother took the flask from Malise, he said cunningly, 'Mother, how old *are* you?'

Grainne spluttered into the flask, and Malise burst out laughing. Francis said, 'Old enough not to have uisquebaugh burn a hole in her throat, shrimp, so let her alone. Time enough for that sort of thing when you're older.'

'Oh, all right,' said Jasper, with the cheerful resignation to adult decree which was one of his most endearing characteristics.

Grainne handed the flask to me, and I raised it cautiously to my lips and swallowed a bigger gulp than I had intended. Liquid flames seared my throat as I swallowed convulsively, and then simmered down into warm comfortable embers somewhere below my ribs. 'I did warn you,' said Malise, as I wiped my streaming eyes. 'It isna weak, yon hell's brew of Archie's.'

I gave it to Sim, after another sip, and settled down in the cool grass, listening to the Scots voices all around me, their accent and emphasis and intonation so different from the Suffolk sounds I was used to. And I was aware, all down that side of me, like being conscious of the sun's warmth, of Francis's presence, of the way he spoke and ate and drank, and never once even lifted his eyes to my face. It was as if I was not there, an invisibility in the grass, and I found it a peculiarly distressing experience. I was glad when Archie said, in the middle of the talk, 'A song, did ye say, Maister Malise? Aye, I'll sing for the lassies. Would ye rather I'd sing o' the auld days, or some love song or sichlike?'

'Sing what you like best,' said Grainne, and Archie cleared his throat, spat into the grass, inflated his meagre chest and sang.

For one so wizened and ancient he had a remarkable voice. I had expected the singing version of his speaking one, dry and thready and cracked, but the mellow tuneful tones were those of a much younger man. He sang a strange eerie ballad about a girl and her demon lover who came for her after seven years' separation and enticed her away from her husband and little son, offering to show her 'where the lilies grow, At the bottom of the sea.' As the last echoes of its tragic ending wound round the high hills, I decided that it was not a song for singing up here late at night. We applauded, sincerely appreciative, and Malise suggested another.

'A muckle sad yin, this,' said Archie, dragging his countenance into even more mournful lines, and embarked upon some long song-tale of a Border reiver slain at his door in revenge for some crime or misdemeanour. I did not find that part particularly affecting: it was the last verse which brought hot tears to my eyes and a deep sudden stab of agony in my soul, so utterly did I identify with the widow's lament:

Nae living man I'll love again,
Syn that my lovely knight is slain,
With aye lock o' his yellow hair,
I'll chain my heart for evermair.

And I had to endure it, to brazen it out, to conceal the grief that I had once felt when I had thought him truly dead, although no more lost to me than he was now. And this was immeasurably worse, to have him living and breathing, so near that I could touch him, and to know that I now meant nothing to him, nothing at all.

Grainne noticed, and touched my arm to send her comfort to me: but pride kept my head high and my face unmoved, until the boy Hobbie came trotting up on a small rotund shaggy bay pony, his long legs dangling down each side of the barrel-like body and brushing the grass. His face fell when Malise explained what we wanted, but brightened when my cousin promised him that a bigger horse would be sent up as a replacement. Jasper, fairly bursting with delight, was lifted up on to the broad sagging hairy back, and with Malise holding him in position was walked three times widdershins around Archie's hut, trying to look as adult as possible, although with the garron's width his legs stuck out sideways in ridiculous fashion. Then, with many thanks to Archie for our entertainment, we set off down the Rig towards Catholm, Jasper still astride the garron, with Malise and Grainne riding close by in case the somnolent little pony took the improbable thought into its head to play tricks. Accordingly, I found myself forced to ride alongside Francis, and he showed me his view of such an arrangement by putting his heels to Goblin's flanks and sending her racing on ahead of us, past the Stones, scattering whaup and peewit and sheep as it went. And before I could have any other thought in my head but anger, The Thunderflash took the bit between his teeth and with an ill-tempered snort stampeded in pursuit.

I had not experienced my mount in full flight before: an exhilarating ride it proved to be, when I was not clinging on for dear life, for the grey had a turn of speed to match Hobgoblin's, and the nimbleness to swerve round or jump over any inconvenient obstacles in his path. Far ahead, I saw Francis halt his horse and turn in the saddle to watch our approach. I sawed on the reins, but The Thunderflash laid his ears flat, stretched out his head with determination, and increased his speed. I had flattered myself, thinking that I was no mean rider, but the horse took no more notice of me than if I had been a midge on its back, and I began to be seriously frightened. My hat had gone long since, my hair whipped and stung my face, and my whole body and brain, desperate and determined not to be defeated, was given over to the task of staying in the saddle. Francis must have seen what was happening, but as I flew past him made no effort to stop us or to come after: and that more than anything lent a furious strength to my struggles. As the ground began to slope downhill I sensed that The Thunderflash was tiring: I hauled on the right-hand rein and was rewarded by his change of course, sweeping wide along the side of the hill and up again towards the place where Francis and Goblin watched. By now the dappled hide was slick and dark with sweat, foam dripped from his mouth, and the great muscles in shoulders and quarters laboured with increasing effort. It was easy to slow him further, and to bring him to a final, welcome halt not a yard from Hobgoblin's beautiful black nose.

'That was a stupid trick to play,' was Francis's chilly, contemptuous comment: and I flushed angrily. 'D'you think I did it on purpose? You must have seen me hauling on the reins, the brute's got a mouth like cast iron. If he'd fallen, at that speed ... After what happened to Orlando, you can credit me with a little more sense than that.'

Orlando had been my horse, long ago at Goldhayes, in the peaceful, balmy days before war intervened so brutally in our lives, and he had fallen and broken his leg as I rode him too fast and furious through the park. Out of that incident had come Francis's first admission of his love for me: and as I saw his face now I knew it had been a mistake to remind him of it. 'You won't win me over by killing another horse, you know,' he said coldly. 'Nor by tears, threats, pleas, anger . . . it is over, madam, over and finished and done with, and I wish you'd cease this tiresome behaviour and go bother some other poor unfortunate with your boring infatuations.' He turned the black mare's head, and my anger and grief and frustration boiled over. I could hit him, I thought furiously, and as the idea crossed my mind my gauntleted right arm swung back and out, almost of its own accord. Venting my suppressed feelings lent my blow a force I had never dreamed I possessed, my leather-clad fist connected with a vicious thud against the side of Francis's face. I saw his look of incredulous fury as his head jerked back from my punch, and then his hand shot out and grasped my wrist, extremely painfully, so that I had no chance of escape, let alone to deliver a second blow. Seething with rage, I tried to pull free, and cried out with the pain as he twisted my wrist to pull me half out of the saddle, his pale eyes blazing coldly into mine. Suddenly my anger dropped away, and I was afraid of what he might do: for my husband Dominic had looked like that once, when I had defied him over my affection for Drake, whom he wanted to kill: and then his hands had come up to grasp my throat. The agonizing pressure on my wrist increased: I gave a small involuntary whimper of pain, and Francis smiled. 'If you want violence, madam, I am ever willing to oblige you, but that is the only thing I will do for you. You will cease following me about, is that understood?'

I was crying now, my face shamefully awash with tears, but on that I would not give in. I shook my head.

'Understood?' said Francis again. I cried out, 'No! No, I won't! You might just as well ask me to stop breathing as to stop loving you, and if you want me to stop trying to get you to see reason and truth, well I won't, not now, not ever, and none of your cruelty nor your torture,' I finished with some drama, 'is going to make me give up, not after all that's happened.'

For a moment longer the alien eyes stared into mine: then he released me, so abruptly I nearly fell from the saddle, and dug his heels cruelly into Hobgoblin's sides. With a snort of surprise at this unwonted treatment, the mare half-reared, stiff-legged, turned on her heels in obedience to his savage tug on the reins and fled away, hooves drumming, down the long Rig towards Catholm.

By now, Malise and Grainne were approaching, Jasper self-important between them and Sim shambling along ten yards behind on his ancient nag. I scrubbed urgently with my uninjured hand at my tear-dabbled face, but there was no point ever in any attempt to deceive Grainne. She said as soon as she came close, 'Did he hurt you?'

Gingerly, I drew off the glove with my left hand. Like a bracelet around my small, bony wrist, the new bruises stood out crimson. 'Flex your fingers,' she said, and I did so. They moved stiffly and painfully, but at least they moved. 'Your wrist's not broken, at any rate,' said Malise, and in his voice was real distress. 'For Christ's sake, is he mad?'

'No,' I said, 'but I must have been. It was my fault really, for I, I lost my temper and hit him. And then he lost his, and I can't really blame him.'

'Nor you,' said Grainne drily. 'I doubt I could have stayed my own hand were I in your circumstances.'

'Doesn't Master Heron like you any more?' Jasper asked me earnestly. 'You were going to be married to him, weren't you, Aunt Thomazine? Doesn't he want to marry you any more?'

'He can't very well,' I said, and then, remembering

the dour presence of Sim, well within earshot, changed what I had been going to say. 'No, Jasper, it appears he likes me no longer.'

'And I don't think I like him either, if he doesn't like you,' said the small boy fiercely. 'Not if he hurts you like that. I hate him!'

'But I began it,' I told him, gently, 'so you must not say that. He has his own reasons, and even if I am angry with him, I can't hate him, ever, so don't turn against him on my account.'

'Well, I think he's horrible,' said Jasper sternly, and would not be shaken from that view despite his mother's protests. It was a silent and gloomy group which wended its way down from the Rig, and at the thought of seeing Francis again, and worse, of Jasper repeating all he had just said to Francis's face – and he was quite capable of it, being as blunt and fearless as his dead father – my heart sank within me.

But that prospect was not, fortunately, to be, for we arrived back to be told of Francis's abrupt departure, not half an hour before. 'He took naught but a cloak and a pair of pistols and some food in a saddle-bag, and he even left his dog behind,' said Sandy, scratching his head in perplexity, 'and he didna say where he was going – in fact he didna say anything at all, and if looks could kill, me and Mam would ha' been dead long syne.'

As ever, the thought of my ferocious and formidable great-aunt being called 'Mam' by her amiable bear of a son almost brought a smile to my face, and I could not but feel relief at Francis's departure. The events of the afternoon had left me emotionally drained and exhausted: he had won this battle in our own tragic little war, and I must rally my forces before any attempt to continue the fight. I could only pray that, wherever he had gone, he would not put himself needlessly into danger, and that he would come back safely. I lived in a constant state of anxiety during the next weeks, waiting for his return, conscious all the while that when he did appear, it would mean again the indifference, the cruelty and coldness that had come near to breaking my heart.

What increased my pain and longing was the sight of Malise and Grainne according so well. Often I would catch him looking at her when he thought she would not notice, and the soft, shy expression in his eyes would twist my heart with sweet glad bitter anguish. Of all my friends, Grainne had suffered the most, and most deserved the love I saw dawning in Malise's face: and yet it heightened my own lovesick sorrow, because I could not command that look from Francis, not any more. And Grainne, for one normally so perceptive, seemed strangely oblivious to him, her calmness unchanged, untempered by the laughter she had shared with Henry. But when Malise announced his intention of going in search of Francis: 'For I've more than a wee inkling of where he's gone and what he's about, and if I'm right he may well be in need of a friend,' Grainne changed abruptly, her shoulders went down, and the smile left her face. 'If you must go, then you must,' she told him, but I could sense her disappointment and, after his departure, could not resist probing her feelings. 'Do you like Malise?'

'Malise? Yes, of course I do,' said Grainne. 'He's worth ten of his brother, after all, and he's been uncommon good to Jasper, teaching him to ride. Why do you ask?'

'Why do you think?' I countered mischievously, and Grainne's lovely green eyes, long-lashed and dark-pupilled in the soft candlelight, suddenly took on the spark and flame of delight, such as I had rarely seen in her. 'You're as bad as Lucy,' she said, referring to Francis's incurably romantic sister, and laughed. Grainne rarely did that, and hardly ever since Henry's death, and I knew then that whatever Malise felt for her, she also felt for him: and, I thought unhappily, Henry had not been two years under the green growing grass in that quiet Oxfordshire churchyard.

'He would not mind, you know,' she said, startling

me as so often before with her perception. 'To love is not to be a dog lying forever in the manger, jealously guarding what it cannot have: and wherever he is, I know he would wish me to take what happiness is offered. When he was killed I thought I could never love again, just as you did when you thought Francis was dead: and now I am learning that I might be wrong. Do you think me disloyal?'

'Less than I was,' I said, miserably honest with myself. 'I had not known of Francis's supposed death for a month when I married Dominic. Oh Grainne, you know I wish you so happy, and I pray God you find love again, but I can't bubble over with joy for you, my own miseries have made me a poor friend. And I have only myself to blame for it,' I added.

'But not only yourself. "As flies to wanton boys, are we to the gods: they kill us for their sport," ' Grainne quoted softly. 'Fate, and thoughtlessness, and malice, and greed, and trickery, have all conspired against you, and raised such a barrier as you feel you may never surmount. Yet you must have some hope, or you are lost.'

'When he comes back, I will try again,' I said. 'I have nothing left to lose, after all, save my pride, and that is better lost, I think. What was it that Montrose said, in that poem?'

' "He either fears his fates too much, Or his deserts are small, That puts it not unto the touch To win or lose it all," ' my friend quoted. 'If that is indeed his key, he will unlock the door of Scotland for the King to walk in: and if that is yours also Francis will not deny you forever. It is his key you must find; you had it once, you cannot have lost it so completely.'

'Perhaps,' I said, and smiled ruefully, carrying the metaphor to its logical conclusion. 'But in the interval the lock has been changed, and I am not a locksmith. Nor am I a thief.'

Chapter 3

The last good-night

Those have most power to hurt us that we love.
(Beaumont and Fletcher, *The Maid's Tragedy*)

The bleak northern April gave way to a gentler, balmier May: and thence to June, when the hills were clothed with fresh new grass and green bracken, young and sappy, and perfect grazing for the black skinny Border cattle and their tiny woolly calves, all leg and liquid dark eyes with a bloom on them like a grape. The herd were up now on the Rig, and the farmers and cottars with them, living in their summer shielings, milking them, making butter and cheese and herding them to the best grazing. Sometime during that month, Francis had a birthday and became twenty-two years old: and I thought also of my baby Kit, who had been ten months on this earth, and would now be crawling and babbling and learning and growing, a personality in the making, and no longer the anonymous infant whose only actions had been to sleep, and feed, and cry. And I would, unless some unforeseen miracle happened, only know him as that tiny child, I would never be able to watch him grow, see the flowering of intelligence and personality that was so entrancing in Jasper. I thought much of Kit during those weeks of waiting for news, and sometimes in my blacker moments I wept, thinking of the child I had abandoned for what seemed to me then to be a vain illusion, a foolish chimera that had lured me away from him to this desolate place, and left me there bereft.

Even during my more cheerful, positive moods, I worried also about the exact nature of Francis's mysterious expeditions. I lay awake often, with my more lurid imaginings processing gaudily and gruesomely through my mind – scenes of squalid seduction and drinking vying with romantic secret conclaves of Montrose's supporters and the vivid horrible realities of the death that might well await one who was too careless of his life. They had just hanged a man who had joined Montrose in Dumfries, along with two other Royalist supporters, and I prayed that Francis would not suffer a similar fate.

In the end, I plucked up the courage to ask Great-Aunt Elizabeth whether she knew just what he and Malise were doing: and her reply was characteristically blunt. 'Spying for Montrose.'

It was what I had half-expected to hear, but my heart still lurched uncomfortably within my ribs. 'Spying? But . . . what will they do to him – them – if they're caught?'

'Hang them, most like,' said Elizabeth, with some grimness. 'If, that is, they get caught. But I doubt Malise will, and Francis, though he's grown uncommon foolish of late, has not I think left his senses entirely behind. If he wants to get himself killed, it won't be at the end of a Covenanting rope.'

'Spying . . .' I said slowly. It had a sly, evil, unpleasant sound to it. 'What exactly do you mean by that?'

'They travel around the Borders, assessing strengths of garrisons, sounding out potential Royalists, gathering support. They've been doing it for nearly a year now, off and on.'

'But how do they get away with it?' I asked, puzzled, for Malise, though obviously Scots, did not have a face and bearing that were easily forgotten, whereas Francis was plainly English to anyone with an ear to listen. My aunt laughed drily. 'Malise, believe it or not, puts a pedlar's pack on his back – he has an arrangement with an obliging man who calls here sometimes, Tam Crozier. And your beloved Francis, who has the Devil's own effrontery, passes himself off as an officer of Parliament's army, come to canvass support for the Scots invasion of England. That is, when he is not pretending to be an itinerant musician . . . you would be surprised,' said my great-aunt, 'how well he can imitate a Scot.'

'No, I wouldn't,' I told her, remembering the gifted actor that jostled with all the other complexities inside Francis's head: and then at the vision of the two of them, improbably disguised, slinking round the Borders and spying for Montrose, my sense of the ridiculous rose up and I could not repress a smile. 'But I would love to see them. They must be quite a sight.'

'They are: as folk say in these parts,' Elizabeth Graham commented, 'they look a wee thing daft. I know what you think, that it is a stupid, reckless schoolboy trick, and it is my thought too, but they have not yet been caught, nor as far as I know even suspected. Folk round Liddesdale are used to accepting things at face value and asking no questions. One or two could give trouble: there's a Graham kin to us down at Netherby at the foot of the dale, who's a friend to the Covenant party and fought for the Parliament at Edgehill. He's come calling once or twice, but no one is likely to tell him anything. Gib is the one who would be expected to support Montrose, but he is very obviously quite uninterested in politics, and Malise has remained deliberately in the background. It is not generally known that he was in Montrose's household at Kincardine for the better part of a year, after Jamie was released from prison. Francis they remember from when he was here as a boy, and he also is accepted without question. No doubt a diligent observer who was prepared to bribe one of our household or play the spy would learn the truth, but of all our family and servants there is only one who is not utterly loyal, and not even she would ever sell her own son to the Edinburgh hangman. Oh yes, it is a dangerous game they play, but if they do get caught, I do not think it will be in Liddesdale.'

This conversation did nothing to assuage my fears. I dreaded to hear news of his capture or death: or of the same fate befalling Malise, for Grainne's sake. And yet

I could not help but admire this ludicrous, romantic, quixotic daring, the bold insolence of the whole operation that smacked so strongly of Francis: I would have laid a heavy wager that the original idea had been his. And I was conscious, despite my strongly practical nature, of a quiver of envy.

And yet I also dreaded to see him on his safe return, within the cold, cruel impersonal armour of his indifference . . . but it was *not* indifference, I realized suddenly. The feelings he showed were too strong for that. It was not that he no longer cared; it seemed much more likely that he did.

I sat up in my bed, gazing into the soft darkness of the June night, wondering with sudden hope. If he did not care about me, why did our meetings always end in such anger, not only on my part, but his? Why did he always retreat, when it was not, nor had ever been, in his nature to do so? It could only be because he did still love me, but for his own reasons, and despite his feelings, was trying not to be involved with me again.

It was a remarkably hopeful view, and one that in all probability would not survive our next meeting – if it ever occurred. But I was filled with a new resolution to win him back. 'I will have him, in the end I will,' I promised myself, wide-eyed and exultant in the warm dark. 'Please God, let me have him in the end, may I make him love me again, for I cannot bear it if I lose him now.'

In the second week of July, Malise came back: unobtrusive, self-effacing as ever, no one knew of it till he frightened the life out of the little maid Bessie by stepping through the door from the Tower into the new wing and asking her politely to bring him some food. Bessie dropped the silver candlestick she was cleaning, with a crash and a scream that brought all of the household within earshot running. Everyone – except of course for Grizel, to whom delight was an unknown emotion – was overjoyed, and none more so than Jasper: he capered round the chair into which Malise had sunk exhausted, saying, 'Oh, Master Graham, now you're back we can go riding again!'

'Hasna Gib been taking you?' asked Malise. His brother, with whom this was a sore point, grunted, 'Oh, aye, I've been taking the wee lad, but he prefers you, it seems.' Gib, who made no secret of the fact that he considered his younger brother something of an ineffectual weakling, had taken over Jasper's riding lessons with the manner of a professional called in to right amateur bungling, and had been most aggrieved to find that his pupil did not appreciate the change.

'Can we go now?' Jasper begged. Malise opened his weary eyes fully and grinned at him. 'No lad, we cannot. There's nae more than an hour to nightfall, and I'm sae tired I couldna climb back on Tanaquill if my life depended on it. Tomorrow, maybe.'

Jasper's face fell. Above his disappointment, I caught Elizabeth Graham's eye, begging her to put the question I did not have the courage to ask, and she obliged. 'Malise, I won't ask you where you've been, or what you've been doing, but where is Francis?'

'Gone south,' said Malise, and then, after a glance round the room to make sure of his listeners, added, 'to see Montrose, tell him of what we've learned in the last few months – that there's no chance of him winning through to Scotland now, unless he comes with an army. And after the battle, there's sma' chance of that.'

There was a sudden, taut silence in the room, and then I said, carefully, 'What battle?'

'Then you havena heard? There's been a great fight by York, a week ago or more, between the Parliament's army and Prince Rupert's – and the Prince was beaten.'

Five words, dropped into the quiet of our listening, only five words: and yet they had the ominous quality of a passing-bell. Prince Rupert, that formidable, bold, tireless and brilliant young man whom I had once met on the slopes of Edgehill, and who had been the guest of honour at my wedding, had had all the invincibility of youth. It did not seem possible, and yet Malise had said it.

'Are you sure?' asked Grainne, speaking for all of us. Malise nodded wearily. 'Oh, aye, I'm sure. He relieved York, which Lord Fairfax was besieging, and then the two armies joined battle near some place close by, called Marston, and it was a botched fight by all accounts, the Prince wasna expecting anything to happen that day and he was taking his supper when the Parliament soldiers charged . . . You remember yon tale of My Lord of Newcastle's Whitecoats, that swore their uniform would be dyed with the blood of their enemies? Oh, those white coats were red with blood right enough, but it was their own, and now there is not one of them left from that last stand, for they wouldna run away . . . and the King's cause is lost in the North, and may never be won back.'

My cousin Simon, who had opposed my affair with Francis so implacably, would have been with that beaten army, and so would Grainne's brother-in-law Tom Sewell, and Charles Lawrence who had been our friend during the siege of Ashcott and afterwards, and all those Suffolk men, nearly sixty of them, who had followed Simon, their landlord, so heedlessly into war. Although there was nothing that I or God could now do about it, since if the worst had happened they had now been eight days dead, I offered up a brief prayer for their safety. I bore Simon no grudge for doing his utmost to split Francis and myself asunder: he had repented afterwards. It was my husband Dominic whom I would hate for ever for what he had done; and into the back of my mind slunk a new, horrifying, shameful wish, that in some battle if not that one, he would be killed; and die slowly, said my vindictive worse nature.

'I dinna ken when Francis will be back,' Malise was saying, as I dragged my mind firmly back from thoughts of vengeance. 'Nor do I ken what Montrose will do now. He was counting on having some o' the Prince's troops

for another invasion, but after the battle there'll be sma'
chance o' that, I'm thinking.'

My days thus far at Catholm had been so wrapped up
in my own thoughts and fears and feelings that I had
had no room to spare for consideration of the progress
of the war, both in England and in Scotland. Now,
however, I began to take more notice of the vague
reports which filtered in to isolated Liddesdale from
the outer world. There was confirmation of the fight at
Marston Moor, and the defeat of Prince Rupert's army:
and a large Parliamentary force under Essex and Waller
had even moved against the King at Oxford, although
Waller's half had been soundly beaten by his Majesty
at Cropredy Bridge near Banbury. On the whole, the
war seemed to be going none too well for the King,
though of course it was difficult to judge the situation
from such a remote far-flung spot as Catholm, and any
Royalist victories in the distant South would of course
be of less interest to our various informants than the
disastrous defeat closer to hand in Yorkshire. Not all the
North was lost: Carlisle was still in Royalist hands, and
since Gib occasionally visited the place, what news we
had of English affairs was filtered through him. Scots
tidings came from a variety of more dubious sources –
itinerant pedlars, including Tam Crozier, local lairds
returned from jaunts to Edinburgh or Hawick or
Peebles, and Master Scott, the Minister – none of whom
could be described as reliable or unbiased informants.
But it was clear that the Scots had effectively blocked
the Border. There were soldiers garrisoned in every
major town and castle, and we began to see some even
in Liddesdale. The Gordon clan, far to the north, had
attempted to rise in the King's support, and Argyll had
brutally squashed their brief revolt. There appeared to
be no hope for the Royalist cause in Scotland, and it
seemed that Montrose, still hovering in Carlisle with a
much-depleted force (Prince Rupert had commandeered
most of it after Marston Moor), waited foolishly and in

vain. But the Border was not so closely guarded that one man could not make his way over the high bleak trackless hills: and ten days after Malise's return Francis rode in.

He looked almost as exhausted as he had during his long terrible illness nearly two years ago, after Ashcott, and Hobgoblin, her beautiful coat dull and mud-caked and staring, was in little better state. Even the ecstatic welcome of Drake, who had pined pathetically during the two and a half months of his absence, was too much: and Elizabeth Graham, assuming her usual dominating role, hustled him straightway to bed. It was enough for me, for the moment, to know that he was safe, and sleeping the sleep of the dead the clock round and more, in the little chamber below Grainne's. I could not muster the courage to seek him out, not yet, however in need of comfort he might be. So I went about my business with an uncomfortable feeling of nausea clogging the nether regions of my stomach, and tried to put any emotion but relief out of my mind.

It took him two days to recover, and then I had again the bitter anguish of seeing him every day, knowing his mind and heart as distanced from me as if we were strangers.

But not quite: for he came upon me, as if by chance, in the mews in the undercroft of the old tower. I had gone there to take out the goshawk, Goldeneye, to join Grainne and Gib and Malise ready and waiting outside, for an afternoon along Hermitage Water, seeking pigeon. I was just coaxing her on to my gauntleted fist when the door from the stairs opened and closed, and Francis stood there. I jumped, and Goldeneye screeched, her yellow irises expanding and her beak opening angrily. In the gloom that enveloped everything more than three feet from the tiny window near the hawks' perches, it was hard to read his face. He said curtly, 'I should imagine that I hurt you, the last time we met.'

'You did,' I said, noting with inward astonishment that my voice was quite calm, and level, and unemotional. 'But I understand why. I behaved badly, and I'm sorry.' I swallowed, and added, 'I will try not to importune you again.'

'It is I who should apologize,' said Francis, and the stiffness in his voice reminded me strongly of his brother Simon. 'I also behaved badly.'

I resisted the urge to do as I had frequently been tempted to do with Simon, and crack that ridiculous unnatural coldness with honest, genuine exasperation. 'Then since we have both apologized, and admitted we were both in the wrong, why don't we shake hands and at least agree to be amicable? All I asked of you once was friendship – is that too much for you now?'

There was a silence, broken by Goldeneye, who gripped my wrist more firmly with her fierce yellow feet, rustled her wings and began to preen her barred breast-feathers. I lifted my face from contemplation of her crisp, beautiful brown and cream plumage, and met Francis's eyes across the width of the filthy stone floor. Something, I would swear to it, sparked for an instant in the air between us, and then died. Flushing and confused, like a bashful village girl of fourteen, I dropped my gaze and muttered, 'I'm sorry. Forget I said it.'

'You suggested we might be friends,' he said. 'I'm willing to agree to that, if you really wish it.'

'Oh God, Francis Heron, anyone would think you were arranging a peace treaty!' I cried, finally losing patience. 'I'm not asking for a beautifully written piece of parchment signed and sealed by the King and Prince Rupert and the Lord General and anyone else who happens along. All I want is to *talk* to you occasionally, to pass the time of day in a civilized fashion and not feel an itch between my shoulderblades. Will you at least grant me that?'

For an instant, unbelievably, I saw a twitch of amusement pulling at the corners of his long mouth, then he said, 'Yes, possibly. But no more.' With that, he went out as abruptly as he had come in, leaving me weak and almost laughing with a kind of ludicrous relief. For the first time since my arrival at Catholm, we had spoken together almost amicably, and now I had some real, actual bricks with which to build up my hope, and was nearly content.

It was a beautiful afternoon, and Goldeneye killed twice, and I went through it all as if bemused by my good fortune, although I had done little more than clutch at straws. Once Grainne leaned towards me as Malise and Gib were busied with a kill, and said softly, 'You look happy. Has anything happened?'

'No, well, yes, possibly. I had five minutes' conversation with him, and we parted on good terms – I think.'

'You never know where you are with Francis,' said Grainne. 'But do you think he's coming round?'

'Oh, I don't know, but at least it's a start,' I said, and felt my wide grin crack my face with my happiness. 'Pray God it lasts, and grows better.'

But during the next week things remained just as they had been before, save that his previous hostility had gone, to be replaced with a dispiriting, neutral indifference that I found, after my initial upsurge of hope, to be almost as daunting as his previous anger. Again I despaired, and not even Gib's suggestion that we go up on to Ninestane Rig one evening for a convivial supper around Archie's fire could lighten my depression.

It would be a balmy night: the day had been hot and sunny, and the earth and air still held a residual warmth. The horses were saddled as the sun went down, and a shaggy garron, hardly larger than Jasper's mount, was laden with a barrel of ale slung over each flank. The child himself, all in a fret to accompany us, had been granted his wish, and sat his hairy little pony in a fidget of excitement, paying no attention to Francis at all. Nor had he done so in the ten days since my cousin's arrival, elaborately ignoring him: and that, I was fairly sure, had hurt Francis more than a little. I could see him now, his eyes on Jasper, shadowed and unrevealing of any emotion, but Jasper, who had cancelled his former loyalty to Francis with alarming thoroughness, was showing off his newly-acquired horsemanship for the benefit of Malise and Gib.

In the dimming light, the sky to our left was a glowing incandescent red and green and turquoise and gold behind the flat shadowy shapes of the mountains, Dod Hill and Stob Fell and Bught Knowe, at the head of Hermitage Water. There would be enough light to see by, until we reached the shielings, and on the way back there would be a new-risen moon, as well as torches, to illuminate our path. We climbed up through the infield, talking softly amongst ourselves, Jasper whistling tune-lessly as he rode at Malise's side. As we ascended the long slope of the hill, I looked to left and right, breathing in the summer dusk, seeing the insubstantial hills lavender and purple in the receding light, the valleys and dales bowls of shadow at their feet, and gently garlanded with ethereal wreaths of mist above the waters. The eerie screech of a whaup echoed above us, and the stars were made new and brilliant in our honour.

The shielings were some way beyond the stone circle, for which I was glad. The fire, fuelled by whin and broom and peats, as well as precious wood from the valley, could be seen from some distance away, and the cheerful sound of singing became audible soon after. As we came close I was surprised to see how many people there were: upwards of thirty men, women and children, most of the latter barefoot, and all so shabbily clad that even in my beech-brown homespun habit, I felt overdressed and out of place. But no one seemed to object to this intrusion of the laird's family at their feast: three scrawny lads took our horses and we were given a warm, friendly welcome, brought to the fire and handed ale in an alarming variety of drinking vessels, made from pewter, pottery, wood or even horn. There were wooden platters to hold our barley bread and oatcakes and cheese, and the hunks of juicy roast lamb, dripping with fat, hacked from the carcasses spitted, crackling and hissing, above the fire. It was all utterly delightful and informal, I thought as I licked my greasily

fragrant fingers, and saw from Grainne's fire-lit, smiling
face as she listened attentively to Malise, that she felt
the same. Jasper, sitting between his mother and me,
was eating with a happy abandonment to sheer greed
that would never have been tolerated at a normal supper
table. And Francis and Gib, on the opposite side of the
fire, had two slatternly-looking girls dancing attendance
on them. As I watched, Gib pulled the more opulent of
the two on to his lap, passing his flask of aqua vitae to
Francis: who drank it off as if it had been water.

All the enjoyment suddenly turned sour. I looked
abruptly away and embarked on a long and involved
game with Jasper. 'I'm going to think of something, and
you have to guess what it is.'

Jasper sucked his fingers noisily, and yawned, showing
a wide row of small even milk teeth. His mother paid
no attention to this display of bad manners, being utterly
absorbed in what Malise was saying. Aware of jealousy
and envy in two directions, I added, 'Are you going to
play?'

'Yes,' said Jasper, his usual enthusiasm rather
lessened by all the food and the lateness of the hour.
'Uh, what colour is it?'

'I can only answer yes or no,' I reminded him. Jasper
yawned again. 'Is it blue?'

'No.'

'Er, is it green then?'

'No.'

Inspiration temporarily deserted him: then he said
abruptly, 'Can you see it now?'

'Yes.'

Jasper cast his eyes round the firelit circle: they lingered briefly on Francis and Gib, who seemed to be trying
to outdo each other in the amount of beer they could
imbibe in one draught, and then passed on. 'Is it something you wear?'

'No.'

'Um . . . is it made of wood?'

126

'Yes.'

'It's this!' cried Jasper, snatching up his greasy wooden trencher from the grass beside him. I praised him, and the game continued, but at last Jasper grew more tired, the cavernous yawns more frequent, and eventually he fell asleep almost in mid-sentence, his small warm body pressed confidingly against me. Across the fire, I saw that Gib and his girl had gone, and his place had been taken by a couple of raffish young Scots, clad in sheepskin jerkins, who were talking animatedly to Francis and the remaining girl. He had his arm negligently across her shoulders, as if by habit, and I realized suddenly that this must be the notorious Kirsty Armstrong, who was so prodigal with her favours. With a sick thump of my heart I looked away to where Archie was preparing to sing. Like many of the company, he had evidently imbibed very well, but it made no difference to his incongruously tuneful voice, save perhaps to mellow it still more. And by some strange unwelcome alchemy, the song he sang was all too appropriate.

Oh, I loved a lass, and I loved her sae well,
I hated all others who spake of her ill:
But now she's rewarded me well for my love,
For she's gone and she's married another.

When I saw my love to the church go,
With bridesmen and bridesmaids she made a fine
    show:
And I followed on wi' a heart full o' woe,
To see my love wed to another.

There were too many memories that song brought back: of the day I had married Dominic, thinking that Francis was dead, and also of another day, at the beginning of my love affair with Francis, when he had sung part of the song to me. As the bittersweet recollection flooded back, I realized that Archie was singing that same strange verse:

The men i' the forest, they askit of me,
How many strawberries grow i' the salt sea?
I answered them back wi' a tear i' my e'e,
How mony ships sail i' the forest?

Involuntarily, I looked at Francis, expecting some sign that he too remembered, and was just in time to see him smooth the girl's riotously tangled yellow curls away from her wet red mouth, and kiss her.

Something had happened to my stomach. I felt physically sick, the oily lamb suddenly queasy within me. Without thought for the slumbering Jasper, I struggled desperately to my feet and ran away from the bright cruel drunken firelight, into the welcoming oblivion of the summer night. I did not care where I was going, I just ran, on and on into the dark, my breath sobbing and the picture still of Francis and that girl, that slut, that whore Kirsty Armstrong, indelibly in front of my eyes like some malevolent will o' the wisp.

Several times I stumbled and fell, over stones or grass-tussock or, once, a somnolent and startled sheep, but always, somehow, got to my feet and went on. My eyes became accustomed to the dark, that here in the North was not so deep, and at last I slowed to a walk, and then halted. For in front of me, flat black against the sky like a mouthful of rotten teeth, were the Stones.

I stared at them, fighting to regain control of my labouring breath. The wind sighed softly in my hair, and in and out of the Stones, like the eerie shushing whisper of the sea: or the wicked Lord Soulis, breathing evilly amongst the Stones where he had met his end. I feared no ghost, I told myself firmly, and I wanted to sit and rest: and where better than against one of the Stones?

I walked in amongst them and sank gratefully down against the largest, which leaned outwards from the circle. Pondering the hideous legends of this place might prove to be a pleasant task beside my recollections of what I had just seen, but was impossible. My feeling of nausea rose again at the thought of Francis, doubtless as Gib had already done, slinking with the girl into the darkness and tumbling her in the heather. Sick with overwhelming jealousy and anger and grief, I drove my fist futilely against the hard impassive mass of stone, and had to suck the salty blood off my knuckles. I could do nothing about them, nothing at all, and that, out of everything, angered me the most. In impotent fury I leapt to my feet and prowled restlessly around the circle, feeling my way from one stone to the next, my fingers registering automatically the minute unseen difference in shape and texture and position, for there was as yet no moon.

There was a light, though, a growing light in the northern sky, and, my attention caught, I gazed at it, for surely the moon would not rise there?

And it could not be the moon. The light was *green*.

I had thought myself an intelligent, educated, rational woman, but I stood rigid, and a thrill of pure superstitious terror lifted the hairs on my back and neck, and sent a shiver running all through me. The wind and the strangeness both brought tears to my eyes. I blinked them away, and stared to the north, fascinated and awed, for now, after that first eerie moment, I knew what it was. Malise had talked of the Northern Lights that set the sky dancing and shimmering twenty times a year on the Borders, more frequently to the north: old Meg had said that the rare displays visible from the hills around Liddesdale were as nothing to the glories to be seen from the Western Isles.

The light grew, and flickered, and tongues of greenish fire began to lick out from the radiant arc on the northern horizon. Utterly entranced, all thoughts of Francis and Kirsty Armstrong totally forgotten, I clung to the stone and gazed at the surpassing beauty unfolded in the sky. The darting, witch-like fingers of light shimmered and twisted and fluttered like banners streaming in an unseen, unfelt breeze between the earth and the stars. As well as green, there were rays of purple and violet and rich rose, shaking and quivering above me like a great windblown curtain of light, and all in a marvellous and utter silence.

I remember I wept from the beauty of it. I do not know how long I stood there, unheeding of cold or stiffness or cramp, spellbound and enchanted as if by witchcraft, until the ethereal lights faded and the radiance withdrew, little by little, before my straining eyes, until there was no more brightness in the north. It was like awaking from a wondrous dream. I became aware again of the small rustles of night, the wind in the grass around the Stones, the stars untouched in their allotted places, of the stone against which I leaned, and my aching legs and painfully cricked neck. With the lights still vivid behind my eyes, I drew deep shuddering gulps of air, as if I had held my breath all the while in awe. Desolately, I supposed that I had better return: if, that was, I could remember my way, for I had come no little distance from the shielings and the fire was no longer visible. I hoped that Malise and Grainne had seen the lights too so that I could share my experience: the view of them down at Catholm, with the bulk of Ninestane Rig interposed, would have been poor at best. I had just collected my wits and was looking round to regain my bearings, when I became aware of a new, dark shape between two of the stones, a shape man-high, that had moved quite silently. I gasped with sudden fear, and backed stealthily towards the edge of the circle, gathering my skirts for a speedy retreat.

'Don't worry, it's Francis,' said his voice, and even in those brief syllables I could tell that there was something strange in the sound of it. But such was my sudden delight – for he must, on purpose, have sought me out, searching for me over half the hill – that I did not heed it. 'Oh, Francis, did you see them, did you see the lights, the lights in the sky?'

'Those? Haven't you seen them before? Though they're commoner in spring and autumn . . . aren't you cold?' He moved nearer, and with incredulous wonder

I recognized in those last words the kind of concern I had never thought to have from him again. I stood stupid with amazement by the stone, and watched his dim shape approaching, coming closer and closer until my straining eyes could discern the pale glimmer of his hair and face and shirt, and the dark shadows that marked his eyes: and then his hands came out to grip my rigid, unbelieving shoulders and pull me against him.

I could not believe it. I wept for joy and relief and overwhelming emotion, crushed against his shirt, while his hands roved over my back and hips and around my waist, and his mouth whispered soft unintelligible endearments into my hair. He guided me backwards until I felt the hard unyielding stone against my spine, and then he disentangled his hands and began to fumble with the buttons of my riding-habit . . .

It was then that I remembered how usually quick and deft were his fingers, and realized that he was drunk. Although I should have been afraid, alone on the moor at night with him in such a condition and his intentions so plain, I was not. It seemed as though my bones were melting and the stars reeled before my eyes as the old desire for him, that I had not felt for nearly two years, threatened to overwhelm me utterly – and I did not care. His unsteady hands finished their task and I gasped, once, at their cool touch on my breasts, and then he smoothed back the tangled hair from my lips and bent his head to kiss me.

An hour earlier, no more, he had employed that self-same gesture to a slatternly girl no better than a whore, clear in my view; and so easily now, and with as little regard on his part, he was planning to seduce me. And I remembered also, on a wave of fear and disgust, the terrible moments in the stable at Nantwich, and the menacing soldier who had wanted my body as Francis wanted me now, with a lust that owed nothing to love or friendship or affection or consent: and was thus no more than an animal's. I had just enough wits left for a stab of perverse anger to taunt me into action. It was as though I had been drowning, drowning in the honeyed deceit of his unscrupulous casual love-making, and had only just in time reached the surface. With the greatest effort of will I have ever needed, I wrenched my mouth from his and twisted and punched and struggled and kicked to win free. Caught off guard, his quick wits fogged by drink, it was easier than I had feared: I plunged to the ground, rolled vigorously over and over, and scrambled to my feet, panting, well out of reach.

'What the devil . . .' He stood staring at me, though in the limited illumination of moonrise we could see very little of each other. 'Come here, you little bitch, and let me have you . . . don't be coy, that's not like you . . .' His voice was soft and slurred and made me shiver with suppressed longing, but my mind was resolute. My shaking fingers groping for the buttons of my bodice, I said, 'No, I won't come to you, however hard you may whistle, for it's plain you only want me for your whore, and I'll not give you my body for your pleasure without having your love in return.'

'You were not so scrupulous with Dominic, were you?' he said, with a new silky, sneering menace. 'You gave him your body, if I remember, and got his wealth and his title in exchange for it, and that's whoredom under a nicer name . . . come here.'

I took two steps backward as he advanced, my heart suddenly thumping unpleasantly as the real possibility of rape became apparent. My heel nudged a stone: on an impulse I bent swiftly and picked it up. It was probably a piece broken off one of the standing stones by frost and weather, and it fitted snugly inside my hand. I said, my voice as firm as I could make it, 'No . . . oh God, don't think I don't want you, but not on those terms, not while you're drunk, any whore would serve you just as well.' I added, unwisely, 'Why don't you go and seek out Kirsty Armstrong?'

'She was not so willing as she promised, and you'll do instead of her for tonight,' said Francis coldly.

'I'm not interested in just tonight,' I said, desperately bunching my skirts in my other hand, 'Nothing less than for ever will do – ah!'

He had suddenly lunged for me, and my overworked eyes had almost failed to see it. I flung myself to one side, and his hands grasped my sleeve. I twisted frantically and with a loud rip of homespun tore myself free. Almost without thinking, I threw the stone with all my strength, not caring how hard it struck him as long as it did. I saw his shape sway forward and fall, whether from a stumble or the stone's force I did not stop to see: I turned and ran out from the Stones, up the long ridge towards the fire and my friends.

When I slowed down to a walk, a stitch stabbing my side, there was no sound of pursuit, and then it was that my cheated body began to regret most bitterly what I had rejected. Dully I buttoned up my abused doublet, exhausted by the wildly swinging emotions that had gripped me within the last hour or so, and reminded myself that I must not weep. I would tell Grainne, but no one else: and I did not think that anyone would guess what had happened.

The fire was almost dead. Heaped around it were several slumbering, snoring shepherds and their women-folk. A uisquebaugh flask was being passed around those still sober enough to tilt it to their mouths. Archie was singing blearily to himself, rocking tipsily backwards and forwards as he sat by the dull peats, and a sleepy-looking Hobbie was holding the Catholm party's horses on the edge of the firelight. Grainne was already mounted and looking around anxiously, her slumbering son a small fire-headed bundle in her arms, but it was Malise who saw me first, and came running clumsily toward me, all but falling flat on his face as he reached me, though he was stone cold sober. 'Thomazine! We were worrit about you. What have you done to yoursel'?'

In the firelight I saw, looking down, the full state of my dishevelment, though fortunately I had managed to button up my doublet successfully in the dark. 'Oh,' I said casually, 'I fell over and ripped my sleeve. It's only the seam gone, it'll mend easy. Oh, Malise, did you see the lights? Weren't they wonderful?'

They had indeed seen the lights, and the discussion that followed served well to divert attention from what I had been doing out in the dark on the moor. It had not been, I gathered, a particularly dazzling display and Malise took it quite for granted. I could see, however, that Grainne had been as spellbound as I. 'And Jasper was mightily impressed,' she added, as we said our farewells and moved away down the hill toward Catholm, safety and sleep. 'Dancing Lights, he called them, which is a very good way of describing them.' She looked down at her son's face, unconscious and abandoned to sleep, still with greasy marks round his mouth. 'It doesn't seem so long since he was a little imp just starting to walk, and now he's almost too heavy for me to hold like this: my arm's aching.'

'I'll take him,' said Malise, guiding Tanaquill close, while Sim brought up his flaming pitch-soaked torch to give the necessary light. Grainne looked at him with a suspicion of laughter in the corners of her mouth and said, 'How can I be sure you won't drop him?'

'I willna do that,' said Malise, with mock indignation. 'Clumsy I may be, but I'm no' daft. Now give yon great lump over here.'

Jasper hardly stirred as he was transferred awkwardly from his mother's arms to those of Malise, and I was deeply envious of such easy oblivion. A huge restlessness was upon me, longing, regret and anger all feverish in my mind, and I was wishing most bitterly that I had succumbed to the sweet drunken touch of Francis's hands. I might be lying beside him now in the dark cool grass between the ancient stones . . .

But I was not, and it did no good to be thinking of it. Malise had dropped behind a little, but not far enough to be out of earshot, and Sim, his torch sending our fantastic shadows dancing behind us like the black counterparts of the Northern Lights, was only just in front.

We passed within twenty yards of the circle, but there were only the usual number of stones, and no additional amorphous shape standing between them; and I wondered with a pang of remorse and fear if Francis might not even now be lying there, stunned by my too-well-aimed stone. But I could not check that he was not without revealing what had passed between us, not only to Malise and Grainne but also to the dour, disapproving Sim. Besides, he was eminently capable of looking after himself, and I did not, I thought, encouraging myself into righteous anger, feel his behaviour unworthy of an uncomfortable night on the hillside. It was warm and unlikely to rain, and he would not come to harm, unless Lord Soulis saw him for a kindred spirit and laid his ghostly fingers on him: and I had no faith in the shade of the Wicked Lord. No, I decided, Francis Heron was probably at this moment sleeping it off in his bed at Catholm, if in his state he had got that far, and deserved no further consideration.

But he was not at Catholm. We walked wearily into the parlour to find Sandy, who had waited up for us to lock the door after, nodding over a tankard of cold mulled ale. 'You're later than I'd thought. Did you have a good look o' the Lights? We didna see much of them at a', down here i' the valley.' He walked over to the door, adding 'Ony more o' you to come?'

'We don't know,' said Grainne, 'Gib and Francis seem to have made their own arrangements – unless they came back before us, of course.'

'No, lass, they havena come back, neither o' them, and I for one can guess why,' said Malise's father, turning the huge key and sliding the bolts. 'Well, I'll bid ye all good night, and make for my own bed. There's a poker hotting i' the fire there, and ale i' the kitchen if you wish for a night-cap, but I'm sae weary I couldna lift it out o' the flames. Good night to you!' And with a friendly, sleepy grin, he lit his candle and shambled off to bed.

I waited until Grainne and I were alone in our chambers, with the ale steaming gently in the hearth and Jasper asleep in a tumble of limbs and sheepskin, and then told her of all that had happened that night. As I spoke, bitter regret washed over me again, threatening to drown me, and I paced restlessly up and down the boards of the chamber. 'Oh, Grainne, did I do right? Will it make any difference? I wanted him so badly, and yet I couldn't, not like that, it wouldn't have been right and when it was over I'm sure it would only have confirmed what he thought of me – that I'm a whore. If I'm going to fling myself into adultery then I don't want it to be a squalid one-night affair with a drunken lover who might just as well have had any woman. I want it to be special . . . and yet,' I added miserably, my eyes on her understanding face, 'I do wish most desperately that I hadn't been so scrupulous!'

'I don't blame you,' said Grainne, 'and yet I'm sure you did right. He has so obviously convinced himself that you're no better than a strumpet, giving yourself *carte blanche* to any man who takes your fancy, that refusing him tonight may, in the sober light of day, give him pause to think.'

'I hope so,' I said, 'and I pray to God I didn't do lasting damage with that stone.'

'If it let some sense into his head,' Grainne remarked drily, 'then I shouldn't waste your worry.'

But my restlessness continued all night. I tossed and turned in my lonely bed, and the dreams that seemed to invade even my wakefulness were all the same, shameful sensual images of Francis and myself, over and over again, that left me weak and shaking and drained with helpless longing, unassuaged and tormenting. At first light I rose with a pounding headache, heavy-eyed and exhausted, dressed in my abused riding-habit and tiptoed downstairs. I felt in desperate need to do something, to submerge myself in activity: and if I should chance to ride up to the Stones, that would not occasion comment.

I had a bannock and a mug of ale from Janet, who

was already up and shovelling hot ashes into the oven in preparation for the day's baking, and then let myself out into the barmkin. There was no sign of life here, except for the fowls gathered round the door in hopes of their morning ration of kitchen scraps. I waded through them and went into the stables.

There was little light, but I could see with a quick glance that neither Gib's mount nor Hobgoblin were there. I walked to The Thunderflash, who looked at me hopefully and nuzzled my sleeve, knowing that I usually brought him some delicacy before a ride. I held out my hand with a broken piece of oatcake on it, and the grey whiskery nose dropped into my palm and neatly slobbered the bannock up, crumbs and all. I rubbed his ears, aware that he was sidling closer and closer – The Thunderflash liked to lean against people, having, for a horse, a pronounced sense of humour – and then I heard a whine. Startled, I looked round and saw Drake, standing a respectful distance from the grey's hind feet, gazing at me with woebegone, appealing dark eyes. Then he whined again, trotted towards the end of the stable, back again, and barked gently. So plainly did he want me to go with him that I gave The Thunderflash a last pat, told him I would be back shortly with his tack, and walked over to Drake. 'Hallo, old boy, what do you want, eh? How did you get in here?' And then I stopped abruptly, for of course Drake had been with Francis last night, and he was unlikely to have got into the stables by himself.

I followed the old dog down the aisle between the horses to the pile of fresh straw and bracken and broom heaped at the far end for their bedding. Sprawled untidily over it, face down and almost anonymous in the gloom, was a dark shape that could only be Francis. My heart thumping, I knelt beside him and took one slack wrist in my hands. It was some time before I could distinguish the slow steady beat under my fingers, and then I broke out into a cold sweat with relief. Drake whined anxiously and thrust his cold wet nose under the tangled pale hair. He was rewarded by a muffled and fortunately unintelligible expletive. Slowly and painfully, Francis rolled over and sat up, one hand clasped to his head and the other trying to fend off his dog, who was attempting kindly to wash any exposed part of his beloved master within his reach. 'For Christ's sake, you bloody dog, get off!'

I obligingly dragged Drake out of the way and made him sit. It was only then that Francis became aware of my presence, and it was obvious from his grey pinched face and set mouth that he was in no state to be circumspect. 'Oh God, not you again.'

'I didn't mean to find you,' I said. 'But Drake pretty well dragged me here. I was going for a ride.' I added ingenuously, 'Does your head hurt?'

'It feels,' said Francis concisely, 'as if at any moment it will split asunder. Did you have to defend your virtue with such vigour?'

'i'll wager,' I said, dodging the question, 'that even if I'd never flung that stone, you'd still have the headache.'

'Take that prim puritan disapproving look off your face, it ill becomes you. You've seen me the worse for drink before, haven't you?'

'No,' I said bluntly, 'not like that. And I don't like it.'

'If I drink myself to death it won't be on your account, I promise you.'

'Oh?' I said nastily. 'On whose? That inviting little Armstrong slut? Why don't you go back to her and get her to minister to your honourable wound – and your other needs?'

'I'll go to Hell my own way if I want to, with no interference from you,' said Francis through shut teeth. 'Now just go away, will you, and leave me in peace; you've got a voice like a scolding old corbie . . . Oh God, woman, will you go away?'

I went, stamping childishly on the stones and slamming the door, with the vengeful thought that if it made his headache worse, I did not care. And at least it seemed I had not done lasting harm . . .

That afternoon, two men rode into the barmkin on tired, ill-groomed horses that, like the Thunderflash, looked deceptively quiet and rustic. Both quite young, one was broad, athletic and unimaginative-looking and walked with a limp, the other a slender youth with a shy, girlish yet determined face, and they asked to see Malise but did not give their names.

When I saw the speed with which their horses were whisked out of sight, and the strangers themselves led hastily into the house by their host, I was suspicious; and more so when the afternoon grew late and they and Malise, and probably Francis as well, had been closeted in the tower for upwards of three hours. I wondered who the men were, and my forebodings were confirmed when Elizabeth Graham, cornered in the barmkin where we could not possibly be overheard, said, 'They are kin to Montrose. The big lame one is Will Rollo, whose brother married his sister, and the other is the Earl of Airlie's eldest son, and Jamie Graham's cousin. What they do here I know not, save that it very likely means our two friends will go a-wandering again.' She eyed me speculatively. 'Have you, as they say in these parts, dinged some sense into Francis Heron's obstinate skull yet?'

'Well, we can argue now without actually drawing blood, metaphorically or literally,' I said, thinking of the conversation, if it could be dignified by such a name, that had taken place that morning. 'But further than that I cannot say . . . Why did those men have to come now?'

'Perhaps they are scouting for Montrose,' Grainne suggested, appearing at our sides. 'Doubtless he still dreams of invasion, but unless he comes with a huge army he will never cross the Border. Perhaps they are canvassing support.'

'He'll get little from the Grahams of Catholm,' said Great-Aunt briskly, 'and none at all from the Grahams of Netherby, or the Elliots of Redheugh and Stobs, and Buccleugh and Roxburgh and Traquair are time-servers and sail-trimmers to a man, and who in these times can blame them? King Campbell and King Covenant rule all Scotland, and if Jamie Graham thinks he can overthrow them he's a bigger fool than Francis.'

Ogilvy and Rollo left that evening. The following morning, still none the wiser as to the purpose of their visit, I came down, earlier than my custom, for the usual informal kitchen breakfast, to find Malise and Francis making ready to travel. My heart sank as I watched their preparations, saw two uncouth, unkempt shaggy garrons waiting outside, and knew they went a-spying again. I caught Malise's eye, and he said ruefully, 'Dinna worry yoursel', we willna be long gone. Tell Grainne no' to fret, and tell Jasper I'll expect to find him jumping the head dyke when I come back.'

'If,' I said. 'Malise . . . Francis . . . be careful?'

'Nae doubt o' that,' said Malise, buckling up his pack. 'There's nae room for the careless in this game. Are you ready, Francis?'

'I'm ready,' said the man, God help me, whom I loved. For a moment his eyes met mine and then looked away: as if he were bidding me farewell, I thought on a moment of panic. 'And wishing to go now, while it's still early.'

'Go where?' Grizel Graham swept into the parlour, as stiff and stark and brittle as a dry stick, her eyes hard. 'Where are ye going this time, eh?' She planted her thin upright figure in front of her younger son, whom I had never heard her address by his name in all the three months I had been at Catholm. Malise looked down at her from his big clumsy height and said, 'That's nae concern o' yours, mother.'

'Spying for that excommunicate hell-spawned Montrose, I dinna doot,' said Grizel, her voice hissing just above a whisper. 'You'll end in Hell, and through the Maiden's embrace like as not, and I'll no' regret it for you're nae true son o' mine!'

'But you willna betray us,' said Malise gently, and it was not a question nor a pleading, but a statement of fact. Grizel seemed to shrink, the light of battle left her stony, blue-grey fanatic's eyes, and she said slowly, with an anguish I had never heard in her before, 'No, I willna betray you . . . I'm your mother yet, dear though it costs me . . . Why canna you leave him and come to God?'

'Because Montrose is my friend, and because your God isna mine, nor will ever be,' said Malise. 'Goodbye, mother. We willna be long gone. Goodbye, Thomazine. Are you coming, Francis?'

'Yes,' said my cousin, and for a moment he looked at me. 'Goodbye, Thomazine. Look after Drake for me, will you? He's shut in my chamber and doubtless bursting to be out.' And he swept me one of his old mocking bows, and was gone.

Well, at least he had said goodbye. It was yet another tiny morsel of hope to cling to in the dreary weeks of anxiety that stretched bleakly ahead: although I did not know which was worse, the strain of waiting emptily for news, or the profligate exhausting emotions that buffeted me whenever Francis and I were in the same house.

All through the next two weeks in the heat of late July and early August, broken by the booming thunder that rolled round the hills and valleys as if invisible giants were playing skittles in the heavens, we waited for news of them. None did we have, though tidings from the outside world became suddenly interesting, full of fearful forebodings. The Irish army, on whom the King and Montrose alike had placed their hopes of invasion, and which had seemed as illusory as a marsh-light dancing over the mosses to lure men to their deaths, had actually landed in the west of Scotland, and was said to be marching inland, burning and ravaging as it came. Now, surely, Montrose must act, or he was nothing but a sham.

Yet the Border was guarded, watched, patrolled; no army could break through.

On the seventh of August, far away in Oxford, my son Kit was a year old. A year ago, I had had my first and last sight of Montrose, and I wondered if I would ever see him again. Despite Malise's evident admiration for the man, I hoped that his invasion plans would come to nothing; for if they did not, Malise and Francis were bound to go with him, and such a crack-brained scheme was certain to fail. Or so Great-Aunt seemed to think, and I had great respect for her judgement. I knew why Malise would follow Montrose, but as usual Francis's motives were obscure. What had happened, I wondered bleakly, to the advanced, not to say revolutionary, ideals which he had professed before the war, and subjugated for my sake? They had been incompatible enough with fighting for the King in England; here in Scotland, where the Kirk had done so much to bring education and enlightenment to the people, it seemed strange to find him on the opposing side. Then I bethought me of the true character of that Kirk, its repressive, joyless inter-fering nature, so utterly alien to all that I knew Francis to be, and realized that, in Scotland at least, he would be fighting on the right side. I wondered what Montrose made of him, and he of Montrose . . . Strange how once, years ago, I would not even have had to ask it of him, and now any conversation beyond a wary, guarded exchange of words was impossible.

He came back with Malise a week after Kit's birthday, and it was quite apparent that neither of them were going to be forthcoming; although Malise walked now with a new air of confidence, even a man-of-the-world swagger to match Gib's (had he not knocked over a tankard of ale or cracked his elbow on the doorpost). And to those who knew him as well as I, Francis's face was a careful noncommittal mask to hide the fire beneath.

Something was going to happen, and it was obvious to me and to Grainne what that something might be, and equally obvious that we were going to be told precisely nothing about it. Seething with anger and curiosity and forebodings, I even tried to revert to my old childish eavesdropping tactics, but a sarcastic comment from

Francis, who caught me once with my ear pressed brazenly to the keyhole of his chamber, soon put a stop to that. I crept away, ears and face afire, like the crawling child he had called me, but it did not put a stop to my burning desire to know what fate hung poised above us all.

The warm weather held. Francis and Malise went riding on the moors, with us or with each other, but there were no more fires by the shielings, no Northern Dancers to shake the stars with coloured icy silent flames. And I had no chance to speak with him alone, he made quite sure of that. Hope, that had buoyed me up all these months, without very much encouragement outside my imagination, began to trickle away. I lost in turn my appetite, my sleep and my sense of humour: and gained despair.

One evening, three days or so after their return, I was in the barmkin with Jasper, having just come back from a short ride. Grainne was inside with Henrietta, who had some childish colic, and all the menfolk were absent on various business. Sim and Holly stood by gloomily as Jasper, for the twentieth time, all but sweated blood in his attempts to unfasten his pony's tack by himself. Seeing his small fingers wrestling dauntlessly with the stiff dirty leather – care of saddlery was to Sim a newfangled untrustworthy modern idea – it was all I could do not to help, but I knew better. Jasper muttered something under his breath that sounded suspiciously like a profanity, and then gave a cry of triumph as the straps and buckles of the garron's bridle finally yielded to his fumbling. 'Here you are, Sim,' he said, proudly removing the tangle of leather, ruthlessly flattening the long-suffering pony's ears in the process. But Sim was not looking: he was staring out at the track leading up to the gate. 'Look yon, Mistress, we've got visitors.'

Three men were riding towards Catholm; two soldiers, with a groom a respectful distance behind them leading a fourth horse on a long rein. My heart thumped suddenly, for what soldiers could be in Liddesdale, save those of the Covenant? 'I'd best greet them,' I said, knowing Grizel to be indoors in the kitchen. And I walked reluctantly towards the gate.

My first thought, as the three approached, was that I knew the first of them, but could not remember where I had seen him. Then suddenly memory flooded back: it was Sir William Rollo, our surreptitious visitor nearly three weeks previously. His companion I had never seen before, however, a tall lean brown-faced man with the indefinable hard-edged air of the professional soldier. And then my eyes went past them to the groom, who was staring at me as if he knew me. I recognized him then: his hair was raggedly cut, his hands filthy and his clothing mud-splashed and threadbare, but there was no hiding that face, clear and calm and resolute, nor the command in the level grey eyes. I almost curtseyed, and then realized that if My Lord of Montrose came riding up to Catholm disguised as someone else's groom, he must have a very good reason for thus being hid.

The Border was guarded against him: no army could win through. But one man, or two, or three might, if they were bold enough: and faint-heartedness was not, I suspected, a characteristic of Jamie Graham's. I said to Sir William, 'I regret that Malise is out, gone over to Gorranberry, but he'll be back shortly. Will you wait for him?'

The two men turned and looked at the 'groom', who gave a barely perceptible nod of his head under its greasy shapeless old felt hat. I thought quickly, wondering if I ought to play hostess myself, and discounted it. I did not want the responsibility for Montrose's capture, should I make a false move, and I was like a blind man groping in the dark, so little had I been told of all the web of intrigue and plans and plotting and allegiances that Malise and Francis had spun between them across half the Borders. 'Jasper,' I called, 'Jasper! Can you ask Mistress Graham – Mistress *Elizabeth* Graham – please to come out and greet her visitors?'

'Yes, if I can find her!' said Jasper, and plunged

eagerly into the house. Sim led the garron and tack into the stables, and Holly, his plain Suffolk face alive with honest curiosity, came up in response to my request and took charge of the four shaggy, unkempt horses.

'So, we meet again, Lady Drakelon,' said Montrose, smiling at me. 'A year ago or more, if I remember rightly, in Oxford: and I brought you a letter.'

'For which I shall ever be in your debt, my lord,' I said. 'Forgive me if I do not curtsey, but I have been told very little about this business, and I do not know who may be watching.'

'And I likewise will not bow. My wish and my thought will have to do instead. May I present Colonel Sibbald, a soldier who has already been of great value to us, and will be more so in this enterprise?'

The Colonel bowed over my hand. 'Sir William Rollo has already been a visitor at Catholm, so he tells me,' said Montrose.

'I regret that on that occasion,' said the cheerful Sir William, 'so swiftly were we whisked in and out, Ogilvy and I, that we caught no more than a glimpse of this delightful lady.'

'Or of this,' said my great-aunt's astringent voice behind us, 'and more's the pity, or this crackpot idea of yours might have been squashed, Jamie Graham.'

I had heard of Montrose's pride, and feared that now, thus addressed, he might withdraw into it: but he was evidently quite accustomed to her ways. 'I fear I am not to be persuaded out of it, madam, so you'd best save your breath now.'

'To cool my porridge, I suppose,' said Elizabeth Graham, with a touch of exasperated affection. 'You had better all come inside before some long-nosed passer-by sees too much. Malise will not be long.'

Inside five minutes, we were all closeted in the tower chamber below Grainne's, which bore the stamp of Malise's untidy personality as uniquely as if he had been there himself: a jumble of books everywhere, piled in the windowseat, on the floor, on the bed, crossbows and longbows and the curious bent sticks that were used in the native Scottish game of golf, though in wild Liddesdale there was small chance to practise it, a lute and a tiny pair of virginals, obviously many years old and decidedly the worse for wear, broken hawk-furniture set aside for mending, and a beautifully carved chess-set. Great-Aunt, with her organizing genius, swept all this paraphernalia off the chairs and stools and windowseat, and from somewhere had conjured up a trayful of food upon which the three travellers fell hungrily.

'We'll not be staying the night,' said Montrose, as they finished. 'We must make all haste we can for the North, before we are pursued.'

'Aye, we've had two narrow squeaks already,' Sir William grunted, stretching out his lame leg with a sigh. 'There was a sharp nosy fellow lurking in Netherby Wood, one of Sir Richard Graham's creatures.'

'We have naught to do with them,' said Elizabeth Graham firmly. 'The King made him a baronet fifteen years ago, and he shows his gratitude by fighting for the Parliament – but then that branch of the family were ever turncoats out for whatever they could get. What was this man doing? Spying?'

'Watching the roads in case anyone with Royalist sympathies was on the move,' said Sibbald. 'Told us what a fine influential man was his master, and how deeply associated with the Covenant and Argyll. Didn't suspect anything though, did he, my lord? Took Will and me for what we claimed to be, and cast never a glance at yourself.'

'And I cast not a glance at him,' said Montrose, wiping his fingers on one of Grizel's best damask napkins. 'So intent was I upon following your excellent advice to hunch my back and hang my head and look less like a Marquis.'

'And when we'd shed his company,' Sir William added, 'we fell in with an old soldier who'd been wounded at Marston and was now making for home.

And that was worse, for God knows how or when, my lord, he'd seen you before.'

'If so much had not hung on it, and hangs on it yet,' said Montrose wryly, 'I might have laughed to see you greet him so courteously and your faces when he ignored you and addressed me by name.'

'Still say we should have killed him,' Sibbald muttered. 'Dead men tell no tales, plenty places round to hide a body and none the wiser.'

'I admit that perhaps it was foolhardy to give him gold and send him on his way,' said Montrose, 'but I could not bring myself to kill him in cold blood at the start of our venture. It would not have augured well for the future, and I think he is to be trusted, drunkard and a deserter though he may be. He wished us good luck, and Godspeed, and we need all the fortune we can win, on this enterprise.'

'You'll not be saying that when you're taken up a few miles on,' Sir William grunted. 'Be it as it may, though, it's done now, or not done, and there's no going back.'

'The most worrying thing to my mind,' said Montrose thoughtfully, 'is that he saw through my disguise so quickly. A fortunate thing indeed that Sir Richard Graham's man had never seen me before, for he was most assuredly not to be trusted. Yet I do not see how the disguise can be embellished: we have done all that's practical already, unless you can think of aught else, Mistress Graham?'

'There was never any hiding you,' said Great-Aunt Elizabeth. She looked at him ruefully. 'Why do you not give over this desperate adventure – for that's all it is, an adventure – and go back to Magdalen and the children?'

'Two reasons, my dearest and most indomitable cousin-by-marriage: firstly, I could not go back to Kincardine openly now even if I wished, I have shown my hand too clear. I would be clapped in Edinburgh Castle before the week was out, and doubtless under the

Maiden before the passage of another. And though it may well come to that in the end, I have much to do before Argyll gets his hands on me. Secondly, I must win Scotland for the King, and no one else can do it.'

It was the statement of a madman, and a conceited madman at that, but he was neither. I looked at him sitting at the table in the gathering gloom of early evening, the calm noble resolute face filled with pride and certainty and his sense of his fate shining in his clear eyes, and knew that if will and determination and ability could prevail, then this man could indeed be master of Scotland.

There was a quick double knock on the door and Grainne entered, curtseying deeply, and her green eyes going at once, assessingly, to Montrose. The men rose and bowed, and Great-Aunt said, 'You plan, I believe, to join up with this Irish army? This is Mistress Grainne Sewell, and she too is Irish.'

'From Cork,' said Grainne, 'though I've not seen it for nearly ten years. My lord, Malise is coming down from Gorranberry, I have just now seen him. Shall I go down and warn him you are here?'

'No need,' Great-Aunt Elizabeth said. 'I told your Jasper to watch for him and bring them up here as soon as they arrived. Is the baby better?'

'Yes, thank you, and sound asleep,' Grainne said. She joined us at the table by the window, tall and slender and thoughtful, in the deep green dress she had made during our enforced sojourn at Nantwich, and when Montrose had introduced his two companions said to Sibbald, 'You are a Low Countries man, sir?'

The impassive brown face broke into a smile, the first sign of life I had seen on his countenance in half an hour of conversation. 'Aye, Mistress, served under the King of Sweden, and the Prince of Orange too.'

'My husband was at Breda,' she said, 'and my father fought for the Prince Cardinal, so I have some recollection of the German wars myself.'

'You are Irish,' said Montrose, 'that is plain in your

voice . . . How do the people here regard you, now that the Macdonells have landed?'

'They think me English, my lord,' Grainne said, smiling, 'for as yet they've never heard an Irish voice, though that of course may change. And since I wed an Englishman, I have given my allegiance to his country and his religion, though he has been now two years dead. Nor am I one of your wild Northern Irish savages, my lord, but an O'Brady from the fair city of Cork.'

The door opened, and Jasper stood there, small and breathless with his bright hair vivid against the gloom of the stairway outside, and behind him Francis and Malise, dusty from their journey up to the head of Hermitage Water and back to enquire of the Elliot who lived there whether he wanted a loan of Sandy's prized Southern cross-bred ram. All three, child and men, bowed low, and Jasper said, 'I brought them up without anyone seeing, Mistress Graham.'

By 'anyone', we all knew he meant Grizel. Montrose smiled at the boy, and then said to Grainne, 'Is he yours, Mistress? There is a certain likeness about his face.'

'For my sins, he is mine,' said my friend. 'And a graceless scamp he is, too. His name is Jasper.'

'Come here, Jasper,' said the Marquis, and the child walked steadily over and stood in front of him, his chin tilted up. For the first time, I saw him with fresh eyes, as Montrose saw him, a boy of five, tall and long-boned and slender, with his father's silky orange hair and freckles and his mother's white skin and green eyes, and I had a brief vision of what he would be like in twenty years' time, with all his promise fulfilled. What would my own son be like, grown to manhood?

'I have three boys of my own, and one is not much older than you,' said Montrose. 'If the Covenant men come riding to Catholm asking for me, what will you tell them?'

'That I've never seen you, sir!' said Jasper instantly, an impudent grin hovering round his mouth.

'And will you hold to that, whatever they may say?'

'They'd have to boil me up on Ninestane Rig like they did to Lord Soulis before I'd tell,' said Jasper with cheerful bravado.

'I don't think even the Covenant men would stoop to that,' said Montrose. 'I am pleased to have met you, Jasper Sewell: I trust our paths will cross again.'

'Thank you, sir,' said Jasper. With the beautiful manners he could always command when needed, he bowed and backed away to a corner by the bed where, released from involvement in adult affairs, he was able to make much of Drake.

'So, it's begun,' said Malise. 'We've been expecting you for a day or two, now, and to be out just when you're arriving doesna seem verra polite . . . Are you staying the night? You're welcome to do that if you wish.'

'No, we must go on as soon as possible,' said Montrose, and told him of the two encounters they had had between Carlisle and Catholm. 'In addition, we heard just before we left Carlisle that Ogilvy and all the men I sent south to Oxford have been captured, and so doubtless it will very soon be known that I did not go with them but entered Scotland, secretly and alone.'

'Only needs that drunken deserter to blab it in the next alehouse, and the hue and cry will be hot on our tail,' Sibbald muttered: Montrose's rash generosity obviously still rankled.

'And so you plan to join the Irish army?' Malise asked. 'How many are they? To listen to some talk you'd think them a horde of many thousands, but I doubt they are that numerous.'

'The King spoke of ten thousand, it's most likely nearer one. That does not matter so much, for they will only be the heart and core of my army. I think that, away from Argyll's influence, the Highlands will rise for me: I carry the King's commission, and they are Royalists at heart. It only needs someone to lead them.' Montrose looked at Malise's deceptively intimidating face, and added, 'And what of you, and Francis? Will you be the only representatives of all the Borders?'

'Most of the Borders have played one side off against the other for so long that they no longer have the courage to make such a choice,' said Francis's dark, mocking voice, speaking for the first time. 'Will you have an Englishman in your army?'

'If you will follow me, and help me win Scotland, I care not if you be Irish, Scots, English or a savage Brazilian,' said Montrose. 'And you, Malise?'

'You dinna need to ask,' said his cousin. 'Do you wish us tae ride wi' you now?'

A brief silence, during which my heart's sudden terrified thumping seemed set to suffocate me. 'No,' said Montrose. 'Three are conspicuous enough, five men together would be too many for safety. Wait two or three days, more if a hue and cry is raised, and then follow. We go to Tulliebelton first – you know it, it's Black Pate's home – and wait in hiding till we have word of the Irish, and there you may find me, or my direction. Now, brief though our meeting has been, I think we must go, for the longer we delay here the more danger are we in. My thanks, ladies, for your hospitality: and goodbye, Jasper.'

That worthy left Drake and ran to Montrose's side. 'Oh, are you going? Goodbye, sir!' He paused and then said, with unwonted shyness, 'Please, if you still want an army when I'm grown up, will you have me?'

'I trust it will not take so long to overthrow Argyll and his cronies, but yes, Jasper Sewell, I will have you if I need you.' He gripped Malise's hand briefly, and then Francis's. 'I will look for you in Tulliebelton, in a week or so. Good luck on your journey!'

'And on yours,' said Malise, and the five men, followed by Jasper, went out and down the stairs to the barmkin, leaving the three of us alone in the darkening chamber.

'You have two days,' said Elizabeth Graham to me.

'If you are lucky, two days. If you still think you can do it . . . tut, girl, weeping won't win him!'

'I can't help it,' I snuffled miserably into my sleeve. Great-Aunt tapped me peremptorily on the arm. 'Then you don't deserve to have him. Faint heart never won fair lady – or gentleman, in your case. Dry those foolish useless tears and think on how you can see him alone, that is your best hope.'

Her brisk lack of sympathy worked: I dried my tears and walked down with her and Grainne to the barmkin to watch Montrose and his two companions ride into the dusk, over the hills and far away into the north, towards what? Death, danger, failure, all seemed probable, and yet as I watched his slender buff-coated back retreating into the gloom behind his friends, a sense of his destiny, of his fate, crept over me, so that I felt I was watching him vanishing out of the realities of our raw modern world and into the insubstantial glories of legend and song and fireside story: a candle in the dark.

> Like Alexander I will reign,
> And I will reign alone,
> My thoughts shall evermore disdain
> A rival on my throne.
> He either fears his fates too much,
> Or his deserts are small,
> That puts it not unto the touch
> To win or lose it all.

'That puts it not unto the touch' – the line from his poem hovered in my head all the next day, to no purpose, for Francis took care to be elusive, and I did not see him until supper time: which with the whole Graham family present, was no time to negotiate a secret assignation. There was only the next day left, for he and Malise were to leave the morning after, and I thought it quite likely that if Francis did go, I would never see him again. I scarcely slept at all that night, and woke from a troubled doze with the first light of dawn. Something prompted me to get up, light my candle and tiptoe across the rough herb-strewn boards of the little chamber to the window. I unfastened the shutters, hearing the sound of hooves, and looked out in time to see Francis and Hobgoblin ride out of the barmkin and take the track which led past the wall, through the infield and up on to Ninestane Rig.

Here was my chance. No one else was in sight, in the first grey, hesitant illumination from the East. I dressed faster than I had ever thought possible, cursing the twenty buttons on the doublet of my riding-habit and the ample skirts which I had to gather up into my hand before descending the stairs. Why he went alone and so early I did not know, nor care: I hurled myself down, at grave risk of breaking my neck or leg, and ran to the stables. The Thunderflash was in awkward mood, practising his trick of inflating his belly while I tried to do up the girth, until I jabbed him in the flank with my elbow and, with a pained look, he let all his breath out with a long blubbering snort. I heaved the buckle two notches tighter, dragged him out into the yard, cursing under my breath, and scrambled on with no elegance and a quantity of riding-boot and stocking displayed to any early riser foolish enough to look out. Reckless of any danger, I urged the grey out of the barmkin and he took off in pursuit of Hobgoblin like a bullet shot from a gun.

All I asked was that if I was going to break my neck, could it at least be after I had caught Francis up. Fortunately, he was unaware of our chase. The Thunderflash bunched himself and soared contemptuously over the head-dyke that bounded field from moor, and raced through the grass: but despite my horse's speed, it was some time before I caught sight of Francis riding unhurriedly a little way ahead.

It took three minutes to come up with him, and another minute to rein in my mount, who was in high expectation of an extended gallop. I said breathlessly, my arms feeling as if they were about to fall from their sockets, 'Do you mind if I ride with you? I want to talk to you.'

'I haven't much choice, have I?' said Francis drily. I thought he looked ill, his face colourless and shadows round his eyes and under his high cheekbones. The cool dawn wind from the west drifted his hair across his mouth, which was set in a bleak uncompromising line. He added, 'Isn't that brute too much for you to handle?'

He probably knew very well the effect that comment would have on me. Aware that he was most likely right, I said indignantly, 'Of course not! Once you get used to all his little tricks Jasper could ride him.'

'Don't let him try. I know how far you'll go to prove a point. Well, what have you to say to me?' He sounded weary and unconcerned: my temper began to rise. 'I think you know. Francis, why don't you ever listen to what I have to say?'

'I am listening.'

'But you don't pay any attention! You – oh, talking to you is like banging my head against a brick wall.'

'And how nice it is when you stop.'

After my sleepless night, I was in no mood to laugh. 'Oh, please listen, please, I won't get another chance. Francis.' I swallowed any pride I had left. 'Francis, I love you. You mean more to me than anything else, anyone else. I always have loved you. I only married Dominic because I thought you were dead and it didn't matter what happened to me if you were dead. I never want to see him again. I never loved him, I tried to but I couldn't, even your ghost was stronger than he was, all the things he told you were lies, all of it, I thought you were dead, don't you see, I thought you were dead!'

He heard my impassioned plea out with a small cynical smile on his face. 'How touching. Lucy would be reduced to tears. I, on the other hand, am less susceptible.' He halted his horse and turned to look at me fully, and I saw, quailing, no sign of any warmth, no opening, no chink of light anywhere in his face. 'Can you understand this? That I have no wish to involve myself with you again, ever, and if that does not suffice to bring your beseeching whines to a halt, then I'll add that you're deluding yourself. You may have loved me once, you may even love me now in your strange time-serving fashion, but for you I feel nothing at all. Understand me? *Nothing*. Nor have I ever felt anything beyond the sort of lust for your pretty little body that your unsavoury husband obviously felt before he found out what you were really like. My sweet coz, you've been gulled, just as Simon knew you had, and I think it's time you understood it.'

'No!' I shouted, my hands over my ears, as if by that means I could stop all my life crumbling around me and under my feet. 'No! It's not true! You know it's not true! Why in God's name are you saying it if you know it's not true?'

'I know it is true – why else would I say it? Do you want me to spell it out plain?' I crossed my arms over my breast as if to protect my heart as he went on, each word falling like a hammer-blow of destruction on the careful edifices of hope I had built up over the last year, and now revealed plain to be all illusion. 'I do not love you. I never have loved you. I never will love you. Does that make me clear to you?'

'You're lying,' I whispered, but it was an empty invocation without meaning or faith. 'You're lying. You must be . . . Oh God, I can't live without you!'

'Then don't live,' he said. 'You may prove your devotion that way if you like, you pathetic little whore, but don't expect mourning from me.'

The Thunderflash moved abruptly: I lost my balance and half-slid, half-fell down his side and clung desperately to his long coarse bushy mane for support, as a drowning man will cling to a splinter of wood. 'Francis, oh God, why?' I could not summon the courage to look at his face, so clearly could I imagine the expression upon it. 'Why? You did love me, I know you did, I *know*, so why are you denying it now?'

'Better to be cruel than kind – you have lived too long with your illusions.'

'But the Unicorns . . . remember the Unicorns – you said once . . .'

'I remember some juvenile sentiments of that sort, yes. But if I ever said I loved you, I lied, and I knew it.'

'No!' I shouted again, at the full pitch of my lungs, as if that power could overturn all he had said and make the world whole again. 'No, no, *no*, it's not true, it can't be!' At the screeching sound of my voice, the grey jerked suddenly, and flung up his head, rolling his eyes to show their whites. Francis's face as he held his mare in check was blank, untouched, only his eyes blazing anger. I took a step towards him, my hands outstretched, with a confused, despairing idea that if only I could reach him, touch him, I could somehow break through to the real feelings that I still, despite everything he had said, could not believe did not exist nor had ever existed. It had *not* been a sham, a performance designed cynically to win me, I knew that as surely as I knew of the existence of the sun or moon or stars, and I knew also that he lied, he must be lying, and I must force him to admit it. But I could not come close enough. Horrifyingly, he took the loose ends of the reins in his hands and whipped them viciously through the air to slash my face. I had just enough wits left to duck: and my restive horse, just behind me, received the full force of the blow across his eyes. With a squeal of anger he reared up, hooves flailing, and one of his iron-shod feet caught the side of my face.

Like a hammer-blow, it smashed me to the ground. I do not think I lost consciousness, but lights to rival the Northern Dancers flared before my eyes, and I could think of nothing but the sudden appalling pain in the side of my head. Unable to move or speak or see, I lay dazed on the ground and without knowing that I did, whimpered in pain and terror and bewilderment, like a small child.

Someone was speaking, but I could not hear the words: all my mind, such as was left to me, being absorbed by the agony shrieking within my skull. I hardly felt myself being lifted and cradled in someone's arms, did not notice as my collar was unceremoniously ripped from my doublet and folded: but the sudden pain as it was applied to the wound made me gasp and flinch away. 'Hold still,' said Francis's voice, swift and commanding enough to penetrate the all-pervading torture that filled my brain. I clenched my teeth and obeyed: and found, to my rather remote surprise, that the world was steadying, the agony becoming bearable. Cautiously, I opened my eyes and saw Francis's blurred image: full recollection of what had just happened washed over me with renewed horror, and I turned my face away and began to sob helplessly.

'Thomazine,' he said, his voice urgent, 'Thomazine, look at me.' I could not: the effort was too great, I had no strength left to fight any more, I was utterly and finally defeated. Painfully, my head was pulled round by the chin. '*Look* at me, damn you!' said Francis, and without really intending to, I opened my eyes. Above me, pale and swimming slightly in my tears, was his face: and what I saw there told me the truth.

'Are you all right?' he asked me, very gently. I could not speak, but moved my head in assent, then winced. 'That thrice-blasted horse was the culprit,' Francis went on, 'but it was I caused him to rear in the first place ... Oh God, I thought I'd killed you for a moment, when you lay there and did not move, and there was so much blood ... ' He drew a long shaking breath, and pushed his hair out of his eyes. I noticed that his hand was trembling, and left a long smear of scarlet across his forehead. With detachment I supposed I must be bleeding. 'I don't know when I've ever been so frightened,' he added, 'and I have never in all my life hated myself so much as now, and God knows that's saying something ... I know that no one would be more justified in hating me now, but could you ... oh, Christ,

I'm not accustomed to beg . . . could you find it in you, perhaps, to forgive me? If not now, later?'

I could say nothing, only stare at him helplessly. On top of the physical blow to my wits, this total volte-face was altogether too much to take in. I could not believe it: had I in reality just been killed, and was now in some extraordinary afterlife where long-held, foolish dreams came miraculously true? The touch of his warm hands on my face, stroking away the tears and the blood, told me I was not, and yet I still did not believe it. I tried to say something; it came out as an incomprehensible croak, and I started again. 'Forgive you? Oh, God, you dear fool . . . you shouldn't need to ask.'

'Are you *sure* you're all right? It's almost stopped bleeding now, but there's a lump the size of a fair-sized boulder on the side of your head . . . don't worry, it's missed your face, there won't be any scar . . . apologies seem rather inadequate, don't they?' he added.

'It doesn't matter,' I whispered, feeling the hot tears washing my face, 'if it led to this it doesn't matter.'

'But it does matter: I was nearly the means of killing you, and whatever else in life that I am or am not able to bear,' said Francis decisively, 'I could never have lived with that. Now listen to me, moi dear, dear owd gal.' I tensed, for he had used that Suffolk expression of endearment to me many times in the old days, before my marriage: never again until now. 'Listen, and mark it well, for you may not have another such declaration from me. I love you, more than I can say: and I always have. All the things I said just now were lies, everything, all lies.'

'But why?' I whispered. 'Why did you say it? You knew, you must have known, that I was none of those things you called me.'

'But for a long time I thought you were. Your thrice-cursed husband, may he burn in eternal damnation, was very convincing, but not so convincing as the marriage-licence. When he showed me that, it was . . . it was as if some part of me, the better part I might add, had been burned away, cauterized, lost . . . it never crossed my mind that you might have thought me dead, and I hated you. And in a way it was easier, afterwards, to believe in your betrayal than to accept that I might, if I had been less eaten up with rage and bitterness, have left my sick-bed and tried to stop the wedding. So I struck my attitude and no amount of reasoning would persuade me into another opinion, and even when you turned up here so desperate, I couldn't allow myself to crack – I couldn't face the fact that I still loved you, and that if your story was true I could have prevented your marriage, and if Dominic's story was true then you felt no more for me than lust, and besides all my trust in you had been so thoroughly destroyed . . . I'm not making much sense of this, am I?'

'If you'd only talked to Grainne,' I began, but Francis found my mouth with his fingers and stopped it, gently. 'You know me. You also know Simon, and the rest of us, and you are a Heron too. The fault is mine, that I could not bear to recognize the fact that I love you: I don't think I can, even now, but I am not going to let you pay the price for my cowardice.' He paused, and then said, almost humbly, 'Do I loom so large in your life then, that you cannot tolerate the thought of it without me?'

Overcome, I nodded my cheek against the scratchy material of his doublet, hardly noticing the stab of pain that accompanied it.

'And can you ever forgive me for my utterly despicable behaviour towards you?'

I gave a muffled hysterical snort of agreement.

'And for calling you whore, and trying my best to rape you?'

I struggled my face away from his chest and sat up, ignoring a sudden pang of nausea. 'That would have been no rape, as you well know. I'm sorry about that stone.'

'Tit for tat, you might say.'

I grinned weakly. 'I – I don't think I've ever regretted

anything so much in all my life, afterwards. Not the stone, I m-mean, but not giving in to you.'

A faint smile lit his face, and his arms tightened about me. 'When I was in a condition to think again, I regretted it too. I always seem to force you into making the choices, whether it's submitting to my lecherous advances or abandoning husband and child and friends to follow me . . . have you lost a great deal of that prickly pride?'

'It's better lost,' I said. 'Francis, I am not the same person you knew two years ago. I have grown up. I have a husband, from whom I have learned hatred, and a child I couldn't allow myself to love and whom quite probably I will never see again. I am not the virgin hoyden you knew before, that's gone for ever. If I stay with you, we can never go back to Goldhayes or Ashcott or Pennyfarthing Street, we will be wanderers in strange lands all our lives . . . like you, I have been through the fire, and part of me is lost . . . do you truly want me?'

'No going back – I do. And together, we may make each other whole again . . . can you forget what I said to you, ever?'

'Yes.'

'And will you promise to love me all the days of your life, even if you don't always do what I tell you to?'

I gave a tentative giggle. 'I will. Do you?'

'All the days of our lives, till death and beyond, I will love you, my dear lady . . . Tell me about your child.'

I swallowed with sudden emotion. 'There's little to tell. I left him before he was a month old. He might look like Dominic, he might not, I don't know. His name is Kit.'

'And Dominic?'

'I think he loved me truly, at first. I thought I could come in the end to feel something for him, till the wedding night.' I shuddered under Francis's steadying hands. 'I panicked, and he raped me. It wasn't exactly a very good start. I thought I hated him then, and he was angry. It was only when I discovered that I was

with child that things mended between us . . . and a
month after, the Widow found that you were not dead
after all, and I resolved to run away after the baby was
born. I wrote to Great-Aunt and she sent a letter back,
by Montrose, to tell me you were here.' It seemed
strange to be telling him all this news, three months
after we had met again, yet it was now that was our first
meeting, and all I had ever dreamed it would be, and
far more.

'Did you ever find out who had betrayed us to Simon,
the night I was flung into the Castle?'

'It was Meraud. She found the letter you sent to me,
and told Simon.'

'For a long time, in my blackest moments, I thought
it was you. So thoroughly did Dominic poison my mind
against you, and only now is it cured.'

'Not only his poison,' I pointed out, 'but your own
stubbornness. You'd taken up your position, and it took
an earthquake to shift you from it.'

'An earthquake in the form of The Thunderflash, that
showed me I could not live without you either. Touché,
my lady, for I am not an admirable character, and it's
a miracle you have been so tenacious in your feeling for
me. I am cruel, stubborn, unscrupulous, too given over
to the pursuit of my own pleasures, I drink too much
and have not a scrap of honour left about me. How,
after all I have done to you, can you still love me?'

'Easily. I don't care what manner of man you are, I
only know that I love every turn of your face, and the
way you laugh and talk, and the touch of your hands
makes my heart reel, and without you there is no point
in anything.'

'Enough said,' Francis told me, and kissed me: and
despite the pain in my head I lost track of place and
time and self, and drowned without a qualm. And when
our lips parted at last, reluctantly, I wept for pure happiness, for at last after nearly two years of grief and hope
I had achieved my heart's desire, and if we died
tomorrow I was content.

I think I must have dozed for a little in his arms, after my sleepless night and the tumultuous events of the morning, in particular the blow to my head: for I next remember his hands stroking the hair from my face, and the old soft mocking tone back in his voice as he said, 'Wake up. Archie approaches and we must be gone.'

I blinked dazedly up at him, aware suddenly of the sun's warmth upon us and the high sweet torrential singing of a lark: the trumpets of heaven he had called it once, and the description might have been made of the exultant delight in my heart, far outweighing any physical discomfort. Stiffly, dizzily, I got to my feet, holding my head, touching gingerly the blood-crusted lump beneath my thick hair on the right-hand side. 'Dear God, it feels terrible.'

'The bone's not cracked, and as with most head wounds it looks far worse than it is. They always bleed excessively. You must have a very tough skull, thank God, for you belong to this world, and your friends, if not to me, and I would not see you plunged untimely into the next.' He kissed me again.

'Archie is looking,' I said weakly. Archie was indeed looking, his evil wizened old face creased with a wicked grin: he was only about five yards away. 'Yon's a bonny sicht for an auld mon on a fine morning! When's the wedding tae be, Maister Heron?'

'I'll make sure you're not invited,' Francis retorted, grinning. 'And don't count your lambs before they're dropped, Archie Graham, for she fell from her horse and I was but offering her comfort. Is that not right, Mistress Heron?'

My own happiness took wings from the laughter in his face, and finally broke free. 'You should know best, sir, for you it was that picked me up.'

'Oh, aye,' said Archie, evidently not believing a word of it. 'Wull, I wish ye both muckle joy, but I wouldna catch Dame Grizel spyin' ye for a' the gold i' the Indies. Good day t' ye.' He planted his greasy old bonnet back on his head and stamped off through the grass, whistling to his dogs.

Hobgoblin was nearby, grazing peacefully. The Thunderflash could be seen further off, eyeing us, evidently wondering if it would be worth his while to be caught. I called him, my voice weak and shaky, and after a moment, so obviously weighing up the alternatives that I laughed, he trotted languidly over to us and rubbed his slobbery whiskery nose down my sadly dilapidated doublet. I grabbed the reins before he could change his mind and Francis, Hobgoblin's long dished nose looking over his shoulder, said suddenly, 'How attached are you to that animal?'

'Very little after this morning. He's fast, he'll go on steadily all day if he's ridden considerately, he's as surefooted as one of Archie's sheep, but he's also as perverse and unpredictable as the Devil – or you. Why do you ask?'

'I was thinking, perhaps it would be best if I left Goblin behind when I go tomorrow, and took The Thunderflash instead.'

Something had happened to my voice, and my overworked heart. Suddenly, my legs did not seem so strong as I had thought them to be and, feeling sick and dizzy, I sat down in the long cool grass. I whispered, 'Are you going to Montrose, then?' Since our reconciliation, I had somehow assumed that he would not. Francis saw my face: he dropped Goblin's reins and came over to sit beside me. 'What is it, owd gal?'

I could not help crying, and despised myself for it. 'I – I did – didn't think you'd g-g-go, n-not now!'

'But I must,' Francis said, capturing The Thunderflash's reins, which were in danger of slipping out of my grasp. 'Can't you see, my dear and only love, that I must?'

'I – I thought you said you had no honour,' I whispered.

'There is a little scrap, lurking somewhere. Oh, God,

what can I do to stop you crying? You never used to – and it's all my doing, all of it. Use your sleeve, there's no one to see.'

'I – I'm sorry,' I said, gulping. 'What a fool I am, an hour ago all I wanted from you was a civil word, no more, and now I have the moon come down for me I must cry for the sun, too.'

'Don't think I want to go, because I don't. If we two were just one little world with no others to intrude, I would never leave you again. But if that were true, none of this coil would ever have arisen. What was it Doctor Donne said? "No man is an island, entire of itself; every man is a piece of the Continent, a part of the main." '

' "Any man's death diminishes me, because I am involved in Mankind; And therefore never send to know for whom the bell tolls; it tolls for thee." ' I shivered, despite the warmth of the early sun. 'And Malise can't go on his own, can he? He would crack his head on the first overhanging branch.'

'He can look after himself quite adequately. That appearance of bumbling incompetence is utterly false, and a very useful cover for all his activities. "Malise Graham?" they say. "Yon chuckle-heided gomerel couldna herd twa sheep togither, never mind work for Montrose." '

I giggled at his remarkably accurate imitation of the local accent. 'And moreover,' Francis added, 'it deceives even his own family, with the exception of his grandmother. We all owe much to her: and you and I most of all, for I suspect that it was she urged you to come here.'

'Not precisely – she was also very concerned to point out what I would be throwing away if I did. But she sent me a hideous report of your activities – and two poems.'

The horses shuffled and breathed and munched the grass: a flying bird's shadow flicked over us. Francis was quite still, his strange-coloured eyes gazing past me into the distance. He said casually, 'Did she?'

'She told me she had found them by chance, discarded, and copied them out for me. I knew they were yours. One was about the Unicorns, but I didn't find that till later, and it decided me finally on coming here.'

'The other one was about you, and it doubtless gave you pause to think before throwing everything away for my sake. I promised you I would find my own voice, but I did not then salute you as you deserved. I will make you another, I promise.'

'But the Unicorns were different, they were beautiful, they made me realize how much I loved you, that I had to make the gamble and come to you, even if you thought you didn't want to see me ever again. I kept the letter by the way, you can have it back if you like.'

'Save for that sonnet, I don't particularly want it – the poem about you brings back too many bad memories and I'm quite sure that Great-Aunt's comments about me would burn holes in the paper, let alone my eyes. I have no copies of either, nor have I written any more. But I might be inspired again, should I have the chance to take up the pen afresh.'

'And if you live,' I said. 'It seems as if you go to certain death – Great-Aunt seems to think it, and she's convinced me. *Why* do you have to go?'

'Because I promised. Because I could not let Malise go alone, both for his sake and for Grainne's, as you will have seen if you have eyes to see, and the one of us will look to the other. And because of Montrose.'

'A candle in the dark,' I said, thinking of what Malise had told me once. 'Does he shine so bright for you, too?'

'I never thought I could find it in me to follow any man for himself alone, and not because of anything he stood for: but I can for Montrose. What do you think of him? After all, you've met him twice now.'

'I think . . . that he doesn't belong now, here, in this age of the world – he's like a figure from a romance, or like Alexander, too bright for ordinary life to hold him. When he went away that evening it was . . . ' I struggled to find words that did not sound foolish fancies. 'It was as if he rode into the past, like that story old Meg tells about the man riding into the hills of Elfland, and when he came out again after a night and a day, three hundred years had passed. Does that sound stupid?'

'No, just fanciful. And yet I don't think Montrose would laugh – he has, I know, a strange sense of his own destiny.'

'Malise said that poem he wrote was the clue to his fate. He will win Scotland, he feels it is what he was born to do, or die in the attempting. And my dear love, please, please do not die with him.'

'The last hero,' said Francis reflectively, as if he had not heard my last words. 'The last hero, from a nobler age than this . . . I swear to you that whatever may befall me, or Malise, or Montrose, that I will do my utmost to return to you unscathed; as far as is compatible with my abused sense of honour, of course.'

I said suddenly, overwhelmed by the adventure and romance and strangeness of it all, 'And I would give the world to come with you and share it! Oh God, how I wish I were a man and could ride with you!'

'And how glad I am that you are not, for then I could not love you, save with the sort of unnatural love for which they burn unfortunates at the stake up here; and I would have to fall back on some Scottish wench with a voice like a see-saw and the shapely figure of a heifer: Kirsty, for instance, and I think you should know here and now that she has never meant more to me than as a body to be lain with, and now we are reconciled she will not even be that. You it is I love more than life or pride or honour: and no one else will ever hold that place. Certainly not Kirsty – or Meraud.'

I grinned, knowing he held the same regard for Meraud Trevelyan, our deceitful conniving cousin, as he would for a venomous viper. 'Or Grainne.'

'Of all women in this world, you are to me the first – and Grainne is the second. To see her falling in love with my friend gives me great pleasure, because she deserves some recompense for all she has suffered. Jasper likes him, too.'

'But not you. He took against you after you nearly broke my wrist up here. That's why he ignores you now.'

'I thought it must be something like that. We must explain to him, before I go, and set it right. Now let's go down: I think Great-Aunt should take a close look at that bump on your head, and while she's doing it we can tell her how all her Machiavellian scheming has worked out in the end. Do you feel well enough to ride? You look very pale.'

My head was throbbing painfully, and the pit of my stomach felt more than a trifle queasy, but I nodded. 'I feel pale, but I'll be all right – as long as The Thunderflash doesn't take it into his head to try throwing me off.'

'Easily remedied. I'll ride him, and you can take Goblin: my dear old lady mare is as steady as a rock by comparison with that hairy brute, and I'll change the saddles over.'

And so it proved. Francis assisted me to mount his beautiful mare, and I was glad of her gentleness, especially when The Thunderflash attempted to unseat Francis twice in the first twenty yards. Somewhat chastened by my lover's firmness, the horse did not repeat his experiments, and we rode down the hill together: and not caring who might see, awkward though it was, we went side by side with our hands clasped like children. We reached the barmkin quite successfully, although I felt a trifle giddy, and the first person we met there was Jasper. His face as he looked up at us was a study in bewilderment. 'I thought Master Heron didn't like you,' he blurted eventually.

'You're right, I didn't,' Francis told him. 'But I've discovered what a fool I've been and we're friends again now.'

'But you hurt her,' Jasper said, frowning. 'Aunt Thomazine was crying, you hurt her so much.'

'It's all right,' I said. 'It was all a mistake, the sort

of mistake adult people are always making, and I've forgiven him for it. Will you?'

Jasper looked from Francis's face to mine, and back, and then at our still-joined hands. 'I s'pose so,' he said dubiously. '*Promise* you won't hurt her again?'

'I promise,' said Francis seriously. Jasper grinned suddenly. 'Oh, good, 'cause I didn't *really* hate you, though I said I did, but I thought I ought to.'

'That would be exactly describe my attitude towards you,' said Francis to me as we dismounted and handed our horses to Sim, who raised a dour grey bushy eyebrow at our hands and my face and stumped off into the stables with Goblin and Thunderflash trailing behind. 'Where's your mother, shrimp?'

'With Hen. Hen isn't well again,' said Jasper gloomily. 'Oh, I *wish* I had a brother!'

Grainne was sitting on the windowseat of her chamber, with Henrietta in her arms. The small scarlet face clashed unbecomingly with the orange hair, and she was grizzling miserably – most unlike Hen, who was normally a cheerful child. Beside her stood Malise, looking as usual large and cumbersome and out of place in this domestic scene; and with a pestle and mortar Great-Aunt Elizabeth was pounding up a powder with the appearance of an energetic apothecary. They all looked up as we entered, Jasper our page to announce us: and Francis closed the door with his heel and deliberately, watching their reaction, put his arm around my waist.

Grainne was the first to respond: one of her swift smiles transforming her face, she rose to her feet, baby still in her arms, and came quickly across to us. 'You've made it up! Oh, I am so glad – so glad for you both!'

'You'd best put that baby down before she's crushed between us,' Francis said. Malise came to take the child, and Grainne put her unencumbered arms around us both, laughing as she so rarely did. Then Elizabeth and Malise added their own congratulations, the former's characteristically spiced. 'I said you were a fool, Francis Heron. Why the devil did you not see sense sooner?'

'I was blind,' said Francis. He looked at Malise, standing smiling at him, though there was a strange forlornness in the set of his face. 'And having been reconciled to my dear and only love, I have told her that I will go with you tomorrow.'

'That you must not!' Malise exclaimed. 'I wouldna take you – not now – I can see the difference in you both and I willna take that from you . . . '

'But you will. You can't stop me going with you, can you, Malise Graham, and I have decided on it. For both of us, and Montrose.'

'And Scotland,' said Malise.

It was at this point that Great-Aunt Elizabeth first noticed the marks on my face, a grimy and unlovely mixture of dirt, tearstains, bruises and blood: and exclaimed, 'What in God's name, child, have you done to the side of your head?'

'The Thunderflash reared up and kicked me,' I said, feeling sick at the memory of those hideous moments that yet had made Francis see reason at last: and divulged no more, for that whole episode was a nightmare that lay only between the two of us, never to be shared nor allowed to interfere with the renewed course of our love: decently buried and forgotten for ever. And I did not need to reveal anything else: instantly the centre of concerned attention, I was hustled straightway to my bed, undressed, comforted with a hot brick at my feet and Drake curled beside me: and my wound was bathed, anointed with some unspeakably foul-smelling paste of Great-Aunt's, and painfully bandaged. Jasper was much impressed by the heroic picture my abused and haloed head presented. '*How* many yards of bandage did Mistress Graham use?'

'Oh, twenty miles at the least,' I told him cheerfully. 'It was a *very* deep cut!'

At that moment Grainne hustled him out, saying that

rest was the most certain cure for a head-wound and that with Jasper's tongue in action I had small chance of getting it: and I was left with Francis, who sat by me on the side of the bed and commented wryly on the fact that whenever we found ourselves in that situation one of us seemed invariably to be in no position to take advantage of it. 'I had the lung-fever in Oxford and was kitten-weak for a month: and now you've Vulcan's own hammer pounding away inside your head. And don't dare deny it, your eyes give you away, owd gal. Cruel I can be, I admit, but never so as to inflict more pain on you, ever. Wait till I come back and then, ah then, I'll show you what love can truly be.'

And the rest of that day passed so swiftly, as in a dream: so strange and unreal, and so delightful, did it seem to have Francis smile at me, laugh with me, hold my hand and kiss me, as in the old days: and we talked of past times and old laughter and distant friends, for the future was too imminent and too dangerous. And when, framed within the little square of window, the summer sky outside grew deep blue and spangled with glittering stars, and the thread of the new moon a sliver of silver hung in the south, I drifted into a peaceful, happy sleep, still holding his hand: and did not think at all of what lay before us.

The dawn came, and with it the terrible, inevitable moment of parting. Grainne woke me and we went down like sleepwalkers to bid our farewells. In the barmkin it was dark still, and Francis only a darker shape in the gloom, till he took me in his arms and kissed me fiercely. 'Don't you cry, love. I'll come back, and then we will truly be together.'

'I'm *not* crying.'

'Liar, I can feel it, the front of my doublet is soaked. Now kiss me again, just once, and then we must go, or we never will: my resolution is failing by the minute.'

This time his embrace was gentle, but none the less passionate for that: and it awakened too late all the old long-dormant fires within us. We parted with desperate reluctance, and I saw in the darkness that Malise was similarly saying goodbye to Grainne. Francis said intensely, softly, 'I *will* see you again . . . I will . . . you must hold to that, ever. Take care of yourself, owd gal.'

'And you,' I said, taking refuge in banality. 'Why do we always seem to be saying farewell? Oh, how I wish I could come with you!'

'Time we were awa',' said Malise. 'Goodbye, Thomazine. May we a' meet again when this is ended.'

'And God go with you both,' Grainne said. We watched them mount up and ride away, on The Thunderflash and an old brown garron for anonymity and safety, to go out of our ken and into the same legend as Montrose . . .

And I did not really believe that they would ever come back.

Chapter 4

Annus mirabilis

Like Alexander I will reign,
And I will reign alone,
My thoughts shall evermore disdain
A rival on my throne.
                (The Marquis of Montrose)

The instant that Francis and Malise had disappeared
from view down the track into the dawn gloom, I was
hustled back to my bed by Grainne, and she and Elizabeth Graham confined me there with direst threats of
the revolting remedies to be inflicted on me should I
dare to disobey. I had much time, therefore, to brood
on Francis's departure during the next few days, reliving again and again in my mind every detail of those
last all-too-brief hours we had shared in love and friendship before war again intruded violently between us.
Nor did I have the comfort of Drake's presence:
although Francis had left his dog tied up without any
intention of taking him to Montrose, the animal had
lost patience at being left behind yet again, had slipped
his collar half an hour after Francis and Malise had
ridden away and had not been seen by us since. I was
limited to books, and the chore of catching up with the
journal I had begun on leaving Oxford, and the conversation of Grainne and Elizabeth, spiced by that of
Jasper and a rather wan and reduced Henrietta, whose
illness had brought her quite low, and was heartily glad
when eventually allowed to lead my normal active existence, several days after my lover and Grainne's had
gone.

There had been no news at all of Montrose's capture,
and now, of course, our chief sources of information
had left us. Gib, self-centred as ever, was simply not

interested, and Sandy was too involved with the preparations for harvest. Grizel had as little to do with us as possible and ungraciously ignored my illness. I began to feel superfluous, unwanted, unwelcome, and Gib's mother did everything possible to confirm that, even to the extent of cornering me one afternoon, the first day of September, and demanding how much longer Grainne and I were going to stay.

I had long ago recognized that Grizel was only dangerous to those who feared her – face her out, and she was defeated. 'I do not know, Mistress. It is very pleasant here, and your husband and sons have made us very welcome. Besides, we are here by express invitation of my great-aunt, and she has not yet made us feel that our presence here is unwanted.'

The hard blue-grey eyes dropped. 'Aye, well,' said Grizel, 'I was wondering if ye planned to bide here till winter. Come November and ye'll no' leave Liddesdale, wi' a' the snow and the cold, till February.' And she walked briskly off, the keys jangling at her waist, the model of a Presbyterian housewife. Not for the first time, I pitied Sandy.

And then the miracle happened. It was the Sunday following that brief conversation, and we heard the news at church, delivered in a voice quivering with anger and a frenzy of indignation by Minister Scott.

Montrose had met with the Irish, in the hills above Atholl. There were just a thousand fighting men, with their women and children. With these, and four hundred bowmen under Lord Kilpont and eight hundred men of Atholl, he had opposed seven thousand well-armed, well-disciplined soldiers of the Covenant, including cavalry and cannon, musketeers and pikemen. And had so utterly routed them that it was said afterwards that a man could walk from Tippermuir to Perth without touching the ground, so numerous were the bodies of the fallen: and just two men out of Montrose's ill-equipped rabble of an army had been slain.

In the gloomy little kirk, the walls running with damp,

the people of Liddesdale prayed for deliverance from the Devil's instrument, the Marquis of Montrose, and his pack of naked Irish savages: and silently, in counterpoint, Grainne and I and Elizabeth Graham prayed for his victory.

When we returned to Catholm, even Gib was shaken far enough out of his cosy self-absorption to say, 'I didna think they would do it, but now they have, let's crack a bottle and drink tae Tippermuir!' And in a mood of delighted, carefree holiday, we did; only Grizel, her mouth a sour line of anger, disapproval and disappointment, taking no part.

'Tae Montrose! Good fortune, and may he ha' more victories!' Gib cried, raising his wine-cup high: and we all, even Sandy and Jasper, echoed it wholeheartedly.

And so began the famous year of victories, the *annus mirabilis*, during which Montrose's ragged undisciplined army of wild Irish kerns led the stolid Lowland Covenant forces up hill and down dale and over the misty, ethereal Highlands like a mocking malevolent will-o'-the-wisp. It was the kind of warfare that called to my own heart and, I knew, also to Francis's: no stern battles with thousands of men dourly swaying to and fro at push of pike, no dreary sieges or interminable manoeuvres: but instead, a kind of sharp and deadly game of hide-and-seek in which the soft-centred Lowland soldiers never knew, in their blundering passage through the alien mountains, where Montrose would strike next; whether that tumble of rocks hid an ambush, or if the ragged skirts of cloud drifting across the mountainside would lift to reveal the inhuman Irish, kilted and bonnetted, armed with axe and spear and knife, musket and bow, hurtling down towards them to the unearthly screeching of the pipes. And I longed uselessly and desperately, woman though I was, to be with them, sharing the freedom and the comradeship, the marches in all weathers, the rain and cold and comfortless lodgings on the cold ground, and the marvellous wild, fey magic of Montrose and the victories to which he inspired them. Malise and Francis had that, and I envied them painfully.

Hard on the heels of the news of Tippermuir came tidings of another victory. Montrose had left Perth and marched north towards Aberdeen. Outside the gates of that city he had met a Covenant force twice the strength of his own, and once more had routed them. The sack of Aberdeen which had followed the battle lost nothing in the Minister's telling; this was the fate meted out to the godly by sub-human Irish savages, and we were all urged to pray and fast most diligently and earnestly for God's intervention, so that the King's Lieutenant would not wreak further destruction on the luckless towns bordering the Highlands. In vain: for Montrose vanished like smoke into the mountains and, despite reports of his death, emerged to plunder and burn Covenanting property: all this with a lumbering enemy army under the Marquis of Argyll, weighed down with superior equipment and inferior initiative, toiling dourly in pursuit. At the castle of Fyvie they finally caught up with him: and Montrose, like the tiger at bay, turned and rent them sorely, and beat them off.

And now winter came down, the Scottish winter of which I had heard vague and terrifying reports. At Catholm the hills were obliterated in icy rain and wind, the bracken again turned to the colour of blood on the fawn slopes, and the cattle and sheep were kept close; the surplus who could not be fed were slaughtered and their meat salted down for the long, dark hungry days ahead. The peat fires in the house burned sullenly and smoked abominably, and I was glad of the warm garments Grainne and I had made at Nantwich the year before. And if it was cold here, so cold that the hard black night sky seemed to crackle and spit stars, and the Northern Dancers glittered and flickered in their frosty, frozen display above a bleak landscape grey with ice, then how much colder must it be amongst the northern mountains, where there could be frost in July and snow in October, and no shelter for a ragged, fugitive army with nothing to warm their limbs or fill their bellies but the warmth of their leader's inspiration and hope and purpose, and the bright comforting memories of their three brief victories?

We craved news, but there was no means of getting it except from the Kirk, and that was naturally biased. The authorities in Edinburgh appeared to share the same casual attitude to the truth as did the Parliament men in London: Montrose's death from fever had been confidently and optimistically reported, and quite often news leaked into Liddesdale of his overwhelming defeat. After a few days of hedging, muttering and fresh tidings from other sources these invariably turned out to be at first not quite so overwhelming, then a stalemate, then an unlucky costly victory, or else no battle at all. Of Malise and Francis we had not a word; when they had ridden away from Catholm that August morning, it might as well have been to Elfland. Nor did anyone at Castleton, fortunately, seem to realize their true whereabouts: Great-Aunt was very industrious in answering enquirers with vague waves of the hand and complaints of, 'Why, somewhere fighting in England, I believe, you know how uncommunicative these modern young men can be.' Thus leaving the curious questioner with the quite unwarranted impression that her grandson and his friend were with Leslie's Scots army somewhere in the north of England. Moreover, Francis was something of a bird of passage to the local people, a shadowy, infrequently-seen outsider, and Malise had for so long been the butt of his more popular, well-known, outgoing elder brother that I do not think that the possibility of his being a 'traitor-rebel' with Montrose ever crossed the minds of any of the Kirk Elders, let alone the Minister.

But news of a different sort we did have, and very welcome it was too. Gib went to Carlisle in early December, half-protesting because of the weather, but persuaded into it by his grandmother's fierce tongue, the long list of household wants and, not least, the prospect of two or three unsupervised carefree days in the town. He came back with two laden ponies, a much-reddened nose, and a letter addressed to Grainne and myself.

It had evidently been months on its journey. The superscription had been much overwritten, rained upon, smudged, smeared with dirty fingermarks and stained with what looked suspiciously like beer, but was still miraculously legible beneath it all. 'To Mistress Sewell and Mistress Heron, Catholm Tower, Liddesdale on the Scottish Borders near Carlisle'. And the hand, swift and flat as if the writer was in too much of a hurry ever to form her letters properly, was my cousin Lucy's.

Lucy, with her warm, affectionate, impulsive heart, her pretty face and exasperating but endearing habits – compulsive gossiping, jumping to unwarranted conclusions, matchmaking with the most unsuitable raw material, desperate passions for absurd and melodramatic stage-plays – was Francis's young sister and, after Grainne, my dearest friend. We had left her in Oxford with her youngest brother Jamie, the acidly brisk Widow Gooch who kept the house, Holly's sister Heppy for their maid, and three people I preferred, for different reasons, not to think about – my husband Sir Dominic Drakelon, our son Kit, who would now be sixteen months old, and my other cousin, Meraud Trevelyan, who more than anyone else had caused the tragedy of my marriage. The separate emotions had existed without her – Dominic's lust for me, Francis's love, his eldest brother Simon's hatred of him – but she had been the catalyst to set everything boiling together, a poisonous brew that had brought grief and rage and hatred in its fumes.

The letter doubtless carried news of all these people within its crumpled folds: and I was half afraid to read it. But read it I must, and Grainne with her usual good humour bore both it and me up to our tower chambers, away even from the children, to open it.

The contents bore a strong resemblance to Lucy's wayward mind (she always took great care to keep her personal appearance neat), being untidy, undisciplined, disorganized and extremely badly spelled for one who read so widely. It was dated from the previous August, 1644, and so had taken four months to reach us.

My dearest Thommazine and Granya, as you cann see from the above we are all still at Pennyfarthing Street, though thatt is no thanks to your hideous husband, Thommazine, who has done his levell best to persuade us to leave lock stock and barrell, but dear Simon called him a Vile Bastard and other worse termms and there was a fearfull Quarrell but since thenn we have not been troubled by Domminnic at all. I do humbly begg both your pardons for not having writ before but I wished to be sure you had reached Cattholmm safe and was waiting for a letter fromm you butt it never came so in the end I lost patience and writ regardless with all our news. First of all, we received tidings nott two weeks ago that my Mother is brought to bedd of a fine boy named Hugh which considdering her Age is verry surprising. It is strange for Simon and Jamie and I to think we have a new little baby brother though of course he is not a Heron but a Trevellyann. I long to hear your news of Francis and if he be well or nott and if your Reconncil-liationn has come about with Success. I wish you would write though of course with this Warr you may have done so many times and the letters gone astray. The Widdow asks me to tell you that Adultery is none so badd as it is made out though how she knows I cannott tell. Simon grieved much thatt you hadd gone away butt I think thatt he understood whenn we told him of what Domminnick had done and he was greatly joyed to find that he had one brother besides Jamie still alive and as I said he has protected us all against Domminnick's rages for Domminnick seemed to think it was all our fault that you had gone, especially the Widdow's and I do believe he would have done her harm except that Simon came between them and thenn followed the Quarrell I told you of. You will want to know what has happened to your child, well after that Quarrell Domminnick removed himm fromm the house to his own lodging and did not even take his Nurse Eliza (this being in October so that Kitt was but two months old) but has engaged a new nurse for him whom I like not for she has a comely face and her dresses are too fine and the Widdow calls her a Brazen Strumpett and Doxy and other names (we saw her once walking with Domminnick in the street she hanging most boldly on to his arm). But a friend of the Widdow who lives nearby them says the child thrives and grows daily more like his father so maybe you are well ridd of themm boath. For ourselves we do well though Meraud is low and listless since we all had a Fever in July, and Jamie talks daily of joining the King's Army though Simon has forbidden him to do anything of the sort. Simon wedd Nann Blagge at last at Christmas and she was quickly with child but miscarried so she was still with the Queen till Her Majesty escaped to France and Nann is now with the baby Princess Henrietta in Exeter and Simon still with the Prince Rupert. He was hurt a little at Long Marston Fight but nott badd so he writes though the Prince's great Dogg Boy you told me of was slain, and thousands of good menn. How I wish this Warr was over and that we were all back at Goldhayes again as we used to be butt I do nott know if it will ever fall thus again and fromm what I hear if we do nott make haste it will nott be a Heron house but a Trevellyann one. Now I am running out of paper so I cann only give you brief news of how it is in the Town which is fearsomely crowded, we have five Officers quartered on us and two of their servants in the stables and whenn it is fine weather menn sleep in the street so there is much Fever as you cann imagine, and in June I think the Town came near to capture for Waller's forces came verry close but we were saved by the Action at Cropredy and now the danger they say has gone. I have no more space save only to say that Captain Ashley writ to me once secretly and I have sent himm a letter assuring himm of my undying Affection and telling himm that Francis is not after all deadd for I know it will please him. I pray for you both every night and we all desire to hear from you, you need nott fear for Domminnick never comes here and Simon knows where you are I really do not have any more room to write so I remain your most loving and affectionate friend and cousin Lucy Heron and Jamie and Meraud and the Widdow send their love.

The last lines were written up the sides of the paper where she had been able to find space, so that the letter was edged like a sampler, and the style and flavour of it brought my dear Lucy, my sister in all but name, back to me like a breath of warm southern air in these inhospitable northern mists. Grainne watched me blink away the moisture from my eyes and said, 'Do you miss them?'

'Oh no, not really. I mean, we can't just go back now, if – if anything happens we might never know about it if we were in Oxford. I think we must stay here till they win – or lose. But just reading it, it's so like Lucy, it's almost as if she were in the room with us. I would so like to see them all again – even Simon.'

'Even Simon. It does seem as though he has had a change of heart over you and Francis. Maybe he has learned his lesson. I'm glad he's married Nan at last, though it can't have been much of a marriage so far.' She eyed me speculatively. 'What do you make of the news from Goldhayes?'

'Worrying,' I said bluntly. 'What did she mean, a Trevelyan house? I thought that Richard was suspicious, you know, there was always something a little too glib and slippery about him – and how keen he was to stay behind peacefully to look after the house while we all went off to war, the underhand rat! And then he married

Mary, and now this baby. I reckon I know what he was after: Meraud was to try her beauty and her wiles to snare Simon and he would be the second line of attack and lay siege to Mary so that if the King failed and dragged the Herons down too, he would be left in possession of the estate. After all, his mother was a Heron, and he's now wed to old Sir Simon's widow, so his claim's good.'

'But isn't everything entailed?'

'Goldhayes and the immediate lands around it, yes, I think they are, and can only pass to Herons in the male line. But there's land elsewhere in Suffolk and in Essex and Norfolk and Cambridge, and property in Ipswich, and ships and a house in London . . . very tempting to an unscrupulous younger son with no inheritance. If Simon and Francis were killed or exiled then Jamie would have the house, but as he's still only sixteen I don't think he'd have the knowledge or the wit to gainsay his mother and stepfather if they gained control of the rest. I don't know. I don't *think* they'd have the boldness to do it, not if the other trustees had any say in the matter, but Ambrose Blagge doesn't care about Goldhayes, John Sewell is getting old and Sir Thomas Jermyn likewise. Oh yes, it worries me, but I can only hope that Simon and his lawyer have wrapped the estate all up so successfully that neither Richard Trevelyan nor the Parliament's men can get their greedy paws on it. And there's John to see fair play, he's honest. And we're too far from it all to do more than sit and worry and raise our choler, and as that won't do any good at all to us or to them I suppose we'd better try and forget it.'

'I should imagine,' said Grainne, 'that any child of Mary and Richard Trevelyan's would not be ill-looking. But I tremble to think of its mental characteristics.'

'An infant Machiavelli, and totally selfish,' I said, only half-joking. 'Always supposing there's nothing wrong with it — she must be all of forty-three or four, and I believe children born of women that age quite often prove defective in some way.'

'I doubt it,' said Grainne drily. 'With those parents, it will be doubtless bonny, blond and beautiful with all the scruples of the Serpent. What a pity it isn't a girl, we could have married her to Kit!'

Despite our rather heartless flippant talk, I felt a twinge of admiration for Francis's mother, a faded over-blown once-beautiful woman who had obviously been very successful in her marriage to a man some years younger than herself. I had never really liked Mary's selfishness and her utter lack of concern for all her children save the eldest, Simon, who was such a credit to her, but I did not believe she knew anything about any plan of her second husband's to cheat the children of her first marriage out of their inheritance. If, indeed, there was any such plan, and it did seem probable that it was a figment of my vivid imagination.

Winter set in comparatively late that year, compared with the last; the first snow fell at Christmas, which was not, of course, a Presbyterian festival. Grizel spent it fasting and praying, but the rest of the family made it a riotous occasion in the big front parlour of the new wing, with Sim's pipes and Archie's lovely incongruous voice, dancing and feasting and drinking while the snow piled up outside, satisfactorily deep enough to deter any Sessions snoopers from descrying any signs of heathen festival on what was supposed to be an ordinary working day.

There was a knock on the door nevertheless: I heard it in a gap in the music (if it could be called that) and, as I was not then dancing, went to answer it. Huddled in the porch was a man all outlined and muffled in snow with a huge pack beside him; a man that after my first startled glance I recognized vaguely. It was Tam Crozier, the pedlar who had helped Malise and Francis with their spying disguises. He grinned wearily when he saw me. 'Good day t' ye, Mistress, and a happy Christmas. Ha' ye a bite tae eat and a wee bit shelter frae the wind for the nicht? I've walked a' the way frae Ewesdale an' I'm sair wearit.'

'Of course, Tam – come in and join in the fun.' I would have opened the door to him, but he laid a roughly-gloved hand to his nose and winked. 'No' just yet, Mistress. I've letters for ye an' they're secret, no' to be shown tae the others, ye ken?' As I stared at him with a heart suddenly thumping wildly in hope, he undid his snow-darkened leather jerkin and brought two letters out from that unsavoury hiding-place. Each was creased, dirty, folded, sealed, and quite blank on the outside. Tam squinted at them. 'There's yin for Mistress Sewell and yin for yoursel', and your name-letter on each, they said, but I canna read them, Mistress.'

I took the letters with a shaking, sweaty hand. Each was marked near the seal, one with a 'T' and the other with a 'G'. Plainly only Tam was to know to whom they were addressed, and I guessed there would be scant clues in the contents of either letter, for safety's sake. But it was all I had ever hoped for, and more, and such was my joy that, when I had secreted them crackling behind the stiff buckram of my bodice, I leaned forward and kissed Tam's bristly, whiskery cheek. 'Oh, thank you, Tam! Now come in, please, you must be starving as well as tired if you've walked all that way in the snow.'

Tam and his pack came in obediently, and greatly enlivened our festivities, for as usual he brought goods both useful and frivolous for everyone to examine with pleasure: sewing threads and needles and pins, bone combs and hair-ornaments, cheap glass jewellery and brightly coloured scraps of material to make shawls or scarves, embroidery silks and frames, knives and spoons, some small quantity of pewter tableware, buttons and laces and rosettes and bundles of foaming creamy lace, and, rather crushed, tiny flowers beautifully sewn out of scraps of velvet and satin and looking, at a distance, almost real; shoe-buckles and hat-trimmings and whalebones for stays and spare cork heels in pairs, sensational chapbooks and a catechism or two, the Scottish version of course; and right at the bottom the inevitable flask of aqua vitae from which he drank greedily before passing it round the company. Altogether it was a most enjoyable afternoon, and all the while the precious letters lay against my heart for me to look forward to.

When Grainne and I were finally alone in our tower, with Jasper and Hen sleeping exhausted with happiness and sticky with food in their beds, I brought out the letters. 'Tam gave me these. There is one for each of us: this is yours. I think I can guess who they're from.'

'So can I,' said Grainne, and her eyes, her whole face, became suddenly brilliant in the flickering candlelight. 'Well, no sense in delaying longer . . . shall we open them?'

I dutifully, eagerly, trembling, broke the seal and unfolded the stiff paper. Francis's writing was as individual as his sister's, vivid and idiosyncratic with flamboyant self-mocking flourishes. The only letter I had ever before received from him was the ill-fated note arranging the meeting for our elopement. Meraud had found that and told Simon, who had had his brother thrown in Oxford Castle. Even the poems he had written had been copied without his knowledge by Great-Aunt to send to me. I gazed for a moment at the close-written page, noting that it contained a poem: and then, saving that mentally for the last, began to read.

My own heart, should you receive this reward the messenger well, for he risks all and for a love letter it is too much, though you and I may not think so. Since you may after all these months be having second thoughts, let me dismay you now by saying that I have not. I love you. I will always love you. Those months when I thought I did not have now only the shape and substance of some terrible, hideous dream, and I look back upon myself with loathing. Hold to that, for I seldom have the grace to present apologies.

We are well. I will not tell you where we are in case this letter should fall into unkind hands, but we are not hurt, though colder, hungrier and considerably leaner than when last you saw us. We also have that thrice-misbegotten cur with us. He caught us up some six miles from the house, and I suppose had slipped his collar. He is too old to make light of the weather and the walking and the snow, but he has augmented our diet by three rabbits, a hare, and two outlandish moorland birds called blackcock, so I have no mind to send him home with his tail between his legs just yet.

We have had now three victories, and I am beginning at the bottom of my cynical heart to admit to a glimmer of hope. One day I trust I will be able to tell you all of it: for the moment I sit chewing the end of my quill and staring at the words dead on the paper, and cannot help but think of how different it would be if you were here in front of me, for I cannot make speeches to a blank wall, and to have your own sweet self to talk and laugh and argue with would bring all my story to life. So my letter must be a poor travesty of my thoughts to you, and for my true feelings and remembrances you must wait until we meet again: as we surely will.

And for the meantime, here is this. The metre is not new, but I owe you a poem for yourself which holds nothing of bitterness or regret. Keep safe, my own sweet heart, my dearest owd gal, and remember this: that I will always go with you. And that I love you more than I can say.

Yours forever,
Francis.

Then came the poem. Tears blurred my vision. I blinked them away and read:

The chains of fate have solemnly decreed
That we should part:
Though all my soul cries out to me my need
For thy sweet heart.

Yet I must leave thee now,
For war and friendship's sake,
But I will not allow
Our love to break.

Look for me not in wintertime to come
Homeward to thee,
Nor listen with wild eyes for tuck of drum
That will not be:
But on some summer's night
Open thy window wide
To guide my homing flight
Unto thy side.

Others have more beauty in their face,
Without thy heart:
To some is giv'n more honour, birth or grace,
And yet thou art
To my thoughts as the star,
That sparks so bright above,
Seems to the moth so far
Yet holds his love.

It was too much. I burst into tears, exhausted by the
energies of the day and the emotions set violently astir
by the letter and the poem. Grainne looked up, a glow
and brilliance in her eyes indicating that she, too, had
received a love-letter. 'Why, whatever is it? Surely not
bad news?'

'No – oh, no, no – oh, how this is stupid, I shouldn't
be crying – he wrote me a poem.'

Grainne waited, unquestioning, as I groped for a
kerchief and blew my nose. At last I said, 'Do you – do
you remember he wrote me one before, and Great-Aunt
sent it to me? It was full of bitterness against me, I
couldn't show it even to you. Now he writes me another,
and it's in the same metre, but it's quite different, it's
beautiful.'

'And that it was upset you.'

'Yes – no – well, not upset, exactly, just . . . I can't explain. Would you like to read it?'

At her nod I passed it to her. She scanned it thoughtfully and then handed it back. 'You are right, it has its own beauty.'

I folded the paper and went to put it in the plain wooden travelling writing-desk where I kept the few letters I had ever received, for I had never previously been so far-flung from my friends, and the journal I had kept in a desultory fashion ever since leaving Oxford: though some of the things that had happened to me since then had been too painful ever to set down on paper. 'How is your letter? It is from Malise, isn't it?'

'Oh yes,' said Grainne, 'oh yes, it's from Malise . . .' She looked up at me from where she sat at the little table by the smoking fire, that slumbered sullenly in the hearth like some weird hunched volcano. 'I could not tell anyone else this, not yet, but I believe . . . I think that I love him.'

'I am so glad, for I like him very much, and I think he's surely worthy of you. You deserve your happiness, after all that has happened . . . does he return your feelings?'

'No doubt of it,' said Grainne, smiling down at the letter. 'No doubt of it at all. I wonder, you know, which comes first, to love or to be loved, and whether one depends on the other . . . I only know that I liked him as soon as I saw him, and that he was kind to Jasper and to me, and then one thing grew and fed off the other until Henry has become like someone beloved in another life – remote and distant and unreal. Only Malise has reality now; and yet quite possibly I may never see him again.'

'You can't say that for certain,' I said stoutly, 'you can't possibly say that . . . let's keep what we have and not fritter it all away in useless speculation and pessimism. They're alive as yet, so far as we know, so let's live for the present.'

'Amen to that,' Grainne said. She gave me a sudden

brilliant smile. 'And now to bed, I think, before Christmas ends.'

In the morning the barmkin was piled high with great heaps and mounds of wet, soft snow, in places as high as the stone walls around it. Somewhere in the elegantly sloping line of drifts opposite my window was the door to the stables, completely obscured. The hills gleamed flat-white like huge painted shapes set against the grey sky, without dimension or distance, so that my eyes struggled to make sense of what they saw. A line of laden dark sticks marked the alders and ash trees along Hermitage Water. As I watched, blinking the moisture from my eyes at the brightness, a small well-wrapped foreshortened figure, probably Sim, emerged from the door of the new wing with a shovel and began to clear a path to the stables.

In Grainne's chamber Jasper was curled in the long window-ledge and gaping out. 'Aunt Thomazine! Do look! Look at the snow!'

'How can I look? You block my view entirely. Anyway, I've seen it from my own chamber.'

'I want to go down.' Jasper retreated all in a rush, and the room became noticeably brighter. 'Oh, Mother, can I go down and go out? I'll put my riding-boots on, I promise, and my cloak and gloves.'

'You may,' said Grainne, plainly seeing it would be unkind, though perhaps wiser, to refuse him. 'But don't disappear into those drifts, some of them must be over my head, let alone yours. Don't go out of the barmkin and when you come in change your wet clothes right away.'

'Yes,' said Jasper, without taking in a word, and hurtled out of the room. I grinned at his mother, who was dressing Henrietta. 'Do you want me to go down and keep an eye on him?'

'There's no hurry, he'll come to no harm. No, Hen, put your arm there, poppet.'

'Ga!' cried Henrietta, waving the disputed arm dangerously near her mother's nose. 'Jasser gone!'

'Yes, he's gone out to see the snow. That's it, good girl.'

'Snow?' said Henrietta. She was nearly two, but not so forward in talking as her brother had been. She had tawny-brown eyes and orange silky hair in wild curls around her freckled face, and was altogether a replica of her father, Henry Sewell, who had died before she was born and after whom she had been named. 'Wassnow, Mumma?'

'I'll show you,' said Grainne, and carried the child to the window-ledge, letting her stand there to look out, her dimpled hands pressed to the leaded glass. Henrietta stared out at the scene for a long moment and then let out her breath in a huge gusty sigh. 'A-a-a-h! Jasser! See Jasser! Jasser da!'

Her brother's small figure capered in the cleared snow behind Sim's labouring shovel. An erratic snowball shot from his hands and hit the implacable bulk of the tower. I prayed he would not aim one at Sim, for with the latter's uncertain temper he risked being clouted with the shovel.

'Go down! Hen go down! Mumma, Hen go down!' the baby begged, stamping her feet in agitation. Grainne, still in her night-rail, lifted her down. 'No, sweeting, I can't yet, I'm not dressed.'

'Go down! Go down!'

'I'll take her,' I said. 'Hen, I'll take you.'

'Go down!'

'Only if you say please,' her mother warned.

'Please go down!' said Henrietta, with no diminution in volume. I hurried into my room, pulled on my boots and cloak and gloves and went back. 'Come on, Hennypenny, you're coming with me.'

'Down?'

'Aunt Thomazine is taking you out to see the snow — isn't that kind of her?'

189

Henrietta had had a thorough grounding in manners. She gave me an ecstatic smile. 'Ack-oo.'

We swept into the new wing, Henrietta in my arms for convenience if not for the ease of her carrying, for she was a very solid weight, opened the front door and went out. There was no wind, but the cold struck like a wall. A snowball smacked into the door and Jasper shrieked like a madman. 'Nearly got you!'

Henrietta's wriggles indicated her wish to get down. I set her small feet on the snowy path and watched her crow with delight as she picked up the snow in her hand and then, in the time-honoured manner of babies, put it to her mouth. 'Cold!'

I watched Sim clear the drifts away from the stable door. Nothing moved in the yard save for him and the two children. I hoped the sheep, some of which might be near to lambing, were safely folded in their stone-ringed pens on the edge of the infield: most of the cattle, I knew, were in the end of the byre, and the fowls were not buried under these six-foot drifts but warm and cosy in the kitchen.

'Watch out, Hen!' Jasper yelled. He was approaching with a huge lump of snow clutched in his hands. 'I'm going to get you, Hen!'

'Don't you dare,' I warned. 'Leave the poor little thing alone — Jasper!' For the boy, who quite often went too far with his little sister, had flung the snowball. Fortunately it broke up in flight, so that only a fraction of it thumped into Hen's chest, but she squawked with surprise, sat down with a bump on her bottom, and began to howl. I was pleased to see that Jasper, fleeing from my wrath, fell over some unseen obstruction and disappeared face-first into a snowdrift. Somewhat abashed, he emerged sniffing and brushing off the snow, presented his apologies to his sister, and we all three went inside to dry off by the kitchen fire.

There we found several people gathered around Tam Crozier, who was sitting at the table staring greenily into a wooden bowl of congealing porridge. They looked round as we entered, and Janet the cook said, 'Och, Mistress, Tam's no' weel.'

'I'm fair frozen,' said Tam in a dispirited grunt, and I saw as I approached that he was shivering. A touch on his forehead revealed that he had indeed got a fairly severe fever. I looked round at the servants' faces, Janet, Meg, Holly, Jock, and said, 'Is there anywhere warm we can lay him? He has some sort of fever.'

Everyone took an involuntary step back save for Meg who, at eighty or more, feared no earthly foe, even the unseen terrors of disease. I said to Tam, with a memory of Francis afflicted with lung-fever after a long journey in adverse weather conditions, 'How's your chest, Tam? And your throat and voice? Have you been coughing?'

'I've a sair pain in ma heid, Mistress, and anither in ma back, but no' in ma cheist.'

It could be anything. I knew nothing about medicine, I had only helped at various bedsides. I said dubiously, 'Well, he needs to be kept warm and away from the rest of the household. Is there anywhere?'

In the summertime it would have been easy. In the depths of winter, with the rooms above the stables like frozen vaults with no means of heating, there were very few suitable places. But Meg had a room with a fire above the kitchen: the only one of the servants' chambers to be so enhanced, it was hers in deference to her age and honoured status in the household. With what I thought to be considerable magnanimity she offered it up: Tam was duly transported up the narrow back stairs and put to bed in Meg's dark odoriferous lair with a hot brick and two spare sheepskins to add to Meg's blankets.

In the next days I often went up to see how he did. The fever was severe and the poor man tossed in delirium, with only the child Bessie to watch over him when she could spare time from her duties to perform the undignified rites of the sickroom with chilblained fingers. On the third day Grainne went up with me, bearing food, to find him apparently much better: he knew us and could talk cheerfully. 'I'll soon be back on the road, Mistress, when the snaw's melted.'

'I expect you will,' said Grainne absently. She took up his wrist to check his heartbeat, and I saw her long pale fingers stop on something she found. And then, strangely, horribly, all the colour drained from her face, leaving her perfectly white, and staring at me with dazed stricken eyes. She said, her voice forcedly casual, 'You take his wrist, Thomazine, I can feel so little against my own pulse that poor Tam might as well be dead!'

'I'm no' deid yet,' Tam grunted as I took up his wrist, feeling the firm fast thump of his heart against my fingers.

And something else. As Grainne had done, I slipped a finger sideways to feel it. A little lump, like a tiny lead shot under the skin: and next to it, another, and another.

And then I knew what it was that he had: and put down his wrist to stare at Grainne with a similar horror to her own. Not on my part, for I had had the smallpox as a child and was therefore immune to further attack: but for her, and the children, and anyone else at Catholm who had not suffered the disease before.

Grainne put her hand on Tam's forehead, and I could see from her fingers that she found the same thing there. Then she said slowly, 'Tam, think back to the houses you've visited in the last two or three weeks. Did any of them have any sickness?'

I did not see how she could remain so calm, until I saw that she had gripped her hands together to stop their shaking. 'I'm no' sure,' Tam was saying, 'heid-colds and rheums were a' I found in this weather, ye ken . . .'

'Nothing else?' said Grainne's deceptively calm voice: and Tam, obviously visited suddenly by a memory, gave a crowing ugly gasp and cowered back into the straw pallet. 'Sma'pox . . . yin o' the houses had a wee maid wi' the sma'pox, but I niver clapped e'en on her . . . Dear God, Mistress, I havena got the sma'pox?'

'I fear very much that you have,' said Grainne, 'and who nurses you depends on who also has had it.'

'I have,' I said, seeing the terror in his bloodshot eyes, all the jauntiness gone. 'And I will look to you, if no one else will.'

The thawing snow and floods which isolated us were at once a blessing and a bane: they prevented terror-stricken members of the household from fleeing into the countryside to spread the infection, but also meant that we were all forced to live hugger-mugger together, eyeing each other for the first symptoms. To my utter relief, I was not the only one who had previously had smallpox: Meg, Great-Aunt Elizabeth, Archie and Jock and Holly, were similarly placed, as was the child Bessie, as could be told from her face. Elizabeth Graham of course took charge, making sure that the children were kept well out of the way in the tower, and that only those unlikely to be infected came anywhere near Tam's chamber, where he tossed and gasped and moaned, and the dreadful spots grew and flowered hideously on his tormented face. On the eleventh day of his illness, he died: and a grim little party, Archie, Jock and Holly, stumbled out into the rain to hack a rude shallow grave from the rough ground by the ruined chapel at Hermitage: for with the melted snow turning the low lands to quagmire, burial in the Kirkyard at Castleton was out of the question.

The day after that, Janet fell ill: and then it was as if the people in the house became skittles in some gruesome game of ninepins, succumbing in ever-increasing numbers. Grizel: Gib: Sim: Sandy: Henrietta and Jasper.

It seemed a miracle that, although she had not to her knowledge had smallpox, Grainne somehow seemed immune to the terrible disease that would, if she contracted it, destroy her rare beauty for ever. So, by the grace of God, she was able to sit with her afflicted, delirious children, comforting them and easing their torments with a love and devotion that no one else could have matched. This seemed to me to be the final, crowning tragedy, after all the misfortune that had befallen her, and just at the time when new love and happiness seemed to be coming to her. And I was well aware of the hideous irony of it, that a letter from her new love had carried the deadly infection to the children. I feared most for them, out of all those stricken, but with the perversity of fate they seemed to take it the least seriously of all. The spots appeared, stayed separate, faded, all in ten days or so, and then they were both well on the way to recovery, two thin, pale, spotty change-lings who lay weak but safe in their bed while Meg, transplanted from her chimney-corner, crouched witch-like on a stool and told them endless stories. Great-Aunt said that she had often heard it remarked upon that children once past infancy were least at risk. 'Indeed, I believe some parents, foolhardy though it may seem, deliberately put their children in the way of the disease so that they may catch it while young, with less risk to their lives and complexions than if they take it later on.'

'They're braver than I could ever be,' I said, looking at Hen's poor little bumpy blotched face. 'These two will, God willing, survive, and you and I did too, and little Bessie. But my brother Edmund died of it, and so did other children at the same time. I wouldn't have the courage to risk my child, and watch him endure what these poor little mites have been through.'

The children were saved, but the fate of the other sufferers still hung in the balance. The feeling of helplessness is what I recall most clearly. There was no physician within a hundred miles, unless at Carlisle across impassable winter country, and even if there had been, I had no faith in his remedies; the Widow Gooch's robust cynicism about doctors' nostrums had rubbed off on me not a little. Great-Aunt, in whom I placed all my faith and trust, had early disillusioned me by saying that she had had the smallpox as a very young child, could remember nothing of her treatment, and had never encountered it at close hand since in all her seventy-odd years. I thought this rather unlikely, but Liddesdale was after all very isolated, and smallpox most rife in crowded towns and cities. However, she did have a boundless store of common sense and a wide knowledge of herbal and other remedies: but it was Meg who proved most useful. 'Sma'pox? Ye maun mix up a wee paste wi' flour an' milk or cream an' put in on their faces, ye ken? That'll make the marking less.'

Grateful for any help, although at her age Meg obviously could not do any of the actual nursing, we obeyed. Other remedies we tried: dressing the patients in red, though there was little enough of that colour in the house; herbal potions to lower fever; keeping them as warm as we could. A rota was worked out: and Holly seemed always to be on hand, solid, steady, reliable, to lift and turn and watch. At his suggestion we tied mittens on the children's hands, that they might not scratch off the scabs and risk worse scarring. Another of Meg's remedies I was too squeamish to try; thirty live toads, burned to a cinder, and pounded into a powder. Besides, as I remarked to Holly, where in all this alien wilderness of bog and icy winter water, would we ever find thirty live toads?

'That cellar's full on 'em,' said Holly, with a flick of his old humour. 'But I reckon thass no reason to say nawthen to owd Meg about that, Mistress.'

Some we could not save. Grizel died quite quickly, calling on her God in her ravings: a terrible fate, to die unloved, unmourned, unlamented even by her husband. She was buried beside Tam in the old Papist Ladykirk, by Hermitage, and doubtless lay unquiet in such surroundings. Her elder son was sorely afflicted, and it was almost unbearable to sit by his bed, hearing his breath as it rasped and stumbled through his half-blocked throat, and his muttered ramblings as the fever crept higher and higher, and to know that neither I nor Great-Aunt could do anything to help him. Yet against all our expectations and fears, he did not die, but at last turned the corner to recovery: and I was glad, for womanizing tippler though he was, I liked Gib.

Sim died too, but Janet, the first of the household to fall ill, seemed to throw it off with ease and after ten days had lost her fever, the pocks healing nicely. Meg's flour-and-milk paste, bizarre as it was, appeared to have had some effect, for it seemed that her scarring would not be as great as the severity of the illness had warranted. Sandy, to my relief, also recovered quite quickly, and accepted his transformed face cheerfully. 'I'm no' fretting, lass. I'm no' as young as I was and I dinna mind if my face frightens the lassies awa'! Puir Gib willna be best pleased tae look at himsel' though, I'm thinking.'

No one said 'Poor Grizel', and it was noticeable how much happier the house was without her. Little Bessie, who as a downtrodden lowly maid had suffered most from her bullying, looked quite a different child and fairly whisked round her tasks: Gib's jokes grew quite indecent and even the widowed Sandy could on occasion be heard to whistle a profane ditty. It had been nearly the end of January before Gib was out of danger, and almost April before all the convalescents were able to resume something like a normal life. Meg was most gratified by the results of her treatment, and was heard to mutter that if only we had tried the toads, all lives would have been saved.

Jasper's sixth birthday was held at the end of March amidst general gaiety in the big kitchen, everyone at Catholm being present. In a pewter mug on the table stood a bunch of woolly-tailed powdery-yellow catkins, first sign of spring, for although the snow had gone from the dale there were still white streaks over the hills. But the warmer weather was coming, lambs were being dropped, and a few days later Sandy rode over the Rig, down to Slitrig Water and so to Hawick. He returned full of news. Montrose, taking advantage of the unusual mildness of January, had marched from Atholl over the mountains in the west, and fallen upon the rich domains of the Campbells, around the lochs and inlets of the western shores. Argyll himself, the head of the clan, had fled ignominiously by sea from his castle at Inverary, leaving his people undefended and disorganized to face the wrath of Montrose and his Irish and Highlanders, all of whom had a long-standing feud with the Campbells. Then, laden with booty, they had marched once more into the winter-shrouded mountains (where a large part of their force had dispersed to take their plunder home), pursued after an interval by three thousand furious Campbells. Montrose had marched over the mountains for two days and doubled back, to arrive unseen above the camp of the enemy. Then there was a night-long wait, frozen, moonlit, weary, before the attack. Before it could be launched, Sandy reported with a grim triumph and contempt, Argyll had again deserted his forces, and Montrose and all his army stood revealed by the dawn, hanging in the hills above them like a falcon in the air, waiting to stoop for the kill.

The Campbells were utterly crushed by the ferocity of Montrose's attack. Hacked and butchered by the savage Irish and Highland charge, they were pursued along the shores of the River Lochy for miles: and ahead of them, like some evil bird of ill-omen, sailed their leader, the MacCailein Mhor, in his black galley, heading for the freedom of the open sea.

The Covenant had tried to make light of this crushing defeat, but in vain. Scotland, as well as maintaining an army in England, now had a home war on its hands: and not unnaturally needed a great deal of money. So the spring brought officials demanding assistance, taxes, war loans, which Sandy did not dare to refuse to pay. Best not to draw attention to Malise Graham's mysterious absence.

Then in the middle of April, the blow fell. Montrose, it was said in Hawick, in Selkirk and Peebles and Kelso and the other Border towns, had suffered ignominious defeat at Dundee. Four or five hundred of his men had been killed including, so rumour had it, his Irish Lieutenant Alastair Macdonell, the great Colkitto: and the scattered remnants of his army had melted back into the Highlands.

For a week or more, with sunken hearts, we believed it, until by some mysterious alchemy the truth infiltrated all at once, so that Gib, on his first outing since his illness, was able to return cheerfully from Hawick market to tell us, 'Yon report of Dundee was a lie, they're saying. Nae defeat at all, and nae more than half-a-dozen men lost. The rest was all exaggeration.' And we breathed again, not knowing then the true incredible story of how Montrose, refusing to abandon his drunken soldiers as they caroused in Dundee, had cajoled and beaten and threatened and forced the men staggering through the eastern gate of the town just as the advance guard of the Covenant's forces rode in through the west gate; and then shepherded, guarded, pushed his inebriated men into the safety of the hills, just ahead of the pursuing forces.

If the news from the north was heartening, that from England was much less so. Vague rumours were rife of Parliamentary gains, of some New Model Army that was supposed to have been raised and organized in a novel and rather terrifying-sounding way, generalled by Fairfax and the rising man on the Parliament's side, Oliver Cromwell. And to Gib's intense annoyance, Carlisle had been besieged, so that tidings of the English war were distant, vague and too filled with rumour and speculation to be wholeheartedly believed.

The spring flowered into summer, warm sunshine and soft, frequent rains to contrast with the cold of December. After the tragedies of the winter, we revelled in the freedom of the weather. Jasper, the smallpox scars almost indistinguishable if you had not known where to look, ran wild on the hills, and Holly, who could seemingly turn his hand to anything, spent much time with the boy and his shaggy garron when he was not helping with the farm-work; for with Sim gone and Gib still weak Sandy was short-handed. Indoors, Grainne and I became less ladies of leisure and took on ourselves as much of the daily running of the household as Great-Aunt Elizabeth would allow.

I had written to Lucy, giving her a brief account of the past eighteen months. It did not seem possible that it was so long since I had seen her; we had never before been apart for longer than a few hours since we were ten years old. I gave no hint of where Malise and Francis were, since there was no telling whose prying eyes might scan even a gossipy letter such as mine. Fortunately it had been sent on its way some time before Carlisle's besieging, so I had some hopes of its reaching Oxford intact, though much scantier expectations of receiving a reply. Nor, after Tam's death, were there any letters from Malise and Francis, but we did not feel the lack: for as the summer marched on so did Montrose and his cause, sweeping on the edge of a dizzy exultant wave-crest of victories, one after the other. Auldearn, Alford, Kilsyth, with each one the Covenant men grew more desperate, reprisals against friends of Montrose, like the Napiers, increased, and the might of the Scottish army dwindled and faded away. There were disquieting tales of a major battle in England, somewhere in the Midlands, which had ended in utter disaster for the King; but in Scotland his cause still flowered bright with hope and victory. Montrose, fresh from his crushing defeat of General Baillie at Alford, reinforced by High-landers who, inspired by his success, had joined his army, prepared to march south to make himself master of all Scotland in the King's name. And at Kilsyth, just north of Glasgow, he met the Covenant's forces under Baillie, and utterly defeated them. The overwhelming nature of the victory was due not a little to the fact that a Committee of Covenanters, including Argyll, insisted on directing the battle despite Baillie's frantic protests. And as ever, the soldiers, the levies from Fife and the Lowlands, suffered for their leaders' mistakes. The Committee, well-mounted, got clean away. Six thousand Covenant soldiers were slain without mercy, for the loss of half-a-dozen of Montrose's men.

Glasgow opened its gates to him, towns and counties sent their representatives to assure him of their support. The nobility, who had held back all this while, the Border lords, Traquair, Home, Roxburgh, flocked to join him, all the fair-weather Royalists came to grovel and promise their undying devotion to Montrose, the new ruler of Scotland. All the country was his; now he could turn his attention to the invasion of England, for the King was in such desperate straits that Montrose's army was his last hope of salvaging some victory from the jaws of disastrous, utter defeat. I thought much during that long warm summer of our soldier friends in England – Simon, Francis's eldest brother, Grainne's brother-in-law Tom Sewell, Charles Lawrence who had shared the siege of Ashcott with us, and Dan Ashley, the Parliament captain whom Lucy loved. There was also my husband, Sir Dominic Drakelon, but I preferred not to think of him – save for a small, evil, understandable whisper in the back of my mind, that would not be stilled, and wished over and over again for his death.

But of Francis and Malise we did have news; not much, it was true, but as Grainne said, better than nothing. A boy of fourteen or so, mounted on a surprisingly good bay horse, came slithering down the track along Hermitage Water, having ridden from Bothwell Brig, near Glasgow, where Montrose's army was at present encamped. He brought a letter for us both from Malise: and when he had been carried off to the kitchen by the kind-hearted Janet for 'a wee sup o' my barley broth', Grainne opened it with suddenly unsteady hands.

They were both well, Malise reported, and in high spirits; and as he had some leisure to write, being troubled with a head-cold, whereas Francis seemed to be eternally busy with the cavalry, he had been the one to put pen to paper. There followed a brief description of the battles, culminating in Kilsyth. 'I have never seen such slaughter,' wrote Malise with distress. 'More than six thousand of theirs were slain, so it seems, but scarce six of our own men dead. Yet such a massacre by the Irish I can in some measure understand, for a month ago or more some of their womenfolk had strayed from the army in Methven Wood, and were most brutally and hideously killed by Hurry's cavalry. So it is likely that thoughts of vengeance were upmost in their minds at Kilsyth.' But it was the last paragraph of the letter which gave us the most pleasure. Montrose was making preparations to invade England as soon as possible: and when his army marched towards the Borders it was probable that Francis and he would be allowed to slip away briefly to visit us at Catholm.

We had not seen either of them for a year. As we sat in the fading afternoon light in the parlour it all seemed to me impossible, a dream, a miracle, a wild fantasy of legendary warriors: that Montrose, with two companions, had crossed the Border a fugitive, hunted, without any tangible support save rumours of the Irish somewhere in the northern mountains, and in one year, the *annus mirabilis*, had, with his wild Irish and Highlanders, made himself master of Scotland in a series of brilliant battles. I remembered Malise saying, long ago, 'If anyone can do it, he can: and I want to be there when he does.'

Well, Malise had had his wish, and Francis too had been part of the glory of that year: and I longed more than ever to be with them, to share their triumph. It was almost unbearable to think that I would only ever know of that story at second hand. To be a woman, encumbered with skirts and femininity and convention, seemed at that moment particularly irksome – especially as I in no wise considered my mind to be the inferior of any man's simply because of my sex.

Women had taken part in that victory; the Irish women, wives and camp-followers, had followed their menfolk and taken their children with them all through the winter campaigns. I envied them most desperately: and had that moment come again, to watch Francis and Malise ride off to join Montrose, I would, like Drake, have slipped my leash and followed them.

With bated breath, we waited eagerly for further news, or best of all to see their familiar dear-loved figures riding up to Catholm. August slid gently into September: the harvest came around again and Grainne and Jasper and I helped to gather it in, remembering similar times at Goldhayes long ago when the world was not at war. There were Montrose's men recruiting just to the west, amongst the Maxwells and Johnstones of Annan and Nithsdale, to replace those of the Irish and Highlanders – including Alastair Macdonell – who in time-honoured, but potentially disastrous fashion were abandoning the fight to return to their homes in triumph – or in Alastair's case to pursue his family's feud with the Campbells.

With his much depleted force, Montrose began his march – striking first towards Edinburgh, so we heard, and then south to the Borders. At the same time, the Minister at Castleton let it be known, exultantly, that General Leslie, hurrying back from the English Midlands on hearing the news of Kilsyth, was near the Borders and would, once he had caught Montrose, smite the ungodly traitor-rebel and his inhuman army of savages from the face of the earth.

But he would not catch Montrose, that will-o'-the-wisp elusive figure from the northern fastnesses. It was unthinkable, a horrible possibility which seemed so unlikely that we refused to entertain it. However small his force was he would surely be able to dodge Leslie's men and slip back to the Highlands; or with that lovely magical alchemy of victory, sweep down on the Covenant army from the hills, as so often before.

We heard that Montrose was at Jedburgh, barely sixteen miles away across the hills, and waited with tense eagerness for the visit that must surely come. But a day, two days, went by and no riders came down the Rig from the north-east; nor did we hear any news.

Towards the evening of the second day – the thirteenth of September, exactly a year after Montrose's victory at

Aberdeen — I decided to go for a walk up on the Rig. We had been in the house all day, helping Janet to brew the week's supply of ale and bake a batch of bread, and now I felt I would run mad if I did not have freedom and fresh air, even if only for an hour. Grainne would not come with me, for it was Henrietta's bedtime: and besides, she said, should Francis and Malise come then at least one of us would be there to welcome them. So I borrowed Janet's plaid, a length of gaudily-woven cloth to wrap round neck and body against any evening chill, put on my stoutest shoes, and walked out of the barmkin and up the hill. Somewhere out on the Rig were Jasper and his garron, and Grainne had asked me to send him homewards with all speed should I spot him. There was no real fear that harm would come to him, and after close on eighteen months at Catholm the child knew the hill like his own hand, but Grainne I knew had always a nagging fear and anxiety about him at the back of her mind.

I climbed the head-dyke and turned to look down at Catholm, small and grey and dim and peaceful in the shadow under the hill, the smoke from the kitchen fire winding languidly into the evening air, and then picked up my skirts and ran the few steps down the other side and on to the rough moorland. The sun still struck here, gold and slanting, and a few late, lazy butterflies drifted up from my feet as I walked. I began to whistle, an unladylike habit I had learned as a wild child at Ashcott, and then to sing softly, affected by the warm quiet beauty of the evening.

It was when I paused for breath at the end of a verse, flushed by the effort of the climb, that I heard a voice, Jasper's high unmistakable tones, over the shoulder of the hill. It carried a long way on the calm air: I could not see him, but cupped my hands round my lips and shouted. 'Jasper! Jas—per!'

There was silence, then an unintelligible screech in reply. The next moment, two horses appeared, walking down the slope towards me. One was the garron, with

Jasper perched on top. And the other, grey and feather-footed, instantly recognizable, was The Thunderflash.

It was Francis. I jumped and shouted and waved my arms, and then dragged my hindering skirts to calf-level and ran, tripping and stumbling up the hill towards them. But my climb had told on me: my vision of hurling myself into his arms vanished in the reality of a parched throat, wobbling legs and seared chest. I stood, gasping, a mere hundred yards or so further on, and only then could I see and hear them clearly.

'It's Thomazine,' said Jasper's high, carrying voice, 'it's all right, she's here, *please* don't fall off, she's coming . . .' And Francis was obviously only held upright on his mount by sheer force of will, his hands gripping the horse's mane, visibly swaying in the saddle. I stared at them in horror, for something had evidently gone badly wrong: and where, oh where, was Malise?

They reached me. I believe I ran to grab the gelding's bridle: some memory seems to linger of my uttering inane banalities: 'What's happened? Are you hurt? Where's Malise?' But all that I really remember is his face, as he lifted his head to look at me, utterly unguarded, weary, desperate, the green shadowy eyes haunted with a new knowledge of horror. 'Malise is safe – but we've been beaten,' he said, and even his voice was different, altered by fatigue and despair.

I saw in one frantic glance that there was a blood-stained rag tied round his arm, and longer to recognize it as Jasper's shirt: the boy wore only his unbuttoned doublet, revealing a flat pale scrawny chest nicked here and there with smallpox scars. 'Beaten? Montrose, beaten?' I said stupidly. 'In God's name, how?'

'In a battle,' said Francis, 'at Philliphaugh, it's near Selkirk. Leslie caught up with us, this morning, trapped the whole army, army, that was a joke, not a thousand men did we have . . .' He clenched his hands in the thick coarse tufts of the grey's mane. I said, 'Jasper, go down to the house, tell your mother and Mistress Graham, tell them to make ready for Francis, say he's hurt, can you do that? And tell them Malise is safe.'

'I will!' cried Jasper, his eyes bright with grief and fear, and clapped his heels to the round bay barrel of the garron. The pony, startled, tossed its head and shambled into a trot. One of Jasper's screeches, and a slap of the reins on its shoulder, urged it into a reluctant canter. I took The Thunderflash's reins, noting automatically the utter weariness of that normally lively horse. Francis said carefully, 'If you walk by his side, I can put my hand on your shoulder. Is that all right? Otherwise I shall surely fall off, and after keeping in the saddle all day, that would be a pity.'

'Is it just your arm?' I asked, taking refuge in my selfish relief at having him at least returned to me, if not exactly safe or sound. 'Is that Jasper's shirt?'

'He's a good lad,' said Francis's altered voice. 'He thought of it, I hadn't the wits left . . . Malise is safe, he's with Montrose. They got clean away . . . more than could be said for the Irish.' He was leaning more and more heavily on my shoulder as we stumbled slowly down the hill: I wondered with some detached part of my mind, how long I could support him thus. 'You must go,' he went on, and as I incautiously turned my head to stare at him, added, 'you must get away from here, first light tomorrow, that's why I came back to tell you.'

'But why? We can't go! What about you?'

'I doubt I'll be able to come with you, but whatever happens to me, you must go, do you understand, go, get away, leave, flee to England.' His hand clenched again on my shoulder, more painfully. 'If they find her here, they'll kill Grainne.'

In total astonishment and horror, I stopped dead. Francis nearly lost his balance, but stayed upright with a visible effort. His eyes burned into mine as I stuttered, 'K-kill Grainne? *Grainne?* Why? In God's name, why?'

'She's Irish, isn't she? They killed all the Irish women this morning. They killed them, they ripped up the pregnant women, they slaughtered the children and sang psalms to the glory of God as they did it. May they burn everlastingly in their own stinking hell,' said Francis, his voice shaking with fury and grief as I had never in all my life heard it before, 'for what they did at Philliphaugh in the name of their God. And to my own everlasting disgust, I skulked in a ditch and watched them do it.' He closed his eyes briefly upon the unbearable memory. 'They know Malise was with Montrose – there were Argyll's creatures thick at our camp at Bothwell, spying. They'll come here in search of him, or me, and if they find Grainne and discover she's Irish they'll kill her – and the children too. *Now* do you see?'

I was crying, the tears running soundlessly down the side of my nose. I smeared them away with my sleeve. 'I won't go without you. They'll kill you too if they find you here.'

'I can be hid easily enough. You and Grainne and the children are another matter.' He twitched the reins and the horse began its weary shuffling walk again. 'You will leave tomorrow morning, is that understood? Don't worry for me for God's sake; after my heroic performance this morning I'm not worth it.'

'Don't say that!' I cried, hearing the bitterness and self-loathing in his voice. 'You couldn't have done anything to save them, you'd only have been killed yourself and it wouldn't have done any good and I'd rather have you a live coward than a dead hero.'

'That's as may be,' said Francis, quietly, 'but it doesn't stop me thinking that perhaps I could have saved . . . Oh God, if ever ghosts walk this earth, they will walk and groan and wail at Philliphaugh.'

We had reached the head-dyke. I dragged the gate aside for the horse to go through, and to my relief saw Sandy and Gib, followed by Jasper, running up from the barmkin towards us. 'Promise me you'll go?' said Francis, and his sound hand grasped mine as I stood by him. 'Oh God, you dear stubborn fool, I can't let you take the risk – *promise* me you'll go!'

Feeling as if my heart was being wrenched from me, I whispered in despair, 'I don't want to leave you, I don't *want* to . . .'

'Grainne can't go on her own . . . you will leave for her,' said Francis, his fingers tightening on mine. 'Promise me?'

'Yes!' I cried, recognizing the inevitable. At the same moment Jasper hurtled up to us, being a faster runner at six than were Sandy at fifty or Gib at twenty-eight, shouting, 'Master Graham's here! I've told them and they're getting bandages ready and things!'

'Good lad,' said Francis, and from somewhere produced a shadowy grin for the child. 'And thank you . . . did you tell them Malise was safe?'

'Yes, of course I did,' said Jasper. He looked up at Francis suddenly, his round high brow wrinkled in puzzlement. 'Oh, where's Drake?'

There was a pause, filled with Sandy's approaching panting breath as he lumbered up the track. 'Drake's dead,' said Francis gently. 'They killed him too, this morning . . . he didn't suffer anything. I'm sorry, Jasper.'

'Dead?' Jasper demanded. 'You mean, like Mistress Grizel? Won't he come back, ever?'

'No, not ever,' said Francis, and suddenly, foolishly, I felt like weeping in earnest. Philliphaugh had been a disastrous defeat for Montrose; Francis was hurt and a fugitive, having been a helpless witness to a most hideous, appalling, barbarous slaughter by men who professed themselves Christians; and yet what brought me close to breakdown was the thought of Drake, friendly, harmless, ridiculous old Drake, killed by Covenant soldiers. The tragedy of Philliphaugh eclipsed by a dead dog in a ditch.

But then Sandy and his elder son arrived panting, taking charge, lifting Francis down from The Thunder-flash – 'Ye maun be crazed, lad, ye canna go on riding in yon state' – taking one arm while Gib took the other, supporting him as they stumbled down the track three abreast, leaving me with The Thunderflash and Jasper, sobbing bitterly into the damp dewy grass of the dyke.

I said all the stupid platitudes about how no one can live for ever, and a glorious death in battle – as if Jasper cared about that – and about Drake's age: 'He was eleven, Jasper, and that's a good age for a dog, he'd have died soon anyway, perhaps slowly and painfully with some illness. It's better this way, really it is.'

Jasper, obviously already beginning to be ashamed of his unmanly grief, sniffled into his sleeve. He said, rather muffled, 'I hate them! Why did they have to kill him?'

'Perhaps it was by accident,' I said, although something about the way Francis had said 'They killed him' had implied no such thing. 'Now come on, we've got to go down, perhaps they need our help and it's getting dark.'

We walked slowly down the track, The Thunderflash limping wearily behind me, and Jasper obviously wrapped deep in thought. At last he said, with great seriousness, 'Where *do* people go when they're dead?'

'Why, to Heaven of course,' I said, deciding to leave out theological complications like Hell. Jasper said slowly, 'Did Mistress Grizel go to Heaven?'

'I should think so. *She* thought she would, anyway.'

'But I thought Heaven was for *nice* people.'

'Well, it's an unfortunate fact, shrimp, but good and godly people aren't always very nice – not to ordinary folk like you and me, anyway.'

'Will you go to Heaven when you die?'

'I doubt it,' I said, thinking of the massed ranks of my sins.

'You ought to go to Heaven,' said Jasper, with the sometimes flattering directness of six. 'You're nice. Who decides who goes to Heaven, then?'

'Well, I suppose God does. And I suppose we do, too, by choosing whether we're good or bad.'

'If God doesn't let you into Heaven then I don't like him,' said Jasper. Shocked despite myself by this evidence of a precocious infant atheist in our midst, I said, 'Then I don't suppose he'll let you in either.'

'That's all right then, 'cause I'll be with you in Hell,' Jasper told me unanswerably. Uncomfortably aware that in this argument at least, he had had the last word, I changed the subject. 'Would you like a dog of your own?'

In the deepening night, the great green eyes turned to mine with delight. 'Ooh, yes, yes, I would! Do you think Mother would let me?'

'I'm sure she would. We must find you a nice puppy that you can train properly to be obedient.'

'Drake never was,' Jasper reminded me. He added, 'It'd be nice to have a dog all my own, like a friend, *my* friend.' And I was reminded with a faint pang that his childhood so far had been a lonely one, no small boys his own age to play with, his only childish companion his baby sister, and all his conversation held with adults. If we ever get back to Oxford or Suffolk, I thought as we entered the barmkin, Grainne should send him to school before he becomes too much of a misfit brat to mix with other children.

At my suggestion, Jasper took The Thunderflash into the stable, highly delighted at the thought of attending to the horse himself. With a suddenly thumping heart, I walked into the house, to find an ominous silence. Guessing where Francis had been taken from the lighted window I had seen from outside, I went into the tower and hurried up the winding stairs to the first floor.

In the chamber that Malise had had, all the candles were lit and the room was crowded and hot. Francis sat on the edge of the bed, stripped to the waist, and Elizabeth Graham was bathing his arm while Grainne held a basin of water. His face was white and set as his aunt probed and prodded, muttering to herself. 'I see the bullet is still in there . . . was there much blood?'

'Some,' said Francis, with characteristic ironic understatement. 'Until that admirable child sacrificed his shirt . . . I trust you don't mind that, Grainne?'

'Of course I don't mind,' said Grainne. 'Tell me what happened. Are you sure he is safe?'

'I saw him ride away, unscathed. We – the horse, with Montrose – we were safe enough, we could escape, but the Irish could not, they were trapped. There were a hundred or so of us, with Montrose, we charged their dragoons, we tried to break through to join the Irish, but it was hopeless. We lost more than half the horse, and Montrose, I could see it, we all could, he wanted to die. They persuaded him, Dalziel and the others, to give up fighting and flee. The fifty of us left split up, Malise went with Montrose but he knew I was hurt, he begged me to come here to warn you. They know we were with Montrose, you see, and their vengeance will be terrible. They killed all the Irish, the women and the children, the cook-boys and the camp-followers, all defenceless and screaming for mercy . . . and they will kill you, Grainne, if they find you here.'

'Why?' Grainne asked, and her eyes, so like her son's, stared at him in horrified bewilderment. 'Simply – because I am Irish?'

'For no other reason than that. Because you are Irish, and to them a sub-human savage, and because they were humiliated by the Irish soldiers all this past year. They want to wipe out that humiliation with blood, and it needs no other pretext.'

'But they are supposed to be men of God! The ministers . . .'

'Are encouraging them. I saw them; like black carrion crows they were, screaming all the while for slaughter.' He winced as Elizabeth Graham scrubbed at the bullet-hole, still sluggishly leaking blood in his upper arm. She said briskly, 'That is quite enough of your talking for the present. That bullet must be got out. Is the knife ready, Bessie?'

The little maid, crouched by the hearth and the new smoky fire within it, looked up. 'Aye, Mistress Graham.'

'And you'd best have some of this,' said Gib, who was sitting by the window, and he proffered a flask of spirits.

'It'll dull the pain a wee bit, ye ken.' Francis shook his head. 'I have proved my cowardice once already today, and I've no mind to reveal it a second time.'

'You're a fool,' said Great-Aunt roundly. 'This is no time for misplaced heroics.'

'Ah, but you need my advice,' said Francis, with a shadowy smile. 'And you won't get it if I'm fuddled with uisquebaugh ... bring on the instrument of torture, Madam Executioner.'

I slipped to his side as Great-Aunt brought the knife, dull and smoky with heat. His hand gripped mine. 'Hullo, owd gal. In at the kill, as usual ... Great-Aunt, you have my permission to get it over with.'

I had not thought myself particularly squeamish, but that messy unpleasant operation was almost more than I could bear. I could practically feel the knife, as if it were in my own flesh, more painful even than Francis's other hand that clenched round mine with such force that I bore the bruises for a fortnight. But whatever he had wanted to prove to himself, it succeeded: the strength of will that lay like steel under his quicksilver, changeable personality would not let him flinch or make a sound, the only signs of agony the grip on my hand, and his grey, taut face. There was a lot of blood, wiped away by Elizabeth with profanities I had never before heard on her lips, as she probed and levered with the necessary callousness of a surgeon. Then a final rush of blood and her fingers came up, stained and running red, clutching the bullet in triumph. 'Thank God,' I whispered, and Francis, his body suddenly awash with sweat, grinned faintly with relief. 'No, not God – thank Great-Aunt.'

The wound was staunched and washed in wine and bandaged, Elizabeth Graham saying cheerfully that it was a clean one and should heal with no trouble, and Francis commenting darkly on her obvious experience in dealing with such injuries. Then, evidently in no state to protest, he was tucked into bed like a child and fed broth and milk. When Bessie had taken the bowl and cup away to be washed, Great-Aunt said, 'So you think Grainne and Thomazine should go?'

'I do, and tomorrow morning at the latest,' said Francis. Propped up on pillows, the now red-glowing fire giving his face colour, only the quietness of his voice betrayed his weakness. 'Thomazine has promised me she will go.'

'But where?' Grainne asked. 'I cannot believe they would kill me in cold blood, I cannot believe it. Perhaps in the heat of battle, but not here, not an execution . . .'

'Believe me, they would, and your children too. Do you want to put them in such hazard?'

It was the clinching argument. Grainne slowly put her hands to her mouth, her eyes, bleak and anguished, filled with tears. 'No, no, I'll go . . . Oh God, poor Malise, and Montrose . . . to be defeated just when victory seemed assured, all those marvellous battles gone for nothing, all that year wasted . . .'

'No, not quite wasted,' said Francis. 'I have a feeling that this year will not be forgotten, by Covenanters or Royalists. And Montrose still has an army, Alastair Macdonell is still in Scotland. He will try again.'

I asked the question that I had been too afraid to ask before. 'And you . . . if we go, to Oxford or Suffolk, what will you do?'

'He cannot possibly go with you,' said Great-Aunt. 'He would not ride a mile like that, he will need at least a week or ten days till he's fit to travel.'

'You can hide me in the shielings,' said Francis. 'They will surely search the house, but if I am on the hills they're unlikely to find me. Hobbie can look after me, or Archie, and now autumn is coming there'll be no one else up there to betray me.'

'It's the best plan, I can see that,' I said. 'But it will break my heart to leave you now . . . will you follow us south?'

The candlelight illuminated the wry twist to his mouth. 'I don't know. My loyalties are torn two ways, though my love is not. If it seems that Montrose is carrying on the struggle, then if I can I will try to join him. If not, then I will see you in Oxford.'

'You have much to do, said Great-Aunt firmly to me and to Grainne. 'Leave him now to sleep, and go make yourselves ready for the journey.'

'Gib or I can tak' ye as far as Carlisle,' Sandy offered. 'Set ye on your way. Ye can tak' Jock too, he's a strong lad and canny.'

'No, thank you, it's all right,' I told him. 'We'd be grateful enough for a guide to Carlisle, but we came here safely enough with Holly Greenwood for an escort, and I know how short-handed you are. We wouldn't dream of taking Jock.'

Sandy did not press the offer, and we bade goodnight to Francis before going to make ready for our departure. 'I won't go without saying goodbye,' I promised him, as I kissed him cousin-fashion. Francis grinned faintly. 'I never thought you would ... Goodnight, owd gal, and sweet dreams.'

Our last night at Catholm was spent mostly in packing, only a few hours left over for sleeping. Our belongings were few, but more than when we had arrived, and it was a job to fit everything into the bags and boxes we had brought with us. Then Holly and Gib and Sandy carried everything down to the stables, ready to be loaded on to the baggage-horse the next morning. Janet, sentimentally tearful, had made up a basket of long-lasting food, cheese and bannocks and dried meat and fresh apples from Sandy's precious two trees, and promised more for our midday meal. In the middle of all this, a sleepy Jasper appeared barefoot in his night-shirt, hair tousled and thumb in mouth. 'What's happening, Mother?'

Grainne explained that we had to leave at dawn, because the soldiers might come and we would be in danger if they did. 'You'd like to go back to Oxford, wouldn't you, and see Orange again?'

Orange was Jasper's beloved cat, obtained as a kitten and left behind at Pennyfarthing Street with our friends and the Widow Gooch. Jasper nodded uncertainly. 'But what about Francis? Is he coming with us?'

'He can't, chicken. He's hurt and he has to rest. He'll come later. Now go back to bed and get some sleep, we have to be up very early.'

Great-Aunt woke us before dawn had even begun to light the eastern hills. We dressed ourselves and the children, and Bessie brought us breakfast in our chambers. Then, when all else was ready, I went to Francis with anguish in my heart to say farewell.

He was awake, and looking a great deal better. There was a fresh dressing on his arm, and a mug of ale and some bread and cheese by the bed. Wordlessly we kissed, long and lingering, savouring every second still remaining to us: and then he gently drew away and studied my face, smiling. 'There is no need for tears, you know, my dear and only love. We will meet again.'

'How can you know?' I whispered, heart-broken. 'We're always saying farewell, always parted . . . one day it will be for ever.'

'Oh ye of little faith . . . I have made my decision. I will follow you to Oxford. I have followed Montrose for a year, and now it is your turn. Neither he nor Malise would understand, for they are like Simon in that, they put honour and duty before the private longings of the heart, but I have had enough of being honourable, and dutiful, and incomplete . . . Look for me in Oxford, my own sweet love, or in Suffolk, and we will surely be together then.'

' "Look for me not in wintertime to come Homeward to thee," ' I quoted from the poem I knew by heart. 'I shall keep that always, I have had no chance to tell you before how much I loved it . . . though that letter could have brought us disaster.' And I told him about Tam, who had carried smallpox to Catholm.

'So Grizel is dead. I thought the house seemed brighter . . . I am glad the children came through safely. They aren't badly marked, are they?'

'No, they were barely touched. And Grainne was so lucky to escape it altogether, for I think she feared that to lose her beauty would make a difference with Malise.'

Francis smiled. 'She has little cause to fear. "Love is not love Which alters when it alteration finds." If he survives all this, he will marry her, and I can think of no one else who will suit him better.'

'Then why doesn't he come for her?' I said. 'I can't really understand . . . if he *truly* loved her, surely he would leave Montrose now.'

'That shows how little you understand him. He can't desert Montrose now, he is far more bound up with his cause, heart and soul, than ever I was. He won't leave Montrose until all hope of a recovery is gone. He is not like you and I, to lay everything aside for love.' He kissed me again. 'Now you must go: and let this be the last of our partings. In Oxford or in Suffolk, I will come to you, and all you must do is whistle . . .'

'But what of Simon, or Dominic? Catholm was the only place we could be together, and now that's gone . . .' I held his eyes, feeling the first onslaughts of despair and grief. 'Will we never be together?'

'My own dear sceptic, a way will be found . . . a way *must* be found, or you and I may as well leap now from that window, and put earthly cares behind us. We have our love, and with that we are richer far than those who lack it. I promise you, I will be with you soon.'

There was a knock at the door. Francis grinned. 'Your summons. Kiss me once more, and then go. I can look to myself; my fears are all for you. Go as quickly as you can, and if you are ever challenged say you are English – don't let Grainne say a word.'

Time for one last kiss: time to stand by his side as Grainne and her children came in to say goodbye, and to hear him repeat his advice. Already light showed round the shutters: Sandy called from the bottom of the stairs. The children scampered out, eager for the adventure of the journey, then Grainne, calling to Hen to be careful going down the stairs: time for yet one more snatched kiss that only heaped fuel on the sullenly burning, unsatisfied fire of our longing. I backed unwillingly to the door: Francis said, 'Keep safe, and happy, and don't whatever you do give up hope. Goodbye: and remember, I love you for ever.'

'And I love you,' I whispered, and fled before my resolve and control could break.

And so we left Catholm, and Liddesdale, and Scotland, our home for nearly eighteen months: a strange little procession, Sandy on his nag, myself on a borrowed horse, The Thunderflash being still too exhausted by the ride over the hills from Philliphaugh to embark on another journey so soon. Then Grainne, with Hen in the basket strapped to her crupper, on the sway-backed comfortable old mare she had ridden from Oxford, and Jasper trotting by her side on his garron. Holly brought up the rear, leading the Widow Gooch's baggage-laden white cob. All of Catholm turned out to see us go, Great-Aunt, Gib, Jock, Bessie, Janet, even old Meg hobbled from her chimney-corner to mutter a Gaelic charm – I hoped it was for good luck – over each of us. And at a window in the grey ugly tower Francis, watching. My eyes blurred with tears, I blew him a kiss, a spuriously merry gesture, and then we rode out in the gathering light, between the tawny, cruel hills whose beauty I had at last come to recognize and acknowledge: south towards gentle green England, and safety, and home.

part two

The cruel mother

How sharper than a serpent's tooth it is
To have a thankless child.
                    (Shakespeare, *King Lear*)

Chapter 5

Returnings

Seek home for rest,
For home is best.
   (Thomas Tusser)

We had left Liddesdale on the fourteenth of September: it took us a month, to the day, to reach Oxford, in contrast to our previous journey, and that month was not uneventful. At Catholm we had had the vaguest rumours of the course of the war in England; on our travels south, we were brought face to face with the brutal reality. The King's power was in ruins: the battle at Naseby, three months before, had destroyed most of his army, and Prince Rupert had surrendered Bristol and been accused by his royal uncle of treachery, causing a conflict which split the remains of the King's forces. In all of England, it appeared, only parts of North Wales and Cornwall were still held for the King, with garrisons clinging on in towns like Newark, Oxford, Worcester and Chester. All over the countryside, life seemed to be returning slowly to normal; the harvest gathered in, October ale being brewed, goods taken to market. Often we met soldiers, not the rapacious thieves of our earlier encounter outside Nantwich, but precise, courteous, chilly men who demanded our destination and business and questioned us as to our origins. But two women, two children and a groom were hardly a suspicious group: always I quoted our destination as Coventry, and Grainne, as instructed, never spoke. Several times Holly had to roll up his sleeve and move his arm to demonstrate that he was unfit for military service, since officers were always on the look-out for fit young men to join their regiments: particularly ones already supplied with a horse. Fortunately, it was obvious that Holly's right arm was incapable of wielding a sword effectively, and I was relieved to discover that at least two of the Parliament officers who would have pressed him into service were prevented also by their own scruples about leaving two women to make their way unprotected across England. It was heartening to discover that Lucy's beloved Dan Ashley was by no means unique on the Roundhead side. Only in Carlisle had we known fear, and that was because the garrison, after the ending of the siege, was composed of Covenanting Scots; but since the citizens thoroughly detested them, being as they were unpaid and compelled to live off free quarter, we were not in a minority and with Sandy's help were able to leave in safety.

And now on the fourteenth of October, we approached Oxford at last, down the golden road from Banbury in a yellow afternoon sunshine that lit the turning leaves with fire: and my heart lifted from the gloomy depression in which it had been wallowing since leaving Francis. For this land was mine, gentle and green, rich and comfortable: and in the evening we would come to the two-gabled stone house in Pennyfarthing Street, by St Aldate's Church, and see Lucy, and Jamie, and Meraud, and the Widow Gooch. I refused to think of Dominic, presumably somewhere also in Oxford with our son Kit, who would be two years old now, and the child's nurse who was also my husband's mistress.

Banbury was still in Royalist hands: so was Ashcott, I saw from the hill above my toy unwarlike castle. There was no time to do more than gaze briefly, though Grainne was able to visit Henry's grave under the yews in Adderbury churchyard, and to pray there for a moment. I wondered if she prayed for his forgiveness and understanding, wherever he was that she had found another love.

And then we rode into Oxford, lovely city of yellow stone and soaring spires, filled with townsfolk and soldiers jostling home before the evening curfew. Almost faint with weariness after the long journey, I let the shouts and cries of the shopkeepers, the fire-blackened buildings in Butcher's Row, the usual huddle of women around the fountain at Carfax, all pass by in a daze of relief. There was St Aldate's, and the walls of Christchurch, and Pennyfarthing Street: and we halted our horses before the tall stone house with the two gables, my house, where we had spent almost a year at the beginning of the war.

Holly knocked on the door. People stared curiously: I saw one or two whom I recognized raise their hands in uncertain greeting. Grainne and I dismounted stiffly: Henrietta, who had ridden all the way from Scotland in a wicker basket, begged to be let down, and Jasper slid off his round uncouth pony and jumped up to the door in excitement.

For a moment I thought with horror that the house was empty: then we heard bolts being drawn back, and a crack appeared through which we could see a narrow rectangle of Heppy Greenwood's freckled face. She gave a shriek of joy, the door was flung wide and she hurled herself into her brother's arms. Behind her stood my cousin Lucy, my dear, exasperating friend who had been close as a sister to me since we were ten years old: and I realized suddenly how sorely I had missed her exuberant, romantic, generous nature, her confidences, her boundless optimism: and how very glad I was to see her again. She was saying doubtfully, 'Who is it, Heppy?' Then, peering shortsightedly, she saw us, and chaos was complete.

In the midst of our tearful, joyful reunion, with half the street looking on with interest, came the familiar astringent voice of the Widow Gooch, who kept the house but was much more to all of us than a mere housekeeper: indeed to me had been almost the mother I had never had. 'Oh, so you're back, are you? Well, don't stand there telling all your news in public for everyone to gawp at, get those horses round to the stable, Holly Greenwood, or I'll give you none of my new October.'

Laughing, talking, we allowed ourselves to be drawn inside. Holly obediently took the horses off to the stables at the back of the house, which could only be reached by going round to the street behind, and his sister ran for refreshments. We stumbled down the dark passage to the kitchen at the end, still obviously the roosting-place for the Widow's hens, and here we were joined by Jamie, the youngest Heron, and Meraud Trevelyan.

In contrast to the vivid, still tearful Lucy, Meraud's welcome was cool and unemotional, her prim cousinly kiss on my cheek a reminder of her betrayal, more than two years previously, of Francis and myself. Grainne was my dearest companion, Lucy like a sister and at once as infuriating and closely loving and supporting as any sister could be, Heppy a most loyal friend and servant, the Widow my shrewd and wise guide, mentor and adviser, and the four of them now surrounded me once more, on my side. But one look at Meraud's cold, untrustworthy blue eyes was enough to convince me that, however polite her protestations of welcome and affection, she was still against me, my enemy: and so nothing fundamental had changed.

But in Jamie, at seventeen two years younger than she, there was a most marked alteration. He had shot up to his brothers' height, and the soft, untested roundness of his face at fourteen had been fined down, sharpened, strengthened. He was very like Lucy, with her heart-shaped face and dark curling hair and vivid eager blue eyes, and he had grown a moustache, rather ragged and new-looking, that nevertheless added an air of distinction to an already handsome countenance. He kissed us both and swung a surprised but happy Jasper up to the ceiling. 'And here's little Hen! Do you know, the last time I saw you, you were on your back in a basket saying ga-ga!'

Henrietta gazed at him with round, tawny eyes, and then turned to Grainne. 'Mamma, who's that man?'

'That's Jamie,' said Jasper, who was rapidly ceasing to use 'Master' and 'Mistress' when referring to the assorted Herons. 'And that's Meraud, and that's Lucy, and that's Heppy, she's Holly's sister, and that's the Widow Gooch, she's a witch really.'

'No, she isn't,' said Henrietta, already at two and three-quarters a prosaic, down-to-earth child.

'That one's got some sense, then,' said the Widow, plunging a red-hot poker hissing into mugs of spiced October ale. 'And still no flies on young Jasper, I see. Here, have a mug of this, you must be worn out.'

We sat gratefully at the big scrubbed wooden table and sipped the hot smoky drink. Lucy leaned forward, all curls and glowing eagerness. 'And now tell us all your news. Do you know, I didn't have *one* letter from you, Thomazine Heron, not *one word*, all the time you were gone! At least I sent you one – did you get it?'

Slightly guilty, I said that I had, and claimed mendaciously to have written two that had presumably been lost in transit. Lucy swept on. 'Tell us – why have you come back? And where's Francis? Is he all right? Did you find him in the end?'

It took a long time to tell. Outside, the darkness grew deeper: the Widow lit one candle, and the cheerfully glowing fire, over which our supper bubbled aromatically, provided the rest of the light. The hens, roosting on pots and pans, clucked and sighed contentedly: Henrietta climbed on to her mother's lap and fell asleep. The story of that strange eighteen months, and the wonderful *annus mirabilis* of Montrose's victories, and the final agony of his defeat at Philliphaugh, unfolded again in vivid pictures, almost visible in the air between us. When we had finished, Lucy let out a long sigh, her eyes bright with tears. 'Oh, what a marvellous story! Like something out of a play! You . . . and Francis . . . and all those wonderful battles . . . oh how I *wish* I'd been there too, with you!'

'We weren't at any of the battles,' I pointed out. Lucy dismissed this as irrelevant. 'Well, you were *almost* there. You have had an exciting time, and here have we been, dull as ditchwater, immured in Oxford.'

'You've no news, then?' Grainne queried with gentle mischief. Jamie grinned. 'Oh, she's bursting to tell you really. The best bit, from your point of view, Thomazine, is that Dominic has achieved his just deserts.'

My heart gave a huge leap into my throat. Ashamed of myself for my hope, I said carefully, 'What do you mean, "his just deserts"?'

Jamie laughed, cheerfully callous. 'He was wounded at Naseby – quite seriously, so Simon says – and taken prisoner. The last we heard, he'd become a Protestant and paid his fines and made his peace with the Parliament and gone back to Yorkshire, and sent for that thinly-disguised whore of a nurse and Kit to join him. So you've no fear of meeting him here in the street.'

'And good riddance,' the Widow added briskly. 'The only pity is that the bullet in his chest didn't do enough damage to kill him. Probably only missed his heart because he hasn't got one. What's the matter, lass? Regretting you ain't a widow like me?'

I pulled my face into a guilty smile. 'It's horrible to say it, but yes, I am. It would solve all my problems.'

'I must say,' Meraud remarked in her soft, insinuating voice, 'I think you all forget that he is Thomazine's husband, and that her place is properly with him.'

'In her place,' the Widow said acidly, 'my only reason for going after him to Yorkshire would be to finish off what that Roundhead soldier failed to do. Then she could marry her Francis as she deserves. Where's he? Following behind, did you say? Better not let His Lordship Simon catch him.'

My heart sank suddenly. Simon, whose jealously obsessive loathing for his brother Francis had been at the root of all the evils that had befallen my lover and me, was one person whom I shrank from meeting just yet. True, he had been most full of remorse for his appalling and unreasonable behaviour when he had thought it had led to Francis's death, but I knew his sternly rigid moral code and doubted very much if he would be able to restrict himself to polite conversation with me after I had deserted both husband and child and run off to join my lover in what he would assume to be adultery. My mind quailed at the prospect of enduring one of his unpleasant, bigoted, forceful lectures on my lack of moral scruples: and I hoped earnestly that I would not be brought face to face with him before I had had time to gather my mental defences.

'But Simon was overjoyed to find that Francis wasn't dead after all!' Lucy was protesting indignantly. The Widow gave a vigorous flick to the stir-spoon in the broth. 'Resurrections are all very well in the abstract. Oil and water those two are, and together in the flesh don't mix. Good thing he's in Newark with the Prince.'

'That was terrible,' Lucy said. 'Did you hear about Bristol? Prince Rupert had sworn to hold it but once Fairfax laid siege he could see he had no hope. So rather than lose his army in futile resistance, he surrendered it.'

'And the King was a trifle annoyed,' added Jamie, with the kind of ironic understatement that Francis often employed. 'He cancelled the Prince's commission, told him to leave the country, and dismissed the Governor here, Will Legge, who's a friend of his.'

'But what made it so suspicious,' Meraud put in gravely, 'was that while the Prince and Fairfax were negotiating terms, his brother the Elector Palatine was being voted large sums by the Parliament. So you can understand why the King had doubts about Prince Rupert's loyalty.'

'If he'd had the sense he was born with, His Majesty would never have entertained any such thoughts,' said the Widow: and added irreverently, 'but then, if he'd had the sense he was born with, there'd never have been no war. Prince Henry now, his elder brother that died, now there was a young man after everyone's heart! But this one, gracious gentleman though he may be, was never cut out for a kingdom: trusts all the wrong people and mistrusts his true friends. Listening to that angelic little rat Digby, and then trying to arrest the Prince –

who, if he'd given him the rope, would've tied up the kingdom for him a year ago.'

'Why is the Prince at Newark?' I asked. 'Is he a prisoner, then?'

'Not as far as we know,' said Lucy. 'The King is there, you see, and Prince Rupert and Prince Maurice set out there a few days ago to try and put their case. They took about a hundred loyal horse with them, including Simon. We've heard nothing yet about what's happened.'

'Nor likely to: the country's crawling with this New Noddle Army the Parliament have raised,' said the Widow. 'News ain't going to come through in a hurry. Poor Mistress Nan is fretting her heart out over in her lodgings – oh, she left the little Princess Henrietta months ago and came back here when she was expecting her second baby, and now she's lost that one too, never thought she was good breeding stock that one, too narrow in the hips. We'd have her here with us save that the attics are full of soldiers.'

'But they've gone out on guard duty,' said Jamie. 'Captain Webber didn't expect they'd be back till tomorrow morning, so you'll have a quiet first night at least.'

'Probably the only one you'll get,' the Widow warned. 'If I'd any say I'd throw the lot of 'em on the street tomorrow, but these days you've no choice who you have foisted on you.'

'Captain Webber is nice enough,' said Lucy, 'though he drinks like a fish – his nose is like a beacon, Thomazine, I'd swear it glows in the dark – but Lieutenant Stevenson is the one I don't like, he, well, *looks* at you as if he can see right through your clothes, and he's like Dominic, he thinks that all women should fall swooning with pleasure into his arms.'

'Or bed,' the Widow added. She chuckled. 'Lucy won't tell you, but I will. He sneaked into her chamber one night, oh, last March it was, while she was getting ready for the night, and tried to seduce her.'

Lucy grinned. 'I was no heroine. I just couldn't believe anyone could have such effrontery. When he started pawing me I cracked him over the head with the warming-pan.'

'Then he tried to do the same thing to me the next week,' Meraud added, 'though you'd have thought a broken head would have taught him his lesson. He came upon me in the parlour. I knew it was no use screaming, for everyone was either in the garden or out at market. Nor was there anything handy to use as a weapon. Fortunately, though, I had a queasy stomach from eating stale meat, and I, uh . . .'

'What she means,' said the Widow, 'is that she was sick all down his nice white military coat. Worked better than the warming-pan that did, he's never so much as eyed either of 'em again.'

'And if he ever does,' Jamie added, looking hawkish, 'I'll have his blood for it!'

The Widow ladled out bowlfuls of thick lumpy broth. 'We still eat quite well, but ready money's scarce and those parasite soldiers contribute little or nothing. Simon ain't been paid in months, and Mistress Nan's had to sell some of her jewellery. Make no mistake, the end's near now. Won't be long afore Fairfax or Cromwell come knocking at our gates, and there's no heart left to resist. The only heart left was in Rupert and his friends, and the King's snuffed that out with a vengeance. And with that Scots friend of yours, that Montrose, being defeated, it don't take two good eyes to see the King's cause is doomed. I give it six months, at the outside, afore there's no resistance to the Parliament anywhere in the kingdom.'

'And what will become of us then?' Lucy demanded. 'You know what Simon is. Dominic may have paid their fines and made his peace, but Simon, never! What will he and Nan do? Go into exile? What will we do? Go back to Goldhayes where Richard Trevelyan rules the roost?' She stopped, her eyes shooting to Meraud, whose uncle he was. The blonde girl said impassively. 'You forget, Lucy, he is only a trustee, looking after the estate till Simon can return. And he is not the only one, there's Master Blagge, and Master Sewell, and Sir Thomas Jermyn, and Lady Heron too.'

'My mother is not Lady Heron any more,' said Lucy, bleakness woven into her voice. 'Oh, Meraud, I'm sorry, I didn't mean to imply . . . but you must admit it will be strange at Goldhayes, to have him for my stepfather, and a new baby half-brother.'

'Now if I was you I'd leave off worrying about what can't be altered and have some of this afore it gets cold,' said the Widow. 'Then you can go where you've been longing to go this past hour, young Jasper – bed.'

But later, I was able to snatch a few moment's conversation alone with Lucy and Jamie, while Meraud and Heppy were in the rear parlour making a bed up out of a mattress and assorted bedding for Grainne and her children: so cramped for space was the house now with all the soldiers within it. In a few moments we would have to go up to the chamber where the three of us, Lucy, Meraud and myself, would have to share a bed, and I was anxious to get my facts correct. 'What exactly *is* happening at Goldhayes?'

Jamie frowned, but Lucy said urgently, 'That's just it, no one knows for sure. I know Simon is very worried. He didn't mind Mother marrying again, but now he's altered, he was very shocked and horrified to hear about the baby, somehow it seemed to make it much worse for him. Now he's talking about sending us back soon, not only because sooner or later Oxford will be besieged, unless some miracle happens, but because he wants someone to keep an eye on Goldhayes. You know what Mother's like, she'd agree with Beelzebub if she thought it'd make her life easier, and I think Simon fears that the baby may be intended to supplant the Herons in some way. John Sewell wrote a letter that made him very concerned . . . by the way, did you know Tom was a prisoner? Yes, in London, he was taken after Naseby and hasn't been able to buy his release like Dominic, though John's been trying to get Richard Trevelyan to use his influence.'

'To hear you talk, Lucy,' said Jamie, unable any longer to keep silence, 'you'd think Richard had some dastardly plot afoot. Of course he isn't going to supplant us, that's ridiculous, he married Mother because he liked her.'

'Not even you can use the word love,' said Lucy hotly. 'I'll wager love never entered into it. He wanted Goldhayes and she wanted a warm bed, and that's all there was to it, and the reason you're so biased towards Richard Trevelyan is because you're in love with Meraud.'

Jamie went a hot and guilty red. I took pity on him. 'Come on, our first night back is no time for arguments, and I for one want to go to bed. Are you two coming or not?'

Glowering at each other, the brother and sister followed me upstairs and effected some sort of truce on the landing. Then, suddenly weary to the bone, I almost fell into the crowded bed: and did not for once mind sharing my dreams with Meraud.

I had foolishly expected life in Oxford to be exactly the same as when I had left it, more than two years ago. The first week after our return soon disillusioned me. Within the house, of course, there were the six soldiers, noisy, out at all hours, returning drunk from tippling-houses and brothels long after curfew and disturbing the whole street, lounging about the house with too little to do. Part of Dutton's Whitecoats, a regiment of foot who had been garrisoned in Oxford since the beginning of the war, they suffered from a lack of action; it was the garrison cavalry, on flying raids to Thame and Basing and other enemy strongholds or sieges nearby, who saw most of the fighting. The presence of Captain Webber, like a Puritan caricature of a Cavalier, and whose nose was even more luminous than Lucy had implied, with his comrades meant that the house was no longer our own, there was no privacy, no peace either from them or from each other save in the evening, and that was only a respite before their drunken return at midnight or later. The little house that had seemed so spacious and neat with ten or so of us living there in 1642 was now, with seventeen, cramped and overcrowded, the maids and the Widow sleeping on pallets in the kitchen and the rest of us packed in the rear parlour and in the six chambers upstairs. Now, too, money was short – the rents from Ashcott which had kept us supplied earlier in the war were much reduced, and anyway not truly ours, since Ashcott had passed to Dominic on my marriage. Simon had ensured that a trickle still flowed into Pennyfarthing Street when Dominic had returned to Yorkshire, but it was not enough. The soldiers paid for board and lodging for the most part with worthless promissory notes, and many of the more valuable items in the house – musical instruments, the lantern clock in the rear parlour, silver candlesticks, books and paintings and tapestries – had been sold to provide money for the basic necessities of life. No one went hungry, but for the first time in their lives, my cousins had been faced with the necessity of counting the pennies. The Widow Gooch eked out the sums by doing illicit brewing and baking for sale to friends and neighbours without the knowledge of the guilds, but life was not easy.

There were changes in Oxford, too: more soldiers, less food in the markets, leaner, gloomier looks on the faces of the people in the street, a general air of hopelessness, demoralization, depression. Even the irrepressible newspaper *Mercurius Aulicus* no longer exuded the old impudent, racy, defiant air. Defeat for the King was in the wind, and the Royalists in Oxford knew it. As autumn advanced, bleak and chilly and windswept, the town took on a dreary, disenchanted look that I found miserably dispiriting. Bad news came in: Basing House had been stormed and taken, with some brutality, by Cromwell's Ironsides. Prince Rupert had failed to put his case to the King, and in his grief and anger had begun a mutiny amongst the Horse at Newark that had further split the King's remaining army: and Lord Digby had, with his usual over-confident nonchalance, managed to lose the King's entire Northern Horse in farcical confusion in Yorkshire.

And there was no sign of Francis. At first I did not worry: then unease began to gnaw at my mind. By the time the King returned from Newark on the fifth of November we had been in Oxford for three weeks, and I was beginning to be seriously alarmed. Then, Mistress Mander, the landlady of the Blue Boar round the corner in Fish Street, brought a letter for us which had been left with her for passing on. Brought by a succession of carriers and travellers all the way from Carlisle, it had taken a month to reach us, and was a brief and, at first, cryptic note in Great-Aunt Elizabeth's writing.

My dear Thomazine, Regarding that baggage which was to follow you on your journey, I regret very much that it has not proved possible for me to send it on as quickly as I would have wished, it proving alas unfit for travel and needing to be packed and made ready afresh. Also, since several rogues have expressed interest in its whereabouts, I have had to keep it close from prying eyes. However, all is still well and you may expect to see your possessions within a month or two, God willing. I trust your journey was a pleasant one, and without incident, and that you are now safe at your destination. Please excuse the brevity of this letter, for there are many calls on the time of your affectionate Aunt, Elizabeth Graham.

The meaning was clear. Francis had not made as speedy a recovery as had been optimistically forecast, and would not be with me for some time: and although the Covenant men had obviously been seeking him, he had been successfully hidden so far. I was bitterly disappointed, but at least now I had less cause for anxiety. He could not possibly be expected in Oxford before Christmas, and I would have to swallow my impatience and endure the necessary wait. At least he, and Malise and Montrose, had escaped the dreadful fate of the prisoners of Philliphaugh – the Irish infantry slaughtered out of hand in cold blood, to the hand-rubbing insistence and approval of the Ministers; and the other prisoners, whether boys or men, wounded or whole, ruthlessly hanged as traitors.

But at last Prince Rupert was reconciled with the King. The proud, arrogant, indomitable whirlwind who had so nearly won the war for his uncle, and received small thanks for it, humbled himself and was welcomed back to Oxford, though given no command. With him came his most loyal companions, among them Captain Simon Heron.

He and Nan came to see the household at Pennyfarthing Street, fresh from their own reunion. As tall and dark and grim-faced as I remembered him, he stooped through the doorway of the front parlour with an exclamation that was not a particularly joyous one. 'Thomazine! Well, I see you've returned at last!'

Nan, his wife of two years, the younger sister of Tom Blagge, Governor of Wallingford and our neighbour in Suffolk, took the sting out of his welcome by smiling her wide, shy smile and holding out her hands. 'Pay no mind to him, he is pleased to see you really. I told him you were here.' In the seven weeks since our arrival she had often visited us, and we her, so we were no strangers: nevertheless, I thought she looked even more unwell than usual, her plain, pleasant face grey and drawn, and the shabby cornflower-blue gown failing to hide her gaunt, painful thinness.

Simon, with some recovery of civility, spent some time asking Grainne and myself about our experiences in Scotland. I could see that he desperately wished to discover the details of my new-found relationship with Francis, but was too polite, or prudish, even to refer to his younger brother by name. Finally, I took pity on him and said bluntly, 'I know what you really want to be told. Francis is well, though he was wounded at

Philliphaugh: and Dominic did such a thorough job of poisoning his mind against me that it was four months before we could even have a civil conversation together. So you need have no fear for my virtue.'

Simon flushed darkly. He had always, but for his loyalty to the King's cause, and to Prince Rupert, seemed as if he would have been more in place amongst Puritans. Alone of his family, he took after his father, and had a rigid and strict code of morality which he had tried, with tragic results, to enforce upon Francis and myself. I had hoped that the shock of his brother's supposed death, combined with the deceitful and despicable behaviour of Dominic, who had been his favoured suitor for my hand, and augmented by the softening love of Nan, might have brought him to a more humane, tolerant view of our family's tangled web: but this appeared to be only partly true. His sombre brown eyes lifted to mine. 'I trust that your customary bluntness, Thomazine, indicates honesty. However much I deplore Dominic's conduct in this sorry affair, the fact remains that you are his wife, you wed him for better and for worse, and you have deserted not only him but your child. To deny the actual act of adultery in those circumstances seems almost superfluous.'

'Well,' I said firmly, 'I do deny it. Simon, whatever you may think, you cannot rule my life for ever. I would rather go on the streets than return to Dominic, and anyway I doubt he'd want me, from all accounts he has a doxy warming his bed for him.'

Simon sighed, but did not make again the mistake of reproving me for my plain-speaking. 'So I have heard. I agree that the chief fault in all this is his, and you at least have my sympathy for your actions, if not my approval. I am truly glad to hear that Francis is safe and well, and has in part redeemed himself by fighting for Montrose. It is your own affair now, I suppose, if you choose to cling together in defiance of your marriage vows and all the rules of God and man, but I would like to say that Dominic was most grievously hurt at Naseby, and is like to be a very sick man for some time yet. He too deserves some sympathy, for he fought bravely, and although I am unhappy that he so meekly paid the Parliament's fines and withdrew from the struggle, yet I cannot blame him, for he has now no strength to carry on the fight. Also, he has his son to rear, and without a mother that is a difficult task for an ailing man.'

'I'm sorry,' I said, looking into his resigned, unhappy face. 'I'm sorry for you, and I will always feel regret and guilt for abandoning Kit, but I can't find it in my heart to forget what Dominic did to me and Francis, and no power on earth will make me go back to him, though I know how much it would please you.' I spoke gently, for I was fond of Simon, despite his efforts to drive Francis and myself asunder, and could respect his ideals. My cousin gave a wry shrug and even, amazingly, a half-smile that gave him a curious look of Francis. 'Well, I have done my best to persuade you to go back to him, and I will never again attempt to force something on you that is repugnant to you. Like you, my chief anxiety is for the child, though I can tell you that while he was in Oxford he was well cared-for, and bids fair to become a charming boy. You may come to feel that you have as much deprived yourself as him, I don't know.' His face was suddenly full of longing and pain. 'I can understand something of your feelings, though Nan and I have as yet no children.'

The Widow brought in refreshments, biscuits and cakes and a little precious wine that had been hidden under the kitchen floor, away from the greedy eyes of our unwelcome military 'guests'. For a while, talk became almost light-hearted, Grainne telling of Henrietta's first encounter with Orange, now a flat-eared bristle-faced tomcat in undisputed mastery of the neighbourhood felines: which had begun with her attempts to pick him up and cuddle him (Hen was already showing signs of strong maternal feelings) and had ended with a furious cat and a screaming, bleeding child whose odoriferous clothes had had to be hastily stripped off her and thoroughly washed. Nan recounted her most recent story of her landlady, who was a gentle and timid soul, fearfully absent-minded. 'She'd lost her spectacles, searched all over the house for them, she was certain some wicked soldier had broken in and taken them. "We'll all be murdered in our beds, Mistress Heron!" she kept crying, until I pointed out that the reason her search had been unsuccessful was that she had them still perched upon her nose.'

'I wonder if Mother still holds out against wearing them,' Lucy mused, 'when we left she was determined not to stoop to having a pair made for her even though she could scarcely see clearly more than an arm's length in front of her nose.'

'You will have the chance to see for yourself, if I have any say in the matter,' Simon told us: and as the chatter died and our faces turned in surprise towards him, he added, 'I have been considering it seriously, as you know, for some time, and I have come to the conclusion that as soon as this cold weather eases a trifle, you must all return to Suffolk.'

'Why?' Jamie asked hotly. 'The King's not defeated yet, there could be help from Ireland, Wales, Montrose, anything!'

'No,' said Simon, 'His Majesty has not yet surrendered, and I am determined for myself to carry on the fight for as long as I am needed, especially since I am greatly honoured to count myself a friend of Prince Rupert. Nan will stay here with me, she has already assured me of that, but I am convinced that the sooner the rest of you go back to Suffolk, the better. Here in Oxford you face hardship, penury even, the possibility of siege or sack, and the virtual certainty of defeat. You may be abused, threatened, taken prisoner or even killed. May I remind you that Cromwell's men did not scruple to kill defenceless priests, and even a woman, when Basing House was stormed in October, and I have no reason to believe that people in Oxford, should it come to that, would fare any better. At least at Goldhayes you will be safe, you will have no fears about money or war or the dangers of living in a house full of soldiers, and Mother will be only too glad to see you all again. I know it will come hard for you, Jamie, to leave the sinking ship like vermin, but I am thinking only of your safety and happiness. Goldhayes is safe from them, and you can claim that as you are under age, you were not responsible for your actions in removing to Oxford.'

Jamie looked sulky and mutinous. I knew how he still cherished illusory hopes of even now, at this late stage, being able to take up arms for the King: and I would not have put it past him, if he thought that Simon was going to cheat him of his long-held ambition, to run away to war before he could be despatched back to Suffolk. But Meraud saved the day: she came to kneel by his chair in a rustle of rose-pink satin – I noted sourly that the reduced circumstances at Oxford had not prevented her from obtaining a new dress – and put her hand over his. 'Oh, Jamie, I know you've always wanted to be a soldier, but surely you can see it's too late now? You'll only get yourself killed to no purpose, but if you come back to Goldhayes with the rest of us then we can be happy again, just like we used to be before the war. Please, Jamie?'

Jamie had flushed a deep vivid red: his eyes flicked sideways to her, reluctantly. Meraud's breathtaking blue gaze devoured his, her hand moved caressingly. 'Oh please, Jamie, come back with us!'

No one watching the scene could have entertained the slightest doubt as to Jamie's feelings for her. He gave a small, apologetic, resigned grin which turned somehow into a fatuously adoring smile. 'Oh well, perhaps you're right,' he said, his reluctance visibly thawing by the minute. I glanced at Simon, to see how he was taking all of this, and saw only a relieved paternal smile on his melancholy features. 'I trust that's all decided upon,' he said. 'Lucy, I take it that you too will be sensible?'

Lucy glanced at me, swallowed, and nodded. Simon turned to me. 'And you, Thomazine?'

236

It was a hard decision to make, but knowing that the possibility of return to Suffolk existed, I had been thinking it over for some weeks. 'No. Francis will expect to find me here, so I'll wait for him.'

The silence was brief: Simon's brows drew into a frown. 'I've already told you that it's your own affair if you choose to fling yourself willy-nilly into adultery. But I refuse to entertain it in the same house as myself. When you have all gone, Nan and I will move into this one, and when Francis does appear he will doubtless come here too. Had you some expectations of continuing your relationship with him in Oxford, then? I see you had. But on that score, I fear, I am adamant. If you want to fornicate at Goldhayes, provided you can do it with a clear conscience with my mother in the house, and young children near you to be corrupted, then I consider that it is your own business. I admit that you have been wronged in the past, and that is why I have made my mind up to be more lenient now than I might otherwise have been. But I want no part of it, no knowledge of it, no sight of it. Do you understand me?'

I looked at his implacable face and admitted defeat to myself. After all, Francis had said Oxford or Suffolk, and there was only a hundred miles between them. I could return with Lucy and Grainne and the others, and look forward to Francis's arrival in due course. My conscience would be clear, for my imagination leaped into the future to a cottage in Bradfield Tye or in Bury, conveniently glossing over the myriad problems involved in so doing. And however appropriate from the point of view of travelling and timing, I could not relish the prospect of trying to embark on a passionate illicit affair under Simon's cold, disapproving, unromantic gaze. Better by far to do it with Grainne's blessing and Lucy's exuberant connivance: if I am bound for Hell, I thought, I might as well go merrily and whole-heartedly down the road to ruin.

It was so easy to sit in the cosy parlour at Penny-farthing Street and weave tantalizing daydreams about my future and Francis's: and then I bethought me of Simon, who was to stay on in Oxford, in the bleak, defeated, dangerous hereafter he was sending us to Suffolk to avoid, out of his regard for duty, and honour, and loyalty. I knew his strict moral code, and doubted very much whether it would allow him to do as Dominic had done, and pay his fine to the Parliament for resisting rebellion against his lawful King. The Simon I knew so well would not thus meekly bow to the assumption that he had thereby been in the wrong. He would rather, I felt, looking at his grim resolved face, go into exile than submit to rebels. And yet he had been prepared, in despite of that rigid sense of decency and honour, to condone my affair with Francis, albeit at a distance. I remembered his almost insane behaviour which had culminated in him using his position in the army to have Francis flung in prison for attempting to run away with me, and realized how unpleasant he could have made himself now. Perhaps he had learned from his past mistakes: perhaps he realized that short of killing us both there would be little he could ever do to drive us asunder again. But I felt, as I glanced at Nan's thin, plain, essentially nice face, that it was more likely that now, after two years of marriage, he had reached some understanding of what it was like to love someone, and to receive their love in return.

So it was with a renewed affection that I smiled at him. 'I understand, Simon, what your feelings are, and I thank you for your generosity thus far. I will do my very best not to abuse it: I can't promise anything, mind you, but I'll try.'

Almost unwillingly, Simon smiled back: and then, amazingly, he put out a hand and touched my shoulder. It was an awkward, perfunctory display of affection, but from Simon, always so undemonstrative and reserved, it was a gesture that meant a great deal. Then he turned brusquely back to the rest. 'And you, Grainne?'

'Oh yes,' said my dear friend. 'Have you not yet learned that where Thomazine goes, there go I?'

That brought a smile even to Simon's face; the tension relaxed. We began to make plans for the journey, with a lightheartedness astonishing in view of the gravity of the military situation. I marvelled at us all as we joked cheerfully about avoiding Roundhead patrols, and how it would be best to dye our clothes black and sing psalms all the way, and what we would say should we encounter the Parliament officer who, so it was said, swore he only requisitioned Popishly inclined horses. Then the conversation naturally turned to that ribald lampooning Royalist mouthpiece *Mercurius Aulicus*. According to Jamie, a Cavalier colonel had been reported in London as having been buried in Oxford 'with a great deal of Popish pomp', to which the living, breathing colonel's reply was that he 'desired a bill of the funeral expenses'. And Lucy, grinning, capped it with the tale of Sir Jacob Astley who, 'lately slain at Gloucester, desires to know was he slain with a musket or a cannon bullet?' So we made merry, and our laughter had a bright, hard edge to it like light on the rim of darkness: for our circumstances were too dangerous for us to be solemn.

Over Christmas, and well into January, the frost continued, iron-hard, bitter, unrelieved by any thaw. Rivers froze, birds starved, the roads were all but impassable, the ruts like rocks against which a waggon wheel could overturn, or a horse's leg be broken. The land was iced into immobility, and the armies were too: only light raiding parties moved about the countryside. Bad news still came in intermittently: Hereford fallen, Chester in dire straits (Lord Byron's beautiful wife had come to Oxford to plead for help, but in vain), Fairfax advancing on the last Royalist strongholds in Cornwall. Simon obtained passes for us that would, he hoped, discourage any Royalist plunderers looking for easy pickings on the road: our bags and boxes were packed, and our means of transport arranged. We still had the horses which had brought us from Scotland, none of which could be described as a cavalry officer's dream, but there was no mount for Lucy, Jamie or Meraud: every horse in Oxford over fourteen hands and capable of moving at a gallop over some distance having long since been drafted into the army. The Widow, who had what she called 'Useful Friends', procured three disreputable-looking animals that might at a pinch be capable of a day's journey. Simon paid for them, without hesitation, with his precious watch, a pair of Nan's earrings set with pearls, and a barrel of the Widow's ale thrown in. The maids, Betty and Heppy, would have to ride pillion behind Holly and Jamie, and Henrietta expressed high indignation at the prospect of once more travelling in a basket. 'Don't want to go in that! Want to *ride!*'

'Don't be silly, you can't ride, you're too little,' said Jasper, with the rich superior scorn of one but three months off his seventh birthday. But it was his turn to protest when Grainne, with unshakable firmness, told him that no, under no circumstances, never, would he be able to take his beloved cat, Orange. 'Can you imagine, a full-grown tomcat in a covered basket all the way to Suffolk? *No,* Jasper, it would be cruel, very cruel. He'll be quite happy here with Mistress Gooch to look after him, and when we get back to Goldhayes I promise you, the next time one of your grandfather's dogs has puppies you can have one.'

That removed the clouds from Jasper's white, freckled, angry face. He hugged Grainne, shouting thanks, and rushed out into the snowy garden to release his exuberant delight in running, shrieking and hurling snowballs at any moving target. I wished, wryly, that all the problems that beset us, and Simon, and the Royalist cause could be so easily relieved.

Despite the weather, which would render any travelling extremely difficult, Simon insisted that we leave Oxford as soon as all was ready: for, as he pointed out, it might be too late if we waited for the thaw. Reluctantly, we agreed: and to cheer our leaving, several friends came to share an informal supper the night before our departure. Simon and Nan were there, of course, the cause of her unhealthy looks now revealed as a third, and so far successful, pregnancy, due in June. Another guest was Charles Lawrence, who had been at the siege of Ashcott with us, and was now a 'reformado' in the Oxford garrison; a shortish, likeable young man with curly brown hair, lively brown eyes and a long-standing tendre for Meraud which, I was somewhat perturbed to see, appeared now to be returned in full measure: for my blonde cousin had seated herself next to him and her pale, enchanting face had been turned avidly up to his for some time, to Jamie's obvious displeasure. Not for the first time, I wished she would make up her mind as to the identity of her quarry: and felt sorry for Jamie, and sorrier for Charles. Hastily I turned my eyes away from that little scene to Tom Blagge, Nan's elder brother and the Governor of Wallingford, whom I did not particularly like. He was loud-voiced and blustering with a very inflated opinion of himself, and his undoubted bravery and loyalty to the King were balanced by a hot-tempered, choleric rashness that wavered on the border-lines of stupidity. His wife Mary, one of the Norths of Mildenhall, was a self-contained, plump little woman who had retained her looks despite the tribulations of such a husband: she kept her eyes on her plate and contributed little to the talk, but I had the impression that without Tom's overbearing presence she would be much more forthcoming. Next to Mistress Blagge was another Suffolk face, Tom's step-brother John Snelling, a shy, stuttering man who had been of great service to Jamie and myself on the field of Edgehill. Altogether we made a merry company, despite the overwhelming personality of Nan's brother, swearing loudly and bombastically that he would never surrender Walling-ford until the last crust was eaten, the last drop of blood shed. I looked round at the laughing, animated faces, and saw all those bleak eyes, drowning foreknowledge of defeat and humiliation in one night's forced gaiety. And I thought of the faces that were missing: Tom Sewell, Grainne's brother-in-law, still a prisoner in

London because there were no Roundhead captives to exchange with him, a mere lieutenant. And Simon and Lucy's brother, Edward, the sensible, unimaginative soldier whose death at Edgehill Fight had probably done much to cause the final rift between Simon and Francis. And, of course, Malise: and Francis himself.

But we had much to be thankful for, despite all our misfortune; of all the Heron family and their friends only three – my father-in-law, Sir Roger Drakelon, Edward, and Grainne's husband Henry Sewell, Tom's brother – had been slain. And the horror afflicting other families, of father fighting son, brother against brother, had not touched us: Francis, although in sympathy with the Parliament, had fought for the King, and it had not been for his politics that Simon had hated him. Only Lucy loved someone from the enemy's ranks, and I had a guilty, unworthy hope that once back in Suffolk she would choose another to love from the fine young men, Gages or Harveys, at Hengrave or Ickworth, and forget Daniel Ashley. But I knew my Lucy, and I realized that, like Francis, where she gave her love it would be for ever. If Dan never came back to her, I doubted she would ever marry.

Tom Blagge was proposing toasts, to the King, Queen, Prince of Wales and all the usual subjects. I saw Jamie's flushed, handsome face glowering at Meraud (vainly, for all her attention was still fixed on Charles' long amusing story of his smallest sister), and John Snelling shyly, awkwardly talking to Lucy, and was conscious of a great pang of sadness. Despite everything, there was still a spirit of comradeship, of cheerfulness, of unity amongst our friends: and tomorrow we would be leaving it all, going away from Pennyfarthing Street, and the Widow's unique, witch-like, cynical face, and the golden, snow-laden city. And though with my practical mind I looked forward to a return to Goldhayes, so beautiful and comfortable and serene, my sentimental heart yearned to stay, to greet Francis just that much earlier, and to share, as we had all shared so much, the final, useless, defiant glory of holding on until all hope had gone. And I would miss the Widow, and her dry no-nonsense comments.

But it was no good: we had to go. We stood at the doorway of the house to see our guests stumble out into the glimmering snowy darkness – a darkness not dense enough, unfortunately, to hide the entangled, whispering figures of Charles and Meraud, giving each other a more private farewell in a patch of deeper shadow not far off. It was so obvious what she was about, rejecting Jamie's impoverished calf-love for the more assured attentions of Charles, who had lands and his Warwickshire manor-house to his name, that I could not believe how men – some men – were taken in by her. Mentally consigning the two of them, and the cheated, disappointed Jamie standing disconsolately by my side, to the furthest corners of perdition, I said my goodbyes to everyone with a growing sense of despondency. At the final moment of parting, even Charles, at last, tearing himself away from Meraud's ivy-like embraces, I watched them all go with tears in my eyes, with an overwhelming sense of witnessing a moment, an era, walking away, never to be recaptured, and certain that some of them, at least, I would never see again.

Simon took us out of Oxford the next morning when we had bidden farewell to Nan and the Widow, with Lucy shedding her usual abundant tears. And though the rest of the journey to Suffolk has receded into my mind in an uncomfortable, uneasy blur, I remember that first morning as if it were yesterday, as we rode north towards Banbury to pick up the eastern road to Buck-ingham and thence to Suffolk. Despite an earlier thaw the snow still lay thick upon the ground and over the hedges and the branches of the trees; but the previous night had seen a freezing fog which outlined each bough, every twig, every dried umbrel of cow-parsley or spear of grass, every leaf of spiky holly with glittering white, so that from a distance the groups of trees, their main branches black by contrast, looked against the glorious blue sky as if they had burst overnight into silvery unseasonable flower. And the air literally sparkled, for as the sun cleared the mists and our breath hung smoking dragon-like on the frosty air, we could see the last remnants of the freezing fog like glittering silver dust, dancing in the light. And everywhere, black boughs and blazing blue sky contrasting starkly with the unutterable, unbearably brilliant whiteness of the snow, blue-shadowed, so that my eyes stung and smarted and overflowed with both the pain and the beauty of it.

I looked for Francis, in a final vain hope of seeing him riding at last towards me as in my dreams: but we reached the turning, and there was no sign. We said goodbye to Simon, and he gave us last-minute instructions for the journey, especially to Jamie and Holly who would be our protection: and as he kissed his womenfolk for the last time, told me not to fear, for he would tell Francis where I had gone, and would send him on his way with no hindrance. We left him and two of his troopers sitting their horses on the Oxford road, black and forlorn against the brilliance of the snow: and rode slowly away, in a mood of desperate gloom, towards the safety of Suffolk.

It took us a fortnight, though the delays were due to the weather and the conditions of the road rather than to any interference by soldiers of either side: for the snow soon thawed in earnest, rendering large portions of the way into sloughs of watery mud some feet deep, in which a man could easily drown. But we came at last to Bury, calm and untouched by war, with its wide market square bordered by the old Abbey gateway, and the Angel Inn opposite; and so to Goldhayes.

We stopped at the Home Farm first, the ancient little house where lived Grainne's father-in-law John Sewell, who had had the day-to-day running of Goldhayes in his capable hands for many years: and finding him out, we saw instead his garrulous housekeeper, Joan. She fell weeping on our necks and especially upon Jasper, who stood bewildered and affronted as she told him at length and in broadest Suffolk how much he resembled his dear dead father and what a poor little orphan he was, and then turned her attention abruptly to the startled Henrietta, while everyone else shuffled their feet, embarrassed, in the homely kitchen I remembered so well. Then, reluctantly leaving poor Grainne and her children to Joan's tender mercies, we set out on the last lap in the growing early dark of winter, cold and damp in the steady icy drizzle. We rounded the bend in the drive and Goldhayes lay at last before us: glowing even in the dim light, windows here and there lit up, all so dearly familiar, the copper green-capped turrets on the outer corner of each projecting wing, the stone porch with the Latin motto on the sundial, the neat box-edged flower beds in the front court already, hesitantly, sprouting spring bulbs. Once again, in a blur of tiredness, we went through the ritual of homecoming: the knock on the door, the startled maid answering it, and then the appearance of Mary, formerly Lady Heron, beautifully dressed and much plumper, to greet us with something, miraculously, more than her usual polite indifference. Beside her stood her husband, Meraud's uncle Richard Trevelyan, looking very much the same as when we had left him nearly four years earlier, tall and self-possessed, with blond hair and Meraud's untrustworthy blue eyes. His greeting was all that it should have been, and he was obviously very pleased to see his niece once more, but I could not rid myself of my suspicions. Nor, I suspected from the way she had peered at the condition of the park and the house, and was now eyeing the furniture in the Hall where we stood, could Lucy.

But Goldhayes itself seemed just the same: still the familiar evocative aroma of sunlight and wood polish and herbs and flowers in the dark-panelled Hall, with the beautiful Van Dyck portrait of the Heron children, painted fourteen years ago, in pride of place above the mantel. As Mary summoned her maid to organize supper and beds and the welfare of the horses, I found myself looking at those five enchanting children, charming and graceful in bright satins and wide, cool lacy collars, their natural human personalities translated by Van Dyck's style into symbols of delightful childhood. There was Simon, thirteen and childishly grave, and Edward, a year younger, standing firm with his hand protectively on his sister's shoulder: Lucy herself glowing as fresh on the canvas as she did in life, seven years old, and Jamie, at four still in petticoats, happily clutching a puppy. Only Francis, the blond one amongst a dark-haired family, had by his individuality defeated the artist's brush, his ten-year-old face secretive and unforthcoming, the green-grey eyes dreaming into space. I wished I had known him then, I wished I had spent all my life with him, and I longed suddenly with a new urgency for the moment when I would see him again, and at last we would be together, indissoluble, inviolate, safe.

We supped with Mary and Richard, who listened politely to our accounts of the events which had seemed so momentous to us, and to them had surely been as distant and detached from their reality as a dream. One detail was clarified for me before we had been in the house an hour; and that was, that whatever had been their reasons for marrying, whether they had been as coldly cynical as Lucy had implied, Richard and Mary had now a real affection for each other. Mary indeed was at times almost as animated as her lively daughter, a great contrast to her former languid, uninterested manner, and the final proof of her alteration came when she urged us, before we retired for an early and much-needed sleep, just to have a look at little Hugh. Obediently and with some astonishment, we all four trooped upstairs and were led reverently into the chamber which had once belonged to Simon and Edward. A round, kindly faced girl, obviously his nurse, rose from her sewing and curtseyed: and we were shown to the cradle.

Hugh Trevelyan was eighteen months old, and as fair as both his parents. For the rest, since he was fast asleep, it was difficult to vouch, save for the obvious two eyes, nose, mouth, and two small clenched fists above the covers. 'Is he not beautiful?' said Mary softly, and in her voice was a maternal tenderness I had never before suspected in her. This was the woman who had cheerfully handed all her other children over to the dubious care of village wet-nurses the moment they were born, and neglected their subsequent development except where it directly touched upon her quite undeserved standing as a good mother. Now, evidently, she had discovered at last, in her mid-forties, that it was possible to feel love for one of her children.

We tiptoed out again, leaving the nurse to watch over her charge, and Mary said again, 'Do you not think he is perfect?'

Lucy drew a long breath, glanced significantly at me, and said slowly, 'Oh yes, he looks delightful, Mother, quite sweet . . . can he talk yet, and walk?'

This was the wrong thing to ask, for Mary at once launched into a list of her child's accomplishments, his entire vocabulary (some ten words), and the longest distance yet covered unaided on his unsteady legs (half the length of the Long Gallery). After about five minutes of this, we made our excuses and retired to our several rooms – Jamie and Meraud to the chambers they had had before the war, Lucy and I, by mutual consent, to the room we had been used to share, overlooking the courtyard garden below. Going into it was like stepping back ten years in time, so little had it altered, and Lucy and I undressed with Heppy's assistance, and climbed into bed with a warm nightcap of mulled ale, and settled down to talk.

'I can't believe how she's changed,' said Lucy, cheerfully unaware of how she had changed herself; the old, naïve Lucy would never have uttered that remark at Oxford about her mother wanting to marry Richard Trevelyan to warm her bed. 'And that baby! I'll swear he's no more beautiful than ever Jasper was, and far less intelligent, even judging from what she was saying.'

'You're jealous,' I told her. 'She's lavishing all the affection she never had for you and the others on that little brat, and you're jealous. I would be too, in your place.'

'I'm *not* jealous,' said Lucy indignantly. She caught my sceptical eye and grinned suddenly. 'You're right as usual, aren't you? I *am* jealous, really. I suppose as well that I resent it that they've stayed here all through the war, nice and cosy and comfortable, living off the fat of the land, while poor Simon is giving heart and soul to the King's cause, and if I know Simon will end up starving in some Dutch or French garret rather than give in to them.' She heaved a long, gusty, Lucyish sigh, and leaned back against the pillows. 'Do you know, I was looking forward so much to coming back, I thought it would all be just the same, I was carrying a sort of picture in my mind of how it used to be when we were all so happy and carefree before the war, and it's not the same at all, it's all changed. I miss being at Oxford, there you were in the centre of things, you knew what was happening, and Goldhayes is such a backwater really. It isn't the same without Simon, or Francis, or Tom, or poor old Edward – oh, I do miss Ned still, after three years and more. We used to laugh such a lot, and I don't believe Mother and Cousin Richard have half a sense of humour between them. And I feel like a stranger here, like a guest, they don't want us back intruding on their nice little domestic snug, we're not welcome and it's our home!' she finished, her voice quivering on the verge of tears with her disappointment. I said slowly, for I had felt much the same thing myself, 'It's not so bad as all that. Since when has Mary ever had much time for us? At any rate there's still Jamie, and Grainne and the children, and I should think Tom will come back soon and Francis should arrive shortly, and then it'll be better. You'll see.'

To my surprise, Lucy's big blue eyes overflowed with tears. She said in a wobbly, tragic whisper, 'You are lucky. You – you *know* he loves you, he's coming home to you, and Dominic doesn't matter. But I've only had one letter from Dan, ever, and that was two years ago and it wasn't very . . . it was the sort of letter a brother or a friend might write, not a lover's letter at all.' And she burst into hopeless, flowing tears.

I had of course to comfort her, whilst trying tactfully to hint that in view of their long parting – it was now nigh on three years – it was possible that Captain Ashley's affections had cooled. But Lucy would have none of it, preferring to believe that Dan might be slain, or hurt, or that there were other good reasons why no letters had reached her. And at last she turned round, her tear-drenched face still comely, and said miserably, 'It's all right for you. Francis is coming to you, but I know Dan never will, I know it!'

'You're not the only one in that boat,' I said, keeping my patience. 'Grainne is in a worse case. At least Dan has the good sense to be on the winning side!'

Lucy gave a sniffle of rather hysterical laughter, and then was quiet for a while. At last she put her arm about me and drew me close. 'Oh, Thomazine, I'm sorry, I've been very tedious . . . Oh, how I wish Francis would come, at least he could make us laugh again.'

It was indeed strange to be back again at Goldhayes, and the first few weeks were extremely disconcerting, so utterly dear and familiar and unchanged were the house and its surroundings, and so altered were its inhabitants. Many of the servants had gone to the wars, others, including Mary's gentlewoman companion, her aunt Margaret Bryant, had died – although the ancient chaplain and tutor, Dr Davis, lingered on in defiance of time and rheumatism. The same was true of the surrounding villages. Rushbrooke and Bradfield Tye still mourned those who had marched away with us nearly four years ago and never returned, though Holly Greenwood's miraculous restoration to his mother and numerous small brothers and sisters was a nine-days' wonder. There were new faces: the Bradfield Tye parson,

Master Eldritch, had been ejected and replaced by a dour black-gowned Presbyterian to Richard Trevelyan's taste and no one else's, and the same thing had happened at Rushbrooke. There were others missing: Sir Thomas Jermyn had died full of years and respect, leaving a young widow, his second wife, and two small children to be provided for; and his two sons were absent, Thomas with the Prince of Wales in the West Country and Henry with the Queen in France, leaving Rushbrooke to be desolately populated with women and children, along with one or two male cousins tucked away in bachelor apartments in that huge house. Ambrose Blagge and his wife and three remaining daughters – his sons Tom, Henry and Ambrose and his stepson John Snelling all being away at the wars – still pursued a sparse, gloomy existence at Horringer: and the Gages and Herveys (with the exception of Sir William Hervey's eldest son, John, who was also with the Prince of Wales), danced and bowled and feasted with unrepentant vigour at Ickworth and Hengrave. Soon Lucy, Meraud and I, and Jamie, were cheerfully reabsorbed into the old hectic social round of the years before the war. I, of course, being wed, was fairly safe from the attentions of the young Gages, John, Edward and Henry, but Lucy and Meraud were extravagantly courted. I liked best of that company Tom Hervey, a cheery young man my own age, and his sisters Judith, Keziah, Mary and Sue: the Gages being altogether too much like their overbearing mother to be to my taste. Lady Penelope was still organizing bowls matches and was not above seeking out prospective players herself, wherever they were and whatever they might be doing, with no regard at all for their wishes. 'She has a finger in every pie and poor Father organized down to the last button on his doublet,' said Tom of his stepmother ruefully. 'But although she has Ickworth and Hengrave both running like clockwork, I do wish she wouldn't attempt to run me likewise!'

I liked Tom very much, but he was no substitute

for Francis. And January gave way to February, and February to March, and still he did not come. Every day I gazed expectantly down the drive, or returned to Goldhayes from one of our jaunts in hopes of finding him arrived in my absence – all in vain. It began to seem as if all my life with him had been made up of saying farewells, and waiting, ever waiting, for him to come back to me. Now, yet again, history was repeating itself. And the most wounding injustice of all was to see Meraud's smug, smiling face as letter after letter came to Goldhayes, addressed to her in Charles Lawrence's quick untidy scribble, and all presumably bearing impassioned words of love. It seemed so unfair, that her amours should be running so smoothly when once she had done her best to wreck mine. Somehow, I kept my feelings hidden, for I knew, none better, the misery of life at Goldhayes amidst the bitterness and malice of a family quarrel. Once, long ago, Francis and Simon had thus ruined the tranquil, lovely atmosphere of the house, and I was not going to start it again by launching a feud with Meraud. It was bad enough to see Jamie, normally so ebullient and cheery, sink into utter despondency whenever a letter arrived, and his yearning, hopeful, hopeless eyes following Meraud's every move like a hungry dog at the dinner-table. I would not interfere: and besides, I longed most desperately for Francis.

For the first months at Goldhayes, I seemed to move in some kind of limbo, my soul suspended, numbly inanimate, while the shell of Thomazine Heron spoke and laughed and flirted like an actor in a stage-play, repeating well-remembered and meaningless lines in a long-familiar scene: lost without my lover. Then, as the newsless weeks went by, I began to grow anxious: and really worried when a letter arrived late in March from Simon, telling us that Francis had come to Oxford a week after we had left, in good spirits and health, with his horse Hobgoblin, and had stayed but a few days before setting out for Suffolk. 'I trust he is safe with you now,' Simon wrote, 'and pray convey to him and to my mother and all at Goldhayes our sad news, that my dear wife has again miscarried, of a child that would, had it come to full term, have been a boy. Though she is very low in spirits, yet she accepts that it is God's will, and that His ways are mysterious to us. Pray give my humble regards and affectionate wishes to my lady mother, and to Master Trevelyan, and to the child . . .'

It could not possibly have taken two months for Francis to travel from Oxford to Suffolk, even over winter roads. Something must have happened, I knew, with a sick feeling in my stomach as I laid down the letter, hands suddenly unsteady. Illness, or soldiers, or footpads – or death. But I would know, I thought wildly, I would surely know if he were dead; for that night in Oxford when he was nearly killed escaping from the castle, I had known, I had woken from a dream of horror and thought that I had shared his death. If he were dead now, it seemed inconceivable that I would not have known of it; but his ghost had never visited me, nor had my sleep been shattered by nightmare.

As usual, I took my troubles to Grainne, and her father-in-law, listening, had a practical suggestion to offer. 'I hev to go to Cambridge next week on that road, and I can easy enough ask for news of him, thass no trouble. He still ride that little owd black mare, do he? Well, that shoon't be too hard to find word of what's become of him, and that'll kill two birds wi' one stone, collect the Lady Day rents from they two manors by Cambridge, and look for Master Francis for you. And I'll tell you this, Mis—, Lady Drakelon, I'll be suffen glad to see him here. That Master Trevelyan, he be a godly man I suppose, but he don't know nawthen of farming at all.'

'Neither does Francis,' I said. John Sewell shook his head. 'Thass true enough, but he *know* he don't know nawthen. Master Trevelyan think he know suffen, and thass dangerous. And Francis, he be sharp as a needle, he don't let nawthen slip by *him*.' And further than that cryptic remark he would not go.

He was obviously worried about Richard Trevelyan, and at first it was difficult to understand why. There were no signs, to my indifferently experienced eye, of bad management either in the house and garden, or at the Home Farm. Everything was neat, tidy and prosperous; assessments and taxes, fifteenths and twentieths seemed to have had little effect. The cows were sleek and fat, the fields weeded and sprouting green with the summer's harvest, the farm buildings in good repair, the village tenants thriving. War had scarcely touched Suffolk: the only signs were the soldiers quartered in Bury, and the paucity of riding-horses to be seen about the place. They had taken most of Edward's beloved breeding stock, even the ageing Arabian stallion, The Saracen, for the Parliament's army; but The Saracen's best offspring, the grey Boreas whom I had named, and who was also Hobgoblin's only foal, had fortunately proved impossible for them to handle. He lived now in the orchard paddock by the Home Farm, lazily cropping the lush grass, his only exertions the occasional gallop around his domain, and covering the mares belonging to Goldhayes and to neighbours and farmers from some miles around who wanted to improve their stock.

In the week of John Sewell's absence I went down to see the stallion, walking down the path as the child Thomazine had done, eleven years before, with Tom Sewell and Francis Heron, turning somersaults to impress them. I wondered wryly if I could perform such a feat now, at the ripe age of twenty-one, and after having borne a child. I was on my own: no one was in sight up or down the narrow, hedge-lined path, and no one was likely to see my probable humiliation. Feeling ten years younger, and sillier, I took off my shoes and stockings, remembering too late that although the sun was warm, it was only just April and the ground was damp and chilly. Then, hoping fervently that there were no curious eyes in the hedge, I kilted my skirt up to my knees, breathed deeply, and ran. I had forgotten, but my body had not: muscles and skills long dormant came to my rescue and I achieved, I was never sure how, something resembling an airborne somersault, and managed to land on my feet, even if I did fall over immediately afterwards. Swearing at my own foolhardiness, I picked myself up and beheld Grainne's son, staring at me in some astonishment. 'Damn!' I said, with feeling.

'It's all right,' Jasper assured me, 'I won't tell anyone if you don't want me to. Could *I* do that, if you showed me how? Please?'

'It's the first time I've done that for ten years,' I told him, 'and I don't think I could show myself how to do it again, let alone you. I don't mind if you tell people: I did manage to do it, even if it wasn't very good.'

Jasper, unbidden, sprinted back to fetch my shoes and stockings, and politely turned his back while I put them on. 'Have you seen the horse yet?' he asked.

'Boreas? I was just going there now. You remember Hobgoblin, Francis's black mare? He's her foal. Do you know, he's two years younger than you are?'

'He's much bigger than me,' said Jasper wistfully, flicking his orange fringe out of his eyes. Despite Joan's claim that he resembled his father, he grew daily more like Grainne, with her long oval face and high, prominent cheekbones taking shape under the round curves of childhood: and of course those extraordinarily vivid green eyes, blazing with curiosity and eagerness. 'Isn't it funny, that he can be younger than me and still bigger?'

We came to the gate of the paddock, where Boreas stood, ears pricked, and watched us. He had the short straight back, proud plumed tail, and charmingly dished face of the Arabian, and the coat that had been so woolly and dark at his birth, when Francis and Edward had laid bets as to whether he would be black or grey, was now sleek and delightfully dappled, his long mane and tail a silky, shimmering white. He regarded us thoughtfully, and blew through his nose. Jasper climbed up on to the gate and reached to pat his neck, while I tried not to appear alarmed. 'I wish I could ride him,' he said. 'But Grandfather said I couldn't. Good boy, beautiful boy, have an apple?' He held out a shrivelled tiny fruit that was hardly fit even for equine consumption, and Boreas, the North Wind, took it with all the graciousness of a king. Uneasily, I said, 'You know he's not broken, don't you, no one's ever been on his back. That's why he's still here, the Parliament men would have taken him if he hadn't been wild and dangerous.'

'No, he's not,' said Jasper, turning a mischievous grin on me. 'Grandfather told me about that. He *has* been ridden, often, but of course Grandfather didn't want them to take him, so he got Joan to let one of the farm dogs out when they had him in the yard to look at him, and Boreas doesn't like dogs, so he kicked out all over the place, and they decided they didn't want him after all.' He giggled. 'So he's quite safe, aren't you, Boreas?'

The stallion tossed his head under Jasper's stroking hand, and turned restlessly away. We watched him showing off his beauty, as if he were fully aware of our admiration, prancing, tail high, through the new-growing grass. Jasper, watching as intently as once Francis had watched Hobgoblin in the same paddock, drew a deep spellbound breath and let it out in a long sigh. 'Oh, I *wish* I could ride him!'

We walked back down the path, and listening with half an ear to Jasper's chatter, I bethought me again of Richard Trevelyan. Why was John worried? The estate was not suffering, the land was well managed – John's doing, that – there was no sign of the draining of resources like timber that was supposed to be typical when someone was milking an estate.

But then, of course, I realized, Richard Trevelyan would not milk Goldhayes. He had the running of it, he and his wife enjoyed the monies from it, it was as if it were his own land. But not for ever. Sooner or later, unless tragedy or unforeseen disaster intervened, Simon would return to claim his lands: and accounts would have to be rendered.

At any rate, Richard thought that Simon would return: I suspected that neither he nor Mary knew enough of her eldest son to guess that he might prefer to go into penniless exile rather than make his peace with rebels and traitors. And even if Simon did not return, there was Francis, and after him, Jamie. It was already beginning to seem unlikely, after three miscarriages, that Nan would bear Simon any children: and I realized suddenly that Francis was bound to me, and that Jamie was painfully, obviously, in the first throes of calf-love with Meraud, despite her recent interest in Charles Lawrence.

Simon might have no children, would be disgraced, in exile; Meraud knew his character, even if her uncle did not. Francis was an uncertain, dubious quantity, quixotic enough to take a sudden fancy to going off to the Americas or the Indies, and moreover in love with a woman already married. And so Jamie, heedless, naïve, gullible, enthusiastic, was the key to Goldhayes: I thanked God that Meraud's efforts were directed elsewhere, for surely she had only to beckon to have him for ever enslaved at her feet. And if Simon did come back, I would be willing to wager that Richard Trevelyan had managed to abstract a tidy sum of money from the estate and invest it somewhere against that rainy day when he would again have to fend for himself, and with a wife and child to keep. How many manors had he bought thus?

I was suddenly frightened by these Machiavellian complexities. I told myself sternly that they only existed in my mind: I had absolutely no proof that Richard Trevelyan had stolen any money at all, and certainly the idea of marrying Jamie for his prospective inheritance did not appear to have entered Meraud's scheming silver-gilt head, although I suspected that might only be a matter of time. I did not trust Richard, and his niece even less, but I could not believe he would stoop so low as to cheat his stepsons of their rightful possessions.

'Thomazine? Thomazine, are you listening?' Jasper's insistent voice, rather whistly at present because he had no front teeth, broke in. I looked down at him, grinning, and consigned the Trevelyans and their supposed iniquities firmly to the back of my mind. 'No, sorry, I was miles away. What were you saying?'

'You're not miles away, you're here,' said Jasper cheekily. 'And Grandfather said that Blackie, you know, his youngest dog, she's going to have puppies in a few weeks and I can have one for my very own!'

'That will be lovely,' I told him, 'now you'll have a friend, like you always wanted.'

'Another friend,' Jasper said seriously. 'Don't forget, there are all the Jermyns too.' One of the great advantages of a return to Suffolk for Jasper had been his discovery of Sir Thomas Jermyn's children at Rushbrooke. Tom, the eldest, was a dull priggish child, but Henry, always called by his given name to distinguish him from his uncle, the notorious Harry Jermyn, was a round-faced, fair-haired scamp of ten who led his sisters and little brother Charles, a year younger than Jasper, into all sorts of mischief. Into this new world of childish companionship Grainne's son had been cheerfully absorbed, and the fact that he made so little of all his exciting wartime experiences in Oxford and Scotland delighted them. I was pleased that he had made friends so easily, for I knew that Grainne had been worried about how readily he might fit in with other children: and it was a solitary life at the Home Farm for an energetic small boy, however much his mother and grandfather might indulge him.

John Sewell returned two days after this, and when he had delivered the rents safely into Richard's hands, came straightaway to me, still muddy and tired from his journey. 'I've no news for you, I'm afraid, nawthen at all, though I asked at every village and inn from here to Cambridge and beyond.'

I kept my hands still by clamping them together, and from somewhere dragged the voice to say, 'Are you sure, John? Nothing at all?'

'I'll tell you exactly what I did,' said John, sitting

down on the chair I indicated in the Long Gallery, where we could not be overheard without our knowing. 'I asked in pretty near every inn and alehouse between here and Cambridge and got nawthen. Hev you seen a young gentleman, I asked, tall with fair hair, riding a little black Arabian mare? And none of them han't seen nawthen, nawthen at all. I even went two-three mile past where I had to go, but din't get nawthen for that. I don't know what's happened to him, my lady, I can't think on it, and thass a fact.'

Nor could I think. Had he had second thoughts after leaving Oxford and returned to Montrose? It did not seem particularly probable; I knew him too well to believe him capable of such an inconsistency as that. The only certainty was that somewhere on the road between Oxford and Cambridge, two months ago and more, something had befallen him; accident, illness, death, the possibilities jostled frantically in my mind and threatened to overwhelm me. I fought them down and thanked John gratefully for his kindness and help: wishing that I could make the journey back again along that road to Oxford, to find out myself what had happened.

But I had months of agonized waiting, in bitter and anguished frustration, for now the jaws of the trap forged by Fairfax and Cromwell were set to close upon the city, and there could be no question of travelling that way yet. In March the remnants of the King's army in the west had surrendered to Fairfax, followed by the last Royalist force in the field, a mob of raw Welsh and Worcestershire levies under the veteran Lord Astley. The King, astonishingly, gave himself into the hands of the Scottish army besieging Newark; and at the end of June, Oxford surrendered. The war was over at last: and still there was no news or sign of Francis, and I despaired.

In early August, after the most miserable six weeks I think I have ever experienced, worse even than Catholm, two letters arrived. One, a brief note from Simon brought by one of the Suffolk men who had joined his troop at the beginning of the war, told us of his intention to go with Nan into exile, following Prince Rupert and Prince Maurice, and carry on the struggle from overseas. It would not, he told us, be a lonely existence, for there were Suffolk friends aplenty to join him: Harry Jermyn, now elevated to the peerage, and his brother Thomas were already in France. Tom Blagge had surrendered Wallingford – on terms so advantageous to himself that his officers all but mutinied, or so we heard later – and was also going abroad, leaving his wife and small daughters to fend for themselves in England. Simon apologized for deserting his own family in such a manner, but wrote that he could not in all conscience do otherwise: and my forebodings were confirmed.

So Simon and Nan set off for Holland, and I looked in vain for signs of satisfaction from Richard: so sincere seemed his expressions of regret that I began to think that I had misjudged him. But Meraud was another matter: I did not think it was purely my imagination that interpreted her reactions to Jamie as being rather more encouraging than before. A subtle change had occurred since the news of Simon's exile, a change from indifference to the kind of sweet, innocent-seeming friendliness that only Meraud could use to such effect: and wholly spurious. My disquiet was increased when a letter from Charles Lawrence arrived and was treated by Meraud with a casual brevity very different from the avid lovelorn way she had read his previous epistles. For was not Goldhayes, the jewel of all Suffolk, a greater prize by far than poor Charles's scant acres and insignificant house?

And then all such thoughts were driven for a while from my head, when Lucy in her turn received a letter: from Daniel Ashley.

It had come by the Post, now restored almost to its pre-war efficiency, and John Sewell picked it up with other letters that had as usual been left for our collection at the Angel in Bury. When Lucy beheld it, she turned first scarlet, then white, and looked to my concerned eyes as if she were about to faint. I pushed her into one of the chairs in the Long Gallery, where we had been sewing, placed the white oblong in her hands, and said, 'Open it.'

'I can't,' said Lucy, 'it might be . . . it might be saying he's forgotten me.'

'Be logical,' I said ruthlessly, 'he wouldn't be writing to you if he'd forgotten you, now would he? Come on, open it.'

Lucy, with shaking hands, slipped a fingernail under the seal. I said, 'Do you want me to leave you alone? I will, if you–'

'No, stay, please,' said my cousin, her eyes greedily devouring the Captain's neat, simple hand. She let out a great sigh of relief and delight that warmed my heart: for, awkward though it was for her to be so enamoured of an enemy Roundhead, I knew now that he was the one she would love until death. And I could not be so mean-spirited as to fail to wish for her happiness, for after all, had I not also fallen in love with an equally 'unsuitable' man?

'He says he is well,' Lucy told me at last, obviously realizing that some statement of the letter's contents was called for. 'And he is a major now, in Colonel Ingoldsby's Foot, and it's part of the Oxford garrison. So he has been to see the Widow again, and listen, he says, "She was no whit cast down by the siege and occupation of the city, and complained mightily to me, when she discovered my rank, of the Parliament soldiers we have quartered in that house, saying that it was hard at her time of life to be rid of one military burden only to be straightway inflicted with another (though as you can imagine she did not employ quite those words), and adding that she held neither with the drunkenness of the Royalists nor the robust and vigorous godliness of my own soldiers, each being as bad as the other!" '

We laughed reminiscently, and Lucy said, delighted, 'I can just hear her saying it, can't you! He says how "going to Pennyfarthing Street brings back such warm and happy memories of the brief weeks of hospitality and kindness which you and your cousins gave to me", and that as soon as he can be free of army duties for a space, he'll come here to visit us!' Her great blue eyes glowed into mine, joyous and elated. 'And that can't be long, can it, with the war ended!' I doubted it myself, since majors in garrison regiments commonly have, by the nature of their task, very little time to spare for going on private courtesy calls to Royalist households a hundred miles distant, but Lucy, of course, was ever the optimist. She turned again to the letter. 'Oh, it doesn't seem more than three years since I've seen him! And he signs himself, "Your affectionate and humble servant," – does that seem like someone in love to you?' she added dubiously.

'We can't all be as exuberant as you. At least he feels affection, and you must remember what he's like, he's not one to show his emotions readily.'

'I suppose so,' said Lucy. She peered again at the postscript, holding the paper, as was her myopic habit, some six inches from her nose. 'Why, this is strange, listen to this. "I have some news of another mutual friend which may be welcome, should you be anxious to know if he be safe and well. I saw him last week, a trooper in Whalley's horse, as they returned after the surrender of Worcester: and though much changed it was certainly he, though I know not by what means he has come to be in that regiment, which has the reputation of being a nest of sectaries and Independents. I had no chance to speak with him, but discovered by careful questioning of his captain (for I did not wish to reveal how I had known him at Ashcott), that he goes not under his own name, and joined the regiment when it was besieging Banbury, earlier this year. Apparently he was taken by them, and given the choice between imprisonment in London or service in the regiment: and not unnaturally chose the lesser evil. Why he was given that choice, I do not know, but the captain hinted at some 'crime' he had committed, and I believe he may have tried to aid some fleeing Royalists. But at any rate you can be assured that he is safe, and that for the moment his subterfuge remains undiscovered." ' She looked at me, her round brow wrinkled in puzzlement. 'Can he – can he mean *Francis*?'

'Who else can he mean? Well, at least we know he's safe,' I said, hugely delighted. This development, while by no means welcome, was so much better than many of the awful possibilities that had tortured my mind for months that for the moment I cared nothing beyond the discovery that he was well, and safe. Lucy, still bewildered, said, 'But *why*? Why did he join the army? Surely they wouldn't force him to choose that, would they?'

'Well, Dan seems to think they did. Pray God Simon doesn't know. And if his real name is ever found out, and that he once fought for Montrose, and the King . . .'

'They won't, because only Dan can possibly know who he is, and Francis is much too clever to give himself away so easily,' said Lucy. 'But how terrible, he was coming to you, and then to be taken into the army . . . Still,' she added, leaping up and hugging me, 'at least they're both safe and they can look after each other!'

'If Dan's a major and Francis a trooper, and in separate regiments, there'll be small chance of that,' I said. 'Well, with any luck the army will be disbanded soon, and we might have them both here before too long. And Lucy, don't, please don't, tell anyone that Francis is in the Roundhead army, it might lead to all manner of complications if it was generally known.'

'Don't worry, I won't,' Lucy said. 'And let's hope you're right about the army being disbanded.'

But my prediction proved an exceedingly naïve assumption. Lord Astley, sitting on his drum at Stow-on-the-Wold, with the King's last army prisoner around him, had told his captors, 'You have done your work, boys, and may go and play – unless you will fall out among yourselves.' And his words had been prophetic: for a gulf was rapidly opening out between two sections of the victorious Roundheads. The New Model Army, led by Cromwell and Fairfax, was full of what their enemies, and Dan Ashley, called 'sectaries', men of every shade of extreme religious opinion (or none) – Anabaptists, Baptists, Brownists, Seekers, all generally lumped together under the name 'Independents'. Against these were ranged the Presbyterians, altogether more narrow-minded and intolerant of differing views. They were to be found to some extent in the Army, to a greater degree in Parliament, and were, of course, extremely thick upon the ground in Scotland. And the Presbyterians' hatred and fear of the Independents, as is usual in these matters, created the very threat of which they had been so afraid. The growing trouble was fuelled by the irrepressible John Lilburne, stirrer of sedition before the war, who had published two pamphlets attacking half-hearted Parliament soldiers such as the Earl of Manchester, and the House of Lords. The Lords, in exasperation, committed him to the Tower, and failed entirely to silence him or to diminish his enormous popularity with ordinary Londoners. And his friends still at liberty continued the struggle for the rights of the people, who had endured or fought the war and now desired a greater share and say in the running of the country. Even in Suffolk there were repercussions. Arguments raged in alehouses, taverns and on street-corners, not all of them ignorant or stupid, on an enormous variety of subjects: freedom of religion, Presbyterianism, the Scots, the eventual fate of the King, the liberties of the people versus the rights of property owners and, closer to home, the recent witch-trials in Bury, or the iconoclast tours of Master William Dowsing. He had ordered the church at Bradfield Tye to be made as plain and bare as any barn, the Doom painting whitewashed over, the communion rails and the rood-screen hacked down and burnt, the carved angels in the roof defaced and the painted glass smashed. He had even wanted the monument to Sir Christopher Heron, founder of the family and more than a hundred years dead, abused because the marble effigy was clasping a Papist cross: but on that subject Richard Trevelyan had been adamant, and a good dinner (one of Monsieur Harcourt's most inspired creations) had persuaded Master Dowsing that Sir Kit was best left in peace.

But even in Suffolk the Parliament supporters did not have it all their own way. Discontent among the apprentices and rougher elements in Bury was rife, and the harvest in 1646 failed disastrously. That December, there was a riot in Bury caused by resentment at shops opening on Christmas Day, treated by all good Puritans, here as in Scotland, as just another working day. The 'prentices, deprived of their holiday, attempted to 'persuade' the shopkeepers to close, and only prompt action by the local magistrates and constables prevented serious damage and injury. Nor did the New Year bring better times: prices rose, the poor began to go hungry, and anger flowered in the Army when it was discovered that the Presbyterians in the Parliament wanted to send some regiments to Ireland, and disband the rest without giving them their arrears of pay.

I would have liked nothing better than the disbanding of the Army, but even I could see that this unbelievably foolish action would set the spark to the bonfire with a vengeance. Knowing Francis to be amongst them, I had already been taking a covert interest in any news concerning the Army: and had rapidly come to the conclusion that this force was unique, bound together as no army before, not only by its un-English discipline and sinister ruthless efficiency, but also by loyalty to aims and ideals not generally shared by those in authority, and for which they considered they had been brought into existence to fight – peace, freedom for the people from tyranny, injustice and oppression, and the preservation of the laws and liberties of the land and the subjects of the King. And when it seemed that the Presbyterians in Parliament were conspiring to pervert and smother those aims, the Army reacted. I knew that Francis, whatever he felt about his enforced presence amongst them, would be wholeheartedly with the soldiers in that, perhaps even one of the 'Agitators', the representatives of each regiment chosen by the men to air their grievances: for the ideas now flying back and forth between Lilburne and his friends in London and the Army men were very similar to Francis's own, the same concern for the poor and oppressed, the same desire to live in a country untrammelled by religious repression, where people could think and speak and write what they pleased without fear of reprisal. For too long, I guessed, Francis had suppressed this side of his character: now at last, for the first time in his life, he would be able to give free rein to his opinions, and to have the chance of acting on them. Once, I had been dubious of his ideals, seeing a threat to the stable little world of luxury that I had inhabited: but that had been before the war, and things were very different now, the King defeated and imprisoned, many of his supporters fled or impoverished, the country frothing like yeast with new ideas, the world, as old Royalists gloomily and disapprovingly put it, turned upside down. And I saw with my own eyes the poverty around me that I did not share, and knew that I was in a privileged position which I had done nothing to earn. And if I, with my strong will and hot temper, had been born into some squalid hovel with no hope of adequate sustenance for body or mind, no future save miserable unremitting unrewarded toil for all my days, which would most like be far shorter than my wealthy well-fed self could hope for, with none of the intellectual delights of music and books and poetry and plays – if I had lived in that environment, I knew full well that I would be in rebellion too.

So, I began to sympathize with the Levellers, as they were later called, in London, and the Independent faction in the Army, and thus found myself at odds with the rest of the family. Lucy, of course, cared nothing for politics, though her soft heart was always touched to generosity by a beggar: even less could be said of her mother. Jamie was at one with Simon in his support for the established order of things: and as deep thought was rather alien to his nature, I doubted he had considered the matter very thoroughly. Meraud supported her uncle and he, whatever his ideas had been before the war, when he had consorted with Prynne and Pym and written seditious pamphlets, was now in possession of Goldhayes and unequivocally on the side of authority and the *status quo*. The people in the villages around grew used to seeing me riding up to their doors and hearing me enquire after their welfare: and where I could, offering medicines, advice, food, even money borrowed from John Sewell or Grainne, who were both sympathetic, and doing what I could to alleviate any suffering. I also tried to act as a mediator between them and Richard Trevelyan, since John had already failed in this task. I attempted to persuade him to raise wages, to take on unemployed villagers, to help improve the worst of the village houses, to increase his contribution to the Poor Fund, and found him distantly, implacably, courteously declining. The crisis came when, in the spring of 1647, he decided to raise the rents of the Goldhayes tenants. For many small husbandmen, after the disastrous harvest of the previous year, it was the final straw. A deputation, led by Holly Greenwood, whose reputation as the local Jeremiah made him the natural choice for this role, trooped self-conscious but determined up to Goldhayes to put their case. Unfortunately, the question of tithes somehow arose as well, and all their simmering grievance at having to pay these not even to maintain a minister of God, but to keep Richard Trevelyan in luxury (for Goldhayes and Bradfield Tye had once been Church land and the tithes had since the Reformation gone to the Herons), rose abundantly to the surface. There was a fine exchange of words, and Holly's little band were ignominiously ejected with the threat of arraignment by the Justices hanging over them. Holly, whose resentment was entirely heaped on Master

Trevelyan and who bore no grudge against any Heron, told me that feelings ran very high in the village. 'They be a-saying now in the Sun-rising that Master Trevelyan hev stolen the land away from Master Heron, and some on 'em be a-talking suffen wild, like.'

'What sort of things are they saying, Holly?' And then, as he went red and shuffled his feet, I added, 'Oh, Holly, surely you can tell me? Aren't I to be trusted?'

'I'm sorry, Mistress,' said poor Holly. 'Thass suffen okkard, like, for you, I can see that . . . Some on 'em be saying as how they'd like to set the ricks afire, or even the Hall, unless Master Trevelyan goo back on what he said.' He looked unhappily at me, and I said, 'I'll talk to Master Trevelyan about it.'

In the end, John and I both went to see him. We put the villagers' case logically and compassionately, and when Richard frowned and began to speak of all the extra drains and taxes and expenses on the estate that the increased rents would pay for, I said, 'I am sure Simon would not agree to it, were he here. He always had a care for the wishes of his tenants, and I know Master Blagge feels the same: *he* hasn't raised his rents, though of course he has always been very careful of his money.' I gazed sternly into Richard's face, hoping that he could read the tacit message I was sending him. Stop this, my look said, or we shall warn Ambrose Blagge and Simon of what we suspect is going on.

If he had been innocent, I knew, he would have clung to his plans: but he backed down with alacrity. 'I am sorry, Thomazine, John, I had no idea of how matters stood . . . this has all been a very sorry misunderstanding, and I am glad you have made matters clear to me. You may tell the villagers, John, that I will not after all raise the rents this year.'

So we left him, victorious, and the breach between Hall and village was healed: on the surface at any rate. After that episode, Richard seemed to realize his danger, and in his serpentine manner slithered on to safer ground. He did not again attempt to go against John's advice, and although he did not go out of his way to help the poorer labourers and cotters, he did nothing more to antagonize any of the tenantry. But John and Grainne and I knew now that our suspicions were confirmed: the intent to cheat the Herons was there, surely, but the methods and present position remained obscure. I hoped that we had discouraged him, but was cynical about our chances of permanent success.

Two or three months before this, the King had been handed over to the Parliament by his Scottish captors, in exchange for large amounts of back pay for the Scottish army. They were now free to go home, to a Scotland relieved from war, for the King had, in the summer of 1646, persuaded Montrose to abandon the struggle and go into exile, taking with him a few loyal friends. I wondered if Malise Graham was amongst them, and if he would ever be reunited with Grainne. The Royalist dream was ended for good: there remained only the squabbles of Army and Parliament over the governing of the Kingdom, and the perennial question of, what was to be done with the King?

Parliament had him in their custody, but when the Independents virtually seized power in the Army, in May of 1647, they took care to seize the person of the King as well. After all, whatever one's political views, it was obvious that his fate would be a key factor in any decision that was reached: to the Presbyterians, someone to be negotiated with, and eventually replaced on the throne to restore equilibrium to the wildly rocking boat of the traditional order: and to the more extreme of the Independents a particularly noxious example of that despised breed, monarchs, who should be brought to account for his tyranny and misgovernment. All that summer and autumn the battle of words continued: the Army leaders, Cromwell, Fairfax, Ireton, supporting their soldiers in their demands for radical reform for just so long as it suited them to do so. There was a Council of War at Bury, and soldiers quartered throughout Suffolk:

and, so it was said, that the regiment guarding the King after his seizure by the Army was Whalley's. And still there was no word from Francis, no sign that he remembered me or, indeed, was still on this earth to love me: and the old sharp, wild pain of despair had dulled long since to a resigned acceptance. As in my childhood, I must make the best of things: and hope.

The country watched and waited as, with the Presbyterians routed, the Agitators of each regiment and their chief officers, known rather derisively as the Grandees, struggled for supremacy. Then, in November, the King escaped – it was rumoured with Cromwell's connivance – and the debates in Putney church that had argued over the governing of the kingdom with passionate belief on both sides had to be broken up. Cromwell had to defeat the Agitators and their supporters in the regiments, for only the Army stood between England and the anarchy of further war, and it could only be in that position while he and the officers remained in control of it. The Levellers were outmanoeuvred: the Army was ordered to rendezvous in three different places, and with the Agitators divided and disunited, it was easy for the Grandees to reassert their authority. Mutiny died: the King at Carisbrooke on the Isle of Wight negotiated with Parliament on the one hand and for a Scottish rising on the other. The threat of the Levellers and their plans for democracy was in temporary eclipse as civil war loomed again on the horizon.

Fascinated as I was by all this political ferment, I could not ignore what was happening at Goldhayes. For during that year it became more and more obvious to me that what I suspected, and dreaded, was the truth. Meraud no longer pursued Charles Lawrence: his letters went unanswered, possibly unopened, as she continued gently, oh so subtly and insinuatingly, to bind Jamie to her for ever. Not a difficult task in itself, since Jamie's open-mouthed adoration had never diminished during all the time she had ignored him, and now increased daily: but it must be done carefully so as not to draw the attention of the rest of the family to the abrupt volte-face in her affections, and hence to the probable reason for it. I was able, with a detached, sardonic and prejud-iced eye, to watch the gradual steps in her seduction: the speaking glance, the rapt attention on his every word and gesture no matter how foolish, the artless linking of her arm in his, the brilliant smile for him alone. All these were employed in full measure, and I could not believe anyone could be ensnared by artifice that, to me, seemed so blindingly obvious.

But Jamie was: and proof of the extent of his thralldom, if proof were needed, was amply given to me one warm summer evening late in August when I strolled unawares into the walled garden, just over the moat from the west side of the house. It had always been one of my favourite parts of Goldhayes, a quiet, sweet-scented and secluded spot where the loudest sound was usually birdsong or the drowsy hum of the bees. In the aromatic air I heard voices murmuring ahead of me, a woman's laughter, a low and intimate sound. My curiosity aroused, I gave way to the temptation to indulge in my bad old childhood habit of eavesdropping. Moving stealthily along the grassy edge of the gravel walk, I approached noiselessly until I could identify the voices: and discovered to my consternation that it was Meraud and Jamie.

They were in the little arbour, entwined with honey-suckle and roses, where once I had sat with Francis long ago on just such a sweet summer's night as this, the night when Richard had brought us tidings of war, and our peace was gone from us. I crept over to the apple-grove which stood nearby and offered a concealed vantage-point, and peered through the leaves, allowing myself a hypocritical pang of contempt for my despicable behaviour. It was hard to be sure of anything, since the gloom of dusk obscured much and the figures in the arbour were almost in darkness: but I could see enough to be sure that they were lovingly entangled, and that every so often the soft intimate lovers' talk was broken by a kiss. Despising myself even more, I crawled backwards out of the grove and crept away from the little garden whose happy memories I had thought to belong to myself and Francis alone: feeling that it had somehow been violated. I felt sorry for Charles, now finally discarded, and yet also thankful for his sake, that he would not be for ever shackled to Meraud: and even more sorry for Jamie, who would. I could not believe that she felt any affection for him at all, I was sure that all that sweet show of loving was false, and that her only interest in him was as the potential heir to Goldhayes: and I was angry with Jamie, because he, a callow boy of eighteen, could not see her as clear as I.

But there was nothing I could do about it: nothing at all. And all my secret suspicions were confirmed a week or so later, when Jamie and Meraud went coyly hand in hand to see Mary and Richard Trevelyan: who gladly, joyfully, happily gave their blessing to the marriage.

It was arranged for December. Jamie would be nineteen by then, and his spouse two years older and quite plainly the dominant partner. She sailed amidst the preparations for the festivities – drains on the estate or no, Richard Trevelyan was making sure that his niece would be married in fine style – with an expression reminiscent of a cat who has just raided the cream-pans and got away with it. Jamie, who was after all marrying a minor heiress (even if her Cornish lands had suffered greatly from the depredations of both sides in the war), and moreover the most beautiful girl in all Suffolk, as he did not fail to inform us with tiresome frequency, wore a not dissimilar expression. Lucy, of course, thought it most romantic, and would always support the course of 'true love', but I could not share her optimism. Neither party would ever be open to any discouraging persuasion, so I congratulated them and kept my misgivings to myself: but I was extremely dubious about the prospects for the marriage. Jamie, even at the comparatively mature age of nineteen was, by comparison with

Meraud's cool assurance, still a young boy, despite his handsome presence, and I could foresee that she might quickly become tired of him, Goldhayes or no Goldhayes. And would the strong antipathy to adultery, which she had once stated so pointedly to me, be altered by her own circumstances? I took my futile, scurrilous speculations to Grainne, as ever, and found her in the Home Farm's little front garden, taking advantage of an unseasonably sunny day to tidy the dead flowers and leaves of November and to gather rosehips for jelly. Henrietta, now nearly five and a practical, methodical child, was rendering valuable assistance with a little basket of her own. I thought involuntarily of Kit, not so much younger, far away in Yorkshire and doubtless very different in appearance from this robust, freckled, rosy-cheeked little girl with her riotously curling red hair and soft, light-brown eyes. I helped Grainne for a little while, talking as I did so, and at the end of it she sat back on her heels, absently brushing the dirt from her oldest gown, and said, 'I agree with every word you say, but there's precious little we can do about it: and anyway they're not children, and we have no right to interfere. You of all people should know that.'

It was the nearest she could ever come to reproof, and I acknowledged it. 'Yes, you're right – I'm fast turning into as great a hypocrite as I accuse Meraud of being. And what's more, I'm jealous. I can't help asking myself, why should she have the happiness that she with all her trickery denied to me? Do you realize, it's over two years, two years, since I last saw Francis? And that he has never once written to me or sent any word? Oh, I know this separation isn't her fault, but it's true to say that if it hadn't been for her interference we would have been wed years ago . . . But you know, it's strange, although this is the longest we've ever been apart, I don't worry about him as I did in Scotland. Oh, I miss him, I miss him terribly, I can't wait to see him again, but I no longer fear for him. Even if he is one of these Agitators or whatever they're called, I know he is safe from death

– or as safe as anyone can be. And somehow, I don't know how, intuition maybe, I can sense that he must be happy, or as happy as he can be without me. He said once that he didn't want to go through the world without leaving his mark on it somewhere, and I suspect that he is taking the chance to do it now.'

'It's a dangerous game, politics,' said Grainne. 'Cromwell had one of the Army mutineers shot a few weeks ago, didn't he? And Lilburne must know the inside of the Tower of London better than his own house. Laudable as their aims may be, I think their chances of success are slender now. The possibility of a new war looms much larger: and I'm beginning to agree with the Levellers when they demand that the King be brought to trial, for I think that he'll be stirring up trouble all his life. The Royalists have been defeated, Cromwell holds the power now, and the country is trying to return to peace and normality. Why can't he accept that and agree to the Parliament's demands? It's not much to ask, for God's sake.'

'If he was a man to compromise, or give way, or profit from his past mistakes, we would never have had a war at all . . .' I pinched off the dead heads of a row of marigolds with as much feeling as if I were snipping off the King's head. 'Like you, I want peace: and then Francis and Dan and Malise would most like be restored to us, and Simon and Tom Sewell might return from the Hague or wherever they are now, and we could pursue our cosy, peaceful existence again, instead of worrying about our absent friends and lovers.'

'We have a visitor,' said Grainne, looking round at the sound of hooves: and I followed her gaze. A stranger, mired and filthy from travelling, sat his weary horse just beyond the gate, and doffed his hat. I stared at him, puzzled, for he had the look of a responsible servant and I could think of no far-distant friend who might send us such a one. 'Can I help you?' Grainne asked, rising.

'Aye, Mistress, Ah'm lookin' for Goldhayes Hall,' said the man, in an accent so broad and Northern that it was difficult to understand him. 'Ah've message for Leddy Drakelon, be her Leddyship there?'

'I am Lady Drakelon,' I said, my voice stumbling over the hated, unused title. 'What message do you bring?'

The man looked dubiously at my grubby, disreputable dress and earth-stained hands, and then dismounted with an awkward bow and fumbled in his doublet. 'Ah've letter from Sir Dominic, Leddy Drakelon.' And I watched, heart suddenly pounding, wondering what this meant, why after four years he had troubled to contact me again, as the clumsy hand brought out the letter.

Someone had edged it, carefully, in black ink.

My first thought was, it's Kit, Kit has died: I stared at it in horror. 'What . . . who . . .'

The servant looked sadly at me. 'It's his last letter, me leddy, t' last thing he ever wrote. Poor Sir Dominic died last week.'

Chapter 6

Kit

'O sweet babe, if thou were mine,
I'd clad thee in the silk so fine.'

'O mother dear, when I was thine,
You did not prove to me so kind.'
                    (Traditional ballad)

The garden blurred and swayed before my eyes: I grabbed the gatepost for support. I heard my voice, thready with disbelief, saying distantly, 'Sir Dominic? *Dead*? No, it can't be, it must be a mistake . . .' Then Grainne's arm was round me, steadying me, and the Yorkshire servant said, his hands crushing his hat, 'Eeh, me leddy, Ah'm right sorry, Ah didn't mean t' break t' news so sudden, like.'

'It's – it's all right,' I said, terribly ashamed that the emotion beneath my astonishment and disbelief was only joy: no sorrow, only delight that now at last I was free. 'Tell me how – what happened? Was it to do with his being wounded at Naseby?'

'Aye, me leddy, that were it. He never got better from that, he were never well, and then two weeks ago he came down wi' t' ague, and that were that. He knew he were going to die when he wrote that letter, you see, me leddy, an' he wanted you to know what was t' be done wi' little Master Kit. Eh, Ah s'pose he be Sir Christopher now.'

From somewhere, I found the strength to say, 'Thank you, er . . .'

'Smith, me leddy, Adam Smith.'

'Thank you, Adam, for bringing me such sad news all that way, and so quickly . . . I am grateful for your concern. If you carry on up this track you will come to the Hall, go round to the stables and tell them to look after your horse and you, you must both be weary. Then I shall talk to you some more about all this.'

'Eh, thank you, me leddy,' said Adam Smith, bowing. 'Ah'm right sorry t' bring you such ill news, Ah am that.' He mounted his horse and rode off down the drive towards Goldhayes: and I burst into tears.

Grainne led me to her upstairs chamber, away from Joan's insistent curiosity, and lent me her kerchief, while Hen stared at me, wide-eyed and solemn. 'I don't believe it,' I hiccupped into the white cambric. 'I can't believe it, it must be some cruel joke . . . he c-can't be dead!'

'I would have thought,' said Grainne, gently, 'that you would be glad of his death.'

'That's exactly why I'm crying!' I told her fiercely. 'I *am* glad, I feel nothing except pleasure at the thought of it, and I am so ashamed of it!'

'I can understand why you wish for the death of someone like that – it solves all your problems, I know, yet it is horrible, evil, unchristian . . . but human,' said Grainne, watching me blow my nose furiously. 'You will have to come to terms with your feelings, for you have to live with yourself, however callous you feel you are . . . and now there is Kit to think about. What does the letter say?'

It was exceedingly ill-written, in the blotched uneven hand of a very sick man, but it was short, curt and to the point.

Madam: when you receive this, I shall be dead. Doubtless you will be overjoyed. I will order my son, and his nurse, to be sent to you when I am buried, that he may know a mother's care for the first time. I have willed him everything I possess, such as my great necessity allows, the Parliament being something greedy for my estate: save, of course, for Ashcott and the Oxford house which form your jointure as was agreed at our marriage. I pray you do not neglect the child, for he will prove a lasting reminder of

Your husband,

Dominic Drakelon.

But even that characteristic, hostile letter did little to convince me that he was really dead. My mind torn in two by guilt and relief, I half-persuaded myself that it was all a cruel plot to punish me in some way for my desertion and infidelity. Even Adam Smith's vivid account of his master's final hours, and the funeral two days later, with the little Kit the centre of pity and attention at the graveside, did not entirely convince me. I wondered about the estate, until Adam informed me that his cousin, who had been Sir Roger's steward, was more than qualified and able to carry on the running of the house and lands at Upper Denby, as well as those manors and possessions which had come to Dominic with me upon our marriage. But Ashcott was truly mine now, though by all accounts virtually a ruin: for when its garrison had surrendered to the Parliament at the same time as did Oxford, all walls, battlements and fortifications had been dismantled or demolished.

So the chief responsibility which Dominic had passed on to me was one which I had, as he had accused, neglected for four years and four months: our son Kit. And it was a duty I did not intend to shirk. In the week or so until his arrival I thought constantly of the child I had never expected to see again, never thought I would ever care for: I conjured up again the hairless, placid baby, less than a month old, whom I had left behind in Oxford in September 1643, remembering what other reports had said of his appearance: a thriving child, one to be proud of, a good-looking boy who greatly resembled his father. All my old guilt and grief at deserting him, however necessary for Francis's sake, however justified by future events, welled up in me again, with a passionate maternal longing to devote myself to him

277

from now on. And I promised him faithfully, fiercely, every night whispered to the thick warm dark of the bed I shared still with Lucy, that I would make it up to Kit, ten times, eleven times over for the mother-love I had failed to give him before.

He arrived four days before Jamie and Meraud's wedding. The coach swayed and jolted up the drive to halt in the front court, just as I had once come as an orphan child to Goldhayes. With a painfully banging heart and sticky hands, despite the cold, I walked out, with Lucy and Grainne as moral support, to greet it.

The four horses stood blown, steaming, heads down. The coachman leapt down to open the door: I watched with joyous welcoming hope as a small, immaculately dressed figure climbed down and stood solemnly five feet from me.

For a moment, frozen, we stared at each other. He would see a small young woman, trim and neat, for once, in decorous mourning black: though I was not so hypocritical as to don full widow's weeds, as Mary had done after her first husband's death. And I beheld a boy, small for his age, but already breeched, in a black suit with a miniature sword and black-plumed hat: an astonishingly beautiful child, with his father's black hair and large vivid blue eyes, rimmed with a sweeping abundance of lashes. There was little sign of me in his face, save perhaps for the pointed little chin and the rather wide, sulky mouth. He gazed at me, with a self-possession that caused my initial impulse to sweep him to my maternal bosom to die before it had scarce been born: and then said in a high, hostile treble, 'Are you my mother? My father said you were a bad woman, but you don't *look* like a bad woman.'

My voice seemed to have stuck in my throat, but somehow I managed a smile, and said at last, 'Yes, Kit, I'm your mother.' And I knelt on the gravel, my arms outstretched in welcome. The child, his lower lip pushed out, retreated a pace: shrilly, he said, 'You're a bad woman! I don't want you, don't touch me, I hate you!'

Tears of rage glittered on his lashes and trembled picturesquely at the edges of his eyes. Appalled, rigid, I stared as a young woman, dressed in mourning, descended from the coach and folded the child into her embrace, patting his shiny head. 'Ah, you're tired from the journey, aren't you, poor little Kit? Never mind, Peg will look after you, don't worry, Peg's not going to go away and leave you.'

I rose to my feet trembling, and met the young woman's eyes. I had forgotten that Kit's second nurse had also been Dominic's mistress: and I saw in the round, pretty, petulant face, framed in a crisp, white embroidered coif and graced with unlikely golden curls, that I had an enemy. I said, anger and bitterness in my voice, 'I collect that you are my son's nurse?'

The woman Peg straightened, Kit's dark smooth head still pressed into her skirts which were, I noted, made of fine satin. 'I am, Lady Drakelon. Your husband entrusted sole care of his son to me. He would not entertain any thought of us being parted.' She smiled, her position assured – no longer Dominic's mistress, but still the indispensable nurse of his sole heir.

I kept the rags of my temper and said, 'You must both be very tired after such a journey. There is a chamber set aside for you, and a supper prepared, and Mistress Trevelyan's son is waiting eagerly for you.' In sudden desperation, I touched my child's shoulder. 'Now you'll like Hugh, Kit, he's just a year younger than you and he's longing to see his new cousin . . .'

Kit's shoulder hunched away from me. He said, muffled, 'I don't want you! Go away!'

Peg made no attempt to admonish him for his rudeness. As if he had done nothing wrong she said, 'Now, come inside and have your supper. Come, hold my hand.' She took the small pale paw in hers and led him indoors: I tried briefly to grasp the other, but with a sound of protest, through clenched lips, Kit jerked it away. Horrorstruck and humiliated by a total rejection I had never expected, I stood rooted to the gravel and watched Peg lead him briskly inside the house as if she owned him.

'Dear God,' said Grainne, 'if he were mine I'd have him over my knee and spank him . . .'

'It doesn't look as if I'll ever get the chance,' I said bitterly. 'That doxy of Dominic's has had her claws into him for too long.'

'Oh, Thomazine,' Lucy wailed, clutching me, 'how awful, to welcome him at last and have him behave like that!'

'It's not his fault,' I said, walking determined to the house. 'It's mine, for leaving him to their tender mercies: and if it's the last thing I do, I'll put it right.'

When we reached the nursery, which was Hugh's domain, we found that young man in a state of high excitement, scarcely restrained by Rose, the ample friendly Rushbrooke girl who had been his nurse since his infancy. Despite my previous doubts about him, I had become very fond of Hugh, who was an engaging, fair-haired, cherubic child with more than a passing resemblance, surprisingly, to his half-brother Francis. Most disconcerting were his eyes, far-set and the same shadowy-green, obviously inherited from somewhere in his mother's family. He bounced up to Kit, who stood sullenly close to Peg, and bowed. 'Hullo. I'm Hugh.'

My son glowered at him: rather disconcerted, Hugh frowned slightly. Then Kit said angrily, 'I don't like you!'

I felt it was high time to intervene. I grasped his shoulder and turned him to face me, forcing him to pay attention to me. 'Kit, that was very rude. You can't possibly dislike him, you've only just met him! Now say you're sorry.'

Kit twisted away from me. 'No! No, I won't!' I tightened my grip, losing my temper, and instantly he began to struggle wildly, his hands clawing at mine. His foot lashed out and caught poor Hugh on the shin: too astonished to cry, although it must have hurt more than a little, the younger boy took a step back, over-balanced and sat down with a plump of petticoats. Suddenly my rage boiled over, and with my free hand I slapped Kit's rump as hard as I could.

It stopped him, certainly. Incredulous, his limbs ceased flailing; it was as if no one had ever spanked him before. I tightened my hold further and slapped him again. 'I'm sorry, Kit, but you are a very rude little boy, and you've hurt Hugh.'

The great blue eyes stared at me and then dropped, spilling with artful tears: a sob trembled in his throat. It was a performance designed to melt the stoniest heart, but I knew that, once having asserted my authority, I must not give in. 'Now say you're sorry to Hugh. Go on, say you're sorry.'

Hugh had struggled to his feet and stood gazing open-mouthed at this extraordinary apparition: he had never seen such bad behaviour before. Kit looked down at the ground, his lip wobbled pitifully, and then strengthened. His voice came clearly in the expectant silence. 'No.'

'Kit, say you're sorry,' I repeated: and again came the stubborn reply, 'No. Let go of me!'

'Not until you say you're sorry.'

'Let GO!' Kit cried, suddenly coming to life again. He wrenched himself free and hurled himself at Peg, who seemed to welcome his frantic clasp of her skirts. She gave me a chilly smile. 'I think he is tired and overwrought, Lady Drakelon. It would be best if I gave him his supper now and put him straight to bed. You must remember that he is very young, and has just lost his father and his home.'

'I am well aware of that,' I said angrily, 'but I would have thought that however young and weary and bereaved, a properly-reared child would be better behaved. I shall speak to you about it in the morning.' And almost too furious and disappointed to speak, I turned abruptly and went out.

Lucy and Grainne, silent and sympathetic, walked with me down the Long Gallery to the windows at its western end, shafted with red light from a sullenly setting sun. We sat down on the chairs grouped there, and stared gloomily at each other.

'I made a mistake,' I admitted at last. 'Pray God not an irretrievable one: but I don't think I should have hit him.'

'You could do little else,' said Grainne drily. 'I have never seen a worse-reared child . . .' Or a more ill-natured one, her silence added. I felt suddenly utterly weary, exhausted by the brief encounter, so longed-for and so totally disappointing. 'What can I do?' I said hopelessly: for knowing only Grainne's friendly, open-hearted children, and the endearing Hugh, I had no conception of the power that such a thoroughly spoilt, indulged and bad-tempered infant could wield; just such a power, perhaps, as his father had possessed as a child. 'Whatever shall I do with him?'

'Get rid of that nurse, as she calls herself,' said Grainne immediately. 'As soon as possible, and tomorrow for preference. While she is here you will have no influence over him at all, he will go from bad to worse, and end by being thoroughly detested by everyone – and he deserves a better fate than that, for he's as much your child as Dominic's.'

'He does look like you, a little,' Lucy put in. 'He has your mouth, only more bad-tempered, and your chin too, though the rest is pure Dominic. If he didn't behave so badly, he'd be quite adorable.'

'But if I get rid of the nurse – I mean, he so obviously loves her, she's been as good as his mother for most of his life – I couldn't – it would be so cruel.'

'But kind in the long run,' said Grainne, who had, after all, borne three children and reared them largely single-handed. 'You will just have to replace her with yourself, and harden your heart. The first thing to remember with a child like that is, don't give in, for once you start indulging their tantrums they become worse tyrants than Tamburlaine. Be kind but firm. If you love him sufficiently, he is little enough for that to win him in the end. But pray he has not your stubbornness, for if that is so, it will be a long, hard battle.' She grinned at me suddenly, friendly and encouraging. 'I will give you all the help and advice I can, but in the end it will all be up to you – for you are his mother, you want him, and you cannot let someone else do your fighting for you.'

I could see the logic of that, and felt better for her sympathy. A four-year-old child was, after all, no more than a baby: Peg would soon be forgotten, and in her absence he would surely turn to me. As I ate my supper with the rest of the family, beguiling images of that shiny dark head pressed confidently, affectionately, against me, just as Jasper and Hen did, kept interposing themselves between me and the rest of the company. But first, I had to send Peg packing, and after all my speeches to Richard Trevelyan about employing the poor and justice for labourers and servants, it seemed the height of hypocrisy to cast her out. She had obviously been a good nurse, except in matters of discipline, and that could well be Dominic's fault. It would be just like his vindictiveness, even if it sounded far-fetched, to ensure that I had no joy in my child by turning his mind against me. I could almost hear his abrupt voice, paternally softened, death-bed weakened, adjuring Kit: 'Do everything Peg tells you, and don't pay any attention to your mother, she's a bad woman, she doesn't really want you, she went away and left us alone.' So convincing was this chilling figment of my imagination that I shuddered: for the child upstairs was Dominic come again, his ghost, his instrument of vengeance, sent to punish me for my desertion and infidelity.

A morbid, foolish fancy, but I believed it.

After supper I had a brief talk with Mary and then went slowly upstairs, preparing myself for the coming interview with Peg: for I was even more determined now to be rid of her, hypocrisy or no. If I wanted to win Kit, I could not afford to pay the price of my scruples, to have her stay on and continue to dominate him. And if I had needed any further persuading, the small comfortably rotund figure of Rose waylaid me at the top of the stairs, curtseying urgently. 'Mistress! Can Oi talk to you a minute?'

'Yes, of course, Rose. What is it?'

Rose glanced round and then lowered her voice confidentially. 'That *nurse* – Peg, she call harself. That in't right, Mistress, what she tell your little mite, and Oi thought that was best to come and tell you, what she say.' Her brown cow's eyes gazed at me anxiously. 'You won't tell her as Oi said suffen to you, Mistress?'

'No, of course I won't,' I assured her. 'What is it?'

Rose took a deep breath, her face eerily lit by my flickering candle. 'Well, Mistress, Oi hard she tell that little mite as how he warn't to dew nawthen you tell him to dew, and as how you was a bad woman, suffen terrible it was an' all, Oi din't know what to say. A proper botty bitch, her be, and Oi doubt Oi can get along of she . . .'

'You won't have to, Rose,' I said, liking her earnest simplicity. 'Do you think you and I could persuade some sense into Kit, if she wasn't there?'

Rose grinned at me. 'Oi dunno, Mistress, but Oi reckon us'll hev a hack at that. Is you a-gooin' to git rid of she, then?'

'I am indeed,' I said grimly. 'And don't worry, Rose, it's nothing to do with you, I've had it in mind for an hour or two. Have you put Hugh to bed?'

'Yes, Mistress, and her's put your little mite to bed too.'

'Then can you tell Peg that I wish to see her now, in my chamber?'

'That Oi will, Mistress,' said Rose, bobbed a curtsey and scurried away.

I lit the candles in my chamber. The fire burned cheerfully, and the shutters and curtains were drawn tight against the chill of December. All around me was the quiet of the old house settling down softly for the night; rustles, creaks, muffled distant voices, and outside the owls shrieking and hooting in the icy park. I heard

Peg's brisk cork heels tapping along the Gallery to my door: a knock, and I ordered her to enter. She did so, very meek, her eyes downcast, and curtseyed. 'Yes, Lady Drakelon?'

Even the faintly insolent tone of her voice was an affront. I said, more sharply than I had wished, 'I mislike the way you have reared my son, Peg.'

'I had Sir Dominic's approval for everything,' she said, not protesting or excusing, but calmly stating an incontrovertible truth.

'That's as may be – but the fact remains that he's spoilt, bad-tempered, badly-behaved, and insufferably rude to all save you. You cannot tell me that Sir Dominic approved of that.'

'Kit was not like that at Denby, Lady Drakelon,' said the confident, deceptively meek voice.

'I should imagine that it was because his every whim was indulged. Now when I attempt to correct him he behaves like an animal who knows no better. Is that because he is unused to correction?'

Her blue eyes flashed venom briefly and then were hidden again. 'He is unused to you, Lady Drakelon. You must remember that he has never seen you before: it is I who has tended him, no one else, since he was a baby. He has always behaved beautifully with me.'

'Have you, by any chance, attempted to ensure that situation continues by telling him to disobey me?'

Another glimpse of those hostile eyes, suddenly wary, confirmed that Rose had spoken the truth. I added, my voice hardening, 'Do you deny it?'

Abruptly her gaze was fully on me, redolent with sneering dislike. 'I do not, Lady Drakelon, and I'll tell you, I'm only following Sir Dominic's instructions. You need have no fear – as long as I have the care of him he will be a credit to you.'

'Then he will just have to cease to be a credit to me – because tomorrow you pack your bags and leave.'

There was a brief, stunned silence. For a moment, Peg looked appalled. I realized with a flash of insight that she had never expected this: secure in the fact that she alone could control and care for the child, she had thought her future at Goldhayes assured. Very likely, Dominic had led her to believe that such a mother as I would not want any close contact with the infant she had deserted virtually at birth, and that Peg could continue to dominate Kit utterly. They had reckoned without the long-suppressed maternal love and guilt that now surged within me. I had possession of Kit's body now, and I had vowed not to rest till I had his heart also.

'You can't,' said Peg, her voice cracking with anger. 'You can't – not after four years – not like that – you *won't* turn me out!'

'I am sorry, Peg, but I'm not going to allow you to complete the process of turning my own son against me. I'll recommend you to a friend of Mistress Trevelyan's in London who's looking for a nurse, so you will not be cast on the streets. The London carrier leaves Bury tomorrow, you can go with him. I will write a letter of introduction for you.'

Peg's face was a white set mask of insolent hatred. 'Why, *Lady* Drakelon? *Why*?'

'Because I want my son.'

'And that's where you are wrong, madam. If you get rid of me I'll see your precious Kit never obeys you, never speaks to you, never loves you – *ever!*'

'I think you've said enough,' I told her, keeping hard rein on my temper. If she had said one word that revealed any love or affection for the boy, I might have had second thoughts: but his only importance to her was as a passport to the security of a good position. 'I repeat – you will go tomorrow. You need have no fears about your future, for I will say nothing in any letter to your detriment. Of course, if you choose to jeopardize your future with Mistress Butler by speaking to her as you have just done to me, that is your own affair. I will do nothing to hinder you, it is up to you from now on. I will expect you to be ready to leave at first light tomorrow morning. You may go.'

Peg gave me one last stare that, if it had been a basilisk's, would have petrified me where I stood. 'You'll rue it,' she whispered, so low and vicious I hardly heard the words. 'I'll see you rue it.' And she flung herself out of the chamber, the door slamming behind her. I had defeated her, for the moment: but she still had power over Kit.

As I dressed the next morning in the trembling candle-light well before dawn, I heard, sudden and unmistakable, the screams of a child in the grip of hysteria. At the same instant, Lucy sat up in bed with her hair tangled over her face and gasped, 'What in God's name is that?'

'I don't know,' I said, fumbling frantically at the fastenings of my skirts, 'but I can hazard a guess. Dear Peg must be saying farewell to Kit.'

Confirmation came as I finished speaking: feet galloped along the floorboards to our door and someone hammered on it urgently. 'Mistress Thomazine!' Rose's voice cried, almost unintelligible in her haste. 'Do you come quick, Peg's . . . she's . . . har be saying all koinds of terrible things to Master Kit, like you've driven she away and all manner of what . . .'

I jerked open the door, still half-dressed, and with Rose at my heels ran the short distance to the children's room. As I burst in, the screams grew louder. In one furious glance I took in the scene, Hugh in his nightshirt standing by his cradle, hands over his ears and his face screwed up in pain, Peg with her meagre baggage, two travelling bags and a wooden iron-bound box, at her side, and Kit, his face scarlet with grief and fury, clinging to her skirts as if she were saving him from drowning. As I approached them, he ducked his face away from me, still bawling, and clutched Peg the tighter. On the nurse's round, curiously childish face, there was a look of triumphant, vindictive spite. 'I am ready to leave, Lady Drakelon.'

It was all I could do not to wrench my son's hands from her skirts and slap her face. I laced my fingers together and said furiously, 'What have you been telling him? Why is he making that noise?'

'I have done naught but say farewell to him, Lady Drakelon.'

'And thass a lie!' cried Rose, forgetting decorum in her agitation. 'Ooh, you botty grumshus owd bitch, thass a wicked lie and you know it! You was telling him not to do nawthen his mother said and you'd be back for him!'

'That's enough, Rose,' I said over my shoulder. 'You'd better look to Hugh, he's all but deafened. Peg. Give me the child and go, before I do something we will both regret.'

By now Lucy, Meraud and Mary, all in their nightrails, were clustered sleepily astonished at the door. Peg's contemptuous glance swept them all and came back to me. 'I fear I cannot release him, my lady. He does not wish me to go.'

'And no wonder of that, he probably reckon you're Owd Scratch himself,' said Rose to me. I knelt by the still screaming child and tried to prise his fingers from Peg's dress, feeling overwhelmingly angry and unhappy, and more than a little foolish. Rose and Lucy came to help me. At the touch of our hands the child went into a fit of hysterical fury so strong it seemed almost like a convulsion, kicking, twisting, biting, clutching. At last, at no mean cost to ourselves in scratches and bruises, we disentangled him from the folds of black satin and half-carried, half-dragged him away. 'Go,' I said to Peg through clenched teeth, and my order was echoed, with quiet authority, from Richard Trevelyan, standing in the doorway with his wife. 'Go now.'

Peg picked up her bags. 'I cannot manage the box on my own,' she said coolly, and with one last glance at her charge for four years, turned and walked out. With a despairing wail of, 'Peg! Peg! Come back!' Kit tore free of our grasp and hurled himself across the chamber to the door. Mary caught hold of him, more I suspect by accident than intention, and he gave a great gasp and became rigid, his face turning purple as he held his breath, his eyes rolling up and his fingers clutching convulsively. 'Dear God, he's having a fit!' Meraud cried, but Rose knew better: she slapped his face once, hard, and with a sharp inrush of breath he began again to cry. No simulated tears these, they streamed down his blotched scarlet face, swollen and uncomely in grief. Over and over again, in between sobs and hiccups, he gasped his nurse's name.

Close to weeping myself, I tried to take him in my arms, but he struck out with clenched fists and screamed his rejection. Nor did Rose or Lucy fare better. Somehow, we got him over to the little truckle bed where he had spent the night, virtually pushed him on to it and held him down. It took four of us to do it: under our firm hands, the threshing limbs grew quieter, and the frantic sobs at last died down into a forlorn, bereft, exhausted weeping which would not stop.

'He'll make himself ill,' said Lucy, staring down at the tiny, frail, trembling body, which yet contained such a strong and passionate will. 'Can't we do something? Shall I go and ask Grainne what to do?'

'Not yet,' I said, reluctant to admit defeat so soon. 'Wait until after dinner, at least.'

'See if he'll have suffen of this,' Rose advised, reappearing with a steaming, fragrant bowl of breakfast frumenty, brought up by one of the kitchen-maids. I saw to my relief, taking stock of the chamber for the first time since Peg's departure, that Mary, Richard and Meraud had gone and that the door was shut. 'Now, Master Hugh, do you come over here and show Master Kit how noice you reckon that there frumenty be,' Rose added.

Hugh, still in his nightshirt, and barefoot, approached dubiously, eyeing Kit's dormant prone shape as if it were a slumbering volcano. 'Won't Kit eat his breakfast?'

'He will if he sees you eating it,' Lucy promised her little brother. Hugh, who was a good trencherman, sat down promptly on the bed with us and spooned frumenty vigorously down his throat, saying at intervals for Kit's benefit, 'That's nice, that is, I *do* like frumenty!' in his surprisingly deep little voice, more than a trifle tinged with Suffolk. Reluctantly, Lucy grinned at me: despite her initial jealousy of his supreme place in her mother's heart, she loved the little boy dearly.

But Kit made no response. Rose took the half-finished bowl and spoon away from Hugh. 'Thass enough, Master Hugh, you'll git poddy if you in't careful, and there oon't be nawthen left for Master Kit. Now, be you a-gooing to eat this here noice owd frumenty, Master Kit?'

No sound or movement in answer. Kit had curled himself up with his back to us on the opposite edge of the bed, his small frame still shaken by sobs. Rose, in the falsely hearty voice she used to coax recalcitrant children, said, 'Now, come on, that in't no use a-carrying on loike that. Sit up loike a good little mite and eat your frumenty.'

Still no reply. Rose attempted to uncurl him and sit him up, but it was like trying to straighten out a hedgehog: and when we did manage to hold him in a position approaching upright, he clamped his teeth shut and refused to eat anything at all. And as Rose came too close to his mouth with a laden spoon in one hand and the bowl in the other, his fists shot out and deliberately, maliciously, knocked them out of her grasp. The spoon spun stickily across the floor, and the earthenware bowl hit Hugh soundly on the head, showering him with the grey glutinous mixture. In the chaos, Kit slithered from Lucy's relaxed hold and made a dash for the door. I was the only one with sufficient wits left about me to give chase. I caught him as his hand grabbed the latch, and tried as gently as I could to pull him away. 'No, Kit, you mustn't do that. Come and have your breakfast.'

At my touch, my son was transformed once more into a threshing demon, an imp from Hell. 'No! No! Don't want it! Let GO of me!' And then, his voice screeching despair, 'Peg! Peg! Want Peg!'

Rose and Lucy rushed to hold him before he could twist himself from my grasp, and suddenly I could take no more. 'No, don't touch him – Lucy, can you sleep elsewhere tonight and for longer if necessary? I think if he and I were alone, for a long time, it might – ouch!' Kit had stretched his head round and bitten my hand. It was not a serious wound, save to my self-esteem, but I was past making any joke of this. I hauled Kit up off the ground, tucked him under one arm and opened the door with my free hand.

'Where are you going?' Lucy cried, grabbing my sleeve. 'What are you going to do with him?'

'Sit with him in our chamber, and watch over him as if he were a hawk,' I answered briefly, and fled.

Easily said – not so easily done. All that day my son and I inhabited that room as if we were prisoners, and I did not touch him, nor make any approach by voice or gesture. After his first tantrum had spent itself, he lay on the bed, a tiny island in its vastness, neither speaking nor eating, exhausted with grief and rage. I knew that, like a falcon, he had to be quietened, soothed, gentled into accepting that I loved and wanted him, and would do him no harm: and I could not have well-meaning interference from my friends. Heppy, hardly hiding her disapproval of my tactics, brought up books, my lute and viol, and trays of food at dinner-time and supper, laden with delicacies that filled the chamber with fascinating aromas. I read, and sewed, and practised my music – hoping especially that this would rouse the child from his defiant despair – but Kit never moved, save to slip silently and unasking to the house of office tucked away between the chamber and Heppy's closet. Sooner or later, I knew, the child's will would break from hunger or exhaustion, but whether it would leave him disposed to transfer his love from Peg to me, I could not predict.

But dusk came, and my book was finished and my hands and eyes aching from sewing and playing my lute, and still Kit had not eaten or spoken, or in any way acknowledged my presence. The fire died to a hummock of glowing ash, and I had to ask Heppy through the door for more wood, and build it up myself. Outside it was a cold and rainy night, and the wind whistled and sang eerily in the roof. Kit lay on the bed, still in the nightshirt he had worn at Peg's departure, and I did not know if he slept or woke. Even with the fire, it was chilly, and I tried to pull a blanket over him: but he threw it off again and curled up into his hedgehog ball, hands and feet blue with cold. I waited until I was certain he slept at last, and very gently drew the blanket up over his still form. He did not stir, and foolishly I felt as if I had won a great victory. I did not wish to disturb his rest; instead I put on my warm fur-lined cassock coat, wrapped it round my feet and snuggled down as best I could to sleep in the chair.

My uneasy slumber was abruptly shattered by Kit's screams. I leapt to my feet, heart pounding, and saw by the firelight that he was sitting bolt upright in the bed, hands stretched out before him, beating the air. Realizing that he was having a nightmare, I promptly scrambled on to the bed and put my arms round his small, rigid, shaking body. And for one glorious moment his over-wrought muscles relaxed and he subsided against me, mumbling sleepily. 'It's all right,' I said softly, 'it was only a bad dream, it's all right, nothing can harm you now, you're safe.'

It was not the voice he had expected. With a sinking heart, I felt him stiffen and then jerk away from me. 'You're not Peg! Where's Peg? I want Peg!'

Against my better judgement, I spoke again. 'Peg's had to go away.'

'You told her to go! *You* did, she said you did, I HATE

YOU!' He started to beat at me with fists and feet as I made a movement towards him. 'I hate you, I hate you, go away!'

I abandoned the struggle. Miserable and defeated, I stumbled back to the chair and my discarded cassock, which had lost all its stored warmth, and huddled into my old position, listening hopelessly to his angry sobs and hiccups dying away too slowly into exhausted sleep. It was a very, very long time before I slept myself.

Morning brought Lucy and Heppy, both anxiously enquiring if everything was all right. I assured them that it was, and asked Heppy for breakfast. A few minutes later, the tray was left outside the door – frumenty, cold herring, bacon, small beer, bread. I was hungry, even after eating well the day before, but Kit had now had no food for thirty-six hours and must have been ravenous. His stony, bewildered, defiant blue eyes watched every movement of my hand, like a starving dog, as I cut bread and bacon: but when I asked him gently if he would like some breakfast, he set his mouth and shook his head, backing away across the bed. Confident that he would come round eventually, I finished my repast and left his portion temptingly on the edge of the table nearest to him: with no result. The morning wore on, and I set myself to mastering a new and difficult lute piece, an Italian Fantasia by Canova that was one of Mary's virtuoso performances. As I struggled with the fingering, a flash of movement disturbed my concentration. Kit, slipping faster than any street pickpocket, had slid from the bed, grabbed the remaining bread and bacon and retreated, his eyes watching me as if he feared I would give chase, and all the while stuffing the food down as though he had not seen sustenance for a week. My heart ached for this misled, bewildered, terrified child, and for what the adults who claimed to love him had done to him between them: myself included. I said gently, 'It's all right. Eat as much as you want, I wouldn't dream of hurting you.' More than ever, I regretted that momentary lapse into fury when I had slapped him. I could have wept, for Kit and for myself: instead I returned to the solace of music, abandoning the tortuous and unsatisfactory foreign fantasia for the songs and dances I, and Francis, loved. My fingers almost of their own accord wove their patterns on the fretboard and gut, and the quiet delicate sounds filled the chamber, merry or melancholy, fast or slow, galliards and pavanes, Dowland and Byrd, 'Britannia' and 'Greensleeves' and 'Light o' Love': and where I could remember the words, I sang.

Go, and catch a falling star,
Get with child a mandrake root,
Tell me, where all past years are,
Or who cleft the Devil's foot,
Teach me to hear mermaids singing,
Or to keep off envy's stinging,
And find
What wind
Serves to advance an honest mind.

Francis had sung that to me, in Oxford. I looked up, and Kit's eyes, blue and intent, dodged away. With dawning hope, I played on, choosing now from the tunes carried in my head the rhymes and songs and rounds and lullabies that had delighted me as a child. My voice grew hoarse, the fingers on my left hand were sore and ridged by continual pressing on the strings, my right hand slowing and fumbling, and my repertoire all but exhausted.

Heppy tapped on the door. The spell broke: Kit retreated once more to the far side of the bed and stared rigidly at the wall. Annoyed, I cried, 'Come in!'

'Sorry, Mistress,' said Heppy, her head coming nervously and disembodied around the door. 'But I reckoned as you'd want this here box, thass got all Master Kit's clothes in that and I reckoned he'd be suffen cowd in that there little shirt and nawthen else.' She dragged in a wooden iron-bound box, like Peg's, and left it by the clothes-press. 'Did he eat that food, then?'

'Yes, he did,' I said, virtually pushing her out of the room, making encouraging optimistic faces at her as I did so. Heppy gave me a grin and a wink in return and shut the door behind her: and I set about the box, talking all the while to myself, and to Kit. 'So this is your box with all your things in it. Aren't you cold after all this time in your nightshirt?'

No reply was given nor, if I was honest with myself, was it expected. Feeling a little foolish, I continued. 'Is this your other suit? It's very nice . . . and your rattle and ball . . . and a hornbook! Do you know any of your letters yet? If you do, you must be very clever, Jasper Sewell didn't learn his till he was five . . .' My voice died away as I lifted it out. The rest of the box was filled with papers, a score or more I saw as I brought them out, and each bore a drawing.

Dominic had been skilled in catching a likeness beyond the common run: under lesser and more fortunate stars he would have made a living at it, but his mother had considered such pursuits beneath the dignity of a gentleman, and had done everything in her power to discourage such foolish pastimes. So Dominic, with his father's connivance, had carried on in secret, and then openly after his mother's death. And here in this chamber were all that was left of his brief, unhappy, anguished existence; his only son, and the proofs of a rare and sensitive talent for portraiture.

They were all of Kit. Dumb, marvelling, I looked through them, laying each one carefully on the floor when I had finished studying it. Our son was depicted in an enormous variety of poses, from the sleeping, bald newborn baby I had so reluctantly deserted in Oxford, to the lively, charming little boy who surely still existed somewhere beneath his new wretchedness: awake, asleep, staring out of the paper or absorbed in some childish task, sometimes several swift sketches on a sheet of the child walking, running, catching a ball or playing with a dog, sometimes one large portrait head, all carefully, beautifully, delicately executed with an economy and accuracy of line and shading that would not have disgraced a Van Dyck.

I had, by deserting Kit so young, deprived myself of the joy and delight of watching him grow and flower, as I had so enviously watched Jasper. Now my dead husband, with these drawings, had given Kit's childhood back to me. Almost overwhelmed with emotion, I sniffed back the tears and stared down at the sheets of paper spread round me: and a great rush of pity, and regret, and grief swept through me. All that tragedy, after all, had not been entirely Dominic's fault: he was not to blame for the fact that his upbringing (and his mother in particular) had accustomed him to getting whatever he wanted, without any thought for others, and without scruples regarding ways and means. He had wanted me, had been promised me, and Francis had been the obstacle which he had carefully removed from his path, as he thought irrevocably. But not as irrevocably as I had believed, because for four months I had thought Francis dead, and when I discovered my mistake it had been too late. And until then I had been quite fond of Dominic, his dash, his overwhelming personality, his charm and his undoubted feeling for me and the child I carried. Easy to remember now those good qualities, as well as the bad, and to regret the fine looks and high spirits that at the age of twenty-eight, had too early been laid into the grave.

The last two drawings were not of Kit. One was the portrait of me as a child, that he had done when I was ten and he had first conceived desire for me: a likeness too faithful for my comfort, seeing now, twelve years later, the bookish, ungracious, self-willed hoyden I had been, and indeed still was. The other was also myself, but drawn sometime during those brief illusory days of our marriage, when I had thought that I might one day come to love him. Like the dress I had worn at my wedding, and never since, the portrait gave me a beauty I did not feel I truly possessed, and yet, like the other, it showed a facet of me, of my personality – large, rather ironic dark eyes, slightly aquiline nose, a generous wilful mouth and small pointed chin, framed in my impossible-to-manage cloudy brown hair.

At some time, someone had ripped the drawing in half. It had been mended, I saw, turning it over and noticing the extra stiffness, by glueing the two severed pieces together on to another sheet of paper, the job done with such care that, save for the additional weight, it was hardly noticeable. I imagined that Dominic must have torn it, but had he also, with that loving precision, put the damage to rights? I did not know, could not guess: all I knew was that, suddenly, the stupid waste and entangled futile hatreds and pointless tragedy of the last five years, for me and for Francis, and Dominic, and Kit, was too much to bear; and I wept.

'Those are my father's,' said Kit's flat, hostile little voice. I started, as guiltily as any chambermaid caught rifling her master's belongings, and hastily smeared the tears from my face. Kit stood before me, barefoot and frowning. 'What are you doing?'

'Just looking at them,' I said. 'They're very good, aren't they? Your father was a marvellous limner.'

'What's a limner?' asked Kit, reluctantly curious. I said, 'Someone who draws or paints pictures of people – usually miniatures, little pictures.'

'Why were you crying?'

To my intense annoyance, I felt myself going red. 'Why does anyone cry? Because I was sad.'

'Why were you sad?' Kit asked. I smiled at him, suddenly consumed with maternal love: for I realized now that his unspeakable behaviour of the last few days had not been typical, but the desperate response of a child whose world had disintegrated into chaos, and who had been bereft of everything and everyone loved and familiar. 'I was thinking of your father.'

'He's dead,' said Kit, with the un-understanding flatness of young children. 'He's gone to Heaven. He said you'd be glad he was dead.' His lip wobbled. 'And Peg said he'd never come back.'

'I'm afraid he won't, chick,' I said, automatically slipping an arm round his stiff little shoulders to cuddle him close. It was a mistake. Kit leapt backwards, tripped, fell and burst into frantic, anguished howls. 'W-want Peg! I w-want to go home!' Any attempt of mine to comfort him brought his fists and feet and teeth into furious combat: in the end, heartbroken and demoralized, I gathered up the drawings, replaced them in the box, and in despair fled the room.

In the Long Gallery was Grainne – all the other able-bodied females probably being in the kitchen preparing for the wedding feast which, I realized with a shock, was now only two days away. As soon as she saw me she rose to her feet and came to greet me. 'You look terrible. How goes it? Not well?'

'No. I thought I was winning, but I keep on making mistakes. He can't bear to be touched, it's a nightmare, I feel so helpless!' I stared miserably at my dearest friend's calm face, silently begging her to provide me with an answer. Grainne shook her head, as always uncannily perceptive. 'No, I said I would not fight your battles for you. But sit with me for a space, while you regain your strength, and tell me what has happened. Kit will come to no harm on his own for a little.'

So we sat in the bay window above the porch, plumping the cushions around us to protect us from the draughts searing through the closed windows, and I gave her a full and detailed account of the events since Kit's arrival. When I had finished, Grainne said nothing for a while, her serene face far away in thought. Then she said slowly, 'I have an idea . . . Hen!'

Her daughter, who had been playing some earnest game with the two dolls that her grandfather had carved for her, looked up. 'Yes, Mammy?'

'Can you come here a minute, and listen very carefully?'

Henrietta put her dolls down, instructing them firmly to be good and not to move, she would be back soon, and trotted over. Grainne sat her down on her lap –

Hen was no lightweight – and spoke seriously. 'Thomazine's little boy Kit has come here, you know that, don't you?'

The neatly-coifed head nodded solemnly, and the abundant fiery ringlets bobbed up and down on Hen's plump shoulders. 'Yes, and Jasper says he's a naughty boy!'

'I don't know where Jasper got that idea, but it's not true. Poor Kit's father has died, and he's had to come here all on his own, where he's never been before, and he's very unhappy and lonely and frightened.'

'Poor Kit,' said Henrietta anxiously. Her heart was warm, generous and unstintingly kind; and on this, I realized, Grainne was staking Kit's happiness. 'Yes,' she said, 'poor Kit. Now tell me, pet, do you think you could make friends with him and play with him? Be nice to him and make him welcome? Could you do that, do you think?'

Henrietta gave her mother a beaming, sunny smile. 'Ooh, yes, yes.'

'Good girl, I knew you would. Now remember, he's very unhappy, and he may not want you there at first, so don't worry if he's rude to you—'

'An' if he hits me I shall hit him back!' said Hen stoutly. She had been reared in Jasper's nimble shadow, and fully expected to have to stand up for herself in male company. 'But don't hit him too hard,' I said, forcing a light-hearted note into my voice. 'He's a lot smaller than you, even if you are nearly the same age.'

'I'll show him 'Mona and 'Phelia,' said Hen, referring to her dolls: she had caught from Lucy the habit of bestowing literary names. And with an enthusiastic wriggle she slid off Grainne's knees and rushed over to collect them.

'She'll be all right,' said Grainne, catching my dubious eye. 'She has all the maternal feelings of a broody fowl, and her two months short of her fifth birthday. Where everyone else has tried and failed, she may succeed. Hen!'

The little girl scampered over, trim and delightful in her green linsey-woolsey dress, with apron and pinner and neckerchief and coif all as crisply new and snowy white as if she had just changed to sit for her portrait, and had not been all day wearing them. 'Yes, Mammy?'

Grainne gave her a kiss on one round rosy freckled cheek. 'Just remember, pet, be nice to him, even if he isn't nice to you.'

'I will,' said Hen, and ran down the Gallery to my chamber. Grainne and I exchanged hopeful glances and after the little girl had shut the door behind her, tiptoed up to it and listened.

'Hullo,' said Hen's solemn, rather breathy voice. 'Are you Kit? I'm Hen.'

No reply.

'I've come to play with you,' Hen explained, and then, her curiosity getting the better of her, added, 'Why are you wearing a nightshirt? Aren't you cold?'

'Yes,' came Kit's flat monosyllable.

'Well, all your clothes are here,' said Hen. 'Why don't you put them on? You *are* silly!'

A muffled protest from Kit: then Henrietta said, '*I'll* help you. I can dress myself, I can. Can't you? How old are you?'

'Four and a half,' said Kit, overstating it somewhat.

'Oh well,' said Hen, 'I'm five, nearly. Come on, I'll help dress you.'

There followed a prolonged and hilarious interlude in which Hen upbraided, cajoled and helped Kit into his clothes. I would have given anything to see it, but was reduced to crouching outside the door, my hand stuffed into my mouth to prevent open laughter. Nor was Grainne more solemn, as she listened helplessly to her small daughter organizing Kit.

'Do you put your drawers on first? Go on, you do it, silly!'

'Don't call me silly.'

'Well, put them on then, and I won't. Where are your breeches?'

'Don't know.'

'Well, let's look. Oh, here they are. You can put them on. There, isn't it easy! Who dressed you before?'

'P-Peg.'

'Who's she?'

'She w-was my n-nurse, but she's g-gone.'

'Well, don't start crying,' said Hen, and added a piece of wisdom gleaned from Joan. 'Thass no use a-cryin' over spilt milk. Is Rose going to be your nurse as well as Hugh's?'

'I don't know.'

'Well, you've got to have *someone* to look after you,' said Hen. 'P'rhaps your Mammy will. My Mammy looks after me. Or p'rhaps *I* can look after you. Would you like that?'

A noncommittal grunt from poor Kit, who was obviously squirming.

'Well, your Mammy will do it I expect, I like your Mammy, she's nice, she sings songs and tells long, long, long stories and I know she's going to like looking after you 'cos she said so.'

'I don't want her to look after me.'

'What? You don't want your Mammy?' Hen sounded quite shocked. 'Why ever not? I'd like her to look after *me*. You *are* silly!'

'I'm NOT silly!' Kit shouted.

'Yes, you ARE!'

'No, I'm NOT!'

'Yes, you are, you don't like your Mammy and that's the silliest thing I *ever* heard – OW!'

'Serves you right!'

'You're horrible,' Hen cried indignantly, 'and I'm going to hit you back, so there!'

'Don't warn him, do it,' Grainne spluttered behind her hand. There was a smacking sound of hand meeting flesh, quickly repeated, and Hen gave a yelp of pain and began to whimper. There was a pause, and then Kit's voice, low and ashamed, said briefly, 'Sorry. I didn't mean to.'

'You did, you hit me hard!'

'I didn't mean to,' Kit repeated miserably. 'I won't hit you again, promise.'

'Promise?' Hen's voice was full of suspicion.

'Promise.'

'Then we can be friends,' said Hen, abruptly restored to normality. 'Now let's put your shirt on.'

'I'll do it.'

'It's the wrong way round,' said Hen after a while, a trace of satisfaction in her voice.

'Oh. Is it? Could,' asked Kit reluctantly, 'could you do it? Please?'

'Course I will. Turn round, thass better.' Like Hugh's, Hen's voice was at times definitely Suffolk-flavoured. 'Now your doublet.'

'I *can* do that,' Kit said firmly, and there was a pause as he evidently struggled with buttons and hooks.

'It's done up wrong,' Hen remarked.

'Oh, shut up, silly!'

'You promised!'

'Sorry. I'll do it, let me do it.'

'All right. Thass better.' A critical pause. 'You look nice,' said Hen assessingly. 'I like your suit. Hugh doesn't wear breeches yet, but he's only three. Are you going to show your Mammy? Go on, show her how nice you look.'

'Don't want to.'

'Oh, go on, please!'

Pause. 'Oh, all right then,' said Kit ungraciously. Grainne and I fled noiselessly back to our windowseat, settling down just as the door opened and Hen propelled the hapless Kit, some three or four inches smaller, towards us. 'Look, Mammy, we've done it all by ourselves!'

I forbore to laugh. My son wore doublet and breeches and shoes, without cuffs, collar or stockings, his hair tangled spikily round his head and the buttons all at odds, but I smiled at him. 'You do look nice, Kit. Will you come and sit with me?'

'Yes, and you can sing us a song,' Hen demanded, 'please sing a song, Aunt Thomazine!'

'Yes, I will, if you can get my lute for me, Kit? Be *very* careful with it, it's so easily broken. Can you do it?'

For a moment hostility struggled with eagerness on the small, beautiful, childish face, and then subsided. 'Yes, Mammy,' he said, and trotted seriously off to the chamber where he had spent so many unhappy hours. A moment later, as Grainne and I stared at each other in growing hope, he returned much more slowly and carefully, carrying the precious lute cradled in his arms.

'Thank you very much, that was most carefully done,' I told him, and was rewarded by the faintest shy glimmer of a smile in response. I tuned the instrument, and Hen and Kit sat on the cushions, one each side of me, with Grainne at the other end.

Music, as I had guessed, was the key to Kit's allegiance: in that at least he took after me, his father having been all but tone-deaf. Hen and I had turned the key between us: now, as we sang songs and catches and my sore, weary fingers laboured on the strings, I saw the guards and defences come down one by one from his face, and his wide, vivid blue eyes at last eager and involved and unafraid. With Hen, encouraged by Grainne, he joined in the singing, beating time with his heels on the wooden panelling under the seat to all the old childhood favourites:

We be soldiers three,
Pardonnez-moi, je vous en prie,
Lately come forth of the Low Country,
With never a penny of money,
Fa la la la lantido dilly.

'We used to sing that on our way home from the Low Countries, your father and Ned Heron and I,' said Grainne to Hen, who, although she had never known her father, had a wide acquaintance with him through her mother's stories. 'And it was true: not only did we have hardly a penny to our names, but we spoke French quite as badly.'

'What's French?' asked Kit.

'It's what they speak in France,' Grainne told him. 'We talk in English, French people speak French, Dutch people from the Low Countries speak Dutch. Would you like another song, you two, or your dinners?'

'Dinner,' said Hen decidedly. ''Nother song, please, Mammy,' Kit said. And as a reward for his politeness, my smile for him alone, I played one last tune.

I'll sing you one O
  Green grow the rushes O.
What is your one O?
  One is one and all alone
  And ever more shall be so.

As I sang the familiar song with its strange words, the others joined in, and Lucy came slipping silently along the Gallery towards us: and Kit shuffled along the windowseat until his body touched mine. It was a small movement, but a highly significant one, as I saw from Grainne's suddenly delighted face. Now at last, after two days of struggle, the door lay open to his heart and allegiance.

Chapter 7

Stones against the wind

Rebellion lay in his way, and he found it.
(Shakespeare, *Henry IV Part I*)

It was, of course, not so simple as it appeared: many months of conflict lay ahead, tantrums and bad behaviour and disobedience, for Kit was not in the least accustomed to being thwarted in any way, and objected violently when I did so. But though there might be screams and tears and stamped feet and beating fists, the foundations of our newborn relationship grew daily more solid. I built up a new world to replace the one he had lost so abruptly; meals, games, visits to the Sewells or to Rushbrooke, elementary lessons with the hornbook, songs and riddles and first rides on Jasper's now outgrown shaggy garron. I had never before had sole charge of any child, but now, so much importance did I attach to our burgeoning attachment, I left Rose to tend Hugh and assumed the care of Kit myself.

This, of course, caused some comment in the household: even Mary, who felt for Hugh all the maternal love dormant with her other, older children, had engaged Rose to look after him. But I had never had much concern for what other people might think of me, and besides, I had Grainne's example to follow. And in the frenzy of preparation for Meraud and Jamie's wedding, no one had much time to remonstrate with me for my unconventional behaviour.

As befitted the standing and position of those involved, it was a lavish and spectacular feast, grander by far than my cramped, hurried marriage to Dominic in Oxford in time of war. Meraud's dress, cornflower silk and gorgeous gold and silver lacing, made her look as magnificent and lovely as a princess in a romance –

or so said Lucy – and Jamie was untypically resplendent in crimson and green. There were all the usual bridal trappings: favours, garters, gloves, musicians, a pageboy – Jasper performing with his usual aplomb the same duty he had carried off so well at my wedding – and, of course, as many guests as the happy couple could think of. Despite the bad winter weather, there were over a hundred: Blagges, Gages, Sewells, Jermyns, Mannocks and even a Barnadiston or two, by virtue of their acquaintance with Richard Trevelyan, and despite their preoccupation with running the county for the Parliament.

There were guests more welcome to some of us, from further afield than Suffolk. The Widow Gooch arrived on her old white cob, having made the journey from Oxford alone: being, as she pointed out, too poor, too old and too ugly to attract the attention of any footpad or thief. And she brought with her a letter for Lucy from Daniel Ashley, still part of the Oxford garrison.

Most of this epistle Lucy, blushing fiercely, refused to divulge, although it was obvious that her hopes were in no way dashed: but there was an item of news towards the end of it that was of great interest to many of us, and in particular to me. Lucy read it aloud to me when we were alone together.

I trust you are still concerned to know the where-abouts of our mutual friend in Whalley's Regiment. He has been made a corporal and, as I discovered, somewhat to my alarm, would have been elected one of their Agitators had he not been such a newcomer to the Regiment, and therefore not so much to be trusted as some. I had some speech with him once by Newmarket this summer last when his Regiment was with the King, and I sought him out to discover for your sake, and your friends', how he did. He said little, but I collect that he is well, and though known for a very convinced and thorough Leveller ('another Lilburne', as said his Captain), yet I would not say he is totally content, though he seemed to profess little interest in the doings of his friends, and when I asked him if there was any prospect of his leaving the Army replied most brusquely, 'None at present'. Since that time, I have not seen him, my place being with my Regiment in Oxford, and his being (up until His Majesty's escape last month) with the King, and so have no further tidings.

That was all the news I had, and more than I had expected. I was still none the wiser as to the reasons for his initial presence in Whalley's Regiment, and still less his motive for staying there. But the penalty for desertion was death, as was common knowledge, and besides that powerful deterrent there would be the lure of political activity, of the chance to influence the course of history. All my old doubts about the truth of his love for me rose willy-nilly to the surface of my thoughts. Surely, a way could be found to come to me, if he *really* wished it? I had felt as sure of him as I was sure of the firmness of rock and yet, after two years with no direct word from him, that certainty began to seen more and more like some marshlight trickery, despite all Lucy and Grainne's assurances to the contrary. Marooned amongst the light-hearted, happy atmosphere of the wedding preparations, I fell into such a despond of longing and foreboding that not even Mistress Gooch's scathing comments could bring me out.

To add to my unhappy thoughts, I had been some-what astounded to learn that Charles Lawrence had also been invited to the wedding, and not at all surprised to discover that he had declined such a crassly insensitive offer. When I thought of how Meraud had led him on to believe it was he she truly loved, and then once out of reach jilted him for someone else with better prospects, my choler rose: for I liked Charles, his cheer-fulness and friendly manner and even his bad jokes and excruciating puns, and it angered me that such an honest, pleasant person should be treated so badly. I hoped fervently that his disillusionment had been complete and that he would not live out a lonely, bitter life for her sake, but start searching for happiness elsewhere. It might be hard to find anyone as lovely as Meraud, I thought, as she paced down from the altar in all her splendour, Jamie's arm firmly trapped in hers: but he would have no difficulty at all in marrying someone nicer.

No question of it, Goldhayes was better suited to such festivities than the little house in Pennyfarthing Street. The high, lovely rooms echoed to music and talk and laughter: there was dancing in the Hall, and in the Dining-Hall a vast selection of Monsieur Harcourt's wonderful food, the centrepiece of the table being a model in carved and moulded coloured sugar of Goldhayes itself, with marchpane ducks on a violently indigo-coloured moat. My misery lifted at the prompting of this large and merry company, and despite my sorrow about Francis, and my so-recent widowhood, I found myself able, to my surprise, to defy convention and enjoy it all. I danced with Tom Hervey, and Jamie, and Edward Gage who was shortly to marry Tom's older sister Mary, and was aware from their freer banter, and especially the interest in John Snelling's mournful spaniel's face, that I was now a widow, young and attractive still, with some few possessions to my name and my son's, and able to bestow my favours where I wished, without constriction of law or convention. I was free, for the first time in my life, to wed where I chose: and suddenly, amidst all the laughter and joy, I felt miserably lonely for lack of Francis, who alone could share my heart and soul. I watched enviously the frenetic gaiety as the happy couple, Jamie flushed, elated and embarrassed, Meraud cool and artful and smiling, were bedded with the usual ceremony and bawdy jokes and lewd good-luck wishes. Then we retreated downstairs to continue feasting and drinking and dancing, leaving Jamie to enjoy his spoils in peace. I allowed myself to wonder, briefly and improperly, how his naïve chivalrous love and Meraud's sophisticated, almost patronizing, affection would deal together in bed, and then, before I could call a halt, my treacherous imagination swept me on, to Francis, and the 'right true end of love', of which we had up till now been cheated, and which seemed to be an impossible dream.

But longing did no good: wishing and waiting would not bring him to me, for now in the depths of winter a renewal of war seemed more and more likely, and the threat of it loomed, a dark and menacing cloud, upon the horizon of the coming year. The debates in Putney Church, where the Agitators from the New Model Army had attempted in vain to persuade their superior officers to adopt the Leveller principles and manifesto, had broken up in the second week of November, and the King had escaped from custody at Hampton Court. He was now at Carisbrooke on the Isle of Wight, as we learned afterwards, arranging invasion with the Scots while still cheerfully negotiating with the Parliament. His Majesty King Charles was nothing if not devious, as the history of the last ten years had amply shown, and Parliament, not unnaturally goaded beyond endurance, at last voted to deal no longer with one who, Royal or no, was so obviously not to be trusted. There was a great deal of unrest in Suffolk that winter – the usual trouble on Christmas Day, Puritan shopkeepers in Bury resolutely staying open, Royalist sympathizers just as determined to close them. There were fears for the King's safety: rumours had it that he had fled Hampton Court so precipitately to avoid assassination, and it was positively asserted that he was being kept closer than a common criminal at Carisbrooke. In Bury, despite the soldiers quartered there, someone built a bonfire, and crowds milled around it crying, 'For God and King Charles!' Similar scenes were reported from other towns in Suffolk, Essex and even in London, where the apprentices had crept out on Christmas morning and decorated the streets with the forbidden, pagan holly and ivy.

Someone did the same in the church at Bradfield Tye: the parson, highly scandalized, ordered it to be ripped down and thrown away at once, but got little support from Goldhayes save from Richard Trevelyan, who had looked on with a somewhat jaundiced eye when his wife, assisted by the rest of the household, decked the halls with boughs of holly and greenery, and made merry with dancing, feasting and the Lord of Misrule. The Widow stayed to enjoy these celebrations and then reluctantly departed, bearing the twentieth effort of a letter from Lucy to Dan, and my private word-of-mouth request to him to find out all he could of Francis, and to send him my love.

After her departure the house relapsed into its quiet, uneventful routine, and I occupied myself with Kit; until one day at the beginning of March, when Heppy came to me as I played with Hugh and my son in the Long Gallery, tossing a woollen ball between us. There were many shrieks of dismay as it bounced through their clutching fingers and slipped across the floor: Kit, his mother's true child, being particularly enraged at his lack of skill. Into this domestic scene Heppy intruded, her eyes wide with curiosity. 'Mistress Thomazine! There's a gentleman downstair, in the Arras Parlour I put him, asking for you, come a long way he hev, and he talk suffen funny, like, and he didn't give no name.'

'Asking for me?' I said, puzzled. Hugh, who had an overwhelming sense of fun, chose that moment to hurl the ball at me, and burst into howls of delighted merriment when I failed to catch it. 'I've got to see a visitor,' I told the children, and with a glance down the Gallery at Mary, dozing comfortably in a well-cushioned chair by one of the blazing fires, added maliciously, 'Why don't you go and ask your mother if she'll play with you instead, Hugh? I'm sure she will . . .' As the two boys, with great glee, hurtled noisily down towards the unsuspecting Mary, I made good my escape, Heppy in tow. Still puzzled, I said, "What does he look like, Heppy?"

Heppy sounded just as bewildered. 'Well, that seem funny, Mistress, but I doon't rightly know. He wear this great felt hat, Mistress, pulled right down over his face so I coon't see nawthen of it, hardly, and a cloak what sweps the floor, like, and all I can really tell you is that he's *big*.'

'You mean tall?'

'That as well, Mistress, but *big* too.'

I had not the faintest notion who this could be, and was wondering, as Heppy announced me to the visitor, if this was not some mistake, or a practical joke of the kind which young Henry Jermyn liked so much: or even something more sinister behind this stranger, standing so tall and shrouded in his black cloak and hat against the shabby faded backdrop of the tapestries. And then, as Heppy shut the door behind her, he turned towards me, smiling, took off his hat and bowed.

'Malise!' I cried, utterly delighted, and with all the old childish impulsiveness I thought I had long ago shed, rushed to hug him. 'Oh, Malise, how wonderful to see you, I had no idea, why didn't you *say?* Heppy! Heppy!'

Heppy's face appeared round the door with suspicious speed. I told her to bring beer and food, and then turned back to my cousin, who was regarding me with the oddly shy, diffident smile I knew so well, and found so endearing. 'Oh, take off your cloak – you look like a villain out of one of Lucy's plays – I thought it might be my wicked past catching up with me, but I never dreamt . . . Where have you come from? Have you come to stay? Have you seen Grainne?'

His face changed: I realized with a flash of insight why he had come here, and not directly to the Home Farm. 'Well, Thomazine, that's just it . . . I havena seen her, I rode past the wee house like a moss-trooper caught in daylight, for I didna ha' the courage tae gae in. Tell me, Thomazine, tell me true, will . . . will she be glad tae see me?'

I took his big, clumsy hands in mine, smiling. 'Oh,

Malise, she'll be more than glad, she'll be transformed. You don't know how she has missed you, and worried about you, and prayed for you . . . Francis said you were safe, after Philliphaugh, and that was the last we ever heard.'

'I'm gey sorry,' said poor Malise, apology and relief and happiness all struggling in his voice. 'I havena had much opportunity tae sit and compose a letter, ye ken . . . Are ye *sure?*'

'Of course I'm sure,' I said with some exasperation. 'I think I know her better than most, and though she isn't one to go wailing her woes to everyone, without you these last years, she's . . . like a, I don't know, like a flower out of water.'

Heppy at this point came scurrying in haste with beer, rather spilt, and a platter of cold meats and a still-steaming pigeon pie, doubtless originally intended for our supper. I told her not to mention my visitor to the rest of the family at present, for I wanted this chance of a private talk before any larger welcome. When she had gone, we fell to exchanging our news. As he ate, I recounted briefly the tale of our journey south to Oxford and thence to Suffolk, and the small news we had had of Francis.

'And yon's a strange thing,' said Malise. 'Forced or no', never to have written nor sent word to you, after all he'd said to you . . . strange, very. You must miss him very much?'

His gentle sympathy made the tears come to my eyes. I glanced bleakly out of the window at the draggled Courtyard Garden alive with sparrows sheltering from the winter cold. 'Oh, I do, of course I do, and sometimes I get so tired of waiting, of longing, of worrying how deep he's got himself enmeshed in politics, and if he really loves me after all, and if I'll ever see him again . . .' To avoid the embarrassment of breaking down altogether, I added, 'But that's enough of us. Tell me what's happened to you, these two long years and more?'

There was not much to tell then, for he would, so he said, leave the story of Montrose's wonderful year of victories till all were gathered to hear it: 'For yon's a long tale, even on a winter's night.' But it gave me time to shake myself back into my usual composure, while he related how, after Philliphaugh, he had returned with Montrose to the Highlands, to rebuild the army; a task thwarted in the end by the petty animosity, pride and obstructiveness of the Gordon family, Huntly in particular, and the single-mindedness of Alastair Macdonnell's pursuit of his feud with the Campbells. The old days, when luck had been his dancing-partner, gracing all he did, were gone; but Montrose did not give up the hopeless struggle until expressly ordered to do so by the King. The remains of the army were disbanded, the soldiers free, by arrangement with the Scots authorities, to return unmolested to their own homes, although many begged to continue the fight. Only Montrose, Crawford and Sir John Hurry had been denied pardon, and had perforce to go into exile. The glorious dream was over, two years after its beginning.

So Malise had returned to Catholm, to make himself, at his father's and grandmother's behest, as inconspicuous as possible and involve himself in the work of the farm. But after the momentous events of the past two years, it had obviously been difficult for him to settle back into cosy domesticity. Nor, I suspected, had his relations with his elder brother been easy, for Gib had always treated Malise with that patronizing mixture of contempt and affection which must have been particularly difficult to tolerate after the time spent in Montrose's heady company. All efforts by Sandy to encourage his elder son into marriage and the production of an heir had failed; Gib was more than fond of women, but most reluctant to cramp his style with a wife. So Sandy had turned to Malise, at first with what passed in him for subtlety, later more openly and mentioning the names of some eligible local girls. Then Malise, utterly surprising his unperceptive sire (but not his grandmother), had revealed that his heart was irrevocably assigned elsewhere.

'I dinna ken what he thought I'd committed mysel' to,' Malise told me, grinning reminiscently, 'but he was verra relieved when I said it was Grainne. Mostlike he'd thought I'd handfasted wi' some Armstrong slut, so an Irish widow wi' twa bairns was a pleasant surprise.'

After this conversation, it had been understood that Malise would journey south to claim his bride, though not necessarily to bring her straight back to Catholm: once having escaped from Gib, I could well appreciate that Malise would be in no hurry to return. And so in February he had set out: and as he travelled further and further south, and beheld the richness of the country, became increasingly beset with doubts, until now, staring in forlorn appreciation at the unthinking comforts of Goldhayes, it was plain he was wondering whether Grainne would ever leave this gentle climate and life of luxury for the hardships of Catholm.

'Go now,' I told him. 'Go and see her now. If she is all you think – and I *know* she is, none better – she will fall with delight into your arms and go with you wherever you will, the children as well. But there's no reason why you cannot both stay here, for Sandy can obviously manage well enough with just Gib to help him, whereas John Sewell is not so young as he was, and has been muttering in Richard Trevelyan's ear for some time about his need for an assistant. He'll doubtless welcome you in that role, if you would like it, and as for Grainne, I know you have no need to worry at all. I *know* her, I *know* she loves you. Don't worry, I'll come with you, if you like, and give you moral support.'

But that was not to be, for Lucy took a hand in her usual fashion, and would brook no argument. I took Malise above-stairs to introduce him to those members of the family who were present, and my cousin, who of course knew the whole story, said at once, 'Oh, how marvellous! Oh, Cousin Malise, she'll be so pleased to see you!'

Eyeing Mary, who had no great affection for Grainne, with some misgiving, I said, 'We were just going down to the Home Farm to see her.'

'Oh no, you won't,' said Lucy, giving me a conspiratorial wink the spit of her brother Jamie's. 'For a start, you know what Joan's like, she'd have her ear pressed tight to the keyhole all through their reunion and half the village would know every detail before an hour was out.'

'Speak for yourself,' I said, a trifle tartly, for Lucy's inability to keep a secret was proverbial. She only grinned at Malise. 'I hope you're not shocked at us, Cousin. We always behave like this, I'm afraid. And for a second reason, you can't lodge there, there isn't room, but Joan will try and fit you in willy-nilly if you show your face. It'd be far better, and much more seemly, if you stay here and we bring Grainne up to see you.'

'And since when have you been so concerned with the proprieties, Mistress Lucy?' I queried. 'But yes, I suppose that is a better plan, really. Joan is John Sewell's housekeeper, Malise, and she's an inveterate gossip – well-meaning but infuriating. You'd have no peace or privacy at all.'

'Then we must find a way to ask her over here,' said Lucy, taking the bemused look on poor Malise's face to be agreement. 'And wouldn't it be fun if she didn't know who was waiting! I know, we can send the children over and they can ask Hen and Jasper to come as well.'

'It's bound to be raining,' I objected, glad that Mary, once the initial greetings were over, had returned to her embroidery more or less out of earshot. Lucy glanced cursorily out of the window. 'No, it isn't. And the sun's out. Kit! Hugh!'

The two little boys ran over. 'Yes, Cousin Lucy?' my son said, grinning at her, breathless and expectant. It had been a good day today, no tantrums, and a delightful willingness in everything he did. It was not always so, and I had a motley collection of bruises on arms and shins to prove it; but little by little, an improvement was becoming more evident. Lucy crouched down to their level, an arm across each child's shoulder. 'Now this is a secret, you two, a sort of game. Can you go down to the Home Farm, and ask Mistress Sewell and Jasper and Hen to come up here for supper as soon as may be. Say it's very important, but don't say *why*, don't tell her about Cousin Malise at all.'

'Why not?' Kit objected, puzzled.

''Cause it's a surprise, of course,' Hugh said with his deep unbabyish chuckle. Lucy hugged him. 'Yes, Hugh, it's a surprise, so don't breathe a word about him, either of you, all right? Go along now, Heppy will let you out of the front door.'

The three of us sat in the window-seat above the porch to wait and talk. The tiny figures of the children, both the same height, one blonde and sturdy and still in petticoats, the other slender and dark and black-clad, scampered down the drive and out of our sight. Mary came over and dutifully joined the conversation: Lucy, with many infuriating nudges and coy glances, managed to convey the reason for the children's errand without stating it in so many words. I could see Malise, now thoroughly ill-at-ease in this frothy feminine company, growing more embarrassed by the minute, and attempted to change the subject by asking about the people he had left behind at Catholm, and about the state of affairs now in Scotland.

All at Catholm, from Malise's immediate family to the villainous ancient shepherd, Archie, were very well; which was more than could be said for Scotland. 'There's some talk now of an agreement the King is supposed to have made wi' Argyll, though how he could thole tae deal wi' that sanctimonious de'il I canna think.'

'What agreement?' I asked, for this was the first I had heard of it, and the others also showed some interest. Malise glanced round the empty Gallery, but lowered his voice nevertheless. 'It's no' generally known yet, ye ken, but twa-three months ago the King agreed tae make England a Presbyterian country, and stamp on the Sectaries. In return, Hamilton and Lauderdale ha' promised, they say, tae invade England.'

So it was all to do again. A chill weight sunk on my heart: I looked round at the other two, and saw my own dismay on their faces. 'Oh, no!' cried Lucy: and her mother said wearily, 'Will they never learn?'

'It'll please Jamie, anyway,' I said wryly. 'He's been aflame for a fight with the Parliament ever since '42, and I don't think he's ever reconciled himself to the fact that he wasn't old enough to take up arms till the war was over.'

'He worries me, you know,' Lucy said, a note of anxiety in her voice. 'Have you noticed, he's taken to visiting Rushbrooke so much more often than he used to, and I know Mistress Rebecca gets secret letters from her husband in France. And he goes to the Angel in Bury every market day and the town's been very restive ever since the trouble at Christmas, even if there are soldiers quartered there ... I do hope he isn't getting himself involved in something foolish.'

I had not previously taken much notice of this change in Jamie's rather mundane habits; now, knowing him as I did, I had a sudden conviction that 'involved in something foolish' would probably be an understatement to say the least. Jamie was a Heron, the last male member of his family left at Goldhayes, and as such could command wealth, contacts, arms, and the loyalty of the trained ex-soldiers who had fought in Rupert's Horse with Simon. Any local plotters of rebellion would certainly welcome him for those reasons, green boy or no.

Mary was saying that of course he would not run himself into any danger, not three months after his wedding, but I caught Lucy's eye and shook my head slightly: she cast her glance heavenwards in exasperation with her young brother. If all our misgivings were true, then perhaps Meraud did not have him on such a tight leash of adoration as I had thought.

'Look,' said Malise suddenly, 'there are Kit and

Hugh.' And sure enough, round the bend in the drive trotted my child and Mary's, still on amicable terms. It was lucky that Hugh was such a good-natured infant, who never bore grudges or resentment, for since his first violent acquaintance with Kit he had frequently been on the receiving end of my son's bad temper, when as often as not he took out his rage and frustration with me or another adult, on his hapless young cousin. But Hugh put up with it cheerfully, as did Hen, now coming into sight pelting at full speed behind them, red curls bouncing. I saw Malise's face suddenly curve into an affectionate smile. 'The wee lass has grown!'

'You wait till you see Jasper,' Lucy told him. 'There he is, with his dog, see?'

Jasper was three weeks short of his ninth birthday, and had grown tall and graceful and athletic; still, though, with the endearing mixture of seriousness and exuberance, enthusiasm and good manners, childish humour, and that sometimes astonishing and unanswerable style of argument. With him trotted Bran, his two-year-old brown-and-white dog, who being a bitch was far more amenable to instruction than poor Drake had ever been; although there were occasions when, in Joan's words, 'There's none so deaf as won't hear.' Now, however, she kept obediently close to his heels, and cast never a glance at the five half-tame deer, four does and a yearling, grazing twenty yards away in the park.

'A grand wee lad, he was,' Malise said. 'I trust he hasna changed?'

'He's just grown up a bit,' I said. 'But he's still the same old Jasper, even if he does try to impress you with his Latin.' In preparation for going to Bury Grammar School, probably in two years' time, his lively brain was being harnessed by the ancient Dr Davis, the family chaplain who had taught me, Lucy and her brothers long ago, and lingered on in spite of his growing infirmities.

'And there's Grainne,' said Lucy, eyeing Malise with the coy, knowing expression she had more than once used on me and Francis. I felt a twinge of embarrassment for the unfortunate, shy Malise, forced to do his courting under the beady and curious eyes of his cousins. I glared meaningfully at her and said, 'Let's get Heppy to show her into the Arras Parlour, and then Malise can greet her there.'

It was Lucy's turn to be swept along by someone else's plans: despite her crestfallen looks, I summoned Heppy and issued my instructions. Malise looked as if a weight had fallen off his back. Below us, Grainne crossed the drawbridge over the moat, drawing her old wine-red cloak round her against a gust of wind, and tendrils of her long, straight, unfashionable black hair floated across her face. Malise's big-boned, freckled hands clenched: then he turned from the window and walked along the Gallery to the head of the stairs. In a few moments Heppy's voice could be heard disembodiedly issuing from below in a stage-whisper. 'Thass all clear now, Mistress Thomazine, I've put Mistress Sewell in the Arras Parlour like you said.' Then feet came scuttering up the stairs, accompanied by Hugh's deep giggle and Hen's fat merry laugh, and the children arrived in a rush.

Hen did not remember Malise: she had only been two when we left Catholm. But Jasper stopped half-way up the stairs, his eyes widening in amazement, and then hurtled the rest of the way, Bran bouncing with him. 'Master Graham! It *is* Master Graham, isn't it? So that's what it was all about!' Remembering his manners, he bowed elaborately on the top step, and Malise said, 'Aye, that's Mistress Lucy's idea, to give you and your mother a wee surprise.'

'And you've come from Scotland? Did you get away all right after that battle? Bran, sit! Hen, get her to sit, could you? No, not like that, you sawny kite, press hard on her rump!'

The unfortunate Bran yelped and sat abruptly, with Hen perched amply on top of her. Malise grinned. 'Your mother mustn't be kept waiting. I'll talk to ye later, perhaps we can go riding and you can show me the park.' And he made his escape, thundering down the stairs with a heedless vigour that made me, mindful of his accident-prone past, fear briefly for his safety and that of the staircase.

Lucy grinned happily. 'So that's Malise! I like him, don't you? Strange how he has red hair when Henry had as well, though it's a different sort of red, of course. Oh, I'd love to see her face when she sees he's come for her at last,' she added wistfully. My sensibilities already somewhat shredded by her behaviour earlier, I said, rather more nastily than I intended, 'I don't think you've any imagination at all! Couldn't you *see* how embarrassed he was at the thought of having to greet the woman he loves under your beady eyes after three years' separation? Can't you respect anyone's privacy? Honestly, Lucy, I think if it wasn't for me you'd be down there now peering through the keyhole, just like you said Joan would do!'

Lucy's blue eyes stared aghast at me. Then, unexpectedly, she burst into tears, floods of them, and her hopeless, despairing sobs carried along the Gallery to Mary and the children. Already bitterly regretting my hasty words, I hugged her and poured out my inadequate apologies into her unheeding ears. It was obvious what she was really crying for, but Dan Ashley was a hundred miles away in Oxford, and out of her reach. Damn the man, I thought angrily, I wish he'd either send for her and marry her or gently disengage himself altogether and cease keeping her on a string of five years' hope. I prayed the Widow had put him right on her return, and not minced her words.

Lucy calmed down eventually: we apologized profusely to each other, she for her tears, I for my unpleasantness, and then joined the others in the Gallery. Just at that moment, Jamie returned from one of his Rushbrooke visits, and with my new insight I listened intently to his conversation with us and with Meraud, who had just joined us and especially to those elaborately casual explanations of his visit. ('Just thought I'd go over and see Martin ffolkes,' – the young steward and the man in charge at Rushbrooke during Thomas Jermyn's absence in France – 'I wanted to ask his advice about something.') Explanations of a sort I had heard before, and which now that I listened with more than half an ear, did not ring very true.

Before I could speculate further, Grainne and Malise appeared in the Gallery, both smiling and happy, but uncommunicative. Jamie and Meraud were introduced, and then there was a good deal of gossip and small-talk about friends and relations until Richard came in and supper was announced. After that meal we returned to the Gallery, now fitfully candlelit, to sit around the comforting warmth of the fire, the children and dogs sprawled sleepily at our feet, and to hear Malise softly, shyly, hesitantly, tell as he had promised the story of the *annus mirabilis*, Montrose's splendid glittering year of victories against all odds and reason and logic, and in which he and Francis had shared and fought, and ultimately lost. Now those few thousand men who had also taken part were scattered, many of the Irish dead and Nat Gordon and other leaders executed or murdered in cold blood: Montrose himself was in Paris, at the French court of Queen Henrietta Maria, and many of his closest friends with him: and nearer to us, Francis with Whalley's House, quartered somewhere in the south-western part of the country. The dream had died in betrayal, futility, feud: but the spell of it lingered on, that chill dark windy March night, until ten o'clock and more, as the tale drew to its close.

The children were woken – except for Jasper, who had been intent on Malise's words throughout – and given a nightcap of hot milk before being taken off to bed. I said goodnight to Grainne as she left with her weary offspring, and then went off to attend to Kit.

'By the way,' said Richard, as I rejoined everyone at the fireside, 'I saw Lady Penelope in Bury this afternoon.'

Jamie groaned. Meraud frowned at him, for such an

important local figure should, in her view, be referred to with more respect. Lucy said, 'Oh, no, *not* another bowls match!'

'No,' said Richard, and he grinned suddenly with a humour I had rarely seen in him. 'No, not one of those for some time, I fancy. She's at her wit's end, so she told me, for her green has been invaded by moles!'

The laughter was long, loud and appreciative. 'She was desperate to know if any of our gardeners had experience in dealing with them, so I said I'd send Old Wat over tomorrow, if we can hoist him on a horse: his rheumatism goes from bad to worse. But the significant part of this tale is that young Henry Jermyn came over with his mother and a couple of sisters the day before the first molehill appeared. I didn't say as much to Her Ladyship, but I wouldn't be surprised if he proved to be at the bottom of this.'

Young Henry was just eleven, and as lively an imp of mischief as was ever found outside Hell. His practical jokes ranged from the harmless but infuriating (glueing one of his sisters' dolls to the floor), through the wasteful (vinegar carefully poured into a half-empty hogshead of wine), to the downright dangerous, when he had stuck a thorn into one of the Rushbrooke saddles so that anyone mounting a horse wearing it would drive the point into the horse's skin. Fortunately the victim of this particular prank had been Henry himself, having forgotten which saddle he had doctored: and he had escaped without any broken bones. But despite this accident, and his exasperated mother's frequent and increasingly severe punishments, his enthusiasm for mischief had hardly been diminished. Introducing moles to Lady Penelope's precious bowling-green at Hengrave was, as Richard had implied, just the sort of thing he would do.

'I'll mention it to Mistress Rebecca when I next go over,' said Jamie, obviously, to my heightened sensibilities, making a mental note to use this as a pretext for some future visit. And more and more, I wanted to know exactly what was going on at Rushbrooke.

Malise quickly became an established part of our family at Goldhayes. Neither he nor Grainne made any mention of any understanding between them – nor, after my outburst, did Lucy or I care to ask – but it was obvious that they were very happy in each other's company. Perhaps, after their long separation, they were exploring anew their relationship with each other. For his part, Jasper was delighted to ride out with him again, though the countryside around Goldhayes, small and green and domestic with its farms and fields and gentle intimate hills and valleys, could hardly have been more different from the barbarous, windswept landscape of Catholm.

A week or so after his arrival, a party of us rode over to Rushbrooke, invited for a small informal early supper to celebrate the fifth birthday of old Sir Thomas Jermyn's son Robert, known to all of us as Robin. Besides myself, Lucy, Meraud and Malise, there came also Grainne and her children, and Kit and Hugh: for this was to be a child-centred affair. The household at Rushbrooke was at present a curious one: old Sir Thomas had died two years previously at the age of seventy-two, leaving his second wife Mary and their two small children, Robin and Bet, who was almost four. There was also Sir Thomas's daughter-in-law, the much-tried Rebecca, and her brood, offspring of the Thomas Jermyn now in France with the Prince of Wales. There were seven of these, ranging from the priggish Tom, fourteen and away at Bury Grammar School, through Kat, Etta, Henry, Beth, Judy and Charles, the youngest, who was seven. These two women and nine young children hardly filled the great house, which was nearly as large as Goldhayes, and very similar in appearance. Malise, indeed, commented on this as Rushbrooke came into view. 'So yon's the Jermyn's great house! It's verra like Goldhayes, wi' yon turrets.'

'It was built at the same time,' Lucy told him. 'And legend has it that the Heron and the Jermyn who built them had a race to see which would be finished first, the prize to be a fine horse.'

'And who won it?'

'Oh, legend doesn't bother with trivia like that,' I said, 'doubtless the race was the thing. They're not really alike – Goldhayes is bigger, and built round courtyards at the back, whereas Rushbrooke is a plain 'E' shape, apart from those turrets. But in both houses you can fish the moat from the windows!'

'They're both very bonny,' said Malise appreciatively. 'I like yon turrets.'

'Lots of Suffolk houses have those,' Lucy said. 'Long Melford Hall, that belongs to Lady Penelope's mother, and Sir Symonds D'Ewes' house at Kentwell, they both have turrets at each corner like that. Probably the same man designed them all.'

'Whatever the truth of it,' Grainne said, 'I still think Goldhayes wins the prize for beauty.'

'Ah,' I said, 'don't let a Jermyn hear you say that – even after a hundred years, the two families are still rivals.'

Mistress Rebecca welcomed us in the entrance hall, a high, gloomily-panelled room that smelt faintly musty. Hugh, who had never been to Rushbrooke without his mother, was rather overawed, despite his irrepressible cheerfulness, and surreptitiously grasped a handful of Lucy's skirts. Kit, who was young Robin's friend and knew the place well, made his bow to Mistress Rebecca with Jasper, and we proceeded through to the main staircase, which led up from a room at the side of the house. Kit trotted up ahead, already in tearing spirits, and half-fearful that he would fall, I followed close behind. So it happened that we were the first to enter the Gallery – a grand chamber, but not nearly so imposing as the one at Goldhayes, for it did not run the full length of the house – and surprise those within. One of them, I saw, was Jamie. The other three were known to me, more or less, by sight or acquaintance: Edmund Jermyn, old Sir Thomas's first cousin, a middle-aged bachelor who had lived at Rushbrooke for several years; John Pooley, Sir Thomas's nephew, who had a house in Bury and had married a daughter of that same Dr Despotine who had saved Grainne's life when Jasper was born; and John Pooley's distant cousin, young Edmund Pooley of Badley, who was the same age as Simon, had fought for the King and had been at Oxford. They were standing by one of the hearths, deep in an earnest discussion that broke off as soon as Kit and I entered. All four men bowed and went through the elaborate rituals of courtly greeting; but Jamie, as transparent as his sister, had flushed a guilty red and would not meet my eye.

The party went off in fine style, save that Kit and Robin Jermyn both ate far too much (in family tradition, they were having a race), and were violently sick. Henry Jermyn, a small, round, fair boy with a merry cheeky face who bore more than a little resemblance, both in mind and looks, to his notorious uncle Harry, the Queen's Chamberlain, seemed not a whit abashed by the episode of the moles, for which he had received a beating – Richard, it seemed, had been quite right. Mistress Rebecca, an old crony of Mary's who was small, prim-faced and plain, told me with a certain satisfaction that all efforts to be rid of the moles had been in vain: Lady Penelope had in the end fetched in a mole-catcher from Cambridge who had finally done the job at vast expense and only after digging up the whole green. She would not be able to mount one of her famous matches for some considerable time, and it was plain that, whatever Rebecca's displeasure at her son's behaviour, she regretted the cessation of those matches not at all.

On the way home in the cool late evening, the four children somewhat subdued after the excitements of the afternoon, I seized the chance of tackling Jamie, who had stayed on, after the Pooleys had left, to ride home with us. 'What were you all talking about when Kit and I burst in on you?' I enquired artlessly. 'You looked very havey-cavey, I must say.'

Jamie swallowed and said casually, 'Oh, nothing

much. We're all going over to Newmarket next week, Edmund Pooley has a horse he wants to race against Boreas.'

'*Boreas?* He's not a racehorse, indeed he's not really a riding horse.'

'Ah. Well. Um, John doesn't know yet, but there's a sizeable wager on it, and if he's agreeable to me riding him, just over a mile, on the Heath, against Edmund's Sampson . . .' Jamie floundered. I felt a sudden wave of anger against these older, supposedly wiser men who had enmeshed my inexperienced young cousin in their snaky underhand coils, and turned my rage on him. 'You're a fool, Jamie Heron. What does Meraud have to say to all this?'

He looked at me sideways, uncertain how much I knew. I was not going to lay all my cards on the table so plain. 'You'd best be very careful, you know, or disaster will surely follow.' I paused, and then added, 'You wouldn't want to face John and tell him his precious stallion – *our* precious stallion – has broken his leg in some reckless and unnecessary race, now would you?'

'Of course I wouldn't,' said Jamie, looking relieved. 'I shall take the greatest care of him, don't you worry.'

But I did. Somehow he won over John Sewell, who gave somewhat grudging permission for the stallion to be taken to Newmarket, and Jamie set off in high spirits, leading the lovely, restless horse to the meeting on the Heath, famous both as a racecourse and as a rendezvous for New Modelled Armies. It was obvious that this race was nothing more than a pretext for like-minded gentlemen to meet together and talk about matters entirely unconnected with horses, but, fuming, I could do nothing. Like Francis and Simon, Jamie was highly resistant to reasonable persuasion, and no other method of dissociating him from his fellow-plotters would be safe. After all, I could hardly denounce him to the County Committee, the only course of action certain to bring immediate results.

Jamie returned from Newmarket in even greater spirits, and with a significantly fatter purse: Boreas having beaten Edmund Pooley's Sampson by a very convincing margin. Now another match, with a horse owned by a Cambridge gentleman, had been arranged for the following week, the last in March, and Jamie was optimistic about the grey stallion's chances. He spoke with an enthusiasm entirely unfeigned, eyes bright and face glowing: now it was not only the excitement and danger of plotting rebellion that fired him, evidently, but also the thrill of riding a superb horse to win.

And I noticed with a pang Kit's hero-worshipping eyes fixed on his young cousin, and heard his high voice asking questions about Boreas with a new and rare eagerness. It was, I supposed wryly, inevitable that my fatherless child would choose for his male idol the only man of dash and presence left at Goldhayes: and Jamie, black-haired and blue-eyed and vivid, could be said to resemble his first cousin Dominic more than a little. Over the last few weeks I had noticed my son seeking out his company more and more, and Jamie, to do him justice, accepted this flattering attention with a good spirit and could often be seen playing with Kit and Hugh, or helping them with their ponies. What caused me far more disquiet was the fact that Meraud, as Jamie's wife, was also now included in Kit's sphere of affections. I could do little to discourage either of them openly: and had to watch in impotent fury as she smilingly tossed a ball to him, or played some gentle undemanding game with an ostentatious sweetness of manner that displayed prominently to all the world the lovely mother she would one day make. And I wondered, with deep foreboding, why she felt obliged to demean herself thus; for Meraud never did anything that could not be turned to her own advantage. But always she had been secretive, hiding her real self and feelings behind that decorous mask of politeness, piety and propriety. I had no hope of discovering any motive for this charmingly false interest in my son, and could only watch and wait, and try my best to remove him unobtrusively from her orbit.

And as March gave way to April, and spring stirred in the new grass and young animals and a fresh, warmer wind, so did the Royalists wake. The first news we had was of rebellion in South Wales, where the Governor of Pembroke Castle declared for the King. Closer to home, on the eighth of April there was trouble at Norwich: an attempt by Parliament's messengers to take the Mayor into custody swelled into riot and revolt in the streets, proclamations in support of the King, theft and distribution of arms, battles with troopers hastily summoned from all over Norfolk, and finally erupted, literally, into disaster when the magazine in the Committee House was accidentally fired. It contained, so it was said, a hundred barrels of gunpowder: scores were buried, burnt or blown to pieces, a hundred and more of the remaining rebels were imprisoned, some being executed, and the trouble died as quickly as it had flared. But it showed that many people, even in East Anglia, were in a mood to listen to Royalist arguments, and to act on them. The comings and goings at Rushbrooke and between Bury and Newmarket grew more frequent: Jamie was rarely seen, save at dusk and dawn, and John Sewell grew somewhat dubious about Boreas's masculine potency after, as he put it, 'All that there racing about.'

Amidst all this uncertainty and apprehension, Grainne and Malise announced that they were to be married. Only Joan was dismayed, and more at the prospect of her beloved Jasper and Henrietta removing for ever to 'furrin parts', than at any insult to the memory of Grainne's first husband implied by such a marriage. But Malise was quick to assure her that there were no plans yet to go to Scotland: John had asked him if he would like to take over part of the running of the estate, with Richard's blessing, and he had accepted. The wedding was set for the middle of June, to give time for Malise's family to be informed, although they would be most unlikely to attend, and to invite such far-flung friends as the Widow and Charles Lawrence. Grainne inserted a message from me into her invitation to Mistress Gooch, asking her to probe, if she could, the nature of Dan Ashley's feelings and intentions towards Lucy. If anyone could undertake such a subtle and difficult task – for Dan was, I remembered clearly, a very reserved character – it was the Widow. I looked forward to seeing her again, even though it was only a few months since our last meeting, and wondered idly if I could channel her brisk down-to-earth common sense into persuading Jamie to devote more attention to his wife.

But even if the Widow were to prove of use in that matter, it was rapidly becoming too late. All over the country, men were restless under the Parliament's yoke, and looking to their old Cavalier generals to provide a lead. In the north, Carlisle and Berwick were surprised and taken, before the end of April, by those names from the past, Sir Marmaduke Langdale and Sir Philip Musgrave. In Norwich, the election of a new Mayor on Mayday passed off without incident, the city still stunned by the terrible end to their abortive rebellion, but there had been disturbances in Colchester, so we heard from Jamie, who had met a gentleman from that town at Rushbrooke. I wondered if it might be Sir Charles Lucas, the Earl of Newcastle's brother-in-law and a zealous, fiery and unpopular supporter of the King. If Jamie's unknown informant was indeed Lucas, then his involvement with the conspiracy – if indeed it *was* a conspiracy, I reminded myself, for as yet I had no proof – took Jamie into very deep waters indeed.

And that proof was quickly and abundantly forthcoming. A day or so after we heard of the trouble in Colchester, I rode with Malise and Grainne into Bury, to call upon Lady May, the sister of that John Pooley who was Jamie's accomplice, and her youngest daughter Isabella, the only one of her large family still living at home. Grainne and I both liked Isabella, a quiet shy girl, very much under her ferocious mother's thumb, who yet had a lively mind and a vivid zest for life and enjoyment away from Lady May's gimlet eye.

As soon as we reached Bury and rode in through the Southgate, it was plain that something was afoot. The place was humming with activity: women standing in doors, men walking purposefully along the streets that led to the great market square in front of the old Abbey gateway at the centre of the town, and knots of 'prentice boys clustered at every corner. With dismay, I realized that many of the men were armed, with sword or stave or cudgel, and one or two, on horseback like ourselves, wore pistols or carbines. Sounds of shouting and cheering filtered through the street noises: Grainne pulled her horse up and stared at me and Malise. 'What in God's name is happening?'

A passer-by heard her question and shouted up to her. 'Thass a maypole, Mistress, they've set up a maypole on Angel Hill.' And to our surprise he cupped his hands round his mouth and bawled to the street at large, 'Do you come and see the maypole! God save the King!'

'A maypole?' demanded Malise, as if it was some Devil's rite – as indeed I suppose it was. 'A *maypole?* I thought your kirk . . .'

'Oh, yes,' Grainne said. 'Parliament banned maypoles long ago, and anyway it's not even May Day. It's just an excuse to show discontent. Shall we go back?'

'Go back?' I demanded. 'Are you faint-hearted, Grainne Sewell? Harm can hardly come to us in such a crowd, we're well known for a Royalist family, and besides Lady May is expecting us and I fear her far more than any riot.' And to make my argument unassailable, I prodded my horse into a walk.

'I'll wager I ken the real reason,' Malise offered, as we rode up Southgate Street amidst steadily increasing crowds. 'You're fair bursting wi' curiosity tae see what's happening, are ye no?'

I grinned candidly. 'Of course I am. Besides, I want to see a maypole, I haven't laid eyes on one for years!'

We passed the two churches, St Mary's and St James's, and so to the Market Square on Angel Hill, where because of the great press of people we could go no further. In the centre of the wide open space, with the great Abbey gateway and ruins on our right, and the old Angel Inn to the left, the promised maypole stood triumphantly pagan and festive above the heads of the populace, and from the flurry about its base it was apparent that some daring spirits were attempting to dance around it. The mood of the crowd was relentlessly merry: there were cheers and shouts of, 'For God and King Charles,' blackjacks and bottles of ale were passed from mouth to mouth, and someone handed a hunk of bread and cheese up to me with the greeting, 'God save the King, and you too, Mistress Heron!' And from the vicinity of the maypole came the wailing and scratching of some musician's old fiddle playing a cheerful tune. A young man and a girl in the crowd nearest to us began to dance, drawing others in with them, young and old, poor and respectable, drunk and sober, until the mass of people became one huge, swaying leviathan. But there were sinister undertones: I could see not only the simple townspeople and country-folk drawn by curiosity and the sheer fun of such an occasion after years of war, poverty and repression, but armed men, a ruffianly-looking lot, many of them the worse for drink. There was no sign of any regular soldiers, nor of the County Committee, whose meeting-place was in Bury: and despite the holiday mood of the crowd, I felt it could very easily swing from gaiety to violence.

We guided our horses round the edge of the square, and so eventually arrived at Lady May's house in Abbeygate. We were greeted by our hostess, a formidable lady who, most improbably, had once inspired Master Aurelian Townshend to write a poem praising her smile: I suspected that it was the extreme rarity of such an expression on her forbidding countenance that had driven him to such excessive flights of fancy. She seemed much pleased at the tumult outside, and made mention many times in her abrupt snappish voice of her hope that this was but the beginning, and that the King would shortly sweep back to power on just such a wave of popular support. I remembered that her brother John Pooley was very probably involved in the conspiracy, and attempted to press her further for details, but she was vague as to time and place, saying only that there were ten thousand honest men in Suffolk and Essex wanting but one word to rise for the King and oust the Committee and Parliament and Army men who dared to impose their will – and, worse, their impropriations and fines – on loyal gentlemen.

We had a substantial dinner, during which Malise was again urged to tell of his adventures with Montrose, and then adjourned to the parlour for a cutthroat game of whist 'To keep you young people amused,' while Lady May sat with benign severity and stitched at a cushion-cover.

The game was almost ended – Malise and Grainne winning handsomely – when there was a knocking at the street door, and presently a manservant admitted Sir William Pooley, the elder of Lady May's two brothers, who lived out at Boxstead. A big man in his forties, he was red-faced and perspiring with exertion and anger, and after bowing briefly to Isabella and the three of us, turned immediately to his sister. 'Have you seen John?'

Lady May looked at him narrowly. Sir William had married a daughter of Sir Symonds D'Ewes, a noted Member of Parliament and devout Presbyterian, and he could by no means be described as hot for the King's cause. 'Is he not at his house?' she enquired cautiously.

'No, Judith, he is not, and his wife and servants say they have not seen him all day. He's making some mischief in this tumult, I don't doubt: the word is that some of the trained bands tried to disperse them and were laid hold of for their pains, and now there are groups of armed men in every church and gate in the town, and the powder magazine has been seized. It only wants some fool to be careless, and Bury will be blown heavenwards as was half of Norwich. And you do not know where our brother is?'

'I regret I do not, William – unless he is at Rushbrooke Hall.'

Sir William glared at her. 'Yes, Judith. Yes, he may well be there. I would entirely expect it, since no one in this town claims to have seen him.' He swung round on our little party at the card-table. 'Your servant, ladies. Good day to you, Master Graham.' And, breathing heavily, made for the door. A thought struck him and he turned back. 'Mistress Heron? I regret to have to inform you – if you did not already know, of course – that I caught sight of your cousin James in the thick of the rioters this afternoon. He appears to be taking a leading part in the disturbances, and I would think it wise that his wife and mother be informed of the fact. Good day.' And he stamped out.

We soon said our own farewells to Lady May and poor Isabella, for whom I felt much sympathy, immured in that house with her dragonish mother, and all her brothers, and sister, gone away. However, when I urged her to pay a visit to Goldhayes, she said, a sudden smile transforming and irradiating her rather plain, pale face, 'Oh yes, I should love that; and my brother Bap is coming up from Hampshire soon, so at least I shall have some company.' This with a cautious glance at her mother, who was talking to Grainne. 'But there will be no more bowls matches for a while – have you heard?'

'About Henry Jermyn and the moles? I have indeed. Is the green as desecrated as it's said?'

'It's entirely spoilt,' said Isabella, smothering a giggle. 'But Lady Penelope thinks she can have turf laid so that it will be almost as good as new quite soon – by the end of the summer, she hopes. So we might all meet at Hengrave then, if not before.'

'I trust before, if these troubles don't get out of hand. Are you frightened, here in the middle of it?'

'Oh, no,' said Isabella. 'They may be a mob, but

they're friendly to us; the leaders have often been here, your cousin Jamie too.'

All this was the final confirmation I had been dreading. We rode home through the depleted streets, passing here and there homegoing rioters, and the debris of disturbance; rubbish thrown at the houses of prominent Puritans, branches of may on the fountain, flowers crushed and scattered in the usual filth of the roadway. At the Southgate there was an armed guard, very self-important, stopping, questioning and searching incoming travellers: they let us pass with alacrity, and we rode out in the free evening air towards Goldhayes.

'So Jamie *is* involved with all this,' said Grainne. 'The stupid fool . . . hasn't he anything better to do?'

'You know what he's like. It would be a surprise if he *wasn't* part of the plots,' I said wearily. 'But I wish to God we could get him out of it safely. I don't for a moment believe that this riot will go unpunished, and when all the might of the Army descends on Bury he'd best look to himself, or he may make Meraud a widow before they've been wed six months.'

'Have you spoken wi' him about it?' asked Malise, guiding his chestnut mare Tanaquill round a winter pothole.

'No . . . I wasn't sure until today, and besides I thought it best to tread warily. Meraud and I are old enemies, as you know, and she might not take too kindly to my handing out advice to her husband. Besides, Jamie shares the family failing – or one of them – in that he will not readily accept advice or criticism.'

'I'll ha' a wee talk wi' him, if you think it'll do any good,' Malise said. 'He may tak' it better from me, no' being female, ye ken.' He grinned to make the joke plain: I pretended to lash out with my fist, but had to add, 'It's true, he has this tedious chivalrous notion about women being pure empty-headed creatures who must be shielded from rude reality as much as possible. He thinks I'm a traitor to my sex. That's why he fell in love with Meraud, who gives out this impression of frail and lovely femininity, when actually she's as hard as nails, as calculating as Machiavelli and has all the loyalty and selflessness of Judas.'

'I think you do her a disservice there,' said Grainne thoughtfully. 'Malise, mind that branch . . .' As her beloved ducked, only just in time, she continued, 'After all, she seems to be genuinely fond of Jamie, and worried about him.'

'She could just be worried about the possibility of him being killed before she has a chance to give him an heir,' I said tartly. Malise snorted. 'I know little of the lady, but I'd say, Thomazine, that where she's concerned you have very little Christian charity.'

'Nor did she when she betrayed Francis. I hated her then, and I'll never in my life feel anything for her that's warmer than dislike. But it's not her I'm worried about, it's Jamie – and if you think you can knock some sense into his head then you're welcome to try.'

'I canna promise anything,' said Malise. 'But as wee Rose says, I'll hev a hack.'

But first, the Bury disturbances had to be resolved. Jamie returned to Goldhayes very late that night, when his mother's Dutch clock had struck half-past eleven, stupidly elated with weariness and high spirits. As his figure appeared at the head of the stairs, Meraud rose from her chair – she, Lucy, myself, Malise, Mary and Richard had been keeping a quiet apprehensive vigil with book and sewing since supper – and hurried towards him. 'Where have you been? I've been so worried about you – you never said you'd be so late back – where have you *been?*'

'Oh, just in Bury, helping some friends,' said Jamie evasively. Meraud took his arm and stared earnestly up into his face. 'Oh, Jamie, I know what you've been doing, we all do, please don't go back there tomorrow – I don't want anything to happen to you.'

'Nonsense, of course it won't,' said Jamie, looking delighted and gratified at this evidence of loving wifely concern. 'All the town is quiet and in our hands, and men are flocking in from all over Suffolk, and Colchester too, to lend us their support. We'll have the King in his own again before the month's out!'

'Is it really so easy?' Richard demanded of his stepson. Jamie had in common with his sister an enviable but dangerous ability to ignore inconvenient realities. He waved the arm that was not clasping Meraud as they walked along the Gallery towards us. 'Of course it is! Everyone is utterly weary of the Parliament and those self-righteous prigs of Presbyterians and the Sectaries in the Army trying to turn the world upside-down. Wales and the north are in rebellion already, and the Scots are about to invade. And think, sir, just think! All East Anglia was hot for the Parliament during the war, you know that, none better. So all this support for the King in Puritan Suffolk must mean that loyal feelings all over the country are just as strong, or stronger.'

'You are forgetting that the Sectaries in that Army, misguided though they may be, form the most efficient fighting machine that we have had in our history since the Romans left,' said Richard quietly. 'How can a rabble of Suffolk peasants and yeomen, however loyal to the King, however well led, hope to prevail against them in the end? You are deceiving yourself.'

'Oh no,' said Jamie, and his naïve self-deception shone from his bright eager face. 'They're scattered, regiments quartered here and there all over the country. There'll be so many risings they won't be able to combine, they'll be overwhelmed where they lie. There are Fleetwood's men in Norfolk, Fairfax's in Essex, Whalley's Horse between Cambridge and Newmarket, a score or so of men to a village. All it needs is the organization to fall upon them so that they can't form into their regiments . . .'

The rest of his speech faded into insignificance for me: for Whalley's Horse, in which Francis served, was only, it appeared, a few miles away. My mouth went suddenly dry and my heart lurched and thumped in my breast, as a picture of the sort I had always dreaded leapt into my mind, of Francis and Jamie fighting on opposite sides, and meeting in the heat of battle in the streets of Bury ... I felt Lucy's hand grip mine suddenly, and saw her delighted smile, and knew that, as usual, she saw only the positive side, and that my darker, more morbid imaginings would never pierce the armour of her optimism. I envied her her peace of mind. She leant towards me and whispered, 'Francis is in Whalley's Horse, isn't he? Just think, you may see him soon!'

At Goldhayes, only Lucy, Grainne, Malise and I knew exactly where he was. I had parried Mary's dutiful, uninterested questions with a vague statement to the effect that he was somewhere in England, or possibly abroad with Grainne's brother-in-law Tom Sewell. It said a great deal about her maternal feelings, or lack of them, that this singularly unconvincing explanation and total subsequent silence as to his whereabouts had satisfied her. I could not imagine her reaction – or anyone else's, Jamie's in particular – if her errant third son were to come riding up to Goldhayes dressed in the uniform of a New Model corporal. Nor could I imagine what sort of life he, who had always made no secret of his atheistic views, would have amongst the most fervently Sectarian regiment of the most religious-minded army England had ever seen. But he might have changed, I thought miserably, remembering the hard-eyed intolerant fanatics of Bury and Banbury, and the son of a Horringer gentleman who had turned almost overnight from a heedless, humorous boy into a cold, unforgiving loud-mouthed preacher. Francis was not like William Lucas, but I felt a twinge of fear nonetheless, knowing that even his independent spirit might not withstand such an onslaught.

And after all this time, when I had taught myself to accept what I had once possessed, and not to long fruitlessly for more, the familiar dull ache – of longing, of absence, of my unfulfilled, incomplete, diminished existence – flared up anew into painful life. He was near, and his thoughts must be with me, as mine were with him, and the possibility of his meeting me was the greater. I longed for it, and dreaded it also, remembering the last time we had met after long separation. Had Simon said something to him, led him to believe that I no longer loved him? Was that why he was in the Army? My rational brain did not think Simon capable of such deceit, but a worm of fear wriggled at the back of my mind, and postulated this and other unpleasant fancies, and would not be stilled.

Despite the combined urgings and pleadings of his wife, mother, stepfather, sister and cousins, Jamie rode back to Bury at first light the next morning. As I had suspected, criticism only increased his determination to take a leading part in this rebellion, despite the probability of its failure: a probability he dismissed with what I considered to be a criminally foolish confidence. As we stood at the door of the house, Lucy unashamedly weeping, the same thought was in all our minds. Would we ever see him again?

Meraud was not weeping, although I suspected from her appearance that she had spent half the night begging him tearfully not to go. The set of her face now betrayed a silent but seething fury; she had offered no parting embrace save a cold kiss on his cheek. After all, I thought with my usual prejudiced cynicism, she is saying farewell, possibly for ever, not only to her husband but very like to Goldhayes as well.

He did not return that night, nor the next. We heard through various channels – John Sewell, Ambrose Blagge, Lady Jermyn and Mistress Rebecca – of the events of those days. Word had been speedily carried to Parliament of the disturbance, and the County Members, Sir William Playters and Sir Thomas Barnadiston, were dispatched with all haste to Bury, to try to quell the rebellion. And in case this peaceful stratagem did not work, the nearest soldiers were ordered to march to within a few miles of Bury. There was a faintly comical interlude, according to John, when the soldiers

– under the command of Colonel Whalley, which information made my sorely tried heart leap anew – made such a successful blockade of the place that the Parliament supporters, Sir William and Sir Thomas included, had to beg them to lessen their enthusiasm and let provisions into the town while negotiations were going on. Finally the rebels were persuaded to lay down their arms in the market place, and to give up control of the magazine, in return for a promise of freedom and indemnity from any punishment or reprisal.

With the soldiers ringing the town in strength, the rebels had little choice. The crestfallen six hundred made their way back to their homes in Suffolk, Essex and Cambridge, leaving the troopers and the Parliament men in quiet and undisputed possession of Bury. The real architects of the brief rising remained miraculously undetected, a fortunate omission since the indemnity offered to the rank-and-file rebels would certainly not have applied to the Pooleys, to Edmund Jermyn and the others had their role been known; nor to Jamie Heron.

We saw soldiers even four miles away from Bury in Bradfield Tye; a score or more of them were quartered in the village for ten days while the town was secured. They were troopers of Colonel Fleetwood's Regiment, and the whole village, whether of Royalist persuasion or not, talked of them incessantly; their good behaviour, the minimal damage (one field of new-sprouting wheat ridden across, and a chicken's suspicious disappearance), the promptness with which accounts were settled. The only real note of dissent came on the Sunday, when the soldiers, taking exception to the parson's Presbyterian style, set up a rival prayer meeting in the churchyard, with one of their number a fine and fiery preacher, and a knot of curious villagers forming part of the congregation. But they were no more than a nine-days' wonder. Trouble arose in Stowmarket, and then a rising began in Kent and the troops were hastily moved south by Fairfax to deal with it.

Before this, when Bury had been quietened and all

seemed safe, I rode in on market day with John Sewell, Grainne and Malise, and a dozen fat lambs, bleating to the skies, legs tied and huddled together in John's cart. I did not know what, or who, I hoped to see: for Jamie had returned only a little disconsolate from the débâcle at Bury, and amid his flood of recollections, plans for the future and anger over the tame way the rebels had laid down their arms, he had said, 'It's strange, when we rode out of the Southgate there were some troopers drawn up outside, and one of them looked very like Francis.'

Something had frozen inside me; my heart seemed to stop, and yet my hand went on, drawing the needle in and out of the split seam on one of Kit's shirts as if of its own accord. Jamie said cheerfully, 'Oh, it wasn't, of course, that was plain. He didn't even really look very much like him at a second glance, and he had a beard. And it wasn't as if he recognized me or anything, just looked straight through me like the rest. And what on earth would he be doing there anyway, can you imagine it, *Francis* in the Parliament Army!' He brayed with laughter at the very idea, and a cold sweat broke out on my palms. If Francis was indeed in Bury I had to try and see him, hence my visit with the Sewells and Malise.

The town was quite unchanged. It had after all been a very minor rebellion (despite Jamie's claims), soon over and with hardly any bloodshed – two would-be Cavaliers killed in a sally against the blockading forces. The only signs of any disturbance were the soldiers. They were everywhere, lounging in the marketplace, guarding the House of Correction on the Cornhill, on duty outside the magazine in the Guildhall. But all the faces under the black pot-helmets, smiling, dour, indifferent, young, stupid, intelligent, were strange to me. I discovered from John that they were mainly in Fleetwood's Regiment, with some from the Lord General's, and a scattering of Whalley's men. Nowhere was there anyone who could possibly, remotely, have been Francis. As we rode home, blessedly quiet and lambless, I upbraided myself silently for being so foolish as to suppose I might find him, and thereby most like putting him in great danger of discovery: for however much he could school his face when stared at by Jamie, I doubted very much whether he could guard his expression thus when faced with me.

And yet, despite my anger with myself, I was sick with a deep, bitter and unreasoning disappointment.

To think that the failure of his first attempt at plotting rebellion would deter Jamie from further efforts was to make a grievous error of judgement. Meraud, it was true, seemed to have forgotten her displeasure in her delight at having him returned safe and sound, and for a few days he hardly stirred from the house. Then, his visits to Rushbrooke began again.

By this time we had heard of the rising in Kent, in which Rochester, Dartford and Deptford were seized by Royalists, and the troops round Bury were withdrawn by Fairfax to march south. It did indeed seem that Jamie's theory would come true: the Lord General's forces were spread too thin already, invasion from Scotland seemed increasingly likely, there were risings in Wales and the north, and now discontent in London and the Kent rebellion. The final straw came when the Fleet moored in the Downs mutinied. This was at the end of May, and Jamie was openly jubilant. Malise had made several attempts to dissuade him from further conspiracy, to absolutely no avail. As he confessed to me gloomily, 'He's that obstinate I canna ding any sense into his thick skull. If the King couldna win before, why should they do it now? All he's doing is building castles in the clouds, and he canna see it. Nor can the others, and they're old enough tae know better.' He shrugged his wide shoulders, resignedly. "I dinna ken where all this will end. In a grave wi' muckle grief and moan, I dinna doot. I ha' one last notion though, and that's tae go tae Rushbrooke wi' him tomorrow. It seems tae be an important meeting, ye ken, and syn I can discover what their plans are, and maybe try to put forward something more sensible . . . I dinna ken, Thomazine lass, but I'm sair worrit.'

'Do you think you can do that? Find out what their plans are?'

'Well, young Jamie trusts me, and they've all heard tell o' his Scots cousin who's fought for Montrose. From wha' I can understand they're a fair bunch o' loons,' said Malise, with unaccustomed grimness. 'They'd trust the Lord General himself wi' their plots and plans if he spoke them fair.'

So on the morning of the second of June Malise and Jamie rode the mile and a half to Rushbrooke and the rest of the household went about their daily tasks: cleaning, sewing, spinning, baking, brewing, cooking. I could not help remembering, as I drilled Kit with his hornbook, the events of six years ago, also at the beginning of June, when we had ridden out of Goldhayes with Simon and his troop and gone to war. Since then, that war had brought grief, separation and bereavement to every one of us; and I prayed with all my heart, desperately and earnestly, that these latest risings would swiftly collapse, and leave the country in peace. What did it matter, in the end, if Parliament ruled and the King was reduced to a powerless prisoner? We still had our lives, our land, our prosperity, whichever wielded authority: and if the rebellion was even partially successful, all those things, for everyone in the kingdom, would be put in hazard. I valued my peace far more, now that I had experienced its absence.

Evening came, summer-late and grey with rain, and there was no sign of Jamie and Malise. Supper was a strained affair, with everyone trying, and failing, to pretend that nothing was wrong. We stayed up until midnight, Lucy and I, and then trailed sleepily and apprehensively to bed: Meraud, so she avowed the next morning, hardly slept a wink. And still there was no sign of either of them.

The first news we had came from Grainne. She arrived as we were breaking our fast, after morning prayers, Jasper following her. That in itself was not unusual, for he came to Goldhayes daily for his lessons with Dr Davis: but her air of urgency and anxiety was. She stood at the door of the little Summer Parlour, where we usually took our simple morning meal, and said at once, 'Are Malise and Jamie back yet?'

'No. We haven't seen them since they went to Rushbrooke yesterday,' said Meraud, starting up. 'Have you any news? Do you know where they are?'

'Well, I suppose they're still there,' said Grainne. 'But John's just heard in the village that the Duke of Buckingham came there yesterday with a great many other gentlemen, and a sumptuous dinner for all, so they're saying, and in the evening most of them rode away again. John said that he didn't know if Jamie and Malise were among them ... What *is* going on, do you suppose?'

'Rebellion,' said Richard, helping himself to more salt herring. 'And if he were not my dear wife's son, I would seriously consider denouncing them all to the Committee. What he is doing is not only wrong but foolhardy in the extreme, and I wonder greatly that Master Graham seems to have suddenly decided to throw in his lot with them; he struck me as a young man of sense and moderation.'

'He is,' said Grainne, with a little less than her customary calm. 'He only went with Jamie to try and influence them towards his way of thinking. Oh well, I suppose that we can only hope they're still at Rushbrooke. Doubtless they'll appear before too long.'

But, like the rest of us, she was only putting a brave face on it. And as the day drew on, and there was still no sign of my errant cousins, and no word or news sent from Rushbrooke or anywhere else, I began to be worried, then exasperated, and finally angry. I would not have expected Jamie, in the fine flush of his

343

enthusiasm, to spare a thought for allaying our anxieties, but with the essentially gentle, considerate Malise it was another matter. What on earth had happened to them?

Late in the afternoon, Grainne returned, and even before I saw her weary, anxious face, with the same look of concealed terror as she had worn once, when waiting for news of her first husband Henry, I was determined to act. 'To hell with convention,' I told her. 'We're going to Rushbrooke to find out exactly what is going on. Will you come?'

'Of course,' said Grainne. Her eyes went to Meraud, standing irresolutely by one of the windows in the Gallery, her shadowed, watchful face wearily surveying us. I had never seen the normally ice-cool Cornish girl under such stress before: in the murky grey light of the cloudy afternoon, she looked older, her face wan and pinched, the marks of sleepless nights printed plain in dark smudges under her eyes. I wondered, reluctantly, whether in some corner of her narrow, selfish heart she harboured some feelings for Jamie. 'Come with us,' Grainne offered.

Meraud shook her head, her eyes staring bleakly out at the park. 'No, no thank you, Grainne, I couldn't . . . I don't think I could sit a horse, far less walk . . . I would be very grateful if you could find out something, anything, but I don't think I can muster the strength to come with you. I'm sorry.'

'I'll stay with you,' said Lucy, solicitously jumping up from her chair and putting a sisterly arm about her shoulders. 'Come on, let's do some more of that cushion-cover you were working on this morning.' The two girls walked slowly down the Gallery: despite myself, I grinned. 'That was very noble of Lucy – you know how she hates sewing. Shall we go, Grainne? I want to put an end to this business.'

Jasper appeared at the head of the stairs, his face betraying more openly that he shared his mother's anxiety. Grainne said, 'What is it? I thought you were working with Dr Davis.'

'I'm sorry,' said her son, 'but I've just remembered something Henry Jermyn said . . . I think he might know something about where Jamie and Master Graham are.'

'Henry?' I queried. 'Why should he know anything about it?'

'You know what he's like,' said Jasper, with a rather embarrassed grin. 'He's got a longer nose than Joan . . . he was very curious about what was happening at Rushbrooke and I think you could get him to tell you what he knows if Mistress Rebecca doesn't want to. And Dr Davis has a cold and doesn't mind if I go, and can I take Bran please?'

So the four of us, two women, the boy and the dog went the so-familiar way to Rushbrooke, and talked all the way of things that did not matter. I was wondering whether we were about to make fools of ourselves, and find Malise and Jamie, knee-deep in conspiracy, annoyingly and thankfully alive and well. I prayed that it might be so, and was rehearsing in my mind the scolding I would administer on the way home, as we rode over the moat bridge into Rushbrooke's front court. We left our horses in the care of a stable-lad who had been warned of our approach – as at Goldhayes, visitors were discernible from some way off as they rode through the park – and entered the house.

We were met by Mistress Rebecca's gentlewoman, a faded mouse-like fluttering creature who performed the same function at Rushbrooke, assisting the ladies and teaching the children, as had Mary's now-dead aunt Mistress Bryant at Goldhayes in my childhood. 'I regret that Lady Jermyn and Mistress Rebecca have gone to Hengrave to visit Lady Penelope, and will not be back until suppertime.'

I looked at the woman, one part of my mind trying to remember – what *was* her name, I could never recall it, did it begin with an R? – and the other, almost mechanically, beginning to admit defeat. 'Oh, that is most unfortunate . . . I was hoping she could tell us whether she knew where my cousins Master Heron and

Master Graham were.' Dear God, I thought in anger, I'm even imitating her flustering now!

The little woman wrung her hands apologetically and fluttered her sparse eyelashes. 'Oh, I am so sorry, Mistress, I cannot be of any assistance at all. I know the gentlemen, of course, but I have not seen them since yesterday night . . .'

'They're not here, then?' I demanded. 'Surely you know where they are?' As she shook her untidy head speechlessly, I added, 'Isn't there someone else here who would know? Where's Master Edmund?'

'I'm so afraid, Mistress,' said the unfortunate gentlewoman. 'I'm afraid he has gone too. Everyone left on Friday evening, His Grace of Buckingham, Sir Edmund Pooley, Master John Pooley, Sir Charles Lucas and Master Edmund and your cousins, Mistress.'

'And you don't know where they've gone?' I cried, my anger turned unjustly against her frail form. 'Isn't there *anyone* who can tell us where they've gone?'

There was a silence, broken by the gentlewoman's agitated breathing – Mistress Ray, that was her name, Frances Ray – into which dropped Jasper's small treble voice. 'Aunt Thomazine – can't we ask Henry?'

'I suppose so, if there's no one else,' I said, feeling a sudden dislike for the irrepressible Henry. 'And where is he now, pray, Mistress Ray?'

'Upstairs in the East Wing, Mistress,' said the poor woman, her eyes avoiding mine. I said, 'Well, we'd better go and find out what he knows, if anything. Will you kindly show us the way, Mistress?'

The little woman, her pale hands fluttering, conducted us up the stairs and through bedchambers, past back stairs and down narrow passages, until we came to the East Wing, in which was a suite of chambers set aside for the numerous children of the house. There were eight of them in the wide sunny chamber at the end of the wing, with windows on three sides flooding the room with light, even on this dull overcast afternoon. The elder girls, Kat, Etta, Beth and Judy, aged thirteen, twelve, nine and eight, were stitching industriously away at various articles with equally varying degrees of skill, while their brothers Charles and Henry sat at a desk, quills in hands, the former busy upon some writing from a horn-covered copier, the latter apparently hard at work upon a Latin translation. In a window-seat sat their diminutive aunt and uncle, engaged in some earnest game with marbles.

The appearance of industry, however, was deceptive in Henry's case. His brown, wary glance caught my eye as we entered, and as he bowed with Charles, I saw him looking again. The little girls curtseyed, their embroidery carefully laid aside, save for Judy, who dropped hers. As impatient with all this childish ceremony as I had been when I performed it myself, I marched across the floor to Henry, Grainne beside me. 'I gather you may have some news of interest to myself and Mistress Sewell, Henry,' I said.

Henry Jermyn glanced at Jasper and then, as if reassured, said, 'Yes, Mistress?'

There was a silence. Then Beth, who had the reputation amongst the children of being a tell-tale, said, 'If you please, Mistress Heron, he's been listening at doors again.'

Her eldest sister, a grave, friendly child, glared at her, and Etta, more practical, kicked her on the ankle. Beth's round little face crumpled and she began to cry theatrically. Henry sighed with an air of masculine martyrdom and said, his brown eyes glancing at us to see how we were taking his information, 'If it concerns Master Heron and Master Graham, well, yes. Do you want to know where they've gone?'

I felt like shaking him – an easy enough task, for although more than two years older than Jasper, and much plumper, he was no taller. 'We do indeed,' said Grainne, the expression on her face indicating a similar exasperation. 'And if you have been listening at doors, and heard what you should not, well, that's not our affair. Just tell us what you know.'

'They've gone to Colchester with Sir Charles Lucas,' said Henry. 'There's going to be a rising there, and in London, that's why the Duke of Buckingham was here too. They're going to seize the Essex Committee at Chelmsford and join up with the rebels in Kent and fall on London. Master Graham said it was a foolhardy idea but they didn't take any notice, and he tried to stop Master Heron going, and Master Heron didn't take any notice either, but asked him if *he* was going to desert them in their hour of need and glory, and in the end Master Graham said he'd go as well, "I suppose someone has tae look after ye," he said.' The imitation of Malise's accent was very creditable – rather more so than the boy's lack of repentance at such behaviour. Then I realized that I was nothing more than a prig, and a hypocritical one at that, for listening at doors has ever been one of my more regrettable habits. At least we now knew where Malise and Jamie had gone, and why: although our anxiety was hardly allayed, with all this talk of risings and rebels and falling upon London, without Henry's eavesdropping we would have known nothing at all. The thing I found most curious was, why had nothing been said, no message sent to put our minds at rest? I said as much to Grainne, and there was a gasp from Kat, who leapt to her feet scattering her needlework and cried, 'Mistress, Master Heron gave it to me, and I forgot!'

'Yes, he did, he gave it to you just as he was leaving and told you *particularly* to have someone deliver it to Goldhayes as soon as possible,' said the sanctimonious Beth at once. Poor Kat looked at her with active dislike. 'Well, why didn't you remind me?'

'I didn't think it was my place,' said Beth with a self-righteous meekness that made me long to put her over my knee.

'You didn't happen to see where I put it?' Kat asked her helplessly. Beth, smirking, shook her head. There ensued a frantic search in which all the Jermyn children, and Jasper, participated, growing hotter, more urgent and dustier by the minute, until Judy gave a yelp of triumph and emerged from under one of the window-seats with a scrap of paper clutched in a grubby fist. 'Is this it, Kat?'

It was indeed the right paper, although Kat, by now almost weeping with contrition and humiliation, could not tell how it had come to be there. Smoothed out and deciphered, the message in fact proved to be less informative than Henry's ill-gotten news.

My dear wife, this is just to say that we are safe, and on the King's business, and will be gone from you some days. Have no fear for us, we will have as much care for ourselves as is compatible with our honour, and look for the day when we return to you in triumph. Pray tell Mistress Sewell that Cousin Graham is with me also, though much against his inclination, yet he conceives it his duty to have a care of me, as he says. I pray it will not be long before you again see your loving husband, Jamie Heron.

Half-an-hour later, the message lay in Meraud's hands, Grainne, Jasper and I having ridden back from Rushbrooke with all speed, leaving a somewhat chastened group of children behind us. Now, receiving it a day late, Meraud stared aghast at her husband's hasty scrawl and then, to my amazement, burst into wild hysterical sobs. 'Oh God, I knew it! He'll be killed in this stupid rebellion and I'll never see him again! Oh Jamie, Jamie, you fool!' And she wept noisily, her customary poise completely overset. I had only once before seen her in such a state, when she had learned that Simon, whom she had secretly hoped to marry, would wed Nan Blagge in preference.

Mary was making some attempt to comfort her, telling her not to worry, of course he would take care of himself, and return safe and sound: at which Meraud cried wildly, 'No, he won't! I *know* he'll be killed, I knew it all along, and then the baby will have no father . . . and I never told him . . . I never told him about the baby, and now he'll never know!'

Chapter 8

Bounden duty

You shall seek all day ere you find them:
and when you have them, they are not worth the
   search.
                (Shakespeare, *The Merchant of Venice*)

At her words there was at once a flurry of concern. Meraud, weeping piteously, was led to a chair by her mother-in-law, and so liberally dosed with Mary's cowslip and bezoar cordial – 'This will calm her, I've never known it fail' – that I for one feared that the cure would do more harm than the hysteria. At any rate, her strange and untypical behaviour was explained and, remembering how ill I had felt at a similar stage in my own pregnancy, I could not help, despite my worse and predominant nature, but have some sympathy for her.

But my thoughts went suddenly to Grainne, remembering, as she doubtless had all along, that in a fortnight's time, God willing, she and Malise would celebrate their wedding. Now he was gone with Jamie, swept up in a lunatic dream of rebellion that he himself despised. Out of his sense of honour and duty, he had put himself and Grainne's happiness in hazard for foolish, naïve, gullible Jamie's sake.

So it was with a fresh, desperate anxiety that we scoured the neighbourhood for news, fell upon every chance passer-by or casual visitor to wring them dry of any possible drops of useful information, and waited with a growing sense of helplessness as the tidings of rebellion began to reach us. There was a battle at Maidstone, in Kent, in which Fairfax's men had, after a bitter struggle, ousted the rebels, led by the ancient Earl of Norwich, from the town. The remaining Cavaliers had then made for London, hoping to take it by surprise, but old Sir Phillip Skippon shut the gates against them, and the trained bands and a regiment of Horse – Whalley's, so one of our informants said, and made my heart lurch – were moving against them. So Norwich and his three thousand crossed the Thames into Essex: which county was now in ferment, for the day after our visit to Rushbrooke, the Essex County Committee, staunch Parliamentarians all of course, had been seized at Chelmsford, and that town was reported to be boiling with rebellion.

Into the middle of this taut-strung, desperate household, came two dearly-loved and totally dissimilar personalities; the Widow Gooch, astringent and witch-like, ridden from Oxford for Grainne's wedding, and her mock-reluctant escort, Charles Lawrence. Neither had, of course, any knowledge of the events which had just befallen us, and at first did not seem to take the situation very seriously.

'You mean to say there's to be no wedding?' demanded the Widow of me, a faint, acidly humorous glint in her eye. 'For shame, lass, I shall have to turn round and ride home again.'

'That you will not,' said Charles roundly, running a hand through his curling, dusty brown hair. 'Now I'm here, I'm not going till I've got what we came for – a celebration and a dance with all the ladies.' He grinned at me, and I smiled wanly back, thankful that Meraud, who had once pursued him so avidly, was still confined to her chamber, eating very little, suffering from acute sickness, and saying almost nothing. (I had in fact wondered whether this withdrawal from public gaze had anything to do with her considerable loss of looks over the past few days.) I was further glad to notice that Charles seemed entirely his old cheerful self, and showed none of the pathetic signs of a lovelorn, jilted swain. I prayed urgently that his usual common sense had prevailed, and that he no longer had any interest in Meraud: for even now I did not trust her, particularly with Jamie wilfully absent.

'But seriously, though,' said Mistress Gooch, as she divested herself of her appalling patched rusty-black cloak, 'I'm right sorry to hear about Jamie – and more so about your Scottish cousin. I was glad that Grainne had found herself another husband, after all the pain and grief she's had, and now to have him go off like this . . . I'll wring that young Jamie's neck for him, when – if – I see him again. I suppose you've no idea of where they are, lass?'

'None,' I said, my exasperation with my youngest cousin – not to mention Malise – rising to match hers. 'They've been gone nearly a week now – a week tomorrow in fact – and we haven't had so much as a word, let alone any message to say they're all right. We don't know who they're with, it could be the Duke of Buckingham or Sir Charles Lucas, they were both at Rushbrooke that day, and like you, when they come back I will be perched on the porch with a pole-axe – or two.'

'Not to mention boiling water and hot ashes,' said Charles, obviously remembering Ashcott, and the kettles and buckets and cauldrons of such unpleasantnesses waiting in vain in the gatehouse to be dropped on any besiegers below. 'The wedding's set for next Thursday, isn't it? I hope they remember to come back for it.'

'They'd better,' said the Widow, 'or we'd best go out and look for them.'

And her idea, once taken hold in my mind, grew and flourished and refused all the attempts of my more cautious side to reduce it. For many reasons, the thought of setting out in search of my errant cousins was extremely attractive: not the least of them the white drawn face of Grainne, who appeared at last to have lost hope, and would not admit it. For Grainne, who deserved so much more than life had thrown at her, and whose eventual happiness seemed to have been snatched from her grasp by a capricious and cruel fate at the last minute, I would do much, just as she had done so much for me. And also it would be positive action, a most welcome change from second- and third-hand news, rumours, scaremongering and helpless, fuming impotence and ignorance. And even with my concern for Grainne's private anguish, I could spare a small thought, somewhere, for Meraud, whose need of her absent husband seemed nearly as great, if more broadcast, as Grainne's for Malise.

Two days after the arrival of the Widow and Charles, the final banns were read for the imminent marriage of Master Malise Graham, bachelor, of the parish of Castleton in Scotland, and Mistress Grainne Sewell, widow, of Home Farm in this parish. Since the prospective groom had now been missing without trace for just over a week, the sonorous words of the parson seemed a particularly hollow mockery. Due not a little to the tireless efforts of Joan and her notorious gossiping, the entire village was well aware of the situation, and Grainne, sitting calm and white as if carven in marble, was the object of a hundred avid, curious, greedy pairs of eyes turned in her direction. My heart ached for her, and even a little for Meraud, hollow-eyed shadow of her former loveliness, hunched forlornly beside her: and my resolve to do something positive to help them was strengthened still more. Then we all emerged from the dim little church, still bare and unfamiliar after its stripping by Master Dowsing of any 'Popish' embellishments, and heard the latest news, spread by an excited blacksmith: that Goring was in Chelmsford, that men from Essex and Hertfordshire had joined him and he was apparently planning to march north through Suffolk. My mind was made up: I made sure on our way back that I rode next to the Widow, squat like an old black witch in the sun on her ancient white cob that had carried our baggage all the way to Scotland and back, and chose my moment to open the conversation. 'You remember your suggestion that we go and look for Malise and Jamie?'

The Widow was ever too shrewd for me. She cackled triumphantly. 'I knew it! Well, lass, you've got four days, having taken all this time to reach a decision. Do you want me with you, or Mistress Grainne?'

I had considered this question already, and made up my mind. 'You,' I said without hesitation. 'It's not that I don't want Grainne with me as well, for I do, but she's under enough stress already, and I think that going off in a search that may well be futile will break her altogether.'

'Whereas I have no breaking-point at all? Tough as an old riding-boot, I am,' said the Widow, sounding pleased. 'Well, lass, let's lay our plans. Shall we try Chelmsford first, wherever that is? Sounds the most likely place to me. How do we get there?'

Making plans with Mistress Gooch was not a task to be undertaken at a snail's pace. By the time our ambling horses had come in sight of Goldhayes, she had worked out everything to the last detail. 'And if as you say Chelmsford's too far to reach this evening, then we'd best stop . . . where?'

'Sudbury, or even Colchester if we make good progress.'

'And we'll tell Mistress Grainne where we've gone and she can tell the rest when we've left, or we'll have that Lucy clinging to our feet like as not, begging us not to go,' said the Widow, whose opinion of Lucy's sense, despite her affection for her, was with some justification not very high. 'Now, you'll get us some food, will you, lass, without too much fuss? Remember some money and a good warm cloak for yourself; with the weather we've been having it'll doubtless come on to rain, despite all this sun.'

It was indeed a beautiful morning as we set out furtively from Goldhayes, riding across the park rather than down the drive in full view of the inhabitants. There had only been one problem to overcome, and that had been explaining my departure to Kit.

It would perhaps have been better from my point of view to have gone without any word at all, and left the task to Rose or some other unfortunate: but Kit had been betrayed by me before, and I would not do it again. I found him and Hugh having their dinner in their chamber with the nurse, and felt like a criminal when Kit, seeing my travelling cloak draped over my arm, jumped up and cried, 'Where are we going, Mammy? Are we going to Bury?'

'Not to Bury, no, I'm just going for a ride with Mistress Gooch,' I said, gently. Kit's face fell and his lower lip began to jut out mutinously. 'Can't I come? Why can't I come? Mammy, I want to come too!' Tears glittered threateningly on the ends of his long, sweeping lashes: but after six months it was no longer so effective, and he knew it. I cuddled him, swore I would be soon returning – omitting with some cowardice to mention that I expected it would be at least two days before I did – and promising to bring him back a gift from Bury. So it was that I could leave him, guiltily, with no more than a tear-streaked face and a promise that he would be a good boy and do exactly what Rose told him to: and fairly flew down the twisting break-neck turret stairs to join Mistress Gooch and our horses in the stable-yard.

No one remarked our going as anything special, no one really noticed us riding sedately out under the stableyard gatehouse in the bright, windy June air: a small young woman, plainly dressed and mounted on an ordinary sturdy brown mare, and the Widow, on her white cob that was as much part of her as her dreadful cloak and direct, caustic speech. We skirted round the edge of the park, and stopped briefly at the Home Farm, tying our horses to the fence in front of the house.

Grainne was in the dairy, helping Joan with the butter. I supposed that such a mundane task served to divert her mind from the anguish of Malise's disappearance: at all events, she was heaving the beater up and down and around in the churn with an uncharacteristic vigour that indicated that powerful emotions were being given an outlet. As soon as we entered she stopped, handed the job over to Joan, and fairly dragged us outside, another indication of the degree to which her normally calm, unruffled, dignified nature had been eroded. 'What is it? Is there any news?' she demanded almost before we were out of Joan's earshot – and if ever ears flapped, Joan's did. The Widow, glancing round, said, 'No, lass, no news, but we're going in search of some.'

'What do you mean?' Grainne's wild, haunted green eyes stared at us out of her white face, pleading to give her some hope to grasp. 'Tell me, please, what are you going to do?'

'We're going to see if we can find 'em,' said Mistress Gooch. 'I'm not going to promise anything, mind, but if we *do* find 'em they'll be dragged home with more than a few fleas in their ears. We're going to Chelmsford, that's where Norwich was until yesterday, and if they're with Lucas he's supposed to be there too, and it's as good a place as any to start.'

'But you won't get as far as Chelmsford today,' Grainne said, her voice calmer, 'it's after noon already.'

'We'll get as far as Sudbury at least,' I said, 'and we've another eight hours of daylight. Do you mind us interfering like this?'

'Interfering?' said Grainne. 'Interfering? My God, I ...' She looked at us helplessly and gave a wry, brave smile. 'Thank you. Thank you both, so much. I don't want to come with you, I can't ... I don't think I could bear it if ... if they didn't want to come back.'

'They'll want to come back,' said the Widow grimly. 'They'll want anything rather than the piece of my mind that I'm going to give them. And we both thought it best that you weren't with us. There has to be someone with some sense left behind, and what with Lucy behaving like a character in one of her precious stage-plays, Meraud lost in self-pity and Mistress Trevelyan with her head in the air, you're the only one we can trust to keep a cool head and her wits about her.'

'For that compliment, many thanks,' said Grainne, smiling, and the tears glittered bright and unshed in her green eyes. 'I won't keep you any longer, if you have so far to go . . . and good luck, and may God go with you, and may you find them soon . . . goodbye!''

I hugged her, seeking to transfer some of my own optimism to slacken and relieve the tension in that stiff over-wrought body: and then, quickly as she had begged us, I mounted my stolid mare and rode away with the Widow down the road towards Bradfield Tye and Sudbury, and the rebellious south.

It was a fine day, for once during the appalling weather we had endured throughout that spring and early summer, with high fluffy clouds chasing each other across the deep blue sky, that here in High Suffolk seemed so close and wide. There was a brisk breeze that had all the windmills on our route twirling and clacking merrily as they ground the last of the previous year's grain, doubly precious because of the likelihood that this year's harvest would fail because of the weather: and despite the gravity of our mission, my spirits soared with the wind and I could almost have burst into song, so glad was I to be free of the stultifying, fraught, close-closeted atmosphere at Goldhayes, thick with recrimination and anxiety and fear. The Widow, too, looked cheerful, or as near to it as her nutcracker face would allow. 'You seem pleased with yourself, lass – we haven't found 'em yet, you know, don't count your chickens before they're hatched.'

'And you know all about chickens,' I retorted, grinning. 'But we'll find them, I just know it, I feel it in my bones – it's the kind of day when nothing can go wrong.'

'And now you've said it, everything will,' Mistress Gooch muttered: she had her own superstitions. But the day continued fine in all respects. We rode through the usually busy wool towns of south Suffolk, meeting few people abroad on this Sabbath day: the Widow offering appreciative comments on the fine houses of timber and brick, pargetting and plaster, and the huge churches, high-towered and magnificent in flint and stone. We came through Lavenham with its broad main street, and by mid-afternoon arrived in Sudbury, some fifteen miles from Goldhayes, and a town like Lavenham and Kersey, Lindsey and Colchester, built and prospered on the money from its woollens, 'Bays and Says', and its weavers. Here I obtained directions from a surly disapproving inhabitant, for it was a long time since I had been to Colchester and I was not sure of the way. It seemed the best policy to make for that town, for if we continued to make such good progress we would assuredly reach it by dusk, whereas Chelmsford was at least a day's journey hence: and at Colchester there was most likely to be news, and a good inn. Fortunately we both had considerable reserves of coin hidden on our persons, so it would not matter if we did not run Malise and Jamie to earth straight away: which, as my ever-present practical half reminded me, was after all very probable.

But it was a lovely day, and my spirits took flight with the larks whose song Francis had once called 'the trumpets of Heaven' – and although their sweet high impersonal song was an aching reminder of his absence, I had long ago learned that no loss, however anguished, can be forever sustained with the intensity of its beginning. I missed him still, after nearly three years apart, and never more than at moments like these: but the pain was bearable, something with which I had had to live too long. And yet here, under the beautiful, bustling sky, with the warm June wind sifting through my hair, I had a strange sense of his closeness. Somewhere, not too far distant perhaps, he was under this same sky, maybe also feeling this sense of peace, and I was almost content. Today I seemed to myself to be adrift within the chains of my fate, as if like a chess-piece I was being moved as part of some grand pattern I could not see, and could not alter: and there was some comfort in that feeling.

Colchester lay on a hill, a fair prospect from the Sudbury road, lit slantwise and red by the setting sun on our right. It was an attractive, prosperous-looking town, of Roman origin so it was said: and certainly I remembered the castle, from my one previous visit, as being extremely antique, not to say derelict. The river Colne wound charmingly around it like a piece of reflective ribbon, and if I had not been so utterly weary after covering twenty-five or more miles in perhaps seven hours' continuous riding, with none but the briefest breaks for rest and relief, the town might have represented more to me than a haven for the night. Our exhausted horses stumbled down the hill from Mile End church, over the triple-arched north bridge, and up the short length of road to the Northgate.

To our surprise, there were guards there, and not just the usual couple of bored militia-men but a full dozen sturdy, grim-looking townsmen with the independent air typical of Suffolk and Essex weavers. They questioned us closely, both as to our identity and the purpose of our journey: and at the name of Heron, which after all was not unknown in those parts, the two asking the questions exchanged significant glances. 'Hev yew any news, Mistress?' one of them enquired.

'News? News of what?' I countered.

'News of that there Earl of Norwich or whatever he call himself. At Chelmsford he were, today, and we've been towd off to keep a look-out for him.'

'No, no,' I said, with an attempt at nonchalance. 'No, we've no news. We're just here on family business. Where would you suggest we stay? The King's Head?'

'Aye, the King's Head be the best inn in Colchester,' said the more friendly of our two interrogators. 'Whether they'll have any room for you, Mistress Heron, is another matter, but you can try. Know where it is? Keep on straight up this hill and it's at the top on your right, nearly at the Head Gate on the other side of the walls, can't miss it!' And despite the dubious looks of his comrade, he waved us cheerfully by.

You could not indeed miss the King's Head: the largest, most palatial establishment in Colchester, if not the whole of Essex, it was a fine plaster-and-timber building in the familiar local style, set back a little from the street and reached under an arch. Two boys ran to take our weary horses and mine host, casting a dubious glance at me and a far more doubtful one at the Widow, came out to enquire our wishes.

The sun was setting, its light still shining red on the uppermost parts of the inn, and at that particular moment all I most desired in the world was a horizontal position in one of the landlord's softest feather beds. But appearances had to be kept up, a room had to be requested and his not unnatural doubts as to our respectability (and consequent ability to pay his exorbitant charges) allayed. It was a good half hour before I could attain my heart's desire: and by that time I would have fallen on to the bed fully clothed had not the Widow, whose energy seemed as ever to be almost beyond the human, made me remove my mud-spotted garments down to my shift, and ensured that I was comfortably tucked up in between the sheets. Just as if she were my mother, was my last conscious thought before I fell asleep . . .

It was broad daylight when I awoke to the brisk swish as the Widow drew back the bed-curtains. 'Come on, lass, time you was up and about, it's gone eight o'clock.'

'Eight o'clock?' I stared at her, clogged still with sleep. 'Eight o'clock? It can't be!'

'It can, and it is, and here's something to break your fast and set you up for the day – and you'll need it when I tell you the news that's all round the town this morning, according to the serving-maid.'

I sat upright, abruptly startled out of my doze. 'What news?'

The Widow grinned and deposited a laden tray on my knees. 'There you are, frumenty – you always was partial to that if I remember rightly – and a nice bit of cold bacon and bread still warm from the oven, first of the day's baking, and all done while you was asleep.' She winked. Almost choking with impatience, I said, 'Never mind all this. *What* news?'

'There's some of the Earl of Norwich's men rode into the town an hour ago or more, and they're drumming up support for their cause outside the Moot Hall at this very minute. Added to which, all the rebels are on their way here from Braintree, so it's said, and God knows what Fairfax is doing. Still got his hands full in Kent? Though they're saying that Norwich is being shadowed by some of Parliament's horse, and the name given to me was Whalley's.' She looked at me significantly. 'So, looks like we don't need to move, do it, lass – just sit tight and wait for all of 'em to come to us. And I hope there won't be no unfortunate meetings, whatever happens.'

I knew exactly what she meant: and my first instinctive upsurge of delight at the thought that Francis was not far away, and coming nearer, was tempered by that hideous, ancient nightmare, so far spared me, that one day Heron would encounter Heron, on opposing sides of the battlefield. I pushed that awful vision resolutely from me – after all, coincidence could be carried too far – but it would not quite be killed, and lingered as a vague, apprehensive ache, as the Widow and I waited all that long June day for the arrival of the rebel army of the elderly Earl of Norwich.

The town, as might be imagined, was twitching with feverish anxiety. Very few people were in any way supporters of the King, save for the poor unemployed weavers and certain unruly young men only too glad to have the chance of some action, no matter on whose side: had it been Fairfax drumming for recruits, I doubt they would have been any slower to join. And the name of Lucas, I was not altogether surprised to find, was as mud on the lips of the worthy, sober citizens of Colchester – indeed, his house at St John's had been ransacked by a hostile mob some years ago, very early in the war. So antagonistic was the town towards the approaching Royalists that, when news of their imminent arrival spread through the town in the afternoon, the Mayor called out the trained bands.

As they marched past on their way to face the Earl of Norwich, the Widow and I left our room in the King's Head and, in common with what seemed like most of Colchester, made our way by dint of ruthless use of elbows and knees and our stoutly-shod feet to the best vantage-point, on the ancient crumbling ramparts by the Head Gate, where the London Road left the town. There was in fact little to see, and all the drama took place offstage: the little band of the town's Militia Horse beaten off with ease by the Cavaliers, and the humiliating aftermath as the unimpressive Mayor of Colchester, flanked by the town officials and a clutch of local justices, negotiated an unheroic surrender. The disgusted comments of the townspeople, as this unpalatable truth became known, rose from all around us on the walls.

'I don't believe it!'

'They in't a-gooing to let them in, surely not!'

'Shame on yew!'

'Whoi don't yew stand and foight!'

'Thass roight, kill the Cavaliers!'

'If there are as many of 'em as rumour has it,' the Widow whispered to me behind her hand, 'they ain't got much choice but to let 'em in, lass. Let's pray God those two misbegotten cousins of yours are amongst them, and then we can whip 'em back to Goldhayes and leave this lot to fight it out with Fairfax as they please.'

Privately, I doubted whether even the Widow's powers of persuasion could deflect Jamie from his headlong flight from reality and responsibility, but she as ever had enough confidence for twenty, and I would not have put it past her to carry out her threat to use a poleaxe, albeit somewhat earlier than her original intention. In any case, there was no immediate chance to ascertain whether or not Malise and Jamie were part of the Cavalier army: for although the news spread rapidly through the crowd that, in return for various promises of good behaviour, lack of extortion and freedom for the townsmen from enforced military service ('and I don't reckon as they Cavaliers will keep their word for any longer'n it suits them,' said one cynic not far from us, to a swelling murmur of discontent from his audience), the Royalists had been grudgingly allowed within the walls, there was no room for the bulk of the army, and with a fine irony they were marched into the courtyard of the Lucas house at St John's a few hundred yards away from us in the suburbs. I could see from where I stood the pinnacled outline of the mediaeval Abbey gateway, next to the house.

By this time the drizzle, which had been falling all afternoon, had stopped, but it was growing late in the evening and, resentful, cold and wet, the townspeople were departing in dribs and drabs to their homes. Since there seemed little else we could do, the Widow and I left the walls as well and went back to the King's Head. By now it was almost dark, and the stars were emerging hesitantly one by one, through the clearing cloud, promising perhaps a fine day on the morrow, the day when we would surely find Malise and Jamie, and bear them triumphantly back to Goldhayes, the trophies of our hunt. In good spirits we entered the inn yard and found a huge eddying tide of damp, sweaty soldiery, all talking and arguing at once. In the middle was a well-dressed, stout gentleman in his sixties, pouch-eyed and impatient-looking, who from his resemblance to his son I guessed to be the Earl of Norwich, formerly Lord Goring, and the Royalist leader. Then amid the confused babble of voices – offering advice, prophesying disaster if sufficient provisions were not brought to the men, demanding to know what could be done against Fairfax, who was somewhere in Essex and in hot pursuit – I heard an intonation that was familiar. Like a ferret after a rabbit, I wriggled my way almost unnoticed around the tangled knot of soldiers, leaving the Widow stranded, and to my intense relief beheld, on the doorstep, a tall, red-haired figure, gaunt and clumsy, his raw Scots voice carrying despite his attempts to lower it, as he talked with a comrade. I stood at his elbow, unseen and joyful, for some time before the Widow, joining me abruptly, tapped him on the shoulder – or as near to it as she could reach. 'Are you Master Graham? We want a word with you.'

Malise whipped round with such speed that the scabbard of his sword struck the door-post an almighty and clashing blow. An extraordinary mixture of emotions – astonishment, embarrassment, guilt, pleasure, relief – dodged across his eagle-nosed face: then, endearingly, he blushed. 'Thomazine! By a' the de'ils in Hell, what are you doing here?'

'Looking for you,' said the Widow menacingly. She added, addressing the startled soldier to whom he had been talking, 'Pray excuse us, sir, but Master Graham has much to discuss with us, and it must be speedy and private.' And with her grasp on one arm and mine on the other, poor Malise was towed inside to the dim private parlour, and fixed with the Widow's beady and heartless eye. 'Well? And what have you to say for yourself?'

He had never laid eyes on her before: it was like watching a fly struggling on a hook. I felt suddenly that I did not want to see Malise, whom I loved and respected, thus brought to confusion. I introduced Mistress Gooch, and added, 'We have been worried about you. We want you to come home, with us. Now.'

'Worried?' the Widow snorted. 'The girl you were going to marry on Thursday is near out of her mind with despair, and being Grainne, she won't admit it to anyone, and if that's ordinary "worried" then I'm one of my own hens. I may not know you, sir, but I know her, and I'm concerned for her happiness. Well? Are you going to come back to Goldhayes and marry her like you promised, or are you going to leave us the task of telling her you love soldiering more than her?'

Malise turned abruptly and faced the fire, which in this unseasonably cold damp weather was banked and smouldering sullenly. I was almost sure, in the red-lit dusky room, that I had seen a look of almost unbearable pain cross his face: and despite my exasperation, a surge of intense sympathy overtook me. He said, his voice almost unrecognizable, 'I canna do it. I canna come back wi' ye, I gave my word.'

'You gave your word to Grainne too, and she deserves better than this,' I said quietly, pitching my voice to strike every syllable home.

'I gave my word, and I canna go back on it. I canna leave them now, they need me!'

'But so does Grainne. And it's my bet she needs you more – and you her.'

'I gave my word!' Malise cried, and turned savagely to face us again, his expression contorted with longing and grief. 'I promised yon bunch of chuckle-heided gomerels I'd look to their Horse, I'm commissioned Captain to Sir Charles Lucas, and if I go wi' ye now that's desertion pure and simple.'

'But *why* did you give your word?' I cried despairingly. 'Why, in God's name? You *knew* you were going to be married this week! Why on *earth* did you join them?'

'It was my duty,' said Malise simply. I felt like throwing something – the pewter tankard temptingly close to my hand would have done nicely to vent my frustrations – but restricted myself with an effort to verbal battle. 'I don't give a damn for duty! Where has it ever got this family? Simon and Nan lonely in a Dutch garret, for duty's sake. Lucy, pining for Dan Ashley, because his duty keeps him away from her in Oxford. Ned being killed at Edgehill, for his duty to his King – no belief in the rightness of his cause, just duty. Francis and I separated, because of duty. And now you want to betray Grainne, and all you promised her, for duty. Because you've given your word! Well, you gave your word to her as well, and before you ever clapped eyes on Lord Norwich and the rest, or got mixed up in this lunatic addle-pated rebellion, and to my mind you owe *her* your duty, or your love is all sham and a hollow pretence. Tell your precious Sir Charles Lucas that your betrothed is desperately ill – and that'll be no lie anyway, if you don't go to her – and demand compassionate leave. Do it now, for God's sake, while there's still time to get out of it all and safe back to Goldhayes.'

Malise's face was a study in unhappiness. I said urgently, 'You don't really want to stay here, do you? You really want to come back with us and marry Grainne on Thursday, that's what you *want* to do, isn't it? You couldn't really care less about Norwich and the rest of them, save for Jamie. Where *is* Jamie, by the way?'

'At St John's, wi' the rest o' them,' said Malise. He sat down abruptly, and buried his face in his hands. 'They're hungry, and if the good folk o' Colchester don't bring them sufficient to eat, there'll be a mutiny before long, I'm thinking . . . Oh Christ, Thomazine, you're right, o' course, I shouldna be here at all, I should be wi' Grainne, my dear Grainne, and be damned to all of them . . .' He looked up at us both, the Widow still standing accusingly behind one of the old high-backed wooden chairs, myself nearer and, hopefully, more sympathetic. 'Gi'e me tonight tae think it over, please – and I'll tell ye in the morning, early. Ah, the temptation tae go back is sae sore . . . Where are ye staying? Are ye staying here, the night?'

'I imagine we still are,' said the Widow. 'Our rooms are paid for, but there's others may stake a claim, and we might be put out on the street yet.'

'That ye willna, not if I can help it,' said Malise positively. 'I'll go and make that certain now.' He leapt to his feet, and the chair crashed back noisily against the hearth. Mistress Gooch raised her eyebrows: Malise, already at the door, grinned at her. 'Gi'es me something tae think about, ye ken, something tae do. Wait here, and I'll see the Quartermaster for ye.' And with a whirl of cloak and fringed sash, and the wind from the slam of the door, he was gone.

'Well, so that's Malise Graham,' said the Widow. 'He's not the fool he appears, is he?'

'No,' I said, busy with my own private certainty that Malise's torn and conflicting conscience would eventually come down on the side of the angels. 'Grainne would hardly be marrying him, else. It was the perfect cover for his activities in Scotland, no one took him seriously, and he and Francis spent the better part of a year spying for Montrose all along the Scots Border and were never even suspected. I think – I hope – that we'll win and if Jamie knows he's to be a father, perhaps that will swing the balance a little more in our favour.'

'We'll see,' said the Widow, 'we'll see. What's more to the point just now is, will he persuade their quarter-master to let us stay?'

Within a short while, Malise returned, the light of battle still in his eye, and announced that we could keep our chamber: so that all was well in that quarter. 'I'm glad that's settled,' I said. 'And many thanks – I'd far rather stay here at the centre of everything than be cast out to find lesser accommodation; that is, if we could, with the town full of Royalists. Anyway, perhaps tomorrow we can go back?'

'Gi'e me tonight tae think on it,' said Malise, avoiding my eye and the Widow's. 'Just gi'e me tonight, and I'll gi'e ye your answer the morrow.'

'And what of Jamie?' the Widow enquired. Malise cast us a despairing glance. 'Ye'll get nae sense out o' *him*, he's full o' nothing but his duty to the King, and fighting for His Majesty's cause, and in truth he fought bravely enough this afternoon, and his first fight too. But ye wouldna get him back to Goldhayes save feet first, I'm thinking.'

'He's needed, though, as you are,' said the Widow tartly. 'But not for the same reasons, mind you. His good lady wife is with child, and pining for him, believe it or not: and though our hearts and thoughts are all for Grainne, Meraud deserves some consideration too, from him if no one else.'

'She willna get it,' said Malise bluntly, 'bairn or no', it isna Meraud he's wedded tae, it's the King's cause. I'll tell him you're here, for I'm awa' over tae St John's now, but I canna promise any sort o' reply. Mine ye'll hae in the morning. Good night tae ye both now, and sleep well.'

We did just that, restored to our comfortable little room under the eaves, with the noise of the rain and the rustlings of sparrows in the attics doing nothing to disturb our slumbers. Indeed, the chambermaid's morning entrance was the first thing that brought me to wakefulness, and by then it was full light. As we breakfasted in our chamber, there was no sign of Malise, but a great deal of bustle below stairs and, more distantly, in the street outside. The girl, coming in to remove our plates, informed us that the soldiers, thousands of them so she said, were being marched into the town to be quartered on the townsfolk, the request for provisions having presumably met with a poor response.

'Well,' said Mistress Gooch, as we stood at the window peering at our very limited view of Head Street, 'are we going to sit here and wait about all day, or are we going to seek out Master Graham and young Jamie ourselves?'

'Seek them out,' I said, being likewise more than a little weary of waiting: and we donned cloaks against the rain and sallied forth into Colchester.

There was no one in the King's Head of any note bar the disconsolate Committee-members, who were under guard in their chambers, so we walked out into the wet courtyard. The street outside was full of Royalist soldiers trudging to their new quarters, and a motley crew they appeared: 'prentices and yeomen, gentry and weavers mixed, motivated, by the look of them, more by the desire for violent excitement than by any love of the King's cause. Up and down the street there were fierce arguments being conducted between the officers attempting to quarter their men, and the indignant hostile residents of the town. Loud cries of warning alerted us as we stood irresolute in the gateway of the inn, and through the Head Gate, drawn by teams of horses, trundled two great brazen cannon, destined for

St Mary's church, just behind the King's Head, where an emplacement would be set up. As we watched, a rider came clattering through in their wake and reined his lathered, mired horse in almost at our feet. 'Mistress, is this the King's Head inn? Where may I find Lord Norwich?'

'As to the first, this is the King's Head, and as for the second, I have no idea whatsoever,' I told him. 'Do you by any chance know where Captain Malise Graham is?'

'Graham? No, I know no one of that name,' said the soldier, his eyes sliding already in search of other assistance. 'Sir! Where's Lord Norwich? I must find him urgently – Fairfax is sighted on the London Road beyond Lexden, and we must shut the gates!'

The officer thus addressed pointed away down the street, and the scout sent his tired horse slithering through the mud in the direction indicated. Mistress Gooch grabbed my arm. 'If Fairfax is coming there'll be a fight for certain, perhaps a siege. We must find your cousins straightaway, or we'll never get them away from here in time!'

Then began a nightmare morning as we fought our way through the crowded, bewildering streets of a town I hardly knew, asking every officer we met of the whereabouts of Malise Graham or Jamie Heron, and receiving from those harassed gentlemen at best curt avowals of ignorance, and at worst indifference, hostility and open abuse. After what must have been the fiftieth such response, by the East Gate at the opposite end of the town from the King's Head, I was ready to despair, and the Widow had long since descended to returning incivilities in kind. 'You're no more a gentleman, sir, than a New World savage!' she called after the unheeding back of the rudest captain yet, and then turned to me. 'No better than pigs, most of 'em, you'd think they'd at least be civil . . . let's get back to the inn and find out what's happening. They'll maybe know more there, by now . . .'

But as we plodded back along the High Street, past

the Moot Hall, the drums could be heard calling the soldiers to muster. Soon we were forced back along the edge of the street by the tides of men, some full armed, others wielding only clubs or scythes or pitchforks, streaming to the town's walls, urged on by their hurrying officers, and knew that we were too late. Those citizens around us knew little more than we, save that Fairfax was coming: and their universal hope, which they assumed we shared, was that the Lord General would give the Earl of Norwich and his men their just deserts and free the town of its unwelcome, unwanted visitors. At last, in the wake of the rearguard of the soldiers, we were able to make our way back towards the King's Head: and as we approached, we saw the road around the Head Gate choked with soldiery, and in the inn's courtyard, a tumultuous, seething mass of officers and men, the air thick with orders being issued, and the tuck of drum, the distant shrieking of trumpets, clattering hooves and marching feet. Miraculously, in the middle of all this bedlam appeared Malise, fighting his way through the press by dint of his size and urgency. 'Thank God I've found ye both! Where ha' ye been?'

'Looking for you,' I gasped, suddenly weak with relief. 'We spent all morning looking for you ... what's happening?'

'Fairfax has sent his trumpeter asking for our surrender,' said Malise, 'and Norwich has sent back his answer – he said he'd heard Fairfax suffered frae the gout, and tellt him no' to worry, for Goring would cure all his diseases ... we're making ready now, for he'll surely attack.'

'And what about your answer, sir?' asked the Widow, but I knew, had known in my heart now for a long time, what that would be, for it was too late now for him to turn back. 'I canna,' said Malise, his eyes on the ground. 'Fairfax has seen tae that, if he'd held off another day ... he'll hae the place surroundit if he's ony sense, and there'll be nae escape then, not for ony of us, not for you.'

'Not even for us?' I stared at him stupidly, for this eventuality had not occurred to me: and Malise said, more grimly than was his wont, 'Not unless ye plan tae go now and ask Sir Thomas nicely if ye can go through his lines . . . my advice tae ye now, is, go tae your room and stay there, dinna go out on the street whatever happens, and ye'll be as safe as ye can be. There may be a good deal of fighting around here before the day's endit.'

I would have argued, for I did not in the least relish a tame retirement to our isolated little chamber, where we might as well be at Goldhayes for all the view we would have of events: but Malise took our arms and steered us ruthlessly across the crowded yard, to the main door. 'Nae arguing, now, I dinna want your deaths on my conscience as well as a' the rest. Mistress Gooch, I've heard ye're a lady o' some sense, get it into Thomazine's heid that this is something she can do nothing about at a', whatever she may think about playing God.' And gently but firmly, he opened the door, pushed us in, and shut it behind himself: putting his head round it again briefly to assure us, 'If a' goes well, I'll be back tae see ye both this evening – and I'll tak' care tae bring Jamie wi' me.'

And with that we had to be content, although the fever of angry impatience in which I passed the rest of that day could hardly be described as 'content'. At first, obeying Malise's orders, we stayed in our chamber, glued to the window, before Mistress Firmin arrived to announce that a good view could be had from one of the garrets if we cared to join her. Needing no second bidding, we followed her up a dark, narrow little staircase to one of the servants' rooms, which faced west, and thus afforded a prospect of the battle about to be fought.

As I craned from the window, I could see, quite close on the right, the tower of St Mary's church above the jumble of roofs, and just behind it the town wall, with the houses lower down in the suburbs beyond it. In the middle distance the London Road was visible, bisecting the higher ground of Lexden Heath: and across it, a dark menacing smudge with here and there the sharp glitter of metal, were advancing Fairfax's men.

As so long before, when I had watched the battle at Edgehill from the ridgetop with Jamie, the intense drama in front of me was acted out with a strange remoteness, the cracking of muskets and the distant yells of the soldiers seeming somehow only to add to my sense of unreality. From somewhere the landlady had procured a spyglass, a magnificent brass piece which I suspected to be the property of one of the Royalist command, and the three of us took it in turns to survey the battlescene through this novel device. We saw the clash between the two forces (in this rainy weather there were no clouds of dust to obscure the view, just powder-smoke) and the intense fighting between the two bodies of infantry in the centre. Somewhere amongst the cavalry, on the wings of the Royalist army, were Malise and Jamie, and I prayed silently and desperately for their safety: and then, as clouds of smoke began to blur our view, it became apparent that the Royalists were retreating. The superior weapons and discipline of Fairfax's men were turning the balance, and suddenly the retreat became a headlong flight back to the safety of the town.

Once amongst the houses of the suburbs, underneath the walls, we could of course see precious little, although it was obvious that pursuit was very hot and the fighting, judging by the ever-increasing noise, extremely fierce. Here and there powder-smoke rose in quantity, betraying the locations of the most desperate struggles. It was agonizing and frustrating in the extreme, to have no idea of how the fight was going, and strain my eyes and ears as I would, I was none the wiser. In desperation, I grasped Mistress Firmin's arm. 'The fighting's moved round to the Head Gate, I can hear it, is there somewhere we can see more?'

The landlady was a kindly soul and took pity on me.

'The chamber over the gateway arch will give you a view of the street and the Head Gate if you lean out far enough, but . . .'

'And what will your fine Scottish cousin say if a stray bullet passes too close?' the Widow enquired. 'Not to speak of your other cousins. If you're set on a choicer view I'd best come with you and make sure you don't put yourself in more danger than's necessary . . . and besides,' she added, winking at me, 'how else am I to see what's happening?'

The chamber in question was reached through a labyrinth of interconnecting rooms on the first floor, running round one side of the inn yard. It bore the stamp of military occupation, but the martial sounds outside were a far more immediate sign of the conflict. My first impulse was to fling wide the window, but the Widow fortunately laid a hand on my sleeve. 'Have your wits left you? The fighting's spread into the town, do you want to be shot by some desperate soldier who thinks you'll drop hot ashes on his head? Look carefully, lass, for God's sake.'

The three of us peeped cautiously around the shutters. The street below was a swirling eddy of men, all, from the motley nature of their garments, of the Royalist forces, some in retreat, others, more determined, pushing forward again. Try as I might, I could not discern any familiar face in that shouting torrent, that suddenly as we watched parted to allow the cavalry through: they appeared to have borne the brunt of the fighting, with lathered, mired horses, and many wounded men, stained with blood and powder-smoke. There seemed to be no danger, for the moment at least, and before the Widow could stop me I hauled the window open and leaned out. The movement caught a few eyes and attracted the kind of noises and comments that young men will always give to the young women they see: and suddenly filled with a wild reckless feeling of comradeship with these desperate yet cheerful soldiers, I waved and shouted, 'How goes it?'

'They're too strong for us, but we'll keep them out of the town, God willing!' the nearest called, a sturdy young man with the accent of London. 'We ain't beaten yet, Mistress, we'll hold 'em off, the ranting crew!' And he flung off his hat and roared the Royalist battle-cry: 'God and King Charles!'

All up and down the street, above the shouts and sword-clashing and pistol-shots about the Head Gate, his words were taken up and roared back. 'God and King Charles!' And I shouted it with them. The noise redoubled suddenly, the men pushed forward, my informant was lost to view, and suddenly I saw on my right, down the sloping street, the flash of metal and the blue-grey drifting smoke of gunfire. Fairfax's men were within the gate.

This was no distant dreamlike drama: this was the reality, the first serious fighting I had ever beheld so near, through all the years of the war. Not fifteen yards away, the men who a moment before had whistled so cheerily at me were engaged in the murderous, gruesome confusion of close-quarter fighting. The Londoner, perhaps a waterman or a 'prentice, attempting to do battle with a sickle against the impersonal machine that was a New Model soldier, buff coat and steel helmet and bright-stained sword, as implacable as the onset of night: and falling bloodily down amongst the struggling feet. A Roundhead horseman was brought down by a lucky pistol-shot from a Royalist officer who, I saw with a shock of recognition that turned my stomach over, was Jamie. I screamed his name, but in that bedlam I could hardly hear my own voice, and could not expect him to. Frantically, my eyes followed him, seeing him gather a group of men on the edge of the street, almost opposite me, and ready them for the charge back downhill to the gate. Another Roundhead appeared fighting valiantly, his men pressing behind him, forcing the Royalists back up towards the centre of the town. Jamie, his mouth hurling unheard epithets, led his little band into the side of them, and for a few seconds I hung unseen right above the waving, slicing fierce swords, the blood and stink of sweat and wet leather and the yells of agony and encouragement. Jamie slipped and fell, one Roundhead lunged at him and was cut down from behind, others loomed ... something to throw, I thought wildly, glanced round and grabbed the first thing to hand, a brimming pewter chamber-pot on the floor by my feet. Below, Jamie was almost invisible beneath an enormous buff-jerkined soldier, sword raised to strike. I hurled the chamber-pot, contents and all, as hard as I could: it clanged on to the Roundhead's helmet with a sound I could hear even above the pandemonium of the fighting. He reeled and almost fell, more probably from surprise than from the force of the blow, and Jamie, as quick-witted as his brother Francis, seized his chance and scrambled to his feet and out of that danger. The soldier I had hit was attacked by another Royalist: and then I lost sight of Jamie in the confusion as a fresh tide of Cavaliers, regrouped in the centre of the town, came roaring down the street towards the Head Gate, the tall, dark-haired figure of Lord Capel, pike in hand, running at their head. In seconds the fighting was swept away downwards, leaving the flotsam and jetsam of battle, dead and dying and wounded, discarded weapons, pools of blood, flung across the street like the aftermath of shipwreck: and suddenly overwhelmed with reaction, I sank to my knees, my head in my hands, and did not know whether to laugh or to weep.

Lord Capel's charge drove the Roundheads from Colchester, and the gate was shut against them and barred with his own cane, for they could not find the bolt: and although Fairfax's men, with stones and fire and cannon, tried to break it down, the fury of the Royalists, still vigorously defending from the walls with muskets and stones and hot ashes, eventually drove them back. As dusk drew a merciful shadow across the littered street, the sky glowed red from the sunset, and also from the burning houses outside the walls, fired by Fairfax in a vain attempt to set light to the defiant town. The sinister flickering flames cast their glare upwards at the rainclouds hanging above us, threatening to douse the torches dancing eerily in the street as the debris from the evening's fighting was carried away to surgeon or churchyard. There was no more to watch, nothing left to do, no sign of Jamie or Malise. Too tired and shocked by what I had seen to think any more, I went with the two older women down to the private parlour, where we fell upon a generous supper served by a frightened child of a maidservant, all eyes in a white distraught face, who jumped like a burnt cat at every loud noise from outside. Gradually, the hot food restored me, and my numbness fell away and was replaced by a gnawing anxiety about Malise and Jamie: and as if in answer to my worry, there was a tap on the door as we finished the meal, and their two heads, disparate black and red, appeared round it. 'Good evening tae ye,' said Malise, notably slower and wearier than when I had last seen him, 'I kept part o' my promise.'

'Thomazine!' said Jamie, pushing past him to embrace me in his hearty, heedless fashion, just like his sister. He smelt of sweat and powder and horses, and seemed somehow far taller than the irresponsible boy he had been just ten days ago. 'It's good to see you, but what in God's name are you doing here?'

'You sound just like Simon at Edgehill,' I said, grinning at him in sheer relief. 'What am I doing here? I'm here to bring you back, of course. Jamie, Meraud needs you, she needs you because she is going to bear you a child.'

Jamie gave a delighted gasp, his face burning suddenly with pleased pride in his achievement. 'A child? Oh, that's wonderful, that's such good news . . . Did you hear that, Malise, I'm going to be a father!' Exuberantly, he took my hands and kissed my cheek. 'A baby, a son, *my* son . . . is Meraud well?'

'No,' I said bluntly. 'No, she is *not* well. Oh, Jamie, she is ill, she needs you, just as Grainne needs

Malise. Please, come back with us now, while you still can.'

'Come back? Back to Goldhayes? I wouldn't dream . . . My God, Thomazine, not even you can rule my life, you know, and not for *anything* am I running away now, not when it's just started.'

'Just ending, you mean,' said the Widow. Jamie glanced at her, startled and indignant: she explained herself. 'Yes, ending. You haven't a chance, you know, Fairfax can sit on this harmless, unfortunate little town like a dog at a rabbit-hole until you and we all starve alike, and where's your precious cause then? Properly sunk, and you in prison or worse, and a whole townful of innocent people made to suffer.'

'But that's why we must hold out for as long as possible!' Jamie, his face impassioned, inflamed, strode around the table, cloak swinging, while Malise watched from the shadows, a faint rueful smile on his face. 'Fairfax is their best general, with Cromwell. The best men in their cursed Army are here – Whalley's, Barkstead's, Ingoldsby's – if they're all kept here, and more of them, to besiege us all summer, then there's the Scots, and the Duke of Buckingham . . . Oh, it's not lost,' said Jamie, as ever oblivious to reality, 'it's only just beginning, and we'll win, we're bound to!'

'Why?' demanded the Widow, a douche of cold water that completely missed its target. For Jamie was now, I saw with terror, armoured entirely within his fantasies, and no arguments, no reasoning, no reality, could pierce him.

And Francis was in Whalley's Regiment, and Ingoldsby's had Dan Ashley as its Major. Here, I realized with a dim, formless foreboding, lay all the seeds of tragedy, at the end of a tunnel down which, heedless and headlong, Jamie Heron was rushing.

'Of course we'll win, we've as many men as Fairfax, if not more, and though they're only country lads for the most part, they can fight as bravely as any. You should have seen them today!'

'She did,' said the Widow. 'She was the one that threw the chamber-pot that cracked your round-polled attacker's head in the street out there – so it's her you should thank for your life, and pay a little more heed to what she says.'

'Look,' said Malise, coming forward. 'There isna any point in arguing about that, nae point at a'. There's nae going back now for any of us, we're a' trapped here until the siege is lifted, whether it's by storm or surrender or relief.'

It was only then that the full seriousness of our situation struck home to me. If we were indeed beleaguered within the town, there was no way of letting those at Goldhayes know what had happened to us. They might be able to make a good guess, but they would not know for certain: the Widow and I to all intents and purposes had vanished off the face of the earth. Grainne would have yet another burden of anxiety, Meraud further fuel for her hysterical sickness, and Kit had been betrayed by me for the second time in his brief life. Not only had I left him with false promises of my prompt return: in the tense excitement and worry of these two days at Colchester, I had completely forgotten his existence, I had not thought of him at all, and I had persuaded him to give all his love and allegiance to me.

The enormity of this overwhelmed me in the soft dark of my bed, and oblivious to the Widow's unheeding snores, I wept silently for my bereft, bewildered son: so strongly could I imagine his white, vivid little face at the windows of Goldhayes, like an abandoned puppy, waiting vainly for me to come back to him, and the damage that must surely be done, should I not return soon.

As at last I drifted into a troubled, unhappy, haunted sleep, the chilly summer moon rose over Colchester, and cast its impartial, fitful light through the trailing, ragged clouds and down on to the people within it and without, friend and foe and neither: the Royalist leaders, so certain of the justness of their cause that they would put

379

a whole townful of innocent people in jeopardy for it: and the Army of Fairfax, already building their first fort, settling down for the inevitable siege. Somewhere, too, it shone down upon Francis, and I knew somehow as I fell asleep that he was safe, and close, and in no danger: so that the old ache of longing was soon appeased, and took second place to my fears for Kit, alone and bereft of my love, and left defenceless now against the subtle malice of Meraud.

Naturally, the peaceful daily round in Colchester was rudely transformed by its abrupt and unwanted pitch-forking into national affairs. Its three main sources of income were the market, the little port so busy it was popularly and punningly referred to as 'the Hive', and the manufacture of the famous woollens, the Bays and Says: and with Fairfax's usual speed, all these were swiftly severed, and the town cut off from the world outside. Within it, Colchester itself resembled a hive, aswarm with soldiers, four thousand of them, searching houses for arms and powder, bringing the stores of grain, raisins, oil and starch from the warehouses on the quay at the Hythe, strengthening the weak places so alarmingly frequent along the town ramparts, or setting up artillery bastions on the tower of St Mary's church and on St Botolph's Gate. At first the days were made hideous by the frequent gunfire from St Mary's less than a hundred yards away from us at the King's Head: later, though, as powder grew short, the gunners were more sparing with their shot. From the garret windows at the top of the inn, the Army headquarters on Lexden Heath could clearly be seen, and nearer and more menacing, the steady inexorable building of the forts and ramparts gradually encircling the town, to draw the noose tight.

We were in a privileged position at the King's Head, sharing the accommodation not only with the Royalist High Command but with their unfortunate captives, the men of the Essex Committee, who from time to time made vain attempts to negotiate a peaceful surrender.

We grew to know the Royalist leaders well: the ancient wit, the Earl of Norwich (father of Lord Goring, the young and dissolute Cavalier general who had been no asset to the King's cause), chosen as leader more for his seniority rather than any fitness for the post: Sir Charles Lucas, native of the town and brother-in-law to the Earl of Newcastle, a ruthless, vain and forceful man who reminded me not a little of the overbearing Tom Blagge: and Sir George Lisle, a pleasant, likeable person, always courteous and considerate, with a gentle sense of humour. He was a bookseller's son, unassuming amidst the other more aristocratic leaders, and was on occasions not too busy to pass the time of day with me or the Widow: our calm, civilized conversations conducted with difficulty amidst the noise and hurly-burly of the siege.

If I had ever thought about it before, I would have assumed that a prolonged siege would have been a tedious and nerve-wracking affair: and yet this was not. Despite the terrible weather, cold with almost ceaseless rain, the morale of the ill-assorted soldiers stayed remarkably buoyant, and humour could be found, if one looked, in almost any situation, whether it was the incongruous sight of a windmill being erected on the Castle roof, or the ham-fisted efforts of weavers and watermen at building ramparts and handling stone. The same spirit of camaraderie that had bound us all, friend and foe, together at the brief siege of Ashcott, seemed to grow and flourish here on the stoniest of soils. Men and officers took a delight in making the most ingenious possible use of whatever came to hand. Night forays and daytime raids brought in cattle, sheep and grain from the countryside around: although as the chain of forts fettering the town extended, these excursions grew more dangerous and infrequent. Moreover, since Sir Charles insisted that only known supporters of the Parliament should be thus robbed, even in Northern Essex the foragers' choice was somewhat limited. Both Jamie and Malise, being cavalry officers, were concerned in these expeditions, but despite frequent brushes with the enemy, they both seemed to bear a charmed life: neither was there ever any mention of my particular nightmare, a confrontation in some midnight skirmish between Malise or Jamie on the one side, and Francis or Dan Ashley on the other. Jamie, who for so long had had because of his youth and inexperience to stand by as others fought, acquired a joyous lust for action and excitement that frightened me; for even if all this came somehow, miraculously, to a conclusion that would allow his safe return to Goldhayes and his wife and unborn child, how would he ever settle again to dull domestic bliss, having had such an enthralling baptism of fire?

And Malise, dear, kind, conscientious Malise, who had once been the patient, thoughtful shadow to Francis's bright flame, had no heart for what he was doing and, being Malise, showed it. After one disastrous night-time expedition in which his nervous chestnut mare, Tanaquill, nearly drowned them both in the River Colne and drew the Roundheads' fire in the process, he went to his commanding officer, Sir Charles Lucas, and requested that he serve henceforth as a humble trooper, rather than bear a captain's responsibility when he did not feel himself equal to the task. It had not been the case in Montrose's wild, unruly, brilliant army, when he and Francis had both been caught up in the legend and had given their utmost to further that dream. At Colchester Malise, as he confessed freely to me, was totally unable to do as much for Lucas and Lisle, Capel and Norwich, none of whom could inspire the love and service that Montrose had won, from him and Francis as from all his other followers. His heart was not here but at Goldhayes with Grainne, and he had said as much to Lucas. That gentleman had completely refused to countenance any such arguments, reminded Malise of his invaluable and unique experience, and then, typically, demoted him to Jamie's rank of lieutenant. The two of them were quartered in Master Warren's house, which lay opposite the King's Head, and whenever their duties permitted, they visited us, or conducted us around the walls, pointing out the Roundhead fortifications. Since by this time the Parliament's gun batteries were operational and had found their range with considerable success, this was not the pleasant excursion that had been promised; we had to retire hastily, somewhat bespattered with earth, after the too-close approach of a Roundhead cannon bullet.

This also, as the siege advanced, brought a new insecurity. The Army's gunners, while on the whole alarmingly accurate – as the increasing battering of St Mary's and the cannon atop it showed – had their bad moments like everyone else, and on one occasion a ball actually crashed clean through the roof of the King's Head, from side to side, and landed in the street, its momentum spent: fortunately without any physical injury, although the damage to eveyone's nerves was a great deal more severe. The Committee-men went so far as to complain via a trumpeter to the Army, and received a somewhat perfunctory apology and the pointed observation that if the esteemed gentlemen of the Essex Committee wished to avoid further inconvenience, or worse, it might be advisable in future to fly a flag to display their whereabouts to the Roundhead gunners. So the King's Head sported an ancient standard, fastened somehow to one of the tall brick chimneys: and although the gunners' aim showed little overall improvement, at least there were no more holes in the roof.

But with all these alarums and excursions, Kit was never, ever far from my thoughts. The commonplace sight of a child his age in the street had the power to bring his plight forcibly to my mind: I could not rest until I found some way of letting those at Goldhayes know for certain where we were. At least then there was the hope that someone, perhaps a Grainne relieved by the news that Malise was so far safe, would explain to him that my absence was none of my contriving, and that to all intents and purposes I was a prisoner in

Colchester. A small band of men, Malise told me, were to break out of the town in an attempt to bring in reinforcements from Suffolk, where a small rising had been reported: and when they slipped between the still-unjoined chain of Fairfax's men in the concealing dark, they carried my hastily-scribbled, cryptic note to Mistress Grainne Sewell, of the Home Farm, Goldhayes, in the village of Bradfield Tye, near St Edmundsbury. I prayed desperately that it would reach her somehow, and that she and Kit would gain some comfort from it.

And Meraud, of course, but her bright hollow figure did not intrude on my thoughts: and it was ever a mistake to stop thinking of Meraud.

The night of the fifth of July was clear for once; a half-moon to see by, and no cloud to obscure it. All that day the stinking smoke from the burning tannery by the mill at East Bridge, set afire by the Roundhead troops, had insinuated its noisome presence all through the town till even our clothes reeked, and our food tasted of burning leather even through the spiced sauces with which Mistress Firmin's cook was attempting to disguise the poor quality of the meat. Already food was dear, and growing dearer: butter and cheese, usually selling for a few pence a pound, were now offered at the criminal price of five shillings, meat was tough and of dubious freshness, and vegetables and fruit had vanished from the menu. We were living on credit at the King's Head, Mistress Firmin deferring our charges until the siege ended, for she had, as she put it, 'Not the heart to turn you out of doors when we're all in the same boat when all's said and done.' By this time, her kindness had altogether dispersed my initial irritation at her garrulous tongue: the Widow and I frequently offered our assistance in the running of the inn, for two of the maids had been so overturned by the cannonball episode that they had left to seek their homes in parts of the town not so uncomfortably close to a Royalist battery, and with the inn packed with aristocratic, finicky Cavaliers every available helper was a godsend. What with the work, and the noise of the day's bombardment, and the cumulative effect of too little food of the wrong sort, I found no difficulty in sleeping, and neither did the Widow: and the knowledge that tonight Jamie and Malise were to ride out on yet another foray, against the forces around that burning tannery, did not in the least disturb our slumbers. Just another night, it seemed, the twenty-third of Colchester's ordeal, and I did not realize any different until the violent hammering on the door brought me rudely to wakefulness. 'What . . . who's there, for God's sake?'

The Widow had also woken, and I heard the rustle of the bedcovers as she sat up. 'Come in and stop that noise, whoever you are!'

The door opened to admit a candle, held by the small cheerful maidservant from Master Warren's house, where Malise and Jamie lodged. Her cheerfulness quite gone, her skin was strained and grey even in the candle's yellow glow, and she had obviously dressed in a hurry – no apron, no cap, her bodice laced awry and her hair in a tangled unbrushed aureole around her face. Behind her stood Mistress Firmin in her night-rail and, I was briefly amused to see, curling-papers in her hair. But amusement died almost as soon as it had been born, and my heart stumbled as I realized that something was terribly wrong. 'In God's name, what is it, Grace?'

'Oh, Mistress Heron, Lieutenant Graham, he told me as to tell you as how you'd better come quick, thass your cousin, they just now brought him in and he's hurt suffen terrible, Mistress, there's blood all over the floor, oh please do you come as quick as ever you can!'

I do not remember how I got dressed, nor my headlong flight down the narrow back stairs, heedless of the noise I made in that darkest hour just before dawn, heedless of the sharp unseasonable wind on my skin as, half-clad, I burst into Master Warren's house at Grace's heels, the Widow on mine, and followed the stains on the floor.

It was Jamie, and not Jamie, that they had laid on a settle in the back parlour, lest he lose any more blood by moving him upstairs to a softer bed than this. Jamie, the child and boy and man I had known more than half my life, was there, or the husk of him, drained of blood and the bright infuriating intense and passionate life that had carried him rushing onward to his doom like wind blowing a ship on to rocks.

And now the wind had nearly ceased for ever, and there was only the brief calm before dying. Peace had come at last to Jamie, the exuberant, irrepressible Jamie, and it was that stillness more than anything else, more than the blood on the floor, on his cloak and doublet and, most fatally of all, trickling from his closed mouth, that told me the truth.

Then I saw Malise. He had been kneeling by his young cousin's body, wiping away the flowing blood with those big clumsy hands that were yet so deft and gentle, and at my entrance he turned: and I beheld his face, the expression on it that of a man who has seen his most dreadful nightmares, his most terrible forebodings, risen from the ghastly depths and made flesh . . . 'Oh, Thomazine,' he said, his voice strained and hoarse with the strength of his emotion, 'Oh, Thomazine, my dear lass, and I promised to keep him safe for you . . .'

I stumbled over to the settle and sank on to my knees beside him, the tears running unnoticed down my face, as behind me I heard the Widow's brisk practical voice ordering old sheets and hot water and all the other useful, useless things: while together Malise Graham and I knelt and watched Jamie dying.

It took all the rest of the night, for he had not been cleanly hurt; the Roundhead's sword had run him through, missing the heart but piercing a lung, and he was bleeding both within and without: dying as Henry Sewell had died, drowning in his own blood, but with the last mercy of unconsciousness to ease his passing.

And how that passing was affecting me, how much I would be diminished by this fast-approaching death, was only now made plain to me. For there were two Jamies, just as there seemed to be two of every Heron; the thoughtless selfish boy whose mad ambitions for military glory had landed us here in Colchester, but also the child I had grown up with, warm-hearted and generous in his love, love of people, love of the life that had now been so untimely wrenched from him. He was a part of my childhood, a part of my life, a part of me: and never before had I watched a person I so greatly valued slipping imperceptibly, inexorably away from me into death: so that I longed to clutch his hands, to pull him back from the black river, to use somehow the strength of my own will to make him live.

In an hour, a half-hour, a few minutes, he would be gone, gone for ever. I could no longer sit passively and watch; I grasped his hands, already cold as his heart faltered, and spoke urgently. 'Jamie! Oh, Jamie, Jamie, can you hear me, are you there?'

His uneven breath altered again as I spoke: Malise held my shoulder, at once a warning and a comfort, and Mistress Gooch said something. And then those eyes, Lucy's brilliant lively blue now misted and faint, opened, and he saw me. The white lips scarcely moved, but I knew what he said. 'Thomazine . . . I'm sorry . . . tell . . . tell her . . . I love . . .' His eyelids sank, and for a moment I thought he had gone: then those dreadfully changed eyes opened again, unseeing of me, of Malise, of the candlelit parlour with the dawn just beginning, false hope, to leak through the shutters, birdsong and gunfire the last things he would ever hear: unseeing of everything save the fighting that had given him his death: and the last breath in his lungs lent his voice too much strength.

'No! No, it can't be! No, Francis, not you, oh God, not you!'

And as he died, I knew who had killed him: and what demon now haunted Malise.

part three
A loyal sacrifice

Truth will come to light: murder cannot be hid long.
(Shakespeare, *The Merchant of Venice*)

Chapter 9

Beleaguered

Hold out then stiffly, Colchester, and be
A miracle to all posterity.
                    (Contemporary ballad)

Jamie Heron was dead: the Widow and I laid him out,
and did all the necessary things to prepare this cold
stiffening travesty of a beloved boy for burial: and all
the while as we worked the terrible nightmare, dreaded
for so many years of war, repeated itself over and over
and over in my brain, reduced to this one brief appalling
fact: Jamie is dead, and Francis killed him. Francis killed
his own brother. Jamie recognized him, so he must have
known what he did. And my thoughts and heart being
so close to Francis, I could imagine with hideous clarity
his feelings on discovering that he had unwittingly struck
down his own brother: for the cool flippant cynic was
but the face that the man I loved presented to the world.
Only those who knew him best could see beneath that
apparently careless skin to the vulnerable, passionate
Francis, capable of great affection and love.

He had loved Jamie as he had loved his other brother
Ned, with a strength he had hidden from most: and now
he had killed him. He had failed to save Ned on the
field of Edgehill, and he had cut Jamie down in some
confused night foray outside Colchester.

I did not want to know more, and yet I needed to:
and when the Widow and I had finished our dolorous
task, we went to find Malise. He was in the chamber
that he and Jamie had shared: a bare but pleasant little
room under the eaves, with a charming irregularly
angled whitewashed ceiling, lit now by the early morning
sun. He opened the door at my cautious knock, revealing
a face that was, if possible, even more haggard than that

which had watched Jamie's death, and regarded us with an expression common to those who see their doom approaching. 'Are ye both here? Ye havena left him alone?'

'Mistress Warren prays for him,' said the Widow: and, being her, shut the door and came straight to the point. 'Is it true, what he said?'

Malise turned away from us and went to the window; outside, Colchester was waking up, uncaring of our anguish or his. He said, the words torn from him, 'Aye, aye, oh dear God, it's true enough – they were Whalley's men we fought, and if he's with them he's cause to be proud, they're magnificent soldiers . . .'

'Tell us what happened – please,' I whispered, feeling the helpless tears begin again at the agony in his voice. 'Tell us everything. I want, no, I don't *want*, I *have* to know the truth.'

Malise took a deep, rasping breath and let it out reluctantly. 'It isna a pretty tale, Thomazine.'

'I've doubtless heard worse,' I said, unjustly impatient with his chivalry – so had Jamie been chivalrous, once. The Widow nudged me and frowned: I ignored her and went to stand by my cousin, like him heedless of the world below the window: looking only at that lovely sky, the colour of bluebells, or cornflowers, and the high, white wispy clouds, a sight which Jamie now was for ever denied. 'Please try – please try to tell me.'

All at once his gentle Scots voice began, roughened with grief. 'Ye'll ken a wee bit, I'm thinking, of what a night foray such as yon is like – no' much light tae speak of, a wee bit of a moon, a' shouting and confusion and suchlike. It's simple enough now tae ken how it could ha' happened sae easy . . . we rode out o' the East Gate and down tae the ford over the river; they'd got drakes in the way there, and men in the houses either side, but it didna stop us, we rode through and cleared the street and charged up the hill to the church at the top and scattered them . . . I came up wi' Jamie in the press, trying tae organize the men, we'd gone ower far, and

Whalley's men were on us in a flash . . . Jamie was trying tae fight off one o' them and a' of a sudden he lowered his sword and he said, he said, "Francis!" and he sounded surprised, aye, but pleased as well . . . and Francis ran him through.'

Something had happened to my voice, my legs, the room receded and wavered and returned. I said weakly, desperately, 'Are you sure? Are you *sure* it was him? In the dark?'

'I'm sure,' Malise said. 'The moon was full on his face . . . even under yon cursed lobster-helmet, I'm sure – and he knew, he knew what he'd done, I saw it in his face, and then he saw me as well . . . and he turned his horse awa' and disappeared into the press. Aye, and the horse was Goblin, tae, I'd swear tae it, all black wi' yon proud tail and sweet little heid . . .' He turned and looked at me, his eyes over-bright. 'Thomazine, I canna . . . I canna understand *how* . . . *why* . . . perhaps he didna hear what Jamie said . . . I canna believe he would deliberately kill his ain brother, no' Francis, he wouldna do it, I could ha' sworn tae it . . . and yet I saw it, I saw him do it.'

'We'll like as not never know till Francis tells us himself,' said the Widow quietly, for her. 'And I should think our chances of *that* happening are remarkably slim, lass . . . well, would you go back to Goldhayes and explain that away to Meraud's face?'

Yes, with that on his conscience, would he ever come back to us now? 'She must never know . . . it needn't go beyond the four of us,' I said, thrusting down the waves of nausea and horror that threatened to engulf me. 'We can hold our tongues . . . God knows what she'd do if she ever found out.'

'God will be the one to know, for we won't,' said the Widow. 'As you said, we can all hold our tongues, and let not a word of this go to anyone else. Anyone at all.'

That afternoon, we buried Jamie Heron at St Mary's churchyard, a rushed undignified ceremony punctuated by the intermittent crashing of the cannon mounted on the tower, so that half the words of the service were lost, and the occasional whine and thump of a Roundhead ball better-aimed than the others. Into a shallow, hastily-dug pit the white-shrouded form of my young cousin was laid, and the earth shovelled hurriedly back over him before the next fusillade from Fairfax's battery could violently interrupt the service. I was too weary to weep, I had done my grieving that morning, and when it was over I went back to the King's Head and slept, dreamlessly and obliviously, until the following noon.

Jamie had always had, like his sister, that fragile yet indestructible quality of hope. For them both, a better life, an improvement, a joyous outcome, was always just around the corner, always just out of reach, yet ever desired and ever certain of fulfilment. Without his optimism, at once annoying and yet somehow cheering, our spirits flagged. Nightly, Fairfax's army made small, significant steps – reoccupying East Street, taking the Hythe, attacking and ousting the defenders of St John's Abbey, burning all the wind and water mills, moving their cannon to fresh, closer vantage-points, the better to assail the Royalist guns. The saker on St Mary's tower, which had done much damage to the Parliamentary cannon and their forts on that side of the town, was the subject of increasing bombardment, and was eventually destroyed, with a cacophony of shattered bells and brickwork: along with the one-eyed gunner whose disability had not prevented him from aiming his weapon with a quite astonishing, not to say diabolical accuracy. After that, life at the King's Head became a good deal quieter; but in all other respects, deteriorated.

For as the noose was drawn tighter round Colchester, so the inevitable happened. There were no more supplies of food from night raids or from the warehouses at the Hythe, now in Parliament's hands, no corn from the mills that smouldered sullenly along the river, burned by Fairfax. With no fresh meat in the town, the horses, close on a thousand of them, were the obvious solution.

The civilian animals were the first to be eaten, among them the Widow's faithful old white cob, and my sturdy brown mare. We could not in all honour protest, for it was for everyone's good, but I regretted the passing of that little mare and the Widow, I guessed, was fonder of her old nag than she would admit. Fortunately, several others were slaughtered at the same time, so we were never sure whether or not it was our own mounts we were eating; and by that time we were too glad of the fresh meat to quibble overmuch at its origin.

It was now well on into August, and the siege had so far lasted two months. Two months since I had seen Kit, and my cousins and friends at Goldhayes; two months since, with such high hopes, we had set out in search of Jamie and Malise. Now the grass grew green over Jamie's grave, and the town through which we walked, that grey and dreary morning, had changed appallingly. Everywhere the damage done by the Parliamentary bombardment could plainly be seen, holes in roofs and walls and roads, the people too apathetic in their hunger to repair them. Many houses had had the thatch ripped off them to feed the remaining horses, and life inside them during the seemingly incessant rainfall must have been intolerable. Down the centre of the High Street those horses stood, hobbled and tied, with lowered heads and staring coats and prominent ribs, waiting with dull resignation for the next selection for the shambles. Knots of townsfolk, hollow-eyed and desperate-looking, were gathered outside the Moot Hall, from which any orders or news would be issued, and the soldiers on guard-duty bore the brunt of their obvious but silent hostility.

A small, scrawny, black-and-white dog crept from an alleyway, tail curled under its shrunken belly, and slunk in amongst the horses, its nose questing desperately for any scrap of food that might by some chance be left in amongst the stinking piles of straw and ordure. At the same time, as I watched with Malise and the Widow, a soldier appeared, eyes eager and, to my surprise, what looked like a lump of bread in one hand and his musket, grasped behind his back, in the other. ''Ere, little dog, come 'ere, there's a good dog.' And he held out the bread enticingly.

I realized suddenly what was going to happen to that little dog. It hardly seemed worth the trouble of clubbing it to death, for there would be no meat on it at all. The dog, hearing a friendly voice, turned, dirty black ears pricked, and then slowly, hopefully, the tail uncurled and began to wag. At the sight of that, my weary indifference evaporated entirely: somehow I could not leave that pathetic little bundle of bones to its fate. I stepped forward and whistled.

The dog did not even glance my way. It licked its lips and crawled towards the bread, hunger overcoming its suspicion. The Widow put out a hand to stop me, but I marched over to the soldier, inflamed with a ridiculous compassion: and all for a stray cur, whereas the plight of the people of Colchester had by comparison hardly moved me at all. 'I'll give you a good meal at the King's Head if you'll let me have that dog.'

''Ave that dog?' The soldier stared at me in disbelief. 'And what'd *you* want with it, Mistress? If you're at the King's 'ead you've no need of it, you've 'orseflesh a-plenty there so I've 'eard, and this little bitch'll make a good soup tonight for me and my mates. Or we can sell part of it – they're giving six shillings, Mistress, six shillings, for dogs that are smaller than this one. And what do you want it for, eh? Touched your soft 'eart, 'as it? Well, we've no room for soft 'earts, Mistress, not when we're starving.'

And how I could see the justice of that: but I looked round at the little dog, which was still crouched in the same place, gazing at the bread with a fixed expression. It had a white stripe up its nose and whiskery ginger eyebrows. I had no money on me, I had no money left and neither had either of my companions, but Malise, the kind and perceptive, came to my rescue. 'Trooper Thompson!'

The soldier jerked round to face him. 'Sir!' It was not easy to stand to attention holding both a piece of bread and a musket: he dropped the bread and I snatched it up from the ground a fraction of a second before the dog. And with that the rest was easy: it would have followed me to the ends of the earth for that crust of bread.

'You're a fool,' said the Widow roundly as I retreated to her side, hand outstretched, with the black-and-white bitch following me as if pulled by an invisible string. 'What on earth justifies you pinching that poor man's dinner – which I may say he both needs and deserves far more than we do – and all for some silly sentimental whim? You ought to be ashamed of yourself, lass.'

'I know I should,' I snapped, guilt making me defensive. 'But I couldn't, I just couldn't, stand by and watch, I don't understand why and I can't justify it, but I couldn't let her be someone's dinner, I just couldn't.'

'She may be ours yet,' said Mistress Gooch, eyeing the dog eyeing the bread. 'Feed her up a bit, and she'd be a juicy morsel . . . eh, lass, if looks could kill . . .'

'I'm sorry,' I said with emphasis. 'I *know* all the arguments, I *know* it's wrong, I *know* we're going to be hard-pressed to feed her, I *know* all that . . . but I couldn't leave her.' I brushed away the ridiculous tears, thoroughly ashamed of myself, and to hide them bent down to the dog, breaking up the bread into little pieces and scattering them on the ground in front of her. They were gone in a flash: I had prudently kept my fingers, and the last scraps, out of it and now enticed the little dog nearer, talking gently. She was in reach, her soft eyes speaking hope, her tail wagging, and I snatched her up before she could run away: for loose in Colchester, she would not be so lucky the next time she encountered a soldier. Normally, even a dog that size would have been too big to carry for long, but starvation had made her pathetically light, the bones pressing hard and sharp against her skin. She was filthy and alive with fleas, she stank, she was going to be an embarrassment, and I could imagine only too clearly what Sir Charles Lucas would say should he encounter her: but she licked my face in gratitude, and we were each other's slaves for ever.

Malise, diplomatic as always, soothed the disgruntled soldier with promises that, being Malise, he would keep: and feeling more than a little foolish with the dog lying in my arms, we made our way back to the King's Head. To Mistress Firmin's astonishment, I procured a bucket of water and soap and went to work with a vengeance on my new friend. Several interested spectators with nothing better to do gathered in the yard to watch: among them Sir George Lisle, who came closer, hands clasped behind his back, and remarked through his moustache that he had not thought the King's Head was yet reduced to roast dog. I explained the situation and Sir George, a smile struggling at the corners of his mouth, said gravely that it might not be wise to let the hound run freely, or Mistress Firmin might be tempted to serve a new kind of fowl. I thanked him equally gravely for his warning, and took the little dog upstairs, an animal transformed.

Even the Widow was eventually won over, for she was a dear, sweet-natured little dog, pathetically grateful for the scraps I fed her: keeping me warm at night, entertaining us during the day. And as she grew a little fatter, and the bones ceased to jut so abruptly through her harsh fur, so I kept her close and guarded, for more than ever now would she make a substantial dinner for some cunning soldier. I named her Mab, for she was also quick and mischievous, and yet loved me in the utter, exclusive way of her kind: and save for dear, dead Drake, and his devotion had been first for Francis, I had never been given that kind of love before.

Spurred on by my guilt at keeping and *feeding* a useless dog in my chamber, I tried to help some of the people in our part of the town. But being East Anglians, and thus by nature as stubborn and self-willed as the sea, many of them were by no means willing to be helped. And however keen I was, and however grateful they were, there was at all times a limit set upon what I could do: for there really was no surplus food anywhere, save what I could steal from the Committee-men's supplies, and what there was, was poor-quality stuff, bread made from rye or even peas and beans, starch and raisins boiled up into unhealthy grey-white puddings, said by the optimistic to be a sovereign remedy for the flux now widespread amongst both soldiers and civilians. Among the sufferers was Malise: the hardships and privations of his years with Montrose had had little effect on him, but in his present depressed and anxious state he was quick to succumb. The Widow and I, not in excellent condition ourselves, helped Mistress Warren to nurse him, a miserable, messy and undignified business that was a deep and bitter humiliation to him. After a week or so he made some kind of recovery, although still very weak, and was able to resume some of his duties: a sorry scarecrow figure with grey face and straggling dull-red hair. But at least his earlier help had been justified, for my little dog Mab turned out to be not so useless as I had thought at first: she proved a first-class ratter, the inn yard an abundant source of supply (the rats were unpleasantly, suspiciously fat), and it was a measure of the depths to which the people had sunk that a fine plump rat was a gift of great value. With disease and starvation now rampant within the town, the very young and the very old were the most vulnerable; and people started to die.

But most terrible of all were the scenes now being enacted nightly in the street outside the inn: men, women and children, thin and desperate, demanding surrender, for they were starving. The soldiers on guard, in rather better case since they at least had horseflesh and a tiny daily ration of 'bread', drove off the men. But the women, clutching their babies, and children clutching their skirts, emaciated five-year-old faces with expressions aged by suffering, could not be dispersed, saying they would rather be shot than starved, for at least that death was quick. Evening after evening they gathered there, crying and howling for food, and each evening there were more, so that it seemed all Colchester stood there and begged for the mercy that Sir Charles Lucas's high temper and stubbornness would not allow them. Short of strangling the entire Royalist High Command, I could do nothing, nothing at all: and each night I sat in my chamber, hands to my ears, the tears pouring down my cheeks for the dying children I could do nothing to help. The soldiers were the first priority of Master Quartermaster-General Carter, the citizens of Colchester so many useless mouths whose vocal agonized presence offended the Royalists' aristocratic ears. They had made the Mayor responsible for the victualling of the people and then, very unfairly, had accused him of incompetence: in the circumstances, the poor man could hardly be otherwise.

There was still hope that the invading Scots would come to their relief: and if the town could be cleared of civilians they would be able to hold out for that much longer. So, a letter was sent to Fairfax, asking him to let the people go: but that canny soldier was too old and experienced a hand to accede, for all he had to do was to sit tight and wait for hunger and disease to storm the town for him. Malise, in his private conversations with us, admitted there was no chance of any relief, and that surrender was inevitable. 'They're mad, all o' them, they willna give in, they're just like poor Jamie, a'ways something just around the corner. First the Suffolk rising, then the Duke o' Buckingham's, then Prince Charles with those Royalist ships in the Thames, and always the Scots, the Scots are coming tae save us! Well, I wish this Scot could, I wish tae God I could ding some sense intae their silly skulls, but I've nae more hope o' doing that than I have o' flying. And those people, those children . . . their faces haunt me.'

I knew what he meant, for I too was tormented by the starving babies, like wizened shrunken old men, dumb with misery in their mothers' arms; and the children, the same age perhaps as Kit, or Jasper, or Hen, reduced to chewing soap and candles for their sustendrance, or begging from more fortunate households. There was no compassion, no glory, no mercy, in this subjection of innocent people to such a terrible ordeal: only a useless obstinacy that confused heroics with heroism, and starved children to death for a cause long since expired.

At least those who died for Montrose had been willing sharers in his exploits, and gave their lives for what they believed.

They let, or rather drove, some of the people out of the town when the clamour grew too great, but they were stopped at the Army's lines, now only a hundred yards or so from the walls. They would not go back, and only when some of the women were stripped by the soldiers did the rest retreat – only to be refused entry by the Royalist men at the gate. Eventually, reluctantly, they were let in and dispersed to their homes – but the episode lingered unpleasantly in the mind, proof of the lengths to which Sir Charles Lucas's callousness would stretch. 'For God's sake,' I asked Malise that evening, as we chewed our way through the horseflesh in spiced claret that now comprised virtually all our diet, 'why, oh why, does he not surrender?'

'He's waiting for the Scots,' said Malise gloomily. 'And if the guid Duke o' Hamilton lives up tae his reputation, he'll wait for ever.'

And that turned out to be true: as was discovered the next day, when arrows bearing the news were shot into the town. The Duke of Hamilton, not widely renowned for his competence in matters military, had had the misfortune to come up against Cromwell, and had been resoundingly defeated at Preston in Lancashire, five days earlier. It was only a matter now of negotiating terms; for the garrison of Colchester, unwanted and unwelcome guests, the sands were fast running down. Those last days passed in a ferment: the King's Head alive with restless, hopeful Committee-men, well-fed and lively on their special rations of venison pasties and fresh white wheaten bread, that had caused so much ill-feeling amongst townsfolk and soldiers alike: and the long, tedious, agonized discussions over the terms of the surrender lasted well into the night: but Malise had no chance to join them, even if his inferior rank had permitted it, for he was stricken anew by illness. This bout was not serious enough, yet, to lay him so low as the last time, and he kept his feet with an effort: a lifeless, joyless wreck of the Malise I had known. And the wrangling over the surrender went on for five precious, futile days, while I longed for it all to be over, for us to be free to wing our way homewards to Goldhayes and say farewell for ever to Lucas and Norwich and the Royalist cause that was now as moribund and pointless as a dream of King Arthur's return.

But it was not so easy as that. At first the Cavaliers resolved to cut their way out, but due to a misunderstanding the chance was lost. Then they begged Fairfax to enter the town so that they could fight him, and the old makeshift defences, boiling pitch and water, weapons made from scythes and sickles and pitchforks, and trenches cut across the streets, were prepared; but the Lord General did not rise to the bait. Why should he, for he had only to wait for Colchester's shrivelled apple to fall into his grasp from sheer weakness and exhaustion. At last the Royalist Command accepted the realities of their situation and agreed to the harsh terms imposed by Fairfax, whose previous more generous offer had been spurned earlier on in the siege. The junior officers, and the men, had quarter for their lives only; and the senior men were to surrender to the mercy of Fairfax.

So on Monday, the twenty-eighth of August, Colchester surrendered. The siege had lasted eleven weeks, eleven weeks of undeserved misery suffered by the townspeople, and it had left me, and the Widow and Malise, physically weak and mentally angry and disgusted with the obstinacy of the Royalist Command in general and the callous behaviour of Sir Charles Lucas in particular; for Lord Norwich was an aristocratic old fool, a figurehead and little more, and Lord Capel and Sir George Lisle capable soldiers but without the strong personalities necessary to outface Sir Charles's overbearing nature. But the spirit in the King's Head on that warm, sunny morning was one almost of satisfaction: of pride in holding out so long against such odds, as if it were a point of honour to put all those innocent lives in hazard for someone else's cause. I did not care what happened to them. I cared only for Malise.

The junior officers had to present themselves, according to the terms of surrender, at Greyfriars by the Eastgate at ten o'clock that morning. There was special provision for the sick and wounded, but Malise refused to be counted amongst the former, and although suffering from agonizing cramps in his belly, insisted on taking his place with the rest. No one knew what was to happen to the garrison: I clung to the hope that somehow, by some miracle, he would be set free, perhaps on payment of a fine, as had been common practice in the past. At all events he would be fairly treated, so I said goodbye, and watched him go with the rest, keeping up with them by an effort of pure willpower. They had no horses, of course, some eight hundred of them having been eaten, amongst them Malise's high-strung chestnut mare Tanaquill, and they presented a proud yet pitiful sight marching raggedly off down the street to their fate.

When they had gone beyond our sight, we made our way, hunger and foreboding dragging our feet, to the Head Street to watch the besiegers enter Colchester. The people lined the roadway, grey-faced and haggard with hunger, but at the same time their expressions were eager with anticipation. The siege was ended: the hated Sir Charles Lucas would doubtless shortly be rotting in some well-deserved London prison, and there was the glorious prospect of food – proper food, bread and meat and vegetables and late summer plums and raspberries and early apples, fresh-brewed beer and new butter and cheese . . . my mouth watered at the thought. Whatever happened, by tonight the Widow and I and, please God, all of those about us, would sleep with full bellies. And so, now that the end was here at last, even those who had suffered most were smiling with delighted anticipation.

At ten o'clock the Head Gate was flung open, and the steady marching rhythm of the drummers announced the entry of a regiment of the besiegers, come to claim the town and their prisoners. In contrast to the tatty, unkempt and half-starved soldiers of the garrison, these men were well fed and immaculately clad, their helmets shining, musket-stocks polished, and sprouting a veritable forest of pikes, though there were not so many of them as a full regiment. At the sight of them a sound arose from the throats of the people along the street; not a cheer, but a sort of collective mutter of relief and approval.

'It's Ingoldsby's,' said the Widow suddenly. 'The Oxford garrison they are, I know them all right – and there's our old friend Dan Ashley.'

Daniel Ashley, Major of the Regiment, was marching alongside his men, his eyes looking straight ahead, hardly recognizable under the hat. He looked more than five years older; presumably military responsibilities had deepened the lines on his face, and the light brown hair, sunlit on his shoulders, was now streaked liberally with grey. More than ever, I could not see why Lucy had succumbed to this man above all the other more good-looking, more charming, more lively, *younger* men she had met: why had she ascertained so quickly that underneath that very ordinary exterior lay a person quite out of the ordinary?

But Lucy in some ways was as perceptive as her brother Francis. And I longed to call out to Dan, to remind him that there were Herons still in this part of the world: but this most solemn and ceremonious occasion was no place for social pleasantries. I held my

tongue and watched his regiment march by: and saw
with a lift of the heart one of the imperturbable, highly
disciplined soldiers slip a lump of bread from his snap-
sack and drop it into the hands of a particularly hungry-
looking child at the front of the crowd. At the sight of
this, other children ran forward, crying, their hands
outstretched, and for a moment it seemed as if a riot
would break out; but the officers with their halberds at
the ready pushed the crowds back, and I heard Dan's
voice, quiet and calming, assuring them all that supplies
would be coming into the town for their immediate relief.
That did bring a cheer, and its rough-edged echoes
accompanied the tramping of the regiment's feet as they
marched up Head Street towards the centre of the town.
Following them, in a cacophonous rush, came a great
crowd of civilians, people seeking news of relatives and
friends in the town, farmers and enterprising merchants
with carts of food – for the villages all round Colchester
had been deprived of a market for their produce during
the siege – and the usual ghouls eager to view the signs
of death and disaster. There were plenty of these: burnt
and ruined houses, the thatch pulled off to provide
fodder for the horses; communal graves in the church-
yards for the victims of war, disease or famine; and above
all the pitiful condition of the townspeople, especially the
poor who had not had the more plentiful reserve stocks
of food that richer households could boast. The sellers
of food had barely the chance to set foot inside the gates
before they were overwhelmed by those who still had
the coin to buy; and by those who had not, and hoped
to steal what they could in the confusion. Despite the
gnawing in my own belly, I was not going to brave that
mob: with one accord, the Widow and I turned and
made our way back to the King's Head. There we were
greeted by an ecstatic Mab, who leaped upon me with
a most gratifying joy, uttering little yelps of delight as
she licked my face when I bent down to stroke her.
Mistress Gooch surveyed us, arms akimbo: then she
said, 'And what's to do now, lass? Are we to go home?'

'No, no, we can't . . . not until we've found out what's to happen to Malise . . . and what quarter for their lives means.'

'It may be just that, their lives and no more – but three-thousand-odd prisoners is too much perhaps for even this Army to cope with. It may happen,' said the Widow cheerfully, 'that all we'll need is a coin or two . . . you never know.'

'But we haven't *got* any coin. We've spent all we had, and we must owe Mistress Firmin a fortune, though she's been kind enough to say nothing yet. Unless Dan . . .'

'I wouldn't presume on a five-year-old friendship, lass – although you did once do him the same favour. This Army's different, I've seen it at close quarters in Oxford, and doing favours for an old friend on the opposite side isn't the approved way of going about things, particularly if you're the Major. Whatever we do for Malise, best not to involve Dan in it at all. He'll as like as not be too busy, anyway.'

'But what do we *do* if we need money?' I asked her. The Widow shrugged in her usual down-to-earth fashion. 'Do, lass? Go back to Goldhayes, o' course, and get it.'

'How? Our horses were eaten, remember?' Worry and tiredness had made me sharp. The Widow came over and gave me a motherly embrace. 'We'll find a way, don't you fret, lass. Walk, if we have to, or perhaps there's someone you know on the way home you can borrow a good stout nag from?'

'There might be,' I said, and sighed wearily into her scrawny shoulder. 'And yet I don't want to leave, don't want to go at all. Where do you suppose Whalley's Horse are now?'

'We'll leave that little matter till later,' said Mistress Gooch grimly, giving me a shake. 'At this moment, it's Malise needs our help most, it's Malise we must look for . . . and your cousin will have to wait for the moment. You may well think I'm being hard, lass, but you've waited three years for him and you can wait a few days longer.'

It was precisely because I had been so long without Francis, that suddenly that old ache of separation, of longing, had become almost too much to bear . . . but I knew she was right, and forced myself to smile.

There was a knock at the door which proved to be Mistress Firmin, aflow with bounteous generosity – one of the food-vendors had been persuaded into the inn yard, she had bought all his provisions and would we like an early dinner? After all her kindness, it was not an offer that could so easily be waved aside, and so we shortly found ourselves regaled with an odd-looking apology for a dinner, but one on which we fell with ravenous gratitude: new bread and soft crumbly white cheese, buttered eggs and beer, plain fare but a prince's feast compared to our fare for the past six weeks or so. Amply refreshed after this banquet, we set off with lifted hearts and unusual optimism, to hunt through the town for Malise.

We found him eventually, but it took two hours of dogged questioning and searching the town's churches, where the prisoners had been taken, before we discovered him in St Leonard's at the Hythe. It was plainly obvious he was far from well; he had been plundered of his doublet, in common with the two hundred or so other captives in the cold, damp, foul-smelling little church, and was crouched in one of the darkest corners, his face grey-white and shiny with sweat and his arms laced tightly across his belly. Shocked beyond measure by the change in him in just a few hours, I tried to offer words of encouragement and hope, shouted above the hubbub of the crowded church: but he seemed too far gone in pain and fever to hear me. And words were all I had to offer him, I had not even a cloak, no clothes, food, medicines, no practical help to give him at all. There was only one thing that would help him, I realized, and my weary body quailed before the prospect:

but I told him what I was going to do, pledging myself then and there before faint heart and body could win. 'It's all right, Malise, we'll try and get you free . . . we'll go back to Goldhayes and get a ransom, we'll go now and please God you'll be free tomorrow, or the day after . . . keep safe, please hold on and we'll come back.'

A faint nod was all the acknowledgment I received, but it was enough. Hoping that ransom was indeed possible, the Widow and I emerged into the sunshiny fresh air, gasping with relief after the thick fetid dank atmosphere inside the church, and converged on the bored young sergeant who had allowed us inside to look for Malise. At the Widow's brisk complaint about the plundering of clothes and the conditions inside the church, his mettle was roused: the prisoners were fortunate indeed, so we were informed, to be given shelter from the weather and left with some garment on their backs, and feeling against the Royalists was running so high in the largely East Anglian regiments of Fairfax's Army that they had been placed in the churches as much for their own protection as to hold them captive. And as for the leaders, Lucas and Lisle and the rest, if the Army had had any say in the matter they would have been hanged from the ramparts already.

'And what is to happen to those men in there?' I demanded, my blood also up. The sergeant laughed callously. 'Them? They'll be lucky to get away with their lives, they will – word's out that they're to be sent to the Indies.'

The Indies were a byword for pestilence, and disease, and hardship. I stared at him, appalled. 'Are you – are you sure? The Indies?'

'Well, I'm not sure, not certain sure, but that's what everyone says,' the man told me, ignoring my horror. 'And they last about six months out there, most of them, working in the plantations. *And* it's more than most of them deserve, if you ask me. The Lord General's at the end of his patience, they say, and Black Tom's tether was ever a longer string than the rest of the Army's. If it wasn't for our lads wanting ransom money, we'd say hang them all and be done with it. So I reckon as if you don't want your friend to go to the Indies, you'd best go and get as much coin as you can afford and bring it to our Captain as soon as you can, for I've heard we march them out in a day or two.'

My anxiety for Malise had by now overcome all my weariness, and my one thought was to return to Gold-hayes as soon as possible and beg, borrow or steal the small fortune my fevered mind assumed would be necessary to free someone so valuable to me. The Widow and I thanked our grudging informant and made all haste back to the town, united in our desperate sense of urgency: for we knew that to be sent to the Indies would be equivalent to a death sentence for Malise in his present condition. We were held up for precious minutes at the gate and inside the town by the progress of the Lord General, inspecting the fortifications and defences of the town, and had a glimpse of the great man that, in my frantic haste to return to Goldhayes, I hardly paid heed to at the time: only remembering afterwards the tall, dark, long-faced Yorkshireman on the old white horse, almost as much a legend in the North Country as Montrose had been in Scotland – Black Tom, the gentle, cultured sufferer from various crippling ailments, who yet could fight as brave as a lion, and had nearly as brilliant a reputation for leadership as his fellow-general Oliver Cromwell. Today, his haggard face staring from side to side at the ruined town and its pitiful inhabitants, he looked sickened – and I remembered what the sergeant had said, and feared it boded no good for the captives.

It was past three when we finally fought our way back to the King's Head, threading through the coney-warren streets of the Flemish Quarter as a short-cut and more than once losing our way. At the King's Head all was uproar: angry voices could be heard upstairs from the large central chamber in which the Royalist High Command had debated all their tactics and their final surrender. Then, as Mistress Firmin explained our arrival to the four stout Roundhead buff-coats outside the main door, the thump of booted feet came down the staircase and more of Fairfax's soldiers appeared, an important-looking officer at their head, and captive amongst them, Sir Charles Lucas, red-faced and furious, the gentler Sir George Lisle, head high and calm, and the round-faced little Italian mercenary whose name I had never been able to catch. We watched with a sense of foreboding as they were marched out of the inn-yard in the midst of what seemed like a full company of soldiers, and away from our sight.

But there was not time to speculate on the doom that probably awaited them, though I had liked Sir George for his quiet humour and friendliness. All our efforts had to be for Malise, and when Mistress Firmin heard our plight she proved once more to be an invaluable ally. Waving aside all offers of future payment for our prolonged stay – 'That's all right, you wait till you come back for your cousin, or later still if you can't manage it then' – she scribbled a hasty letter to a farmer out at Mile End, on the road home to Suffolk, a relative of hers who would lend us a horse or two.

We gave her our most grateful thanks and packed our bags in haste, for even with horses there was no chance at all that we could reach Goldhayes before dark, and it was advisable to travel as little distance as possible by moonlight. So we said our goodbyes to Mistress Firmin, and spoke once again of our gratitude that no words could really express: and walked out of the King's Head, and left the suffering, relieved people of Colchester behind us.

Chapter 10

Homing flight

Princes do but play us; compared to this,
All honour's mimic, all wealth alchemy.
              (Donne, 'The Sun Rising')

Mistress Firmin's cousin proved kind and helpful, and his wife, on hearing that we had been within the beleaguered town, pressed upon us so many laden baskets of food that our borrowed mounts looked like a pedlar's packponies. More inadequate thanks and a promise to return the horses as soon as possible, and we started our journey back to Goldhayes.

I had ridden long distances before, I had been weary and hungry before, but never did miles prove so gruelling as those between Colchester and Goldhayes on that late summer's afternoon and evening. The horses were good reliable ones, obedient, well-shod and willing, and we pushed them faster than I would normally have done over such a distance, twenty-six miles or so without any rest save for the necessary stops. Mab on her diet of rats seemed in good spirits, enjoying the exercise, and trotted beside us till we reached Sudbury, where her speaking eyes begged that she be given a lift; from then on she rode on the Widow's or my saddlebow. By this time, the sun was setting, and only an extreme effort of will kept me from taking the coward's way out into the nearest Sudbury inn. Mistress Gooch, a tough and stringy figure hunched on top of her mired and sweating horse, saw my look and cackled. 'You can stop if you really want to, lass – I won't prevent you.'

'No – it can't be more than we've travelled already, three more hours at the outside, and another hour of light. I can stand the pace,' I said, forcing a grin, 'but can you?'

'Of course – can't you remember me saying to you, the day we set out for Colchester, that I was tougher than an old riding-boot? We'll go on all night if we have to, lass, though please God we won't – it's harder to see the potholes in the dark.'

The sunset lingered long and fierily to our left as we plodded wearily on: the horses trotting less frequently now, moving with increasing caution as darkness approached and normal hazards in our way became almost impossible to discern. Apart from these obstacles, there was also a considerable risk of human dangers – two women travelling alone after dark being a sitting target for footpads or other, more sinister, molesters. We rode on the verges where possible and hunched ourselves deep into our cloaks, trying to attract as little attention as we could. And the familiar road became strange and sinister in the gloom, every twisted tree or rustle in the grass a threat to my exhausted, overwrought mind. It became in the end purely and simply a matter of endurance, and by the time we came to the right-hand fork in the road which led to Little Whelnetham, Bradfield St George and Bradfield Tye, I was all but asleep in the saddle and nearly missed it. The moon, almost full, shone cold and brilliant through the trees above us as we saw at last the lights of the Home Farm, and knew we were at journey's end.

Someone had heard the horses: a lantern shone out and John Sewell's dear Suffolk voice called, 'Who's thar?' And I had just enough wit left to answer him.

Then, of course, everything happened at once: barking dogs, Bran leaping up at Mab on my saddle-bow, John helping me down off the horse, Joan's cries of welcome, Jasper, wild and tousle-haired in his nightshirt and Hen with a thumb in her mouth, and behind them all Grainne, her face a mixture of hope and dread, and her eyes asking the questions she dared not voice. And it was for her that I said, 'It's all right – he's safe, he's a prisoner in Colchester and they say we can ransom him.'

I hugged her, and John and Joan, and the children who were pouring out questions, and Mistress Gooch and I allowed ourselves to be drawn inside the farmhouse and given mulled ale and pots of one of Joan's rich, thick broths, while we somewhat incoherently told our story, and that of Malise, and the fact of Jamie's death, though not, of course, the circumstances.

'I had your letter,' Grainne said, 'and it was the only word we had – you might have disappeared into thin air, though we guessed you might well be in Colchester. But Jamie . . . poor Jamie, how terrible, and he was only a boy, and such a likeable one.'

'But he brought it on himself,' the Widow pointed out, 'and dragged everyone else into trouble in the process. Still, if death was the punishment for foolishness there'd be precious few people left in this world. Question is, how will we tell Meraud?'

'And will she care?' I asked dully. Joan looked shocked.'O' course she'll care, poor little maw, an' har loikely an' all . . . that little mite she carry will have Goldhayes one day, I reckon.'

That prediction, so casually and confidently stated, jerked me back to full wakefulness. I stood up with an effort. 'We must go there tonight, tell Richard, we need the money to free Malise, they may be taken away soon.'

'I'll come with you,' said Grainne: amid Joan's protests that we must not think of stirring another step that night save to our beds, and Jasper asking hopefully if he could also accompany us (his mother soon put paid to that request), and John's offer to light the way politely refused, we set off on foot down the moonlit drive, our temporary mounts having been left in well-deserved peace in the Home Farm stables. My muscles ached from riding, so that the walk was at once a relief and considerably painful, my head swam from the ale and my eyes played tricks with the dark. Grainne did not pester us for information, but as we walked I found the temptation to confide in her almost overwhelming: and exhaustion nearly made me succumb. At last the house, the Gallery still showing lights, became close, and I said to Grainne, 'How is Kit?'

'Desperate,' said my dear friend. 'He grew more and more impossible when you failed to return. I tried to explain, when I got your message, what had happened to you, but I don't think he really understood . . . you may find him very much changed, and not for the better. And what's more, Meraud's been taking a great interest in him – she took him and Hugh for a walk in the park only this afternoon, and she often plays with him.'

In anyone else, this kindness might have had a perfectly happy and innocent explanation, but I knew that Meraud rarely did anything that she could not at some time turn to her own advantage. Yet, as before, I could not possibly see what profit she would find in befriending my bewildered, unhappy, five-year-old son, save to use him as a weapon against me at a later date. And with that thought I remembered that he had celebrated his fifth birthday less than a month ago – and that I had no present for him.

It was that, more than anything else, which filled my eyes with exhausted tears as the three of us crossed the bridge over the moat and approached the grey, ghostly house. So tired was I that only the pathetic image of my deserted child filled my mind; the incredulous noisy welcome which we received from Charles Lawrence, Heppy and Lucy, and to a lesser extent Mary, Richard and Meraud, left me unmoved. I heard the Widow, her voice a respectful, sorrowful murmur, breaking the news of Jamie's death to his mother, sister and wife, and I could not face that: instead, like iron to a magnet, I turned unnoticed and doggedly climbed the stairs towards Kit. Behind me, the discordant sorrowful music of grief rose abruptly: but I had already done my mourning for Jamie, and could not face more. I hauled myself up the last of the stairs and moved like a sleepwalker to the door of the children's chamber: and slipped inside.

Their nurse, Rose, was sound asleep on a truckle bed

in the little inner room: her snores drowned the boys' soft breathing. But as the door clicked gently to, one of the children sat up suddenly, gasping, and in the glow of the little wax candle that always burned to lighten their dark, I beheld my son.

He had lost weight, his face thinner and older and, to my over-sensitive gaze, drawn-looking with purple-smudged eyes huge in that waif-like little face. I said, 'Kit? Kit, it's me. I'm back.'

In a flash he was out of the bed and hurled himself against me. With an uprush of relief at his welcome, I picked him up and held him close, feeling the small hands clutch me tightly and the warmth of his body pressed so close to mine. 'Mammy, Mammy, you're back, you're back!' And then, turning his head to look straight into my eyes, he said, 'Mammy, why did you go away? Why didn't you come back sooner?'

'I couldn't,' I said. My legs threatening to give way under his weight, I looked around for a stool and stumbled over to it. It was smaller than usual, a child's one, and I sat down abruptly and further than I had thought, trying at the same time to explain, using words that he would understand. 'I couldn't, chicken, I couldn't. I went to Colchester to find your cousin Malise and your cousin Jamie, and while I was there the soldiers came and we couldn't get out.'

'You could have 'scaped,' said Kit seriously, a hint of accusation in his beautiful blue eyes. 'Cousin Meraud said you could have 'scaped.'

My heart sank. 'What does Meraud know about it? She wasn't there, was she? Believe me, Kit, believe me, I couldn't have got out – I wanted to terribly, I wanted so badly to come back to you . . . but the soldiers would have killed anyone who tried to escape.'

Those reproachful eyes, unconvinced, still stared at me. 'You said you'd bring me a present. Have you brought me a present? Cousin Meraud said you would.'

By this time, if Meraud had knocked at the door I would have cheerfully strangled her, but instead I heard a faint, hopeful scratching. Visited by inspiration, I gave him my best smile. 'Ah, but I have, and she's outside now. Go and open the door, Kit.'

He slid off my lap and ran to lift the latch: and in leapt Mab, as bouncy and devoted as ever despite the day's ordeal. Her tail whirling like a windmill, she bounded at me, licking whatever part of me was in reach – Kit was not the only one to feel the fear of desertion. He shut the door and stared at the quicksilver little dog, which had come near to knocking him flying. 'Is that my present?'

'Yes, that's your present. Her name is Mab, and if you get into bed I'll tell you a story about her before you go back to sleep.'

Kid said mutinously, 'Don't want to go back to bed! Don't want to!' But I took him gently and steered him towards it, feeling his body tensing. 'It's all right, Kit. I'm not going to go away. I'll tell you a story and Mab can sleep on your bed . . . come on now, in you go.'

Reluctantly, he slipped beneath the sheets, beside the still-slumbering Hugh (who seemed to share his half-sister's enviable ability to sleep through anything). Mab jumped up beside him and curled up, pushing her nose against his hand to gain his attention. Kit, used to dogs, absently rubbed her head, his eyes fixed on me. 'Don't go away again . . . please don't go away again.'

'I won't,' I said, promising myself as well as my child. 'I won't leave you again, I swear it . . . shall I tell you how I found Mab? She was very cold, and hungry, and dirty, and lonely . . .'

I was told later by Grainne that she had found me kneeling by the bed, fast asleep, with my head on the bolster beside Kit's and Hugh's, Mab curled up warmly between us. All I remember is someone shaking me, of walking supported to another more comfortable bed: and then a return to blessed oblivion.

I woke quite suddenly and completely, about dawn: a thin, lemon-coloured light leaking through the shutters and the bed-curtains. The bed was my own, and Lucy's: my cousin lay the other side of me, a hump ending in a tangle of dark glossy curls and the tip of her nose. Mab, evidently unaware of the change in her ownership, was lying possessively by my feet; she stirred as I did, opened one eye, and wagged a tail hopefully. I was vaguely surprised, not only at my abrupt awakening, but at my lack of tiredness; a surprise which vanished when I got out of bed and had to clutch the post for support as my stiff and aching legs all but gave way beneath me. The sensible thing to do would have been to return to the warmth under the blankets, but something was making me restless, driving me to the chest whereon my clothes were laid, urging me to slip them on, and calm the waiting Mab, and slide with her out of the chamber, down the stairs, still dim in the early morning light, and across to the front door. Despite my attempts at silence the muscles in my legs made me clumsy: I stubbed my toe on a Hall chair left slightly askew, and swore fervently under my breath. With the next step I trod on Mab's paw – she had an inconvenient habit, born of her devotion, of always cleaving too close to my feet. Her indignant yelp split the silence, but no one stirred: I judged from the dim light that it must be about half-past four. After apologizing to poor Mab, who did not know what she had done to deserve such treatment, but was determined to make amends, I wobbled over to the door and, feeling not a little foolish, reached up to slide back the huge bolts on the front door, with a slam that I thought could be heard all over the house. 'You're either mad, Thomazine Heron,' I told myself, grinning, 'or bewitched.' And I raised the latch, pulled the huge door open with only a small creak and, with Mab following me, slithered through the gap.

In the park it was misty, wet and cold. The trees stood sentinel, shrouded in leaves and damp – it had evidently rained again in the night – and dripped dismally like cold-ridden children. This time yesterday I had been in Colchester, a prisoner still of fate, and now my fate moved me again: walking on protesting limbs, hampered by wet skirts clinging to my legs, through the dawning day. The mist wraithed ethereally around me, and the strange feeling grew within me that I was a ghost, lost in someone else's time. I wandered on, picking a handful of flowers – scabious, yarrow, ox-eye daisies, cornflowers – growing scattered in the drenched grass, and Mab followed damp and devoted at my heels. The deer were out too, feeding busily before full light should come and drive them back to Piper's Wood, where they would lie up during the day: and for a long time I stood with my curious, snuffling dog, unnoticed in the shadow of a young oak, watching their shy graceful movements, and the dancing of the June-born fawns as they played amongst the does. Then suddenly, without a movement from me, every head was flung up in unison, the large ears directed towards the source of their alarm – away from me.

There was someone – something – else in the park.

One of the does barked her warning, and the deer turned and plunged through the grass towards us, ears back, tails up to reveal the guiding white scut on their rumps. I had difficulty in restraining Mab as they swerved around us and raced on into the misty park, out of sight amongst the thicker growth of trees and scrub near to Piper's Wood. Puzzled, I stared after them for a moment and then, with burgeoning curiosity, walked out from my shelter towards whatever it was that had startled them.

I heard the hooves first, the sound of a tired horse clopping wearily up the drive, through the sudden joyous burst of dawn birdsong. Then, slipping through bushes with some care, I came in sight of the mysterious horseman. A soldier he was, one of the Parliament's soldiers, in the unmistakable uniform of the New Model Army: lobster-tail helmet, buff coat, boots, with sword and pistols at his side. I stared in astonishment and foreboding at this unexpected apparition: and then noticed the horse. A small horse, black and mired to hock and knee, with the true sign of Arabian blood in the sweet curve of the white-starred head, hung low though it was with weariness. With a wildly blossoming hope, I raised my eyes again to the soldier: a tall man, lean and wide-shouldered, riding with a so-familiar casual grace, despite his evident exhaustion, that struck my heart with a blow of recognition. I hurled myself from my hiding-place into the horse's path. 'Francis, oh, Francis!'

The black mare was not so tired as she appeared. At my precipitate eruption into her path she shied and half-reared, snorting with surprise, and her rider, unprepared, was nearly flung from the saddle. I grabbed Hobgoblin's reins as he recovered himself and stared for what seemed like for ever at my face, so that I could see my tiny disreputable figure reflected in his eyes, and note the rough unkempt beard and the new hardness in his mouth. Then he let out his breath in a long gasp and spoke his words of welcome, in a voice still recognizably his, 'Christ, Thomazine, do you want to kill us?'

'No,' I said, half-laughing, half-weeping, and my hands left the reins and stretched up to take his, encased though they were in stiff leather riding-gauntlets. 'No, I'm sorry, I didn't think – I *couldn't* think, oh God, I can't believe it, I can't believe you're here.'

'Well, I am, and not by any leave or permission of my captain,' said Francis, and there was a grim note in his voice. 'I've deserted. But there's more urgent work to hand. I've brought Malise with me.'

I stared at him and delight took wings as the last burden and dread lifted from me. '*Malise?* Oh, thank God, you've freed him! But – but where is he?'

'Down the drive. I took him out of one of the churches last night and he was only half-conscious then. I had the devil's own job to get him on to Goblin with me, and after twenty-six miles in the rain we had last night he couldn't take any more. He fainted about ten minutes ago, and I couldn't get him back on the horse. Even after what he's endured, there's a lot of him left. So I wrapped him in my cloak and hid him under a tree. I don't even know if he's dead or not,' said Francis, a flat, drained note in his voice. 'Shall we go see?' He turned the mare and in doing so spotted Mab, who had been following our conversation a safe distance from us, her ears pricked and her face delightfully attentive, ginger eyebrows and white whiskery nose and round dark eyes. 'Is that yours?' For the first time there was a hint of the old ironic humour in his voice. 'I'd need a spyglass to see her clearly.'

'She's mine, her name is Mab, and she loves me because I saved her,' I said, and seeing my chance to tell him, added, 'She was going to be a soldier's dinner. I was in Colchester too.'

Francis stopped Goblin and turned to face me: and for the first time since we had met again, looked at me with thoroughness. 'You were in *Colchester?* Dear God, yes, I can see you were.' His gloved hand reached out, briefly, to touch my cheek: and even that was enough, in my overwrought mood, to set my blood singing dizzily. 'The dog has more flesh than you,' said Francis. 'Tell me later, how you came to be there. For now, we must look to Malise.'

I walked back with him down the drive, noting with a pang of bewilderment this new, strange Francis, who seemed compelled to keep his distance: and wondering with apprehension what we would find under the tree.

Yesterday, a lifetime away in the little church at the Hythe, I had thought Malise looked bad: now, he seemed close to death, the only colour in his hawkish face the startling red of hair and eyebrows and stubbly beard, and the incongruous scattering of freckles across that deceptively intimidating face. To my utter relief, he drew a deep harsh breath and moved his hands across his belly, his body doubling with the pain. I knelt beside him, feeling the sweat of fever on his hot forehead; his sojourn in that damp church, not to mention the long night's journey in the rain, had undone all the good of my nursing and the Widow's in Colchester. But he was here, and we could nurse him again, he was young and strong and above all there would be Grainne, to lend him her own strength of heart and will and make him whole again. And above all he was free – not, please God, for Malise the living death of bond-slavery in the Barbadoes or Virginia.

Unless they came after him.

I pushed that thought away and spoke urgently. 'Malise! Malise, it's Thomazine, can you hear me? Malise!'

He grunted, moved and opened his eyes, bleary with pain. 'Thomazine? Wha' . . . I dinna ken . . . whaur's this?'

'It's Goldhayes, or nearly,' I said gently, feeling my earlier joy at his freedom trickling away at the harsh reality of his physical plight. 'And we've got to get you on the horse again because you can't walk the distance . . . can you sit up?'

'I dinna ken . . . but I'll hev a hack at that,' he said, with that enduring, endearing humour that seemed to appear even *in extremis*. Gently, I helped him to sit up, wincing in sympathy with him, and looked round for Francis. He was bringing Hobgoblin close: he had removed his helmet and the rapidly-increasing light showed an older, harder man than the one I had known, a stranger, the beard giving him an oddly villainous, raffish appearance that the earlier Francis had lacked.

But the man I had known had not killed his young brother.

Malise saw my look and caught my eye significantly. 'Dinna tell him you know till ye see how the wind blaws . . . Ah, dear Christ, my guts feel as though they'll burst!' He doubled over again, retching. When the spasm had passed, Francis and I helped him to sit up again, and then to stand. Francis took most of his weight, but even so I staggered under the burden. Somehow, slowly, inch by inch, the sweat rolling off our faces, we stumbled over to Hobgoblin, who was pulling on the grass a foot or so away. Malise, gasping, leaned on her, his big hands flung over her back; fortunately the mare stood still, her training and temperament telling even through these untoward events. 'Good girl, stand still,' Francis said, and her trim ears flickered and moved to catch the sound of his voice. 'Now, Malise, can you put your foot in the stirrup?'

I still do not know how we managed it: if Malise had not been able to help himself a little, despite his weakness, we would never have succeeded. At last, however, by dint of pushing, pulling and sheer brute strength, he was thrust into the saddle and sat, dizzy with pain, fever and exhaustion, drooping over Goblin's neck.

'Now,' said Francis, 'we walk. All you have to do, Malise, is hold on – and you take the reins,' he added to me. 'I'll walk beside and support him, all right?'

Slowly, our strange little group shambled up the drive towards the house, Mab trotting beside us. I said urgently, 'What are we going to *do* with him? What happens if they come looking for him – or you, for that matter?'

'We'll cross that bridge when we come to it,' said Francis shortly. 'How many of the servants can be trusted to keep their mouths shut?'

War and slightly reduced circumstances had depleted the once considerable numbers at Goldhayes. Those left were for the most part older, reliable men and women who had been in the family's service for years. I said, running through them in my mind's eye, 'Almost all of them, I should think.'

'Good. We'll need their cooperation. Of course, once it's discovered he's gone, and with the help of a deserter to boot, they'll do their best to find him, with the aid of all those soldiers now sitting on their arses twiddling their thumbs outside Colchester. And since his name is known to them now, here is the first place they'll look. And if I'm here too, that will clinch it. Unless . . .'

'Unless what?'

'Unless I shed my erstwhile identity completely, and become Francis Heron once more. I should think it could be done, especially if I shave this off. Goblin will have to be hidden, of course, but John can arrange that if he's still in charge at the farm. Who else is here?'

'Your mother and Richard Trevelyan: Lucy, Meraud, Charles Lawrence and the Widow Gooch, they came here for Grainne's wedding to Malise and Mistress Gooch went with me to Colchester to find him when he and Jamie joined the rebels. And, of course, Grainne herself and all the Sewells at the Home Farm.' A thought struck me suddenly, and I could have kicked myself for not having considered it before. 'Why didn't you take him there?'

'With Joan there? She is still there, I take it? How long do you think his presence here would stay a secret if she knew? I'd give it about three hours before the story was all round the four Bradfields and over to Bury as well. It's too dangerous to risk. And besides, in military parlance the Home Farm is like an outpost to this fortress. If the enemy approaches, we can be warned in good time.'

'But what would we do if they searched the house?'

'Hide him. It can be done, you know, there are places I remember, and if no one talks, and no one recognizes Corporal Jonathan Marshall lurking beneath Master Francis Heron, newly returned from a tour of France, then he will be safe.' He glanced up to look at the house, now in view as we rounded the curve of the drive, a sight he had not seen for more than six years. Malise mumbled something and swayed in the saddle, and at once Francis's hands went up to support and encourage. 'We're nearly there, hold on, we're nearly there.'

There was no more time for talk, a circumstance for which I was secretly grateful. Malise seemed close to fainting again, and my hands as well as Francis's were needed to steady him for those last few yards over the moat bridge and up to the porch. 'Can you find the Widow?' Francis asked as his horse stopped. 'And Heppy, and Richard – there's no sense in keeping this secret from anyone here, let alone him, it's impossible.'

'You do know he's on excellent terms with half the County Committee, Barnadistons and all?'

'I might have guessed it, but we'll just have to trust to his family feeling. Now go!'

I thrust down all my unease about his strange, abrupt, almost nervous mood, and fairly ran into the house. I found the three he had mentioned almost at once; but as Francis had foreseen, it proved impossible to restrict my message. As soon as I had gasped out, rather incoherently, to Heppy that Francis had Malise outside and could she come at once, than Lucy appeared and demanded to know what was happening, and where had I gone this morning, she had been really worried about me, slipping off like that, and Kit had been beside himself . . . and on cue my son arrived, hurtling down the stairs like a bullet and leaping into my arms. 'Mammy, Mammy, Mammy where were you, you said you wouldn't go away, you said, you said, you SAID!' And he burst into howls of grief and rage and clung to me as tightly and desperately as he had once clung to Peg. My mind was much too taken up with the morning's happenings – Malise's freedom, the worries about his health and hiding him, and above all the leaping dizzying emotions that had surged in me again since the first moment I saw Francis riding up the drive – and soothing infant tantrums was not high on my list of priorities. I disentangled him briskly. 'Good heavens, chick, you didn't think I'd gone for ever? I can't spend every moment of the day with you, you know. Now stop that, there's things I must do, you can look after Mab and play with her and Hugh upstairs. Rose?' The nurse-maid, with little Hugh peering round the stairs above her, had arrived in pursuit, and despite Kit's frantic protests I handed him over and in my preoccupation scarcely heard his wails as she picked him up and without more ado carried him struggling back up to the nursery, Mab following reluctantly at my stern order, tail curved under her belly.

By this time more people, family and servants, had

been attracted by the commotion: with the result that a dozen excited helpers hurried into the porch, all eager to offer assistance. Lucy hurled herself into her brother's arms, sobbing incoherently: she had, I realized, not seen him since that terrible night in Oxford, the night of Charles's birthday supper, nearly six years ago. And Heppy, on her own initiative, set off down the drive to fetch Grainne: I hoped she would heed my hasty instructions not to let word of this slip to Joan. Then, supported by Richard, Charles and Francis, Malise was helped inside the house. 'Put him in that chamber at the top of the back stairs, if it's free,' said Francis, and to Lucy, who had not ceased to pour her questions at him, 'Oh, do give over, little sister, I'll say all I have to say later. Let's make Malise comfortable first.'

By the time our Scottish cousin had been installed in the chamber next to the children's, at the head of the turret stairs that led to the kitchen and cellars, the entire household from stable to kitchen to garret must have known of his arrival, brought by the prodigal Francis clad in the distinctive uniform of a New Model Army trooper. Richard, swiftly apprised of the facts, nodded in agreement. 'Yes, you are right, Francis – he must be hid, and can't be moved till he recovers.' He looked at Lucy's anxious, beseeching face, and added, 'I am not such a monster as to denounce him, you need have no fears on that score, especially as he only went to Colchester for poor Jamie's sake. I will give the servants explicit instructions to say nothing about all this to anyone, on pain of dismissal.'

I did not hear those instructions given, having stayed with the Widow to make Malise comfortable, but Lucy afterwards assured me, dubious as I was, that Richard had carried out his avowed intentions to the letter. That, I thought later, as the Widow and I stared down at Malise's exhausted face, misleadingly aggressive even in slumber, was as maybe: but what was to stop him sending a message to one of his Committee cronies?

Lack of motive was the immediate objection, for Richard could gain nothing from Malise's capture, and I had long since ceased to credit him with any other ends but his own, or Meraud's. One of the servants might perhaps talk, either out of malice or, more likely, from carelessness: that would be where the danger would lie.

Well, it was done now, and even had the servants not been informed, I doubted whether they could have been kept in ignorance. I uttered up a prayer for Malise, and for Grainne, and turned away from the bedside. Mistress Gooch was already settling herself, in her usual efficient way, with a pile of sewing by the window which gave out on to the stable yard below: the months of deprivation in Colchester, and the ordeal of last night's ride, seemed to have made no difference at all to her wiry, hard, withered frame, as tough as a dried stick. Just so had she sat once in Francis's sickroom, keeping vigil. She caught my eye and grinned, witchlike and encouraging. 'Well, lass, he's here, and you're free, and he is, and that prudish prig of an elder brother of his is hundreds of miles away overseas . . . What are you waiting for? Go and greet him, I'll warrant you didn't have time for it earlier.'

'I didn't,' I said, my hands automatically piling up the wet dirty clothes we had just peeled from Malise's shivering, thin and pain-racked body. 'But . . . he's changed. Even since Scotland, he's changed.'

'And can you wonder at it? Good God, lass, not even he can do what he's done and come through it unscathed. It's in your grasp, what you've wanted all these long years, don't let it slip now for want of a little courage. And anyway,' she added, with her evil bawdy chuckle, 'he hasn't changed that much. I saw him look at you when we was carrying Malise in here, even if you didn't. Go on, lass, there's no need for fear.'

But there was, and my mind was boiling with doubts and uncertainties as I closed the door softly behind me and went in search of my one-time lover. Seven years had we loved, and now at last no obstacle stood in our way – save those he might place there, out of guilt and grief for what he had done. And I did not know how to tell him that I knew about Jamie's death, and the manner of it. He had to tell me himself, I knew that, and realized that in the next few minutes I would have to tread very carefully indeed, for Francis in this mood was as difficult to handle as a snake: and one with a venomous bite. And as before in Scotland, I felt adrift in an uncharted sea, for unlike love in the poem that once had seemed a perfect mirror for our feelings, he had altered: and was no longer an ever-fixed mark.

I found him in the chamber he had once shared with Jamie in their childhood, and which had been unused since his youngest brother's marriage to Meraud, when the happy pair had removed to a bedchamber with sunnier aspect. The room had a stale musty smell of old herbs and newer polish, overlaid with fresh sweat and wet leather. He was shaving off the beard, stripped to the waist and peering into a tiny mirror propped up on the mantelshelf above the long-dead hearth. The betraying buff coat of the Army lay flung and tangled in the corner. For an instant, before he noticed me, I could watch him: taking in with a sweet sensual appreci-ation the hard-muscled lines of his body, blurred and drifted over with pale gold hairs across chest and arms, and branded with the scars of old battles, Edgehill and Philliphaugh. There was a newer one, red and raw still, snaking down his right arm, that looked ugly against his light-brown skin. And all the long-suppressed desires came tumbling, flooding, pouring back, making me tremble and grip my hands. He saw the movement and his hand jerked involuntarily, nicking his cheek: he turned and stared at me for a moment with disturbing intensity, while I wondered dizzily at this new, nervous, tense person who had always prided himself on his self-control. Then he grinned at me ruefully, making my heart lurch, and said, 'One scar more or less won't make much difference.'

'Did you have that at Colchester?' I asked unwarily,

indicating his arm: and immediately wished I had not. The old impervious mask shuttered across his face again, keeping me out: he said curtly, 'Yes, I did,' and set about staunching the tiny trickle of blood with a scrap of towel. I watched as he finished his task, seeing the old familiar Francis emerge from the bearded ruffianly soldier like a snake sloughing off skin. Only the pale hair, and above all the eyes, shadowy grey-green, were common to both: and would, like Montrose, always give him away. But there was also the clear-marked difference between where the beard had been, pale and untouched by sun and weather, and the tan of the rest of his face. Francis studied himself dispassionately in the mirror, and I wondered briefly if he saw anything of the changes that to me, after three years' separation, seemed so obvious: then he said, 'Do you, with all your housewifely experience, know of anything to make that less plain?'

There was a faint sting in his tone. I ignored it and applied my mind to this minor problem. 'Perhaps . . . Do you remember taking the outer shells off walnuts and trying to get the stains off your hands afterwards? I know the walnuts on that tree by the drive aren't ripe yet, but surely they'd still stain your skin just as efficiently. We can ask the children to get us some.'

'It'll have to be done with care,' said Francis, putting down the mirror and shrugging on a clean shirt. 'Or I shall look like a patchwork Moor.' He laced the shirt up and it became apparent that in the six or seven years since he had last worn it, his frame, always big but sparely covered, had broadened out considerably. The doublet he donned next looked lamentably old-fashioned upon him; too long and elaborately laced and buttoned down front and sleeve, unlike the loose skimpy garments at present à la mode. 'It'll never be believed that you've just been in foreign parts if you go around as badly dressed as that,' I said, 'there must be something of Jamie's you could have.'

A second later, I could have bitten my runaway

tongue, for the change in him was frightening. Half-way through putting on the doublet, he ripped it off again and flung it into the furthest corner of the chamber, nearly taking a pewter candlestick with it, and turned away from me, explosive tension in every line of him. 'Shut up, woman, for God's sake!'

I knew the signs, and steeled my heart and mind for what must come. This was not, unlike those anguished months at Catholm, directed at me: he bore all the hallmarks I had dreaded, the stamp of someone unable to live with himself and what he had done. But although I knew, I could say nothing: from somewhere, he had to find the courage to tell me, and face what had happened. As the tormented silence began to stretch out for ever, I sought desperately for a way to prompt him without it seeming too obvious that I did. At last, tentatively, I moved over to where he was standing, gazing out of the window into the park, which came right up to the moat on this side of the house, rough grass and deer and scattered, graceful trees in the misty morning sun. I glanced once at his brown hands, hardened and calloused by years of holding reins and handling sword and pistol, clenched now on the window-ledge so that the knuckles were white, and spoke softly. 'Something is wrong. Can you tell me?'

'I must go,' said Francis, as if he had not heard me. 'I must leave – it's not fair to you or any of them – forget all about me, I'm not worth anyone's pain.'

'You are! It doesn't matter, you're wrong, it doesn't matter to me, it doesn't matter *what* you've done, *what's* happened, it's made no difference to me . . .'

'But it's made a difference to *me*,' said Francis, a great and desperate grief and anger in his voice, worse by far than his anguish after Philliphaugh. 'Shall I tell you? Do you *really* want to know? Do you really want me to tell you that I killed my own brother, and *knew who he was as I did it?*'

Tears suddenly filled my eyes, spilling over, choking me: I reached out blindly to hold him, feeling the shuddering tension under my hands. 'Tell me what happened, please, tell me. You have to, for your own sanity you have to.'

'I can't,' Francis whispered, 'oh, God, not even you, I can't . . .'

I was trying to regain my calm, to think clearly, realizing that on my reactions and help and support depended which side of the knife's edge he would fall. I had to ignore the awkwardness of my stance, and the crick in my neck as I pressed my face against his shirt. A great tremor shook his body: I said urgently, 'Tell me, I'll make a judgement or not, as you wish, but tell me, you can't let it fester inside you for ever . . . tell me what happened.'

There was a long silence. Beneath my ear, his heart thudded painfully and his breathing fought against control. At last he said, in a voice so quiet and altered I heard it almost inside my head and not with my ears, 'They made a sortie, the Cavaliers, you must remember the night, warm with no rain and some moon to give them light to see. They were going to attack the East Bridge mill which we'd garrisoned a few days earlier . . . but of course Malise must have told you all this.'

'A little . . . it doesn't matter, go on.'

He took a deep shivering breath and went on, his deceptively calm voice telling me once more a story of grief and battle, as after Edgehill and Philliphaugh. 'The forlorn hope carried the bridge and the outposts there, and killed or captured nearly a hundred of the garrison. Then they joined up with the main forces and charged on up the hill to Greenstead Church where our fort was. By this time we had our men on the slopes of the hill below the church, but they charged so strongly we were overrun and retreated back up the hill. There were hedges, we rallied the men behind one of them, tried to fight back and hold the hedges and the top of the hill. It was very confusing – dark, not much moon, people shouting and screaming, powder-smoke and frightened horses – then we heard one of the Cavaliers shout out for more ammunition, so we knew they must be running short and would have to retreat soon. And that was the turning-point. So the colonel rallied us and we charged through the hedge at them.' The timbre of his voice altered slightly and I tensed, knowing that now he was coming to the moment of greatest pain. "We fought hand-to-hand in the dark on the hillside, all mud and uneven ground, Goblin stumbled on something and all but threw me, and while I was getting back in the saddle one of the Cavaliers engaged me, that was where I got the wound on my arm, there was something about him that seemed familiar but I was fighting for my life, I could hardly halt and cry parley and ask him who he was . . .' His voice faltered: he took another deep painful breath and said, 'Then he seemed to waver, he said something and raised his sword a little, I got in under his guard, and then I saw his face, even in that dim light there was no mistaking my own brother . . . and my hand just went on, pushing the sword into him, as if it didn't belong to me, as if he was a total stranger . . . I killed him and I knew who he was!'

I had no words to reach him, to offer my pathetically inadequate comfort, to try and erase this most terrible, tragic death. I could only hold him, just as I had held Jamie as he died, as if by the urgent, desperate pressure of my hands and body I could creep within his heart and share some of that terrible burden. We stood there by the window for a long time, united as never before by our grief and anguish: until at last, someone coughed gently.

We looked round, dragged back at last, unwillingly, to the life which had to go on, and beheld Grainne. She was standing at the door, her unfashionable hair tangled, unbrushed after the night, around her glowing, glorious face. Some of the delight faded as she took in the unhappiness that must have been obvious in our expressions, and then, still smiling, she held out her hands. 'Oh Francis, dear Francis, how can I ever repay you?'

Looking up at Francis's face, that of a man awakening

slowly and groggily from nightmare, I did not wonder that he made no reply. Grainne's hands dropped: she walked forward and gently, lovingly, with friendship, kissed him on the mouth. In all the years I had known her, she had never done anything like that before: but then, never had happiness shone from her thus, like light through a thin curtain. Francis held her eyes, so different and calmer a green, with his and said very quietly, 'It was an atonement for Jamie. I had to do it, or never live with myself again.'

Grainne's eyes went to mine, shocked understanding suddenly on her face. 'For Jamie?'

'For Jamie,' said Francis with difficulty. 'For Jamie, because I killed him, and could have avoided it. So I saved Malise instead.'

'And thereby saved me,' said Grainne. 'Will you tell me what happened? I'll understand if you don't want to.'

But tell her he did, and already, brought into the open and shared, the burden seemed less. And at the end Grainne did not offer excuses or explanations or superficial sympathy for his comfort: only saying, 'I'm not going to apportion any blame, but others might – and I don't think, if you are wise, that this should go beyond the five of us. Now, we must think about Malise, because he at least is bound to be looked for here, even if they have no idea who freed him. What are you going to do?'

Thus was Francis forced to turn from his agony over what was past and done to active, practical consideration of present and future problems. For a moment longer the haunted look shadowed his face, and delayed longer in his eyes, and then his strong will asserted its usual control of his emotions once more. 'He has to stay here, for the moment. He's too weak and ill to be moved, and besides, as long as the Widow's in charge of the sickroom he won't dare do anything but recover as soon as possible. Richard has sworn the servants to secrecy, about me as well as Malise, and I can't think of any of them who'd betray us deliberately. If a permanent watch is kept at the Home Farm or in the village, then we can have plenty of advance warning of any approach of soldiers, but it has to be done without Joan's knowledge.'

'Jasper,' said Grainne instantly. 'He's old enough to enjoy the adventure, and clever enough to do it properly, unlike that Jermyn child. All we have to do is to persuade Dr Davis that he needs a holiday from teaching, and Jasper can be at the farm all day without arousing Joan's suspicions.'

'But where,' I enquired, 'do we hide Malise if the soldiers do come looking for him? And what story do we tell them about you?'

'That one I shall have to think about,' said Francis. He walked over to his discarded doublet and picked it up, with a shadow of his old mockingly rueful smile. 'And as you so rightly said, who would believe I'd been in France if all I wear is something as unfashionable as this? Oh well, it'll do for the moment. Let me show you what we can do when they come looking for Malise.'

Curiously, Grainne and I followed him out of the chamber, down the New Gallery with its windows looking out on to the Courtyard Garden, like a lush well dipped into the centre of the house, past Malise's chamber to the turret stairs, which led up to the garrets and down to kitchen and cellar. 'Could he be got down here?' I queried, peering down into the gloom, seeing the narrow, twisting steps upon which more than one scurrying maid had twisted or broken an ankle.

'That's exactly what I had in mind when I suggested putting him in that particular chamber,' Francis said. 'I know it would be difficult, to say the least of it, but with several strong helpers we could do it, even if he was still too weak to walk.'

'And where would you hide him?' Grainne asked dubiously. For answer, Francis gestured downwards: in the depths a door opened and shut, a gust of warm air laden with cooking aromas ascended, and the scuttering of feet heralded the arrival of Rose with a pile of fresh linen. She curtseyed awkwardly on the stone stairs and then slid past us, muttering apologies in broadest Suffolk. Her appearance reminded me, with a nameless feeling of apprehension, that in the turmoil of the last hour I had completely omitted to tell Francis of the presence of Kit; and a pang of guilt smote me as I remembered also the cursory way I had dealt with the child's greeting that morning. True, the arrival of Malise and Francis was a valid enough reason for thus dismissing him, but Kit was not old enough to understand that: he knew only that his need for my love and the security it gave to him, who was so desperately insecure, overrode everything else in his life. Guiltily aware that I had failed him yet again, I followed Grainne and Francis down the break-leg stairs, past the door which gave on to the kitchen, and down into the bowels of the earth.

The drop in temperature down here was marked, the air chill and slightly musty. This was the oldest part of the house, being crypt or cellar from the Benedictine Priory, offshoot of the great Abbey at Bury, which had first stood on this site. So above us, dim and smeared with grime and cobwebs and dust, sooty with the smoke of centuries of rush dips and tallow candles, were the ancient, sturdy stone arches of the Papist monks who had served God here for nearly five hundred years before being ousted by the combined forces of Mammon, the eighth King Henry and Sir Christopher Heron. As a child, superstitious despite myself, I had rarely ventured down here alone: for no matter how much I had scorned my own foolish fancies, there was no denying the eerie feeling of being watched, the uncertainty of what lay in the great flickering shadows cast by wine and beer barrels, stored food, and the accumulated rubbish of centuries. As well as elderly and anonymous heaps of rusty iron and rotting wood, there lay here and there the lovely carved dust-shrouded stone that Thomas Cromwell's vandals and Sir Christopher's masons had failed to bring themselves either to use or to destroy. Angels, gargoyles, saints, fragments of leaves and beasts and abstract angular carving, loomed blurrily through their mantles of dirt.

'This is beautiful,' Grainne said, her soft voice tinged with wonder as she stared down at the remote frozen face of an angel, winged in glory and imprisoned in stone. 'From the old Priory, I take it . . . Do you know, I have never been down here before, in all my time at Goldhayes?'

'You haven't missed much,' I said, shivering despite myself. Francis walked down between the casks, smiling remotely like the angel, the light from his candle laying huge fantastic black shadows over the rough stone walls as it flicked and jumped. 'Ah, but the ghosts here are friendly – I think.'

'That's not an impression I ever received,' I muttered, following him. He appeared to be walking down the avenue of grotesque swollen barrels towards a blank wall at its end, where the crypt had been roughly walled across with miscellaneous blocks of Priory stone, used anyhow with no regard for aesthetic considerations at all. I was perhaps five paces behind him; then he turned to the left, and vanished. Had the light also disappeared, I believe I might have panicked, brought as I was by recent events and emotions to a pitch of nervous tension: but I could see the faint reflected glow of the candle still, and followed it. 'Francis? Are you there?'

His laugh echoed around the arched vaults. 'Damn. So I haven't fooled you. I thought to vanish completely, you see . . . stay still for a moment, both of you.'

There was the close sound of a creaking door slamming, and all vestiges of light disappeared. The sensation of being watched increased abruptly, and I shivered. 'All right, you've proved your point – now show us where you are.'

Silence. 'He was right,' Grainne said, her voice hushed, 'the ghosts are friendly.'

'I've never felt them so,' I hissed back. The dark seemed all at once very close, muffling right up to my face like a shroud of black cloth, and I disliked it intensely.

The door opened again suddenly, making me start. Francis stood there, half-hidden by the end barrel, his face demonically lit in abrupt light and shadow. 'This is where I thought we'd hide him. Come and look.'

'This' lay through the doorway, low enough for Grainne to have to bend her head to pass under. I stepped inside behind her, curious and apprehensive, but there was nothing but a bare, dirty chamber, vaulted like the rest, with an arch across the end wall that might once have framed an altar. In one corner lay the white, fragile, dust-cloaked bones of a long-dead rat, but whatever bodies had lain in the crypt had obviously been given burial elsewhere – or more likely, hearing the stories of the downfall of the monasteries, scattered to the four winds. Just an empty chamber, some fifteen-foot square, but not a place in which I would have cared to spend time alone.

'Did any light show?' Francis asked, and we shook our heads. 'That's good – it means we can leave him with a candle or two. In fact, this had better be made ready now – and the fewer people who know of it, the better.'

'The three of us, and the Widow,' I said. 'She can be trusted, we all know that.'

'I agree. And no one else. Now, what will we need? A pallet of some sort, candles, food, drink, books perhaps – he may need to be in there some time.'

Grainne said slowly, 'They're bound to search the cellars. It's an obvious place. Why shouldn't they find this?'

'Because when a couple of hogsheads are pulled across and stood upright against the door, you can't see it. Very few people know about this room anyway, and besides, we can lock it. It's certainly much safer than anywhere else.'

Unsatisfactory as it seemed to me, I had to agree. Goldhayes, having been built by a Protestant family, was unfortunately devoid of the priests' holes and secret chambers of houses like Hengrave and Sawston Hall. But I would not like to be Malise, I decided, imprisoned down here in the dark with a hundred monkish ghosts and the fear of discovery to haunt him, and nothing but candles for his comfort.

Before dinner, we carried the chief necessities down: Grainne and Francis with the pallet, taken from an empty garret chamber and miraculously transported down the twisting stairs without either being seen or breaking a limb, and the Widow and I stealthily raiding larder or buttery for rat-proof crocks and containers of bread and cheese, and a couple of blackjacks of beer. All this, placed in the musty chamber on a hastily-swept piece of floor, did not do anything to lessen its oppressive aura; pathetic attempts at cheerfulness, marooned in a sea of dust. Upstairs, Malise slept on, blessedly unaware of the fate that awaited him should soldiers come a-calling: and I still had not told Francis about Kit.

In the event, I did not need to. The Long Gallery was deserted, dinner only a few moments away, and Francis and I had slipped in to see how Malise did. He still lay oblivious below the blankets, sleeping ominously like the dead, but the Widow seemed cheerful about his prospects. Relieved, we slid softly out of the room and round to the Gallery. At the head of the main staircase, Francis took my hands and turned me to face him. 'My own dear heart, do you realize that it's now some six hours since we met once more, and we have not yet kissed?'

'For shame,' I said, the blood rising singing to my heart as always at his touch, 'shall we make up for time wasted?'

If it had not been for the imminence of the meal, I think that kiss, after a greater separation than we had yet endured in all those seven years of partings and absences and reunions, might have served merely as the gateway to those greater delights that we had never yet tasted together. At once a greeting, an exploration, and an affirmation of love, the embrace must have lasted some time, though neither of us was conscious of anything save the wild weakening strength of our desires and emotions; until I felt my skirt being tugged with a rhythmic and increasing persistence, and a small, urgent voice said, 'Mammy! Mammy, who's that man?'

I jerked out of Francis's embrace as guiltily as any city wife caught by her cuckolded husband in the arms of her fashionable lover. Kit stared at us, his blue eyes angry and accusing, the sleek black hair neatly brushed by Rose, who stood, embarrassed and awkward, a few paces behind him with Hugh. With those vivid eyes and the contrast of white skin and dark hair, and above all the suspicious, possessive expression on his face, he had never looked more like his dead father.

There was a long, long moment when he and Francis stared at each other, and my heart felt fit to burst from my ribs. Would my lover accept my child for my sake, or reject him for his father's? And Kit, too, must have sensed that this man meant far more to me than any other friend: a frown appeared between the strongly-marked, peaking eyebrows, and he repeated with growing intensity, 'Mammy, *who's that man?*'

I cast a brief, desperate glance at my dearest love: he was regarding Kit with a strange expression on his face, one that I shied from interpreting. I said quickly, 'This is your cousin Francis, Kit, he's just returned from overseas.'

'Was that why you were kissing him?' Kit demanded: once settled on a course it took an earthquake to divert him – as with his parents. Hugh giggled, if so deep and unchildish a sound could be so called, and was hastily shushed by a red-faced Rose.

'Partly. And partly because I like him.'

'Are you going to marry him then?' said the flat, hostile little voice of our earliest acquaintance. I felt a deep crimson blush, rare and humiliating, wash over my

438

face. 'Now that's quite enough of your questions. Go down to your dinner with Rose and Hugh, I'll follow in a moment.'

Kit did not move. His intense, assessing, jealous gaze dwelt long on Francis's impassive face; then stiffly, formally, as he had done on first meeting me, he bowed low. The corner of Francis's mouth moved upwards slightly, to my intense relief, and then he also bowed. 'Your servant, Master Christopher.'

'*Sir* Christopher,' said the unchildlike child, coldly. Francis's eyes flashed to my face, significantly, and I remembered with a shock that until this moment he had not known of Dominic's death. Then he said, very seriously in the face of my son's implacability, 'I crave your pardon, Sir Christopher.'

'I grant it,' said Kit, unaware of the latent humour in this comical confrontation. 'I will see you at dinner, sir.' And he stalked past as upright and haughty as any court gallant, followed by the flustered and apologetic Rose, towing Hugh, who was chuckling happily to himself. Francis stopped him. 'Are you my new baby brother?'

Hugh turned his long, sleepy shadow-green eyes up to the man who was strangely like him, and grinned. 'Are you Francis?'

'I am indeed.'

'Then I'm Hugh and I'm not new!' said the infant, and his triumphant cackles of merriment could be heard all the way down the stairs, drowning Rose's reproofs.

'I'm sorry,' I said, gazing down at their retreating figures. 'I meant to tell you, but somehow there just hasn't been the opportunity. He's been here since before Christmas.'

'So Dominic is dead, I take it. Did someone murder him at last, or was he eaten up with a canker from within?'

'Neither. He was wounded at Naseby and never recovered.' I shivered as his phantom slithered unwelcome into my mind. 'And I regret to say I did not mourn overmuch – in fact I was glad, ashamed though I am to say it.'

'After the way he treated you, you'd be a saint if you weren't delighted.' He grinned suddenly, and the ghost vanished. 'I believe the correct description of your brat is, "a chip off the old block".'

'Ah, but which block?'

'Yours, of course – he never gives up asking all the wrong questions. Are you going to marry me, then?'

I looked up, seeing in his face an expression that removed all my doubts and reminded me that, after all, nothing essential had ever changed; and all the shadows fell from my heart. 'If you will have me, I will.'

'Despite what I have done?'

'Look,' I said, my voice quivering with exasperation, 'I have told you, my own dear fool, that if you ride in league with Lucifer I will follow you through the gates of Hell and beyond. The past is gone, we can't bring Jamie back, and your atonement has been made: there's no point in torturing yourself further. And I love you – is that not enough?'

'I suppose it might just suffice,' said Francis with convincing solemnity. We caught each other's eyes and burst into delighted laughter, in my case abruptly terminated by the force of his arms around me, driving the breath from my lungs. As I returned his embrace, I heard his voice, soft and deep and rough with passion and longing, against my hair. 'I am yours for ever. Will you marry me, as soon as may be?'

'What does it take without banns being called? A special licence?' My own voice was different to my ears, and not only because I could hardly draw breath within the strength of his arms.

'Whatever it takes, you may depend upon it, I will do it. And my own dearest dear, since it is so soon, will you come to me tonight?'

There was no answer needed: and like a jewel that prospect lay within my mind, illuminating all the rest of the day; not only the usual routine of mealtimes and sewing, reading and recreation, but also those moments that made this day one of reunion, hope and the promise of delight. Frequently, I caught myself staring at him, loving just the way he looked, and wondering afresh that out of all the women on this earth, I with all my faults should have been the one he chose. And something in my cautious nature refused still to let go, to believe, to trust to the benevolence of a fate that through those seven years seemed to have done its best to chain us for ever apart. What, at the last moment, would drive us asunder?

I did think, when Francis fell instantly and soundly asleep on one of the window-seats shortly after dinner, that our plans and hopes would be overturned by something as prosaic as his sheer exhaustion; he had not slept for a day and a half, and had ridden from Colchester through the night supporting a sick man in his arms. Snappishly, I detained Lucy, who had approached him with her typically overwhelming sisterly concern, and diverted her unwanted attentions elsewhere. I was relieved when, after perhaps two hours of sleep, he woke, his usual acerbic self, took Jasper aside when the boy's lessons with Dr Davis had finished, and in a corner of the Long Gallery issued him with his instructions: to return to the Home Farm with some tale for Joan's benefit of his tutor's illness and a pile of books he must read before the aged Welshman's recovery. That would ensure his constant presence in the farmhouse, so that at any approach of soldiers, he would be able to give us warning. 'Take the shortcut across the park,' I advised him, 'it's at least half the distance of the drive, and that should with luck give us a few precious minutes to hide Master Graham.'

Jasper's eyes were brilliant with enthusiasm. 'Where are you going to hide him?'

'Best you don't know, shrimp,' Francis told him. 'Then you won't be able to say anything, no matter how they try to persuade you. And you won't be able to give it away by accident, either.'

'Please tell me,' Jasper begged, urgently. 'They could put me on the *rack* and I wouldn't tell them, I swear it, and I'd never ever breathe a word to anyone, I *promise!*' He added, glaring at Francis, 'And don't you think I'm a bit old to be called shrimp? I'm not five any more, you know.'

'Jasper!' said Grainne, reprovingly: but Francis grinned. 'All right. I'll reserve shrimp for Hugh, or Kit. You can be a prawn now, since you've grown somewhat, but it'll be a year or two till you're a fully-armoured lobster like me. Now get you gone, and don't forget any of what we've said. Master Graham's safety may depend on you – are you man enough for that responsibility?'

Jasper's indignant face was indication enough that he thought himself more than equal to the task. He bowed with more than a touch of Francis's own flamboyance, and fled. Grainne stared after him dubiously. 'I know he'll do his best, he always does, but he's so young yet . . . only nine! And perhaps two lives hang on his quick wits.'

'There's no one else can do the job,' Francis pointed out. 'Not unless you want Joan, and then the whole of Suffolk, to put two and two together and make fifty. Don't worry, he'll be all right, you know damn well he will, and it'll keep him out of mischief.'

Like Grainne, I had my doubts about loading such a burden upon a small boy, even an unusually intelligent small boy like Jasper, but I did not see any neater solution. In any event, the rainy day drew to its close, prematurely dark, without any sign of inquisitive soldiers: and after the remarkable events of the morning, the atmosphere within Goldhayes remained subdued by the news of Jamie's death: Mary and Meraud nowhere to be seen and Lucy draped in black. Yet I had the delight and joy of Francis's presence, ever at my side, and our love no secret here for the first time in my life.

And night brought with it soft golden candlelight and

deep shadows: the house settling into quiet, children in bed, though that in itself was a routine fraught with difficulty this evening, Kit being as clinging and possessive at the moment of parting as he had been all day; his instinct, I sensed with sorrow and alarm, being thus to shut Francis out from me. Gently, I disentangled the winding arms from about my neck and smiled down at him with, I hoped, no trace of the secret anger I had fought so hard against all day: an anger directed as much against myself as against my son, who could not possibly understand the force of this apparently new emotion in me. 'It's all right, Kitling, I won't leave you.'

'You left this morning,' said that flat, accusing little voice. I sighed. 'I didn't leave, little one, I just went for a walk – and I'm sorry if you missed me. Now go to sleep, and tomorrow night I'll tell you the story of the old woman who lived in a jug.'

'Tell me now!'

'No, it's time you were asleep – look, Hugh, is already. Tomorrow, I promise, but only if you sleep now. Good night, sleep tight, and don't let the bugs bite!'

'Aren't any bugs,' said Kit's voice, tottering on the edge of sleep. 'G' night.'

I stood and watched his usual abrupt descent into slumber. Only when I was sure he would not notice did I creep softly from the boys' chamber, exchanging as I did so a wry glance with the long-suffering Rose. Outside, Francis was just emerging from the next room where Malise lay sleeping too, warm and rested, and nourished by Monsieur Harcourt's special restorative beef broth: and feeling suddenly very much in need of him, I slipped swiftly into his arms and was tightly held. 'Is that brat of yours causing you trouble?' Francis asked.

'No, not really – but it took me so long to bring him back to normality. When he arrived here he was miserable and angry and he took all his loss and bewilderment out on me, and even when I'd managed to tame him a little it was a long hard toil to make him civilized again . . . and now in the time I was trapped in Colchester, he seems to have gone right back to his bad old ways again. He was five less than a month ago, and yet in his behaviour he's younger than Hugh, who's only just four. And Kit's no fool – even if he doesn't understand it, he senses that you mean a great deal to me.'

'More than he does?'

I looked up at Francis's face. It wore its habitual enigmatic, uninformative expression, but there was somehow a vulnerability within, a preparation for bad news, that more than anything he could do or say spoke of the strength of his love and need for me. And I answered honestly, as he deserved. 'Yes. Yes, I know I shouldn't say it, but you do. And yet, can you understand this, I don't want to make the choice, I don't want to be forced into a situation where I have to choose between you. I have failed him too often, I owe him some happiness, for it is my fault he is on this earth, not his; and he is not to be blamed for depending so much on me. I'm all he has left.' I swallowed, vulnerable in my turn. 'And since I am thus encumbered, do you still want to marry me?'

For a long moment he made no answer, and my jumping heart suddenly threatened to suffocate me. I turned my face away and buried my nose into the despised, unmodish doublet. Abruptly his arms all but squeezed the remaining breath from my ribs, and his voice, rich with laughter, said, 'Ah, I can't leave you any longer on tenterhooks . . . if you had twenty such brats, I'd marry you willingly still. He's young yet, we'll win him to us by kindness and laughter.'

'And music, he has something at least of me in him, for music is his key.'

'All to the good, for I as you know am a musician of many parts – lute, harpsichord, virginals, flageolet, viol, I play them all, most vilely in the latter case – ah, don't mock, my lady, I mean it most seriously. And talking of brats, when are you going to give me licence to roam your sweet body, after "these long seven years and more"?'

' "And come to seek those former vows, I granted you before",' I quoted softly, a tremor in my voice from love and laughter mixed. My demon lover was edging me towards the door of his chamber, and there was no one to see or to remark upon our sudden absence, most of the household having retired after supper on this day of mourning. And half-exultant, half-afraid, I gave myself into his power and his keeping, and was led within his arm to the room he had inhabited as a child.

Now, in the secret light of one candle, it took on a strange, enchanted air, so that we did not notice the signs of long disuse: having eyes and thoughts only for each other, aware as never before of the sensations of touch and sight and hearing: the glancing contact of his fingers like flickers of fire against my skin, his eyes dark and smoky as he unlaced my bodice, and his voice likewise quoting the words of desire that another man of imagination and power had spoken to his own much-loved lady both long since dead:

' "Oh my America! my new-found-land." '

And as Donne had described, the musty dim chamber, and the enclosed world-within-a-world behind the faded bed-curtains, served only as the background for our long-awaited exploration of the delights of a passion that swept through me as overwhelmingly as it filled him: and the wonder of it was, that it was as though those brief dreadful months in Dominic's loathed bed had never existed, and all my bitter experience of love was made new and fresh and whole below Francis's hands and body, as if I had been, despite my husband's distorted, tainted lust, despite my child, a virgin after all until this magical, spellbound night. And neither was this second deflowering accompanied by the fear and pain of the first, but burst upon me like a sudden summer flower, heralded by desire and attended by joy. And when our hunger was assuaged we lay, still tangled together, dazed by the force of our love, and consumed by its wonder and magnificence.

'I have waited a long, long time for you,' Francis said, so softly that, had my head not lain a few inches from his, I would not have heard him at all. 'And you were all I thought you would be . . . and more. Are you satisfied, owd gal, my dear, dear lady?'

'You shouldn't need to ask . . . it's all right, I weep for happiness, not for sorrow . . . Oh, I love you, I love you more than anything else in the whole world . . . and now nothing can sever us, we are together, now and evermore, no more harm, no hurts, no lies, no deceit . . . our truth at last for all to see.'

And the night was young yet: no one came to disturb our love-making, and the candle sank and guttered as our desire flared anew, for such a wonder and delight should not be tasted once only . . . until at last, very late, my head spinning with happiness and exhaustion and the marvellous, sensual memories and the afterglow of passion, Francis leaned on one elbow and lazily, smiling, traced the lines of the answering smile on my face. 'Even those possessed by Venus must sleep, my dear . . . and there will be many other nights after this, even if they do not have quite the same wonder of discovery. Do you mind?'

I laughed with an unalloyed joy and happiness. 'Mind? I have no more strength than a day-old kitten, your love has drained my senses dry . . . "So roll me in your arms, my love, and blow the candle out." '

Francis did so, laughing likewise, so that in desire and laughter and delight the pattern of our future loving was set, immutable, an ever-fixed mark: his dark, amused voice the last thing I heard before sleep claimed me, capping my quotation:

' "And if we prove successful, love, please name it after me!" '

I woke once in the night, wondering, stupid with sleep, what it was I had heard, to have roused me so abruptly:

and then Francis's voice, reliving old agonies, came out of the darkness. 'Oh God, *Jamie!*' The violence of his movements shook the bed; blundering, I slithered and crawled towards him, finding him in that musty and sheet-entangled expanse more by accident than judgement, and curled my body around his. 'Francis, wake up, oh wake *up!*'

Under the pressure of my arms he moved and shook and then suddenly was awake: I could feel each indrawn shuddering breath, dragging him back from the horrors of nightmare, and love and pity and grief mixed brought tears to my eyes. 'You had a bad dream.'

'An understatement,' said Francis. It was strange, not being able to see him, but the pain in his voice was almost visible despite the dark. 'What did I say?'

'You . . . you called Jamie's name.' I could not see his reaction, but I could feel it, and I went on quickly. 'I know that anything I say, any sympathy, any understanding words, may seem . . . oh, pathetic, hopeless, inadequate, laughable – I don't know. But whatever you think, I am *here*, here now, to take whatever burdens you want to share with me. My dearest love, remember this: you are no longer alone.'

For answer, Francis turned and held me, his face buried in my tangled hair, and I heard his voice, hardly stirring the air around us. 'I know – and of all the gifts you have to give me, that is the greatest and the best. With you, I feel I can face anything – even this.'

There were no more nightmares: we slept again, in each other's arms, and no horrors came to destroy our peace. It was full morn when I woke, as far as I could tell from the lances of light spearing through the cracks in the shutters and the bed-curtains, but such was my sense of languor and well-being that I felt no urge to rise, none of the restlessness that had afflicted me the morning before, as if I had been aware of Francis's approach. Luxuriating in this wonderful sleepy, lazy sensuality, I turned my head and beheld my beloved abandoned in sleep, his yellow hair drifted across his face, and all his tight-strung defences gone. It seemed a shame to wake him: instead, I contented myself with watching him, delighting secretly in the opportunity to do so without attracting his usual ironic attention. These few moments of peace would soon be gone, as the faint noises from outside indicated: and indeed I had only been awake for a little while before my lover stirred, rolled over and saw me watching. 'Hullo, owd gal. Didn't we make a night of it! Come here . . .'

I slid into the circle of his arm, my head resting on his shoulder. 'We did indeed . . . and are you happy?'

'I think I can safely say that never in all my life have I been happier . . . I'll find out about that licence today. Perhaps if we plan it rightly we can have a double wedding with Grainne and Malise!' Lazily, he stroked my riotous hair away from his face. 'You've too much of this, and it tickles . . . Kiss me, love.'

As I did so, I became vaguely aware of a louder noise in the world beyond our chamber. Francis's hand cupped my breast and began slyly to explore further, awakening again a desire that the night had done nothing to diminish . . . and outside, Kit screamed suddenly and piercingly. 'Mammy! Mammy! Mammy, where are you?'

'Oh, Christ,' I said with feeling. 'I wish I could hide . . . Oh, Francis, I'm sorry, I shall have to go, or he'll scream the place down.'

'He can wait a bit longer,' said my lover, cousin, friend, and he grinned. 'Don't tell me you *really* want to go . . . Do you like that?'

I did indeed, and the devil on my shoulder led me thoroughly and easily into temptation. 'He won't find us in here, after all . . .'

And the door burst open. As we sat up, our rising passion rudely interrupted, there was a flurry of the bed-curtains and Kit arrived like a small tornado, hurling himself through them and landing with a thud on the bed. His scarlet, angry face stared from me to Francis and back again, and he cried furiously, 'You weren't in your room! I couldn't find you again! You went away and you *promised!*'

'I didn't go away,' I said, as calmly as I could manage, being at once embarrassed and as angry as he, and also very conscious of the fact that the sheet was a rather inadequate cover for my nakedness. 'I was here, I didn't go away. You mustn't come bursting in here like this, it's very rude indeed.'

'Was *he* with you?' Kit demanded, ignoring my reproof. 'Was he with you all night? And Mab too?' For the little dog, who had spent a somewhat storm-tossed night at the foot of the bed, having sneaked in unnoticed to join us, was now slinking and wriggling up to lie beside me and give me her morning lick. Francis, his mouth set with annoyance, said firmly, 'It's none of your business, Kit. Now get down and go, and leave us in peace.'

'No!' my son screamed at once. 'No! I'm not going! I want to be with my mammy, I want to be with my mammy, I'm *not* going!'

He should have known better. Francis, much though he liked children, was in no mood to stand any nonsense, and I was similarly infuriated. 'Kit! Do as you're told and go back to your room. *Now.*'

'No!' Kit cried: and as Francis, who had for decency's sake wrapped his discarded shirt around his waist, approached him, he shuffled backwards down the bed on his knees. 'No! I'm *not* going! No!' He shrieked as Francis captured him, a hand around each small arm, and was suddenly transformed into a writhing, twisting demon of fury. 'I hate you I hate you I hate you let me GO!'

Francis jerked the curtains back one-handed and pinioned the struggling boy firmly under one arm. Rose stood crimson-faced at the door, which she had fortunately closed, in an agony of embarrassment. 'Oh, Mistress Thomazine, Master Francis, I'm so sorry, that were all my fault, he slipped away from me, he be a strong little mite and I coon't keep a hold of he, but

Mistress Meraud didn't know where you was and she coon't do nothing to calm him down neither. I'll take him, Master Francis,' she added, with such a look of anguish on her face as she tried to avert her gaze from his parlous state of undress that, despite my own feelings, I was hard put to it to conceal a smile. Francis dumped the screeching infant in her capable arms, and with a hasty curtsey Rose, much burdened, opened the door with fumbling fingers and scurried outside. Beyond her, in the New Gallery, I caught sight of a black-clad, silver-haired figure: Meraud, whose unexplained influence over Kit seemed to be as malign as his nurse Peg's had been. I wondered with sudden rage if she had steered him to our chamber, knowing full well what he would find and his reaction to it: then Francis, grinning, swept her a flamboyant bow. The shirt finally slipped from its precarious position, and I had a glimpse of her scandalized, outraged face before my lover shut the door with a flourish, wedged a high-backed chair securely under the latch, and returned to the tangled bed. 'Well, despite that little interruption, shall we carry on where we left off?'

And we did, but compared to the delights we had earlier enjoyed, it was at best an unsatisfactory experience, both of us being thoroughly disturbed by Kit's noisy intrusion and neither of us willing to admit the fact. When we had done, we lay together for a while, silent and unhappy, separated by our own thoughts, until Francis said softly, 'Something will have to be done about Kit. It'll do him no good at all if he loathes his stepfather – and it won't improve our life either.'

Relief flooded me: I had been afraid, wrapped within my own anger and guilt, that he might ask me to make that choice that I had begged should never be forced upon me – but I should have known better. Francis had his own codes and rules which might not have been those of, for instance, his brother Simon, nor even Dan Ashley, but save for those dreadful months in Scotland, I could always trust in his sense of fairness and rightness.

I found his hand and gripped it: Francis said, smiling suddenly into my eyes, 'Did you think then that I was going to change my mind? Ah, my love, you should know me better than that. But I do think that we should begin by taking him away from Meraud's sphere of influence. How in Christ's name does she come to wield such power over him anyway? She's never shown much interest in anyone else's brats.'

'As to why, I'm just as much in the dark as you, but he used to be fond of Jamie, and I think he transferred some of that affection to her. And then while I was in Colchester, Grainne told me, she used to take him for walks, play with him and so on. And because he was lonely and lost and missing me, and Jamie, I suppose he turned to her. He's very gullible, but then he's only little.'

'All the more reason for removing him, and us, out of dear Meraud's way. Apart from anything else, her presence hourly reminds me that I killed her husband, my brother: and I feel that she's quite capable of extracting that information simply by looking at me, those cold, blue eyes seem to pierce right through any dissembling.'

'I know where we can go. We can take Malise and Grainne as well, and Jasper and Hen – we can go to Ashcott.'

'Are you sure that's wise? After all, Ashcott holds many memories, and not all of them are pleasant ones – especially for Grainne.'

'But it's mine, it's my jointure house with the one in Pennyfarthing Street. Everything else I had is Kit's now, but Ashcott is mine and it needs someone to live in it again. Not even the Tawneys are there any more, Will Tawney died last year and his wife and children have gone to live with her brother in Bristol. It must be going to rack and ruin.' I warmed to the idea as I spoke, seeing again in my mind's eye the little golden castle like amber in emeralds amongst the water meadows of the River Swere. 'It would be nice to be there peacefully, no soldiers or garrisons, and you'd be safer from unwelcome pursuit, you and Malise. And if we are all happy with the people we love and no worries about the past, then our ghosts are defeated.'

No one directly mentioned the events of that morning to us, although the Widow commented sharply and pointedly about Kit's lack of due respect: and Lucy, who was, of course, well aware that I had not spent the night in my accustomed place, gave me one of her coy, meaningful looks at breakfast. And Meraud, after my brief, disturbing glimpse of her outside our chamber, did not appear again that morning, not even showing her face at dinner: pleading her grief for her husband's death. Nor did Kit eat with us, for he had been confined to his chamber as a punishment for his behaviour. I had tried to be reasonable with him, tried to explain that there were some things that could not be tolerated, and my reward had been another hysterical outburst followed by a prolonged fit of weeping, his head buried in my breast and his tears soaking my bodice. I did not think it wise to mention Francis, or Ashcott, for the moment: but as a gesture of good will, left him a reluctant Mab for company.

So the only child at dinner was Hugh, the infant wit with the deep, infectious chuckle and the echoes of Francis in his face: would our son, perhaps already conceived, look like this? Francis often had his eyes on him, even engaged him in a solemn, entertaining conversation about his half-brother's shaggy little pony upon whose back, despite its being as broad and flat as a table, Hugh seemed quite unable to stay, and I wondered whether this interest was not only for the child's own sake, but also because he might be a harbinger of Francis's future offspring.

Or perhaps he was also comparing Hugh's cheerful, friendly nature with the unhappy, hostile Kit.

After the meal, we repaired above stairs to the Long

Gallery, for during the morning the rain had begun again and it was drizzling miserably outside. The company was enlarged by Grainne and Henrietta, come to see how Malise did, and most pleasantly surprised to find him sitting up, eating heartily, and all but restored to his normal self, if not to his former robust and sturdy shape. It was hard to believe, looking at him now, that he had been in such a parlous state only the day before, but the good food, warmth and rest had worked a miracle. My blood ran cold, though, to think what might have been his lot had Francis not brought him away from the church at the Hythe, for even a day longer in that fetid unhealthy place might have been too much for him to withstand.

The Widow had allowed him to come and sit with us around the fire in the Gallery, and he bravely took the solid, bonny and bouncing Henrietta on his knees. Kit, allowed to join us, sprawled on the boards with Hugh and Mab playing some game with a ball and a rope ring. Mary and Meraud, black-clad, stitched at baby-clothes; Richard Trevelyan penned a letter on a little writing-desk balanced on his knees; and on my instructions Heppy and Dorothy brought up a selection of musical instruments for myself, Lucy, Grainne, Charles Lawrence and Francis. Music was Kit's key: it had unlocked him before, for me, and my hope now, as Francis took up the lute that he had not played for so long, and drew his long fingers caressingly across the strings in the first minor chords of Greensleeves, was that it would help my lover to gain Kit's liking and confidence. And indeed, as we played and sang softly, in deference to our mourning state, he left Hugh to play with Hen and crept closer to us; but his eyes were on my face, not Francis's, and it was by my stool that he sat. Charles, who was possessed of a pleasing tenor voice, and a deft touch on the guitar, proved a good complement to Francis's deeper voice and the high clear sounds of the three women: when we had played three or four such gentle, favourite songs, he turned to my lover. 'Have you still got that little flageolet you used to carry at Oxford?'

For answer, Francis picked it up from the floor beside him. 'It goes everywhere I go. What would you like me to play?'

'This,' said Charles, and his eyes went beyond our little group to Meraud, demure and sorrowful and virginal above the swelling mound of Jamie's child, due to be born at Christmas, the child she hoped would inherit Goldhayes.

If Francis had not returned.

I pushed that sudden, unwelcome thought from me, and my pity for Charles, still tied to Meraud after all this time, and obviously without much hope of success. He picked out a familiar tune, and at once we all joined in, the lutes of Lucy and Grainne, my own viol, and above us, soaring high and free in descant, the silver flageolet as we played Charles's unhappy, longing, unspoken dedication to Meraud – 'Light o' Love'.

By tacit agreement, we laid our instruments down when the last sweet high haunting notes had died away along the Gallery. Kit picked up one of the recorders and blew it softly and surprisingly tunefully: I had begun teaching him the fingering some months ago, but he had, of course, had no practice in it since June. Lucy rose, stretched her fingers, and strolled over to one of the window seats. 'It's stopped raining. Shall we go for a ride? There's blue sky over there.'

'I don't believe you,' said Francis affectionately. 'You've never been able to see clearly more than a foot beyond your nice little nose, it's probably pouring still.'

'It has stopped!' Lucy cried indignantly. 'I can *hear* it's stopped.' She paused, and then said in a completely different tone of voice, 'Is that *Jasper?* What on earth is he doing riding Boreas?'

Francis, Grainne and I were at her side almost before she had finished speaking, the Widow not far behind. From the direction of the Home Farm, galloping hell-

454

for-leather across the park towards the house, came the dapple-grey Arabian stallion that was John's pride and joy and hope for the future: and perched atop, fiery hair blown out behind him by the speed of his progress, crouched the small urgent figure of Grainne's son, riding bareback.

'Dear God, he'll kill himself,' said the Irish girl, alarmed. 'Why is he riding that horse, John would never let him . . .' Her voice ceased abruptly as realization came to her as to us, simultaneously. 'He must have seen something – Malise!'

Francis turned, swift and decisive as he always seemed to be in moments of crisis. 'Richard – I think we are about to have visitors. Can everyone be warned? I'll get Malise out of the way.' He nodded to me and Grainne, and we hurried over to help. There was a flurry of anxiety, into which Richard's voice cut, quiet and positive. 'It's best if we give the appearance of normality. I'll go tell the rest of the household. Lucy, you go down and see Jasper, make sure there are indeed soldiers coming – it might be a false alarm after all.'

'And I'll go and make sure that room doesn't look too much as though a sick man's been in it,' said the Widow, and bustled off.

It did not take long for the three of us to help Malise down those tortuous stairs to the cellars. There would be no hiding the general direction of his whereabouts, should anyone turn traitor; but at least the exact place would be a close-kept secret. I fought hard to keep myself calm in the ominous dark below the house, feeling the weight of what lay above me, brick and stone, tile and wood and plaster, pressing down upon me as never before. Grainne stood, her betrothed's arm about her, supporting some of his weight, as Francis unlocked the door of the hidden chamber by the light of the candle held in my trembling hand. 'Don't worry, owd gal, it'll be all right,' he whispered to me, with one of his most reassuring, buoyant grins to which it was impossible not to respond: and the pressure seemed to lift somewhat.

He stood aside with a mock flourish for Malise to enter his appointed chamber, and with Grainne's help he stumbled forward, only to trip on a slightly raised piece of stone and fall heavily against the door. With exclamations of dismay we picked him up, ascertained that no major damage had been done apart from a sore elbow, and led him within.

Even the philosophical Malise seemed a trifle taken aback by the place in which he was expected to hide. He stood, leaning on Francis on one side and Grainne on the other, staring round at the grim little chamber, and then with a wry expression on his face walked slowly, unaided, over to the pallet and sat down rather heavily. 'I hardly daur ask it, but do I get a candle?'

For answer, I lit the one we had left with the other supplies by his side, thanking God Francis had had the foresight to think of all this. 'That should last you several hours, and there's another, but I hope you won't need it. When the door's shut, no light shows.'

'We're going to have to lock you in,' Grainne added, crouching down by his side, 'but this is easily the safest place. Don't worry, we'll send them packing soon enough. Will you be all right?'

'I've been in tighter corners,' said Malise, 'but always in the open air before now . . . oh well, I dare say I shall manage. What about you, Francis? They'll be looking for you, too.'

'I can look to myself,' Francis said cheerfully. 'My appearance has changed rather dramatically in the last two days, and I think I can bluff my way through most things – also, I want to be on hand in case of any trouble. Come on, you two, I'm afraid there's no time to linger.'

Grainne snatched a last embrace with Malise and then, with a smile that disguised her fears, hurried from the stone room, leaving him alone with the candle, the dust and the ghosts. Francis shut the door, a very final, ominous sound, and locked it: then the three of us manhandled two of the larger hogsheads in front of it.

As the second of them thudded into place, we heard someone approaching. Francis swore softly, but the prosaic elderly voice put paid to our alarm. 'It's only me,' said the Widow. 'Come to tell you it *is* soldiers, Jasper says. Fortunately he was chatting to that horse when he saw them coming along from the village, so we had more time than we thought, but they'll be here any minute, I reckon. Cavalry it is, half a troop at least, according to young Jasper. All done here, eh? Well, you may think so but I don't – look around you.'

There was little enough light to see by, but we stared dutifully about us. 'Footprints,' said Mistress Gooch concisely. 'Good giveaway they are, all round those hogsheads. Sweep 'em away, spread that dust around a bit, make it look natural. Use your aprons, I would.'

We did as she recommended and obliterated all the signs that were visible in the inadequate light of our two or three candles, and then Grainne and I hid our now filthy aprons behind a pile of carven stones and followed Francis and the Widow up the two flights of stairs to the Long Gallery. There was a creditable attempt at the normality which Richard had sensibly advised, and indeed, to anyone not acquainted with us, it looked very convincing: but Lucy plucking a lute desultorily in the window-seat above the porch was patently on watch, Charles's playing with the four children and Mab just a little too frenetic, and Richard seemed to have lost the fluency of his letter-writing. As soon as he saw his mother, Jasper abandoned his game and came running over. 'The soldiers are coming! Have you hidden him? Was I in time?'

'Yes to both questions,' Grainne said, and hugged him. 'You did very well, and I'm proud of you. Where's Boreas?'

'In the stables, I took him round when I'd told Master Trevelyan about the soldiers.' He glanced at his mother's face and added, more subdued, 'I know I shouldn't really have ridden him like that, and I expect Grandfather will be angry if he finds out, but I did get here much quicker, didn't I, and I didn't even come near falling off!'

'Thank God,' said Grainne, smiling. 'Now, you know what you have to do. Try and pretend everything is just a normal afternoon. Unless something goes wrong, they won't ask you anything, there are too many adults they can question instead! So don't worry.'

'They're here!' said Lucy, sounding raw with nerves. 'Just coming round the bend in the drive.' She paused and then said in a small voice, 'There are quite a lot of them, I think. Cavalry.'

Mary and Meraud went on sewing, calmly, coolly – I supposed with dislike that this, after all, did not touch either of them as it did the rest of us. 'Come on,' I said to Grainne, 'let's go play some more music – it'll help keep us occupied while we're waiting. And we can resist the temptation to gawp at the windows.'

So as the soldiers of the New Model Army approached, silent and inexorable, Grainne and Lucy and Francis and I took up our instruments again and tried to soothe our jangling nerves with our music. My mind as busy as my fingers, I tried not to think of them, but the fears would not be stilled. Were they Whalley's men? Would Francis be recognized? Would Meraud, in her sly and subtle fashion, play the innocent traitor? Would one of the children or servants unwittingly reveal some of the truth? And I sang, superficially, blithely, happily, while all Grainne's and my future, and the lives of Malise and Francis, hung on a thread like a Damocletian sword.

There was the sound of horses in the yard below, distant beneath the music, and a hammering on the front door. Normality dictated that someone at least should glance from the windows, and casually Francis took the flageolet from his mouth and strolled over to look out. I followed him, my heart banging against my ribs and my hands numb and sticky with sweat. The front court seemed full of horses, disturbing the gravel, decorating the ground or nibbling the flowerbeds, and troopers, dismounted and awkward in their heavy riding-boots, were being formed up outside the door. 'Whalley's,' said Francis at once, very softly, and turned away from the window. 'Here we go, owd gal – I shall need all my wits for this one.'

'Can't you hide?' I demanded urgently. 'There's still time, surely – there *must* be places we can hide you – they're bound to recognize you.'

'Like this?' said Francis. He had borrowed a suit of Richard's today, and although it was a sober black, because of our bereavement, it was considerably more stylish than any of the old garments he had left from the days before the war. His pale curling hair looked startling against the sullenly-gleaming satin, and with the white lace and elegant shoes he was altogether the modish Cavalier – a different-looking creature entirely from the weary Army trooper, dour and ordinary, who had ridden up to the house less than two days before. Walnut juice, diluted and used with great care, had rendered the difference between the upper and lower parts of his face almost negligible; no trace was left of the beard that had transformed him. I realized suddenly that he might well be right. After all, they were looking for a sick Cavalier and a deserter from the Army, and nowhere within the house could anyone be found who corresponded in any way to those descriptions. And who would connect that Army deserter with Francis Heron, gentleman, lately returned from a sojourn abroad with his exiled eldest brother, and vouched for by any respectable local figures one cared to ask?

Francis looked over my shoulder to the head of the stairs, and something in the narrowing of his eyes warned me. I turned to see what he had seen, and beheld Richard climbing the last few steps, two Army officers by his side. One, from his buff coat a cavalryman, I had never seen before, but the other I recognized with a sickening lurch of my heart. The only man in all of the Roundhead Army who knew for certain that Corporal Jonathan Marshall of Whalley's Horse, and Master

Francis Heron of Goldhayes were one and the same: and thus held all our fates in the balance.

It was Major Daniel Ashley.

Chapter 11

The worm in the bud

All things move to their end.
   (Rabelais, *Pantagruel*)

I knew that this must be the finish of it all. Dan was like Simon, a man devoted to duty. Our kindness to him at Oxford, any feelings he might have shared with Lucy, were more than five years in the past: and here and now, he was a very important man within the Army, within reach of a colonel's rank, and doubtless on familiar terms with the great, the real rulers of the country, Fairfax and Cromwell. It was unthinkable that such a person, dedicated to the discipline of the Army and the cause it served, should turn a blind eye to the brazen presence, albeit in another guise, of an army deserter under his very nose. Most like that was why he had come in search of the two fugitives: he knew very well where they were, and could readily identify Francis. Army justice would be served, the escaping prisoner taken back to join his unfortunate fellow-captives, and the despicable deserter, who had betrayed his trust and his comrades, would pay the penalty for his crime.

In the New Model Army, as in any other, that penalty was death.

I gripped Francis's hand and received an answering pressure in return: then, in common with the others, we drew near the fireplace where Richard had led the officers. He was inviting them to warm themselves, and ordering Heppy to bring wine and refreshments, as if half a troop of cavalry rode up to Goldhayes every day of the week: and with a commendable appearance of innocent concern, he asked the two officers what he could do to help them.

Dan Ashley's reflective, honest gaze swept us all: it

passed straight over Francis and lingered for a short moment upon Lucy, who flushed a deep, betraying red but did not look away. He smiled briefly at her and returned to Richard. 'I have the honour of being known to some of these ladies and gentlemen here: the fortunes of war threw me upon their kindness some years ago in Oxford, when I was a prisoner of the Royalists. And in return for that kindness, I have come here with Captain Williams in order to spare them any unpleasantness that may accompany our task – especially since I see to my sorrow that this is a house of mourning.'

'Yes – I regret very much that we have recently lost my stepson, James Heron, a dear boy much beloved of us all, and only six months wed to my niece, Meraud,' said Richard sadly. 'You may have known him at Oxford too, when he was but a child. But I was unaware that my cousins were acquainted with you, Major Ashley,' he added, with a glance at Lucy that heightened her discomfort. 'However, that is as may be, and I am glad that your acquaintance is based upon kindness rather than the more usual enmity these days between those who differ in their politics. Now, sir, what is this task that might be unpleasant without your presence, and how may we assist you?'

Dan murmured his condolences for Jamie's death, and gave his answer. 'We have been asked to visit certain houses in this part of Suffolk to search for fugitives from Colchester, which as you may know surrendered two days ago. There are several important men we are seeking, amongst them Colonel Farr, who was to be executed along with Sir Charles Lucas and Sir George Lisle, but escaped before he could be apprehended for the sentence to be carried out. Although he is the one we are most urgent to find, for he it was who persuaded the Essex trained bands to the Royalists, there is also amongst them a man who I believe is known to you – one Malise Graham, a Scot, who apparently made his escape with the assistance of one of our own soldiers. It is that soldier we are especially anxious to make a due example of: his fellow-troopers are particularly enraged at his desertion, and wish him captured as soon as possible so that he may be punished as army discipline dictates.'

Why doesn't he come straight out with it, I wondered with angry despair, why does he keep us all dangling in limbo like this, waiting for the denunciation? He must have seen Francis by now, he knows he's here – why doesn't he say it? They killed Lucas, he's no great loss, but Sir George Lisle I liked, he did not deserve to die for what he believed to be right.

But the whole war, all the last six years of England's, and Scotland's, agony had been caused by people fighting for what they believed to be right. I wished desperately, with a strength that I had never felt before, that all the people who believed in rightness and causes and inflicting their opinions forcibly on everyone else, would go away to some deserted island and fight it out amongst themselves, and leave the rest of us in peace to live and love and laugh and make music as we pleased. Francis, like Lisle, had done what he believed to be right – and in saving Malise had put love and friendship above ideals of honour and duty. And, like Lisle, he would die for it.

'I very much regret,' Richard was saying courteously, 'that I do not know where Master Graham may be found, nor have I any knowledge of any soldier of yours who may have helped him. We have seen nothing of him since he and my stepson James rode away to join the Royalists at the beginning of June – and the only news we have received has been the sad tidings that Jamie was killed during the siege.'

'I remember Jamie from Oxford, and I am most sorry to hear of his death,' Dan repeated quietly. 'You have had much grief from this war. I pray God you will have no more.'

Heppy, with a look of awe on her face that anyone knowing her well would have ascribed instead to sheer terror, brought the wine and cakes, and Dan and his brother-officer were seated before the fire, the steam rising gently from their soaked garments, exchanging pleasantries with Richard, Mary and the rest of us. Captain Williams, a man evidently of humble origins, partook of very little and inspected his hosts and their luxurious establishment with a somewhat hostile eye. I saw him direct some especially sharp glances at Charles, and more particularly at Francis. Plainly he was puzzled, his memory nagged by something he did not understand, and I prayed he would not ask any penetrating questions or, worse still, recognize Francis, who evidently reminded him of someone, as the deserter. For then, surely, Dan, although inexplicably he had said nothing so far, would have to support him: he could hardly do otherwise. At Captain Williams's curt request, Richard gave him our names and various relationships: and at the words, 'My stepson, Francis Heron, who has recently returned from visiting my wife's oldest son Simon and his wife in Holland,' the Captain's nose lifted and his gaze sharpened. 'I have not, then, met you before, sir?' he enquired: and Francis said coolly, 'No, sir, I do not believe I have had that pleasure.'

'I have, though,' said Dan, turning his head and looking at Francis fully for the first time. 'It was on a most inauspicious occasion, as I recall, but I remember you most clearly, Master Heron – or Lieutenant Heron, as you were then. Master Heron surrendered a garrison to me in the first year of the war,' he added in explanation to Captain Williams, who gave Francis one last frowning glance and then said, 'Apparently you know him, Major. I had been puzzled by some resemblance . . . but I see upon looking further that I am mistaken.'

'Ah,' said Dan. He rose, looking round at us all, and added, 'I remember your enthusiastic description of Goldhayes most clearly, Mistress Lucy. May I say that the reality exceeds your pictures of it? I thank you, Mistress Trevelyan, for your excellent refreshments: and now, I fear, we must carry out a search of the house and outbuildings. Would you care to accompany me, Master Trevelyan? And of course any of you who wish, since Captain Williams's men will have of necessity to search even your private chambers and possessions. I regret all this, but it must be done, as I am sure you understand.'

So while some soldiers guarded each exit from the house, so that none could escape, the rest began their search through each of Goldhayes' four storeys, beginning with the attics where many of the servants slept, and questioning (without result) those they found there. I followed them with Francis, Lucy and Grainne, hardly daring to look at any of them, least of all my lover. Captain Williams had been half-way to recognizing him, that was obvious, but Dan had casually, skilfully deflected him: and Francis had been saved. It was beginning to look as if Dan was not after all here to identify the deserter: and yet if that were so, why was he here at all, when he must obviously have had to volunteer his services for such a search?

There was one answer which, if the right one, would mean that all might be well: perhaps Dan had offered to accompany Captain Williams because he knew that his word could save Francis, should he be found at Goldhayes. It was certainly possible that the friendly, honourable Dan we had known at Pennyfarthing Street would do thus; but to whom was his loyalty given now? To his one-time friends who had rescued him from prison? Or to the Army whose discipline he was duty-bound to uphold?

I was still desperately worried, and trying not to show it, as the search spread to the first floor and the soldiers rapped panelling, peered under beds and into clothes-presses and up chimneys: but I could not allow myself to relax. Perhaps Dan was after all on our side, but we could not be sure or certain of that until the last soldier was out of sight round the corner of the drive.

The Widow had done her work well: not a trace remained of Malise's brief occupation in the room at the top of the turret stairs. Everything was neat, bare, normal: Captain Williams gave it hardly a glance. We followed the soldiers and Richard back to the Long Gallery, where the rest of the Herons and associates were occupying themselves with the same tasks or pursuits as they had before the soldiers came, apparently quite unconcerned. Charles was performing sterling service with the four children: evidently with all those younger sisters, he was well-used to infant ways. Meraud had abandoned her sewing and had picked up one of the discarded lutes. She was picking out a simple little tune and, as I watched, Kit left Charles and the other children and quietly trotted over to sit in front of her and watch, owl-eyed and absorbed in the music, a different child entirely from the furious little demon of that morning. Jealousy struck me with appalling strength: I could make no comment, no scene, not now, but my hands clenched almost of their own accord behind my back. The impulse to do Meraud physical violence, for no reason that most people would understand, was becoming worryingly frequent.

My eyes fixed suddenly on something lying casually by Meraud's chair, something long and silvery that reflected firelight and daylight, and to which Kit's small hand strayed as I watched. Francis's little flageolet, which had been his constant companion for years: which he had certainly played to his comrades in the regiment. If Captain Williams's suspicious eye should alight upon *that*, his wonderings would become a certainty. I glanced around: he was walking towards us with Dan and Richard, engaged in conversation. I made a quick decision, not really thinking about it at all, there was no time, and strolled over to my son. 'Hello, Kit – don't you want to play any more?'

Meraud looked at me with those limpid cold, blue eyes, but said nothing. I wondered with a sudden chill if she had deliberately laid that flageolet there in full view, knowing its significance. I scooped Kit up with one hand and the little silver whistle with the other, as casually as I could, and walked down the Gallery towards Charles. 'Here you are, take Kit, he wants to play again.'

'Don't,' said Kit indignantly, 'I want to stay with you, Mammy!' But I handed him over to Charles despite his protests, and at the same time passed the flageolet. 'Can you hide this? Up your sleeve or something, just till the soldiers have gone downstairs and then put it somewhere safe.' I nearly said 'away from *her*', meaning Meraud, but stopped myself in time. Charles was not slow-witted: he grinned, palmed the flageolet deftly inside his doublet and bore the struggling Kit away. I drew breath again: and turned to follow the search party down the stairs to the Hall. So far, so good.

If Francis was perturbed by the fact that he had so nearly been recognized, he was not in any way showing it. He stood below the Van Dyck portrait of him and his brothers and sister: no doubt whatsoever of the likeness between that thoughtful, painted child and the thoughtful, real man beneath. By now, Williams was not even looking in his direction, and the other soldiers, who must have known his *alter ego*, did not take any notice of him at all, being entirely concerned, as before, with peering up chimneys, under tables, and behind tapestries, rapping the panelling or examining the floorboards. As we progressed solemnly from East Wing to West Wing, via kitchen, buttery, scullery and chapel, I began to have trouble suppressing my inconvenient sense of the absurd.

And yet, somewhere below us, Malise lay hidden, waiting for discovery, or the news that all was safe.

I reminded myself firmly of that as Dan enquired what else, apart from the stables, remained to be searched, and Richard told him that only the cellars were left. 'But there's no light, of course – I suppose lanterns must be brought?'

'I regret if that causes you any inconvenience,' said Dan courteously, 'but I am afraid we must go down there: I have to assure my superiors that every effort was made to seek out Colonel Farr and the other fugitives. So, if you do not mind?'

The soldiers, lanterns in hand, trooped gingerly down the notorious steps, peering into the gloom as if they expected any minute to meet toads, familiars, phantoms or even a few ordinary rats emerging. Afraid for quite other reasons, I picked up my skirts and followed them: Grainne, Lucy and Francis came behind me. At the foot of the steps we stood and watched as Whalley's men, by now fairly offhand, conducted their search by stronger, steadier lights than the few, guttering candles we had used not an hour before. In the glow cast by half-a-dozen lanterns, the cellars seemed very prosaic and unremarkable: no ghosts lurking behind the racked hogsheads or the piled stones, and no escaped Cavaliers either. They inspected first the part of the cellars where the hidden room lay, but it was a cursory business at best, and the nearest any of them came to that concealed doorway was when one young trooper, more bored or lazy than the rest, leaned against one of the great hogsheads we had dragged in front of the door, and was sharply ordered back to work by Captain Williams. The lanterns moved on, back round the stairs and away to explore under the eastern part of the house: and by my side, Francis began to whistle softly.

It was a cheery tune, one I knew well, the usual words those he had quoted to me last night before we slept, and smiling in the gloom I remembered them. 'So roll me in your arms, my love, and blow the candle out.'

'*And blow the candle out.*' The significance of that struck me at the same moment as Grainne reached her arm behind Lucy's back and touched my sleeve, urgently. I stared at the concealed door, and saw what she and Francis had seen. That clumsy fall of Malise's must have done damage to the wood of the door-post, for a faint but unmistakeable glow of light was creeping from behind the two hogsheads, through some gap around a part of the door-frame.

Francis whistled the tune again, louder, with the slightest emphasis on the final, telling line of the verse. The soldiers, by the sound of it, were returning, naturally empty-handed, but if one of them were to glance this way, and see the light that, once the lanterns were further away, appeared so terrifyingly, glaringly obvious . . . then it would be a different tale both for Malise and for Francis.

Lucy sensed that something was wrong, and her hand clutched my sleeve as well. 'Thomazine! What is it?'

'Sssh!' I hissed back, under cover of that deceptively cheery, message-laden tune, praying desperately that Malise would hear and understand: and as if in answer to my prayer, miraculously, the glimmering light abruptly disappeared.

We emerged sweaty and shaking from the cellar behind the soldiers, trying urgently to conceal the overwhelming relief of that moment: although Francis was still whistling, the tune had changed to the jaunty 'Packington's Pound'.

In the Hall were the soldiers who had been detailed to search the stables: since Hobgoblin had been removed the day before to one of the Home Farm's more distant pastures, well away from any road, and her military tack thoroughly hidden in John's barn, they had been unlikely to find anything, and so it proved. Captain Williams bowed to Richard, presented his compliments and apologies to all of us, and led his troopers outside. Dan lingered, his eyes again on Lucy. 'I regret this intrusion on your grief very much, and I confess I am glad that nothing was found. We must go on now to search Rushbrooke Hall, so I cannot stay, but I do not think it will be long before I return, and in a civilian guise, for I have resolved to leave the Army – officially,' he added, with a sudden smile at Francis, who for once in his life seemed at a loss for words. 'I told you, I think, of the execution of Lucas and Lisle? That was the final straw that broke the back of my devotion to Army duty. Oh, I'd been wavering already, for a long time, and the horrors of that siege only served to increase my doubts. I know that it was military expediency to return all those starving women and children to the town, when they stood between the walls and our lines and begged to be let through, and we would not, for then thousands would have followed and the Royalists would have been able to hold out for a much longer time, with far fewer mouths to feed . . . I know it had to be done, but I disliked that necessity so much that I decided that I did not want to uphold it any longer. Nor does this task appeal to me, when I know full well the fate in store for those I capture.'

'It seems we have much to thank you for,' Richard said, smiling, and the two men shook hands. 'I shall indeed look forward to your company in happier circumstances, Major Ashley.'

'And I also. Now I must say goodbye to you all. It has been most pleasant to see you again, and to view your incomparable house, if in rather more detail than would normally be the case: and I trust I will soon visit you again.'

'I owe you special thanks,' Francis said softly, coming forward. Dan shook his head. 'I could do no other – and since my action, or the lack of it, would not be approved of at all by my superiors, it's one more most excellent reason for leaving the Army: for I can no longer set my duty above decency and friendship, and am therefore unfit, in my eyes and others', for a soldier's life. God grant your secrets remain hidden – and goodbye!'

Hardly able to credit our wonderful good fortune, and still more Dan's unauthorized kindness, we stood at the Gallery windows and watched them go down the drive and out of our sight. As the last rump disappeared through the rain, Jasper raised one of his screeching cheers of triumph which sent Mary's hands flying to her ears and aroused his mother's ire. 'Jasper, my lad, that's not only impolite and thoughtless, but it's tempting fate as well. Perhaps Captain Williams will be back later, to check that no one's come out of hiding – I for one wouldn't put it past him, whether Dan is with him or not. No cheers, please no cheers, until we're certain all is safe.'

For the same reason we did not immediately let Malise free from his hiding-place, although Grainne slipped discreetly down to the cellars to tell him that, so far, everything had gone well. The light from his candle had seeped through a gap round the door, as I had suspected, damage presumably caused by his heavy fall against it; warned of this, he would now be alert to put it out at the first sound of returning soldiers.

But they did not return: and as dusk approached the rotund cheerful little figure of young Henry Jermyn trotted up the drive on his equally rotund and cheerful pony, to inform us in general, and Jasper in particular, that the search of Rushbrook had similarly revealed nothing, and that the soldiers were now gone on to Bury for the night. 'And I heard one of 'em saying that they'd only got tomorrow and the day after to search all the other Royalist houses round about, because the Colchester prisoners are being taken away on Friday or Saturday and they're needed to guard them.' His sharp brown eyes, keen and curious, flicked over all of us as we sat in the Long Gallery, still hardly able to believe our good fortune in escaping denouncement. 'So they didn't find anything here either? They were very annoyed, you know, Jasper, that Captain Williams kept on saying he couldn't believe there was nobody hidden at Goldhayes.'

I caught Francis's eye and grinned with renewed wonder at our luck. Henry went on quizzing Jasper in his nosy gossiping old-womanish way, but Grainne's son was, even at nine, a fair judge of character and deflected his questions with a deftness Francis himself might have envied. At last, after Jasper had proved uninformative on every point save that of Francis's presence ('I don't suppose you remember him, he's been in France or Holland or somewhere like that for ages, since the end of the war'), Henry had to take his leave, his curiosity unsatisfied, and the Herons and Trevelyans and Sewells trooped down to a happy, relieved supper, plain fare but, after Colchester, with all the savour of a king's banquet. And Grainne slipped out and reappeared a few minutes later with Malise on her arm: a pale, unsteady figure, eyes narrowed against the brightness of the Dining Hall candles, but free, and whole, and safe. 'Thank you, sir,' he said to Richard: and Meraud's uncle said quietly, 'It is not I you must thank, but your friends who cared for you and hid you so well: and Major Ashley, who knew Francis of old, and would not give him away.'

'Nor did you,' Malise said, and grinned. 'The only thing that bade fair to betray me was a wee crack round the door, letting my candlelight through – and a song stopped that.' He looked across at Francis, who finished his wine with a flourish and in explanation whistled a few bars of 'Blow your Candle Out'. 'So,' said the Widow, wiping her fingers on a napkin, 'when's this wedding to be, that we've all been waiting so long for?'

'And is it going to be a double wedding?' Lucy asked me, nudgingly. I gestured at her brother. 'For that, you'd best ask him.'

'A wedding?' said Francis, and his thin ironic face was suddenly transformed with a huge and joyous delight. 'And why would I be thinking of a wedding just now, sister mine?'

'You can't,' said Meraud's still, unexpressive, sibilant voice, cutting through the happiness like a knife. 'You forget Jamie. Jamie is dead. There can be no weddings yet.'

'It would certainly not be seemly,' Richard added, as Malise sat down next to Grainne and accepted a cup of wine. 'I think it would be best to wait some months before we can celebrate anything in this house. Not until after Christmas, at the least. Besides, it might not be safe for you, Master Graham, to make yourself so conspicuous so soon. Best to lie low for a while, and regain your strength.'

'We don't have to celebrate it here,' I said, an idea suddenly taking hold of my mind with force. 'We can go to Ashcott, all four of us, and be wed there, and live there for a while.'

'And who says we are to be married?' Francis enquired, his eyes gleaming, teasing. 'A hedgehog like you, my dear lady Thomazine, all hair and prickles . . . I'd need to wear a suit of armour!'

'*Two* weddings?' said Meraud, as if realizing it for the first time. 'You, and Thomazine, wed at last? I never thought it would happen.'

'Well, I can't think of any better way of keeping her in check than marrying her,' Francis said, grinning at me. 'Oh, by the way, mother, may I have your permission to marry Thomazine?'

Mary looked at him vaguely. 'My permission? Of course, if you need it. But I thought there were to be no weddings yet.'

'At Ashcott,' Lucy told her impatiently. 'They're going to Ashcott to be married.'

'Did you hear that, Kit?' said Meraud, turning to my son, who sat at the end of the table with the three other children, wan, tired and uncomprehending of this sudden adult fuss and flurry. 'Your mammy's going to be married.'

It was not the way I would have chosen to break the news to him. He frowned and then said fiercely, 'No, she isn't!'

'Yes, she is,' said Lucy cheerfully. 'She's going to marry my brother Francis, your cousin. You're going to have a stepfather, isn't that nice?'

Kit's lip wobbled and his blue eyes abruptly spilled over with angry tears. 'No! No, it isn't!' He jumped off his stool and ran round the table to where I sat, his face urgent and pleading. 'You're not going to get married, Mammy, are you? You're not, are you?'

'I am,' I told him. At the simple words his small face crumpled with fury. 'No! No! I don't want you to!'

'But *I* want to,' I told him, 'we'll go to Ashcott and spend Christmas there and you and Francis can be friends—'

'No, no, no, NO!' Kit screamed, his face contorted, his feet stamping in rage. 'No, you're *not* going to get married, I don't want you to, I won't let you, no, Mammy, NO!'

I kept a desperate hold on my temper, aware of all the people around the table watching the spectacle my child was making of himself, and me. 'Kit. I'm sorry if you don't like the idea, but I *am* going to marry Francis: I love him very much, we've wanted to be married for a long, long time, and now at last we have the chance, and we must take it. You'll understand, when you're older, and I know you'll like to have Francis for your father—'

'No, he's not my father,' said Kit, quieter now, but between clenched teeth. 'No, not him. I hate him, I hate him, you love him and you never loved my father, you went away and left him!'

I suddenly could not bear the prospect of all my anguished past being displayed again via the doubly distorted view of my child and through him, Dominic – who, though he had been dead for nearly a year, still had the power to reach out from the grave and influence our son, and me. 'Now that's quite enough. You'll understand when you're older, the truth of all this. I think you'd best go to bed now, with Hugh – say your grace and go upstairs.'

It was not so simple as that to dismiss him, of course: and several frantic and highly embarrassing moments later, he was finally escorted forcibly from the Dining Hall by Rose, a puzzled Hugh yawning attendance. As his screams died away into the distance, I said unhappily, 'I am very sorry about that. I shall make sure he doesn't share our meals again until he's learned to behave himself.'

'He is your child, and you have assumed the responsibility of caring for him,' said Richard, still, after that ringing scene, his usual imperturbable self. 'But I must say, Thomazine, that behaviour such as that should not be tolerated. Were he mine, I'd be extremely firm.'

'If he was like Hugh, you wouldn't need to be – your son's a credit to you,' I said despairingly. 'Mine seems to bring naught but endless trouble, battles, tantrums. I pray God he gets over this.'

'He will, if we take him to Ashcott,' said Francis. 'And I'm certainly not going to let a five-year-old come between me and my heart's desire. Now, may I propose a toast to her?'

In an echo of that long-ago supper at the house in Pennyfarthing Street, my health was drunk, and that of Grainne and Malise also, more wine was called for, and the meal ended in laughter and relaxation and delight. No Simon this time, black-cloaked and menacing, to burst in upon our merriment: and we made our way upstairs for a quiet evening's music which somehow, despite our mourning, became somewhat louder and more jolly than we had intended. And if I had time to notice it, there was one person who did not join in the fun: not Mary, who played her lute with her usual virtuoso skill, nor Richard, joining his light tuneful voice to the part-songs and madrigals. It was Meraud who sat like a spider, black-clad and gross with her unborn child, and yet so beautiful, and watched coldly, with hostility, our overflowing delight at a betrothal that would eventually disinherit her son and Jamie's, and put paid finally to her long-cherished plans to gain control of Goldhayes. All her dreams, destroyed by my love for Francis, and his for me: and so no wonder I saw in her untrustworthy, lovely, deceitful face, as she watched us laughing and singing in our joy, that which chilled my blood within me, and seemed meant to turn us both to stone.

But our love was true, and strong, and nothing now, I knew, could defeat us.

I shared that night again with Francis, creeping to his bed when all were asleep, like a thief, stealing myself from Kit: and once more remade our love, sharing our minds and bodies in glorious, passionate union, like a pair of lutes becoming more in tune with each other every time they were played: and the song we made together had no match, no equal anywhere, and was perfect in tune and harmony and delight. And afterwards, very softly, wrapped together drowsily in the softness of the feather-filled bed, we talked: Francis telling me something of his experiences over the last three years, and of how he had come in the first place to be in Whalley's Horse, despite his desire to follow me to Suffolk. Mixed up in a skirmish near Banbury, on his way home to Goldhayes from Oxford, he had had the misfortune to be taken by them, and had been offered the choice of being held captive in London, with little hope of immediate ransom, as had happened to Tom Sewell, and a ruinous fine at the end of it: or the comparative freedom of service in the regiment. 'They would always welcome an experienced soldier with a good horse, you see,' he told me, his voice thoughtfully stirring my hair. 'And despite everything, despite what I had said to you about wanting peace, and you, there was something in those men that called to me so strong, and that was their desire for political freedom. The sergeant who gave me the choice was a Leveller, the whole regiment is, pretty well, and I saw my chance to make my mark on the world, and took it. And whatever happened after, I can't regret it: despite all the strain of pretending to be someone else, of keeping up the fiction of my supposed Essex yeoman forebears, hiding the fact that I was by no means so ardent a believer in Jehovah and the rule of the Saints as were they. It's not often you have the opportunity of remaking a kingdom there, in your hands, and the power given you to do it – and an exhilarating, heady experience it is. Even now, when the Leveller dream is all but ended – the Royalists put paid to that, Cromwell had to crush us before he could fight the rebels and the Scots – even now, a part of me wishes I could work for everyone's freedom, not just the freedom of a handful of privileged men to run the country as they choose, but the right of *all* the people to decide how they live and work and what their future is to be. And whatever I do in my own future, I shall always remember that, and remember the men I fought with, who were plain and honest and believed so passionately in liberty and justice: and I betrayed their ideas in the end, for my love for you and for Malise proved the stronger. As did Dan's, for Lucy.'

'You didn't betray them,' I said indignantly. Francis kissed my abundant, tangled hair. 'I did, you know. According to their lights, I am a deserter, a traitor – and I regret that more than anything, for they were my friends too, and I respected them and their opinions. But . . . old loyalties, old loves, and you, my dearest owd gal, won in the end. How do you think I could have lived with myself, knowing I had killed my own brother, and then allowed Malise to be marched off captive to almost certain death? I knew what I must do, and the consequences if it miscarried: and so I rescued Malise.'

'I'm glad you did . . . so glad . . . you don't know how it has been, wanting you so much all this time, and not knowing how you were, or why you hadn't followed me. All I knew was from Dan's two letters, and they were cryptic to say the least. I missed you so much,' I said, burying my head into his shoulder. 'Please, please, don't go away again . . . or at the least, do me the courtesy of telling me what's happening if you do!'

'You have the most delightful way of making me squirm with guilt,' Francis remarked drily. 'I did write you a letter, but it must have gone astray, and then events took over. There are, believe it or not, long stretches of Army life when you're altogether too busy by far ever to put pen to paper, and besides I risked discovery . . . I don't know what my fate would have been had my true past been revealed, but it would certainly have been considerably less pleasant than life in Whalley's Horse.' His arm tightened around me. 'Those three lost years are my doing, my fault, and I cannot ever make up to you for the lack of them – but let's try to forget them now, and think of that lovely rosy future that beckons us so enticingly. I have had my tilt at war, and political windmills, and my fill of both of them, and I want nothing more now than to live with you, and make love and music and laughter and riddles . . . and children. Which reminds me . . .'

A while later, our limbs differently mingled, we lay once more in a drowsy sated peace, utterly weary and content. ' "The right true end of love," ' Francis quoted softly. 'How right was Dr Donne, how well he knew all the joys that man and woman can make together . . . and that there is nothing wrong in doing thus. Have you forgiven me, lady, for all I have done, and not done?'

'There is nothing to forgive – for it all comes from you, yourself, and if you were not to your own self true, I would not love you, and so I take the rough with the smooth, the worse with the better, and love you the more, for you and your heart and soul will never change – they are the rocks beneath the sea.'

'And you have poetry in you too, my dear lady: we shall deal well together, something tells me.' He paused and said, on a different note, 'That morning when I brought Malise – why were you out in the park? You must have scarce ridden in from Colchester, you should have been exhausted.'

'We reached here about ten or eleven o'clock the night before, I think . . . but it was strange, you were quite right, I was exhausted but I woke up before dawn, all restless, as if someone was calling me.'

'Perhaps I was,' Francis said softly. 'Our minds are in tune, have you noticed, often we think the same things at the same time, we know how it goes with each other when we're apart . . . I wanted you, and you came: although I did not specifically summon you, no sorcery, you sensed my need, and responded.'

A little frightened, and yet pleased that he also felt

this tenuous link existed, and was not a figment of my vivid imagination, I told him about the nightmares I had had long ago in Oxford, when I thought I had shared his death: and why, therefore, I had never questioned it, though his body had not been found. 'So we'd best be very careful – they've recently been most hot against witches and warlocks, hereabouts. "If thou be'st born to strange sights, Things invisible to see . . . " '

' "Ride ten thousand days and nights, Till age snow white hairs on thee . . . And swear, Nowhere, Lives a woman true, and fair." And yet Dr Donne was wrong in that,' said my Francis, with love and laughter in his voice, 'for there does, and she has bewitched me, and she lies here in my arms, now and for all time.'

The sun shone warmly down, the drenched grass shiny and wet and steaming faintly. I walked dreamily in the walled garden, all in the morning early, my head full of love and songs and poetry, twining late flowers in my hands, at peace with myself and all the world. Easy to forget, this lovely morning, the events of the last few months, to forget the secretive scurry back to my proper chamber, an hour or so previously, so that Kit would not again discover me in bed with Francis: to forget Meraud.

Yet there she was, suddenly, in front of me, stepping out from the honeysuckle arbour I had once shared with Francis, the night seven years before when the threat of war had first intruded upon our peaceful lives. At the sight of her, my happy mood drained away abruptly, leaving only a sick, nameless foreboding. And I could not interpret the expression on her beautiful, kittenish face, so incongruously innocent and childish above the swelling mound of the baby she carried. She had never looked at me before in such a manner: and it was a moment before I deciphered it, with terror, as open, naked enmity and hate.

I was defenceless, alone, everyone else within doors or out on business, and I did not know where Francis was. I took a deep breath, determined not to panic, and said, trying to pretend all was normal, 'Hullo. Isn't it a lovely morning?'

'No,' said Meraud. 'No, it is not.' She was trembling, not, I realized, with fear but with anger, a rage so deep and passionate that her whole body shook with it. 'I want to talk to you,' she went on, her voice hissing hardly above a whisper. 'Here, where we cannot be overheard.'

'Why?' I did not move, and when she grasped my arm, tried to shake it off. 'Why? What do you want?'

The small, fine, perfect fingers dug so deep into my flesh that I gasped with the pain. 'What do I want?' said Meraud, my enemy, in her true and terrible colours at last. 'I want what's mine by right, mine and my child's. And you and that murderer aren't going to cheat me out of it now.'

'Murderer?' I could not keep the horror out of my voice. 'Wh-what do you mean, murderer?'

'I mean Francis. He killed Jamie, didn't he? Oh, yes, I overheard something, the morning he came here, I heard him telling you how . . . how it happened. He *knew* who Jamie was and still he murdered him, killed him in cold blood – and I loved him!'

'Oh, no, you didn't,' I countered, my rage and terror taking control. 'No, you didn't, you've never loved anyone but yourself. You can't tell me you loved Jamie, all you loved of him was his possessions. He gave you Goldhayes, isn't that what you were after?'

'How wrong you have me!' Meraud's voice sunk still lower. 'And you always have, you've always treated me with spite and dislike . . . Oh, I loved Jamie, and now he's gone, slaughtered in cold blood, cut down in his prime, I'm not going to stand idly by and watch an adulterous whore like you, and your fratricide turncoat lover, take Goldhayes away from me and my son – I am *not*, do you hear me?'

'But you can't do anything – as long as Simon is in exile, Francis is the next heir, the one who'll be in charge: and if Nan stays barren, our children will inherit Goldhayes in the end – you can't change that.'

'Oh yes, I can,' said Meraud, and the triumph in her face was terrifying. 'Oh yes, I can, Mistress Thomazine Heron, and I will. You are not going to have any children, you and Francis, and you are not going to marry – because if he does not leave Goldhayes this morning, I will send to Bury and denounce him to Captain Williams – *and Major Ashley and Malise Graham as well!*'

And then I knew defeat. Short of killing her now, there was nothing I could do, nothing I could say, no one I could turn to for help. And she knew it, and laughed, and it took every scrap of will-power and control I possessed, to prevent me from strangling the breath from that pale, slender, lovely neck. I cried in rage and anguish, 'No, no, you couldn't do that – you're bluffing!'

'Couldn't I?' said Meraud, coldly. 'I can, and I will if necessary. I don't care about you or your precious Francis, or anyone else – I care for *this*, my child, my child and Jamie's. All my land in Cornwall is ruined by the war, there'll be nothing for my son and me save Goldhayes, and Goldhayes I will have.'

'But Richard . . . your uncle . . . he'll stop you, he wouldn't . . . he wouldn't betray his own stepson . . .'

'He wants Goldhayes too – why else do you think he married that stupid woman? He just has certain scruples. I do not. He may not have betrayed them yesterday, but he did not know yesterday about the facts of Jamie's death: and if you go to him I will make sure he, and everyone else, knows just how Jamie was killed . . . and meanwhile I will have sent for the soldiers. Do you want Francis shot as a deserter? Do you want Malise taken away into slavery in the West Indies? He wouldn't last the voyage in his state of health . . . if you persuade Francis to go away, Malise will be safe, they will both be safe, though God knows Francis deserves a hanging . . . if you do not, they both die, and Major Ashley is disgraced.'

'I'll go with him!' I cried, weeping now in my fury and anguish. Meraud smiled. 'And leave Kit behind? I think not. I have done my work well there. You have lost, Thomazine Heron, you have lost, and you richly deserve it, and more . . . I give him an hour, before I send the messenger, and you needn't think I will not find anyone to do it, for I have a man waiting in the stable-yard ready. Nor will you tell any others of this, for then I shall have some things to say, concerning murder . . .' She swept me a mocking, triumphant curtsey. 'And thus, for everything, I am revenged. Good day to you, Lady Drakelon, on this lovely morning.'

And she let go my arm and strolled past me, up the garden towards the house, the so-beautiful jewel-like house that had proved such an irresistible lure . . . and left me standing desolate, incredulous, despairing, in the ruins of the future that only a few moments before had seemed so sure and glorious: destroyed by one woman's hatred and greed and spite.

I wanted to think, act, move, find help, but I could not – caught in the grip of nightmare, my hopes slain when I had least expected. And then down the garden, brisk and bustling, came the Widow, ever my rescuer: when she saw me she broke into a stiff jolting run and arrived a little breathless beside me. 'For God's sake, lass, what's wrong? What's that little bitch said to you now? I saw her come away and there was a look of glee on her face to freeze your bones – Thomazine, my dear lass, what's she said?'

And I told her.

At the end of my sobbing, almost incoherent account, Mistress Gooch swore long and fluently, consigning Meraud Trevelyan to the deepest fieriest torments of Hell: and then said, 'I knew she was a hard, selfish little bitch, but not capable of *that*.'

'What do we do? What *can* we do? She'll do exactly as she says she will if he doesn't go – you didn't see her face as she said it, she meant every word, it was horrible . . . and I can't bear to be separated from him, not now, not now when I thought, we both thought, that we'd never be parted again . . .'

'Well, go with him, then.'

'But what about Kit?' I cried. 'I can't leave him behind, I can't take him with me – she's made sure he hates Francis – given a week or two I might have begun to win him over but if I whisk him away with me and Francis now – can you imagine it? And if I go with Francis, she'll still inform the soldiers and we'll be pursued, and Malise will be taken, and Dan disgraced . . . Oh, she's sewn it up so tight,' I said bitterly. 'There's nothing any of us can do, and she knows it – every avenue blocked save the one she wants us to take. And so she's won – and if I were a less civilized person I'd have slain her with my bare hands at the look on her face.'

'It does look as if Francis must leave,' said Mistress Gooch thoughtfully. 'You stay here, I'll go find him – last I saw of him, Hugh was showing him and Charles his pony, so he can't have gone far. We'll think of something, something to make it better.' And she sat me down in the arbour and, still with that stiff stork-like run, hastened up the path towards the house, leaving me with my despairing, frantic thoughts. No way out at all, save for Francis to leave me, leave me with my memories once more, and two nights in which the sun and moon had danced at our command, and for the first time in my life I had known perfect peace, perfect fulfilment, perfect union, perfect joy. Terrible anguish flooded my face with tears: all that happiness, gone, lost, destroyed: my life ruined.

'I'm not dead, am I?' said Francis's dark, humorous voice. He slipped into the arbour beside me and hugged me close while I wept on to his shoulder. 'So there's not much need for that . . . Owd gal, we will find a way, don't worry, even if I have to murder Meraud to do it . . . come on, dry those tears and let's *think*.'

I wiped my face on my sleeve, childishly, having no kerchief about me, and told him what Meraud had said.

Francis's urgent, intelligent eyes stared into mine; beside us, the Widow stood, her own shrewd, wise brain also hard at work. 'If it's all as she says, for the child's sake, then there's one thing as will cook her goose for her for good and all – she seems mighty certain she'll bear a son, but what if it's a girl? All gone for nothing.'

'Yes, the house is entailed in the male line: all a daughter will get is Meraud's lands and Jamie's one or two manors in Suffolk,' said Francis. 'But we won't know for another – two – months, is it? And meanwhile I must go. I must, owd gal, there's no help for it – we can't risk Malise, nor Dan, nor having such a burden of fines for malignancy descend on Goldhayes as will cripple it for ever . . . and it is after all Simon's really, and one day, if the King enjoys his own again, Simon will return. We are only the trustees, the guardians – which is perhaps something dear Meraud has forgotten. One day, if not now, she'll get her just deserts, and I mean to be there to enjoy her discomfiture when she does. Now, I must go . . . and I'll need money, for Whalley's hadn't been paid for months: food and spare clothing, all must be packed, so there's not much time for talking.'

'But where will you go?' I cried, unable still to accept this, to believe the disaster that had befallen us, who had been so assured of our happiness just a short time before. And Francis said, 'With your permission, lady, to Ashcott. Meraud's arm will not stretch there, it's my belief she'll be content to have me gone from you: and she was ever one to use the means at hand to gain her ends, rather than exert herself so far, she's an opportunist through and through . . . No, I'm safe at Ashcott, people there will remember me, and I'll set it to rights for you. And one day, oh my dearest love, you will ride down that long avenue of elms from the Deddington Road, and see it all golden and sunlit framed at the end of the trees, and ringed about with grass and water, and I will come out to greet you, and a happy ending will be ours at last. But for now, owd gal, I must go, to give a happy ending to Grainne and Malise, and perhaps

Dan and Lucy too. We have less than an hour to my leaving, so let's go pack, and if possible, do it without arousing anyone's curiosity, Lucy's in particular.'

That, in fact, was not so difficult as it sounded, for many of the people who might notice his departure had left the house for various purposes: Richard to the village, Mary to Rushbrooke, Charles with Kit and Hugh and the pony. But Lucy, whose appearance I most dreaded (I could imagine only too clearly her curiosity, her questions, her pestering) was in bed with a violent headache, asleep, a misfortune for which I gave heartfelt thanks.

It did not seem possible that Francis could be so calmly, almost cheerfully, packing to leave me once more, with the threat of denunciation and death hovering over him: after all we had endured, and particularly the happiness so briefly tasted, it was almost too much to bear. And yet as I sat on the bed where, last night and the night before, we had had the world and the heavens at our beck and call, and made our music of the spheres in silent harmony, my grief and despair began slowly to dissolve, and I started instead to absorb his own quiet certainty that in some other time, some other place, we would again be joined in love and hope and peace. Not now, but in the future: for even the chains of fate could not fail to recognize and bow to the essential rightness, the truth and beauty of the love we shared.

And so I was able to smile at him, through my tears, and say to him, 'It will not be for ever, you are right . . . we are meant to be together, in the end: despite Meraud, despite her evil, we will win.'

'Brave lady,' said Francis. 'Keep your smiles and your music and your laughter, and win Kit back to you: and remember always, I shall wait for you for ever, love you for ever, need you and want you for ever. Hold to that and we shall never be defeated, for we have what few people on this earth are ever allowed to possess: we hold Venus's flowers in our hands, and we will never let them die.' He smiled at me. 'And then, "Since there's no help, come let us kiss and part." I have said that to you before, I think, but this time I do not ride away to battle: this time our love has been satisfied, though not I think for very long. This time, though it seems so final, I feel, I can see, somehow I *know* this parting will not be for ever. We have the past, and the future too: only endure the present and all will be well. Trust me: "Earth, heaven, fire, air, the world transform'd shall view, Ere I prove false to faith or strange to you." '

'And I also,' I whispered, moved almost beyond speech by the strength of joy and hope which his words stirred within me. 'And God – God grant you go safely, and live in peace, and do not miss me too much, and I will work here for our reunion.'

'It is time,' said the Widow abruptly, with a curt nod of her head to the door: and Meraud stood there, the angel of revenge, meek and demure and terrible in her power, and smiled with a wilderness of malice. 'Yes, it is time: in ten minutes my messenger will go, if you do not go first. You have said enough farewells, and if I were you I would not hope to meet again – my son will see to that.'

I could not kill her, as I wished: instead, I walked past her, drawing my skirts aside as if to avoid contamination, and took Francis's hand, and we went together down the Gallery, sunlit and empty and beautiful, and the carved oaken staircase, and so to the Hall and the porch and the Front Court where Goblin stood waiting, saddled and ready: each step like the beat of a clock, counting away the last minutes that we would have together. We embraced for the last time, our lips and hands entwined, reluctant to let go: until Francis gently set me from him and smiled into my eyes, and said, 'Hope, owd gal, always hope – your candle in the dark – let it shine bright or we are lost – and we do not deserve to be defeated, least of all by such as *her*. Look to yourself, and to Kit, and Grainne and Malise – keep our secret, for their sake, and keep yourself safe.

Remember the Unicorns, and remember also, the chains of fate will not bind us for ever, and the chains of love are stronger. Oh my love, goodbye, and never fear: she will not defeat us, we'll win in the end, hold to that, and never forget it!'

And our handgrasp was broken and I watched through my sudden desperate tears as he mounted Hobgoblin, and gathered the reins between his fingers. ' "And on some summer's night, open thy window wide," ' he said, and smiled as brilliantly as if he were going out for a day's hunting and not into the unknown, far away beyond my knowledge and out of my sight. And then he wheeled the black mare round and sent her galloping down the drive, raising a great halo of sunlit dust around him.

And the hope that had buoyed me up so briefly, his own parting gift, ebbed away as his retreating figure diminished into the distance, and tears blinded me: though not enough for me to miss the wild, flamboyant way he reined in the mare two hundred yards away, and turning made her rear up in salute. Then with that last flourish they were gone, perhaps for ever.

And yet I knew somehow that I would one day have more of him than memories, and the poem that was a measure of his love:

Look for me not in wintertime to come
Homeward to thee:
Nor listen with wild eyes for tuck of drum,
That will not be:
But on some summer's night,
Open thy window wide,
To guide my homing flight
Unto thy side.

Chapter 12

The trumpets of Heaven

Now I will believe that there are Unicorns.
(Shakespeare, *The Tempest*)

Oh, it was a bitter pill indeed to swallow, to return to the house and try, after the last tumultuous three months, to take up a normal, ordinary, everyday life: to go back to that dormant, unawakened Thomazine that had existed, almost happily, here at Goldhayes before Colchester and the ecstasy and tragedy and disaster that had followed on from that terrible siege, a loyal sacrifice to match mine and Francis's, and had touched us so nearly. Hard, indeed, to live again without Francis, knowing now what all his love could bring, and the sweet anguished memories of those two nights – the only two nights in all the seven years of our loving – that we had shared. And hardest of all to remain silent, to keep my own counsel, beneath the bombardment of questions, particularly, of course, from Lucy, who could not understand why her brother – her last brother, as she tearfully informed me, forgetting Simon's exiled, invisible existence – had, after all his talk of marriage, and permanency, then left us all so precipitately. My vague excuses and explanations did not satisfy her in the least: and it was the final turn of the knife in the wound of Meraud's vengeance to hear her subtle, scattered hints that Francis, having achieved his desire and gained my body in his bed, had now abandoned me in search of fresh conquests. Only the brusque, sensible support of Mistress Gooch, ever by look or whisper reminding me of my duty, saved me from crying aloud Meraud's perfidy for all at Goldhayes to hear: and thereby also proclaiming that Francis had killed his own brother.

In those first months I could not have kept my sanity

without the Widow's presence. She alone knew the whole truth and was sympathetic, and I leaned on her gratefully. For never, ever, unless by some miracle Meraud's threats were lifted from us, would I tell Grainne of the bargain we had made for her happiness and Malise's life and freedom. I would place that burden, that beholding, upon no one, not even my dearest friend: nothing, I swore, would now interrupt her own plans for wedded delight.

For, despite our mourning for Jamie, despite Meraud's previous objections to any celebration at this time, their marriage had been fixed for the last week in October, and the Widow and Charles (who had received a succession of increasingly pained letters from his family enquiring why he was so long away from them), would at last, four months late, enjoy the festivities for which they had come to Goldhayes in June. And although the guest-list was small, and the wedding-party accommodated in the cramped and humble surroundings of the Home Farm (Joan having unfortunately refused to entertain Richard's generous offer of the far more suitable facilities at Goldhayes), yet it was a merry, joyous, riotous occasion, with singing, dancing and feasting: Joan's cooking, plain country fare though it was, being one excellent reason to have the celebrations there. And I had some consolation for my sacrifice and Francis's, when I saw the happiness that blazed from both their faces, and knew that at last they had achieved an end to grief and longing.

After the wedding, Charles went home to Warwickshire, but Mistress Gooch, to my intense relief, stayed on: having shrewdly proved herself useful brewing simples, looking after the sick in the household, and generally freeing Mary from those mundane duties she found so tedious, and which Mistress Bryant had been used to do before her death. 'Don't worry, I'll go back to Oxford eventually,' said the Widow to me as we waved goodbye to Charles, a curiously forlorn figure retreating down the drive, his long adoration of Meraud still unsatisfied, unacknowledged, unfulfilled – she had not even bothered to come out and wish him Godspeed. But although I felt sympathy with Charles for his unrequited love, I was also profoundly glad that Meraud was not interested in him – for I would not have wished her as a wife on Lucifer himself.

November brought bad weather, storms and rain and wind, and also at last a secret, cryptic note from Francis, in that unique and typically flamboyant hand, telling me that he was well, and safe at Ashcott, and much more besides: a love-letter that moved me to tears. For now I had news for him, the best of all consolations for his absence, if anything could ever make up for our separation – in November, I became certain that I would bear his child.

I was not ashamed of it, and yet I could not for the moment endure the thought of pronouncing to all and sundry that I was expecting his bastard. I could imagine Meraud's smug face, her plans and deceptions amply justified, for an illegitimate son of Francis's could never inherit Goldhayes, whereas she and Jamie had, of course, been safely wed. And daily she grew grosser, and more satisfied, sitting in her chair in the Long Gallery like a spider at the centre of her sticky web of threats and blackmail and deception; triumphant and assured of her victory.

So my own baby, conceived in such joy and hope and love, was nourished, deep in its dark womb, by my hatred for the girl who had cheated us of that love: and as I had once prayed for Dominic's death, so now I prayed desperately, guiltily, for hers.

In all of Goldhayes, the only person I told of my pregnancy was Mistress Gooch: and she, of course, was delighted and instantly full of plans. 'I'll wait here until *her* baby's born, and then I'll take news of that and your child to Francis at Ashcott, and any letters and messages you want. It'll bring you a little closer together, perhaps. And if you want me to be with you afterwards, I'll come back gladly, lass. Pennyfarthing Street can look to itself for a bit, and anyway I've no chickens to worry about – gave 'em all to a friend of mine before I left in May.'

The day after Christmas, Meraud's pains began: and I was glad, viciously delighted, to see her suffer, and was no longer ashamed of my desire for her death. Indeed, so long and difficult was her labour that death seemed the very likely outcome of it. But Meraud, so tiny and delicate and fragile and childlike, was actually as tough as any man, in body as well as in mind. All day and for most of the night she fought bravely for her baby's birth, awakening even my grudging admiration for her courage: and at last, as dawn broke on the twenty-seventh day of December, in the Year of Our Lord 1648, the infant was born at last, and delivered into Mistress Gooch's capable hands.

'My son . . .' Meraud's voice could hardly be heard. She lifted her sweat-soaked head feebly from the pillows to see the baby as the Widow severed the cord and slapped it into sudden, screeching life. And the look on the old woman's face was one of contemptuous, spiteful triumph. 'Your son, Mistress Meraud? I am very much afraid,' said the Widow with boundless satisfaction, 'that your child is a girl.'

Meraud's expression changed extraordinarily: even in this extremis the rage and disbelief in her face was terrifying. 'A *girl*?' she gasped, struggling to raise herself. 'A *girl*? No, no, it can't be . . . I don't believe you . . . *show me!*'

Mistress Gooch thrust the slippery, bloodstained, wriggling baby almost under her nose. 'A girl it is, my lady . . . not worth all that trouble, eh?'

Meraud fell back gasping on the pillows, her face grey and sunken, all the ethereal beauty utterly vanished. 'Take it away . . . I don't want it . . . I don't want to see it ever, do what you like with it, I don't *want* it!'

Grainne, who did not, of course, know the full significance of the baby's sex, looked appalled. 'What do you mean, you don't want it? She's a lovely child, your own, yours and Jamie's, all you have left of him . . . put her to your breast and you'll feel differently . . .'

'No! No!' Meraud threshed in the bed, her head twisting from side to side in her fury. 'No! I'm *not* having it near me, I swear . . . if you give it to me I'll kill it! Take it away!'

'She's distracted,' said Grainne, staring down at the transformed, hideous, writhing figure on the bed. 'The birth-agonies must have turned her wits . . . Or,' she added, looking closely at me, 'there's more to this than meets the eye – am I right?'

'You are,' I said grimly. 'But now's not the time nor the place to tell you. More to the point, what in God's name are we to do with the baby? For I've no doubt she means what she says.'

'I'll give her some laudanum, clean her and the little girl up, and we'll see if she changes her mind later on when she wakes up,' said the Widow. 'If not, we'll have to find a wet-nurse.' She looked down reflectively at the tiny, unwanted, unloved child, last memento of Jamie's heedless, vivid rush through life. 'Poor little thing . . . what are we going to call you, eh? Name you for your mother?'

'There'll only, I pray God, be one Meraud,' I said bitterly. 'Let's name her for you, you deserve the honour . . .' I paused, realizing with surprise that I had never discovered the Widow's given name. That lady grinned suddenly. 'No, you don't know it, lass, but it ain't a bad name when all's said and done – Eleanor, I was christened, though all my friends call me Nell, and it's served me well enough. Let it serve the babe too.'

Meraud did not change her mind, and so Eleanor Heron, whose sex had cheated her mother of her hopes of Goldhayes, was given into the care of a Bradfield St Clare woman with one babe of her own and an abundance of milk. It took Meraud almost a month to make a full recovery from the strains of that difficult birth: and during the weeks of her convalescence she made it abundantly clear to me that the birth of a daughter did not in the least change her threat to expose Francis and Malise. But somehow, issuing from that chalk-coloured, wraith-like figure dwarfed by the huge bed, her words had lost their former power. The Army had gone now from Essex, the leaders preoccupied with dealing with the perfidious King whose deceit had led to the Royalist rebellions and Scottish invasions, and the prisoners of Colchester long since dispersed to their fates: and the only remaining card Meraud still possessed, I knew if she did not, was her possible exposure of Francis as a fratricide. Malise was safe now, whatever she did, and I could afford to treat her threats lightly. Francis and I were still sundered: but the day of our reunion, as he had foreseen, did not seem so impossibly far away now.

I could not travel to Ashcott, though, for my pregnancy, just as when I had been expecting Kit, made me ill and faint, and moreover this child was so precious to me that I did not want to risk it at all; but Mistress Gooch took the news back to Francis, that he was to become a father, and of Eleanor's birth. She bore also a long letter in which I had given him a detailed account of the events since our parting, now four months ago: and an affirmation of my love for him and my joy at the coming child.

The Widow had promised that she would return soon, but it was only ten days before her indomitable figure, on the bay nag that was the replacement for her old white cob eaten at Colchester, hove ploddingly into sight round the bend in the drive, illuminated by a watery, fitful January sun. She brought the tidings that Francis was no longer at Ashcott: he had, so she had been informed, gone to London in the company of one who, from the description given to her by one of the villagers, could only be Dan Ashley, albeit in civilian dress. And as to why they had gone to London, I had no doubts: for in London, our High and Mighty Sovereign Lord King Charles was on trial for his life.

That trial had a foregone conclusion, and yet, until the moment when the executioner lifted up the dripping royal head and the crowd groaned as if their own life-blood had been spilled, no one really believed that the terrible sentence would actually be carried out. The Lord's anointed ruler, King by Divine Right, had been judicially slain by order of the very human Oliver Cromwell and his officers, and to many it seemed, such was the enormity of the crime, that the end of the world was nigh. Kings in England had been murdered before, killed in battle or furtively done to death in some dark dungeon, but never previously had such a mighty challenge to God been flung down, to do the deed thus openly, with the full ritual panoply of law. I was glad to hear that Black Tom Fairfax dissociated himself completely from this irreversible act of murder: but I also remembered Colchester, and the suffering that more wars and rebellions would bring, and the determination of the King to win back his power by fair means or foul, and could understand the desire of Cromwell and his officers to make an end to His Majesty and his plotting once and for all, and begin their rule of the kingdom unhampered by his intrigues behind their backs.

But I quickly understood, as news from London trickled in its accustomed, unhurried remote way into Goldhayes from the usual variety of sources – letters, carriers, the Jermyns, gossip, rumour – that it would not just be the killing of a King that had drawn Francis and Dan to the capital, hub of England's universe: and also the stronghold of Leveller support. In the Army, Francis had met Levellers, sympathized with them, become one of them and worked for the justice and freedom which they desired for all men – and women, for there were many female Levellers in London – poor as well as rich, peasants and servants as well as gentlemen and merchants. And now, in London, Lilburne and his followers, after their temporary eclipse in the shadow of the King's execution and the purge of Parliament (for what need did the Army officers have of Leveller support, with King and Parliament destroyed and all power in their hands alone?), were stirring again, angry at the 'Grandees' betrayal, not just of themselves but of the people of England. I could well understand Francis's desire to become involved again with those heady, exhilarating radicals and idealists: but feared for him also, because there was not only the strong possibility that one of his erstwhile comrades would recognize him, but also the ever-present danger of imprisonment. Cromwell, knowing he could count on the support of most of the Army, was in no mood to tolerate those who still, so tiresomely, believed in the rights and freedom of the people, and who considered this new government of England by a handful of senior Army officers no more than a military tyranny, as bad as the illegal rule of the King against which the wars had been fought in the first place: new chains for old, as the pamphlets pointed out.

And as my child grew within me, and spring came in obedience to the natural laws which were thought to have been overturned for ever by the execution of the King, so I began, dimly, to perceive that the real tragedy of these times lay not in that death, which then had seemed so significant and was now but a fading ripple on the water, but in the gradual but inevitable failure of the Levellers and their friends to gain their desires. The chances vanished: Cromwell and his cold practical son-in-law Ireton ruled the Army, and therefore the country, and the dream died, illusion's bubble pricked at last by Oliver's pin when a few last intransigent Army Levellers were defeated at Burford in May.

It was but a week or so to the expected day of my baby's birth, and I had long since grown accustomed to the whispers, the gossip behind my back, as my body grew big with the child whose father – though no one could be in any doubt about his identity – I had not married. I did not care about the wagging tongues: what I found hardest to bear was the open disapproval of Francis for, as they all thought, deserting me so callously to evade his responsibilities. And still I could not tell them the truth, still I had to bring out all the unconvincing explanations for his disappearance, knowing that if I or Meraud disclosed the real reason, he would be doubly reviled.

There was, too, the ever-present problem of Kit. Gradually, during the months immediately after Francis's departure, I had won him back to me, weaning him away from Meraud's malign influence by the simple expedient of devoting all my waking hours to him, and totally excluding her: and her daughter's birth, with its attendant traumas, made my strategy easy to carry out. Mab was a great help, too, and soon grew used to regarding Kit as her especial property, sleeping on his bed and clinging as close to his heels as she had once done to mine. By March, our combined affection had made Kit mine again, secure, quieter, more confident by far in himself and in me, the terrible tantrums and clashes of will a thing of the past – almost, said the Widow to me on more than one occasion, like a civilized member of the human race. And I had a tiny lute made for him, and taught him his letters and the notes of the harpsichord, and discovered what I had long suspected, that my son was an infant musician.

Having once regained his trust, and with Meraud a temporary invalid, it was easier than I had feared, to introduce Francis into our conversations – 'This is a piece I learned from Francis.' 'Francis told me this riddle once.' 'I used to sing this with Francis,' – so that gradually he became accustomed to the name, and to the idea that this man, and music, and his mother were all inextricably linked. Although he became strangely silent when I first told him that shortly he would have a little brother or sister, he seemed to accept the idea after a day or two, and it was one of his chief delights to rest his head against my belly, and feel and hear the unborn child within.

At last, I had plucked up my courage, and told Grainne a somewhat edited version of the truth, leaving out entirely Meraud's threat to Malise. To my relief, she accepted my story, and it was very good to know that, apart from the Widow and myself, at least one other person at Goldhayes knew what had really happened, and could still believe in Francis's fidelity. I needed that support: as the expected time for our baby's birth grew nearer, and there was still no word from him, I began, despite my hope and trust, to feel a little gnawing of doubt, the first pangs of anxiety. Surely he had not become so involved in politics again as to forget me and his child?

But of course he did not know about the baby, and I, not having any idea of his whereabouts, could not tell him. The Widow had left a message with one of the more reliable Ashcott villagers, and a more detailed letter for Francis's enlightenment, but unless he returned there he would not have it: or he might have sent a letter that had gone astray, or even been 'lost' into some sinister Government spy network – Rebecca Jermyn had had letters from her husband abroad intercepted. And it began to seem, as the year advanced and Lilburne and his friends fell deeper and deeper into trouble, that a spy for Cromwell might very well take an interest in the correspondence of a Leveller sympathizer, however domestic his letters might be. Even now, I thought, as rumours of Lilburne's imprisonment filtered through to our quiet little backwater, Francis might also be languishing in jail: and tidings of the affray at Burford only served to increase my worries.

And then, one afternoon an hour or so after dinner, Richard Trevelyan fell suddenly and inexplicably ill.

It began, not particularly seriously, as a small pain in his belly: which within hours had erupted into agonizing griping spasms that sent him gasping, vomiting and doubled-up to his bed, an anxious Mary, for once jolted out of her usual smug complacency, at his side. The prescribed remedies, purges and cordials and disgusting compound mixtures made to the recipes of Mary and her cronies, were poured down his throat, and more or less instantly returned. Dr Despotine, who had attended

Herons and Sewells in their illnesses for close on forty years, was now too old and infirm to be called out, but he sent his young assistant to Richard's bedside with a fresh consignment of medicines. But all to no avail. There seemed to be nothing that anyone could do: the pains crescendoed to a dreadful climax, at which, mercifully, he relapsed into unconsciousness.

Bewildered, appalled, we stared at the grey, sweaty, tortured travesty of a man who, only a few hours before, had been his usual unruffled, calm self, talking to John Sewell at dinner. In astonishment, I beheld tears on Mary's plump, rouged cheeks. Never before had I seen her weep in all the years of my acquaintance with her, for nothing had ever seemed to touch this shallow, self-absorbed, distant woman: and now, at the sight of her unaccustomed grief, my own sorrow came to the surface. For despite my mistrust of him, I had come to like Richard Trevelyan: and I would wish such pain on no one – save his niece.

But Meraud, standing pale and shadowy by the bed, exhibited as yet no such grief, only, in the white, pure oval of her face, a disbelieving anger and terror. 'Uncle Richard!' she cried, as he sank back fainting against the pillows. The doctor felt swiftly for the pulse and was quick to reassure her. 'Do not fear, Mistress, he's naught but fainted, and that is surely God's mercy. Now, I recommend that he be bled, may we have the bowl, Mistress Gooch?'

All that night, the doctor and his helpers – myself, Meraud, Mary and the Widow – kept watch by Richard Trevelyan's bed, and did what we could to ease the desperate pains which were too strong to allow him the blessed relief of unconsciousness for long. It was only a short time before Mary broke down altogether, and had to be led weeping from the room by her maid, and comforted by her daughter. For the rest of us, as our sense of helplessness grew, there was no such respite: only a feeling of disbelief at this so hideously sudden sickness that not even the good Dr Wright's knowledge and experience seemed to be able to cure, or even to alleviate, for Richard could not keep down the laudanum we gave him. As morning came fever also made its appearance, and despite the bleeding, the remedies, the leeches, it would not subside: and we all recognized defeat.

Both Mistress Gooch and Dr Wright – who had struck up a brisk, cordially professional friendship at first sight – had seen sickness of this type before. The Widow whispered to me, as I sat unhappily by the sick man's bed, that it invariably, in her experience, ended in death. 'And if I were you, lass, I'd get you gone to bed before you harm that child: it'll do you or it no good to sit around like this, and there's nothing you can do for him: I don't reckon there's nobody can do anything for him now, save pray for a speedy end to his suffering.'

'I can't go, if he's going to die,' I muttered, exhaustion making me stupidly obstinate. The Widow patted my arm. 'Well, he's got a few hours to go yet, poor man. Now for God's sake, lass, go and get some sleep – your Francis won't thank you if you harm your baby now.'

I saw sense at last and dragged myself to my bed, where not even the arrival of Kit and Mab at their usual waking time could do more than half-rouse me from slumber. In the end I was woken properly, late in the afternoon, by a tearful Lucy. 'Oh Thomazine, come . . . come quickly, Richard . . . Richard, he's dying, Dr Wright says!'

I flung my night-rail around my swollen body and made my ungainly way, with as much haste as I could, yawning to Richard's chamber. The late, red-tinged sunlight streamed through the windows of the Gallery, giving its dearly familiar shapes and outlines a ruddy deceptive cheerfulness: save for the servants standing around the anteroom door in hushed, respectful groups, some of the younger, more impressionable ones wiping away the tears. As Lucy and I came to the door, Rose emerged with an unwontedly solemn Hugh in tow. She blew her nose vigorously, curtsied, and hurried the little boy away. His curious, anxious questions, in that serious deep voice, carried back along the Gallery towards us. 'But Rose, *why* is my father ill? *Why* did Dr Davis say he was going away?'

With the sick feeling of helplessness, apprehension and fear I usually experienced at death-bed scenes, I joined the rest of the family as they stood around the bed to make their last respects and bid farewell to Richard Trevelyan, who had tried so hard, and failed at the last, to make Goldhayes his own. There was Mary, her face puffy and blotched with grief, supported by her devoted maid, Dorothy: John Sewell, serious, stout and now quite white-haired, with Malise and Grainne beside him: Dr Davis, shrivelled like an old leaf, praying in the loud toneless voice of the hard-of-hearing: Mistress Gooch, with Dr Wright, easing the dying man's last moments, bathing his brow, giving him water: Lucy snivelling miserably by my side. And last of all, my eyes lighted upon Meraud, her fierce little face staring into her uncle's sunken bloodshot tortured eyes as hungrily as if she were begging the world from him. Still no sorrow showed upon her face, and I wondered if all her vaunted feeling for the man who had endeared himself to her in her childhood by being pleasant and kind to her, was genuine at all.

Richard was gasping for breath, trying to say something. His hand groped outwards and Mary, sitting by the bedside, took it and leaned over him. He muttered something, and smiled at her weakly: and so, on a last rushing, rattling exhalation of breath, Richard Trevelyan died.

For a moment, no one around the bed moved, and then Mary quietly began to weep. Lucy, her own tears flowing abundantly once more, went swiftly to comfort her, and mother and daughter, united as never before by their sorrow, clung together. The chaplain began to pray again, more quietly, as Dr Wright, shaking his head resignedly, leaned over and closed the dead man's eyes. And Meraud, her white face blazing with a sudden, terrifying rage, cried, 'He can't be dead! Not so soon! Only yesterday . . . he was all right yesterday! What kills someone so quick, that way, unless it was poison? Somebody poisoned him!'

Dr Wright, astonished, started to speak: other voices drowned him. 'She's distracted!' Grainne exclaimed. The Widow snorted with disbelief. 'Poison? That was no poison, girl. I've seen men die of such a griping of the guts many a time before. And anyway, who do you think poisoned him, for God's sake? Now be quiet, it isn't seemly—'

'Who poisoned him? Why, *she* did, of course!' Meraud cried, and her shaking, pointing finger stabbed straight at me.

Appalled, I could do nothing for a moment save stare at her in horrified incomprehension. The Widow grasped Meraud's shoulder. 'This is not the time or place, your uncle not two minutes dead, for Christ's sake get a grip on yourself!' But Meraud shook her off and advanced on me, and my bewilderment changed to a great and suddenly overwhelming anger as she spoke again. 'You did it, you hated him, and me, you always have, *you* poisoned him!'

It was not, as the Widow had said, the time or place for such a confrontation, but she had started this and as all my pent-up long-harboured hatred erupted, I knew I would finish it. 'Poison Richard? You're mad, your wits are overturned, if I were going to poison anyone it would be you – for the only venom here is in your mind, and Francis and I are the ones to suffer for your spite and self-seeking and greed.' I glanced round, seeing all the appalled, horrified faces staring at us, and added, 'And I'm sick of pretending, of suffering your lies and taunts, and whatever the consequences, I'm going to tell everyone, here and now, what you did and why.'

'Careful, lass,' said the Widow softly. 'Oh, be careful.' But I was beyond subterfuge now: the truth will out, the saying went, and out I was going to drag it,

unsavoury and sickening as it was, into the light for all
to see: no more lies, however much it might hurt me,
for only this way could Meraud be defeated. I was about
to strip her of her power, and her frozen face showed
that she was well aware of the possibilities. I said,
pitching my words low and clear, 'This sweet, demure
girl came to me in the garden, on the last day of August,
and told me that unless Francis instantly left Goldhayes
for ever, without me, she would betray him and Malise
and Dan to the Roundheads. And that would be as good
as murder, wouldn't it, so Francis had to go. That's why
he left me: he didn't desert me willingly, he went because
she wanted Goldhayes for her child and he was all that
stood in her way – until the child turned out to be a
girl, that's why Jamie's daughter is still being nursed in
Bradfield St Clare, because her mother didn't want her,
she wasn't a boy!'

'Is all this true?' John demanded, astonishment and
disgust plain in his voice. Meraud glanced round at him,
her expression hunted, cornered, and licked her lips.
'More to the point,' he added, 'why didn't you tell us,
Thomazine? We'd have helped you, done suffen . . . why
i' the maim o' the flesh didn't you *tell* us?'

Meraud's mouth opened, to play her last card, from
spite or vengeance for it would do her no good now:
everyone's illusions about her were too thoroughly
blasted in pieces ever to be reassembled. I forestalled
her quickly. 'Why didn't I say? Well, for one thing, my
silence, and Mistress Gooch's, was part of the bargain.
For the other, this may be painful to all of you but it is
true, and it is something for which Francis feels most
bitter remorse. He was the Roundhead who killed Jamie,
by accident in the dark. And Meraud overheard him
telling me, and used it as a weapon for blackmail. If I'd
spoken of her threats, she'd have told all of you that
Francis murdered his brother in cold blood.'

'He's a murderer!' Meraud screeched, her face
contorted and terrifying in its hate. 'He murdered Jamie
– I should have made sure he was captured – shooting's

too good for him after what he did – I should have informed on them anyway!'

'I think you've said enough,' John told her, coming forward. 'Enough to know, Mistress Meraud, that you're none of us and we want none of you, and the sooner you're gone from here the better we'll all like it, I reckon. So you'd best start making plans, because I reckon I speak for all of us when I say I coon't stand the sight of your poisonous little face no longer. Betraying and blackmailing your own kin in't what we do in Suffolk, maw, so do you go back to they furrin parts where you belong.'

Meraud stared round all the faces, grey and strained with shock and grief and horror, and saw in none of them any sympathy or pity or approval: and with an exclamation, or a sob, of fury or terror, she whipped round and ran from the chamber. We listened in utter silence to her frantic footsteps dwindling and diminishing into the distance: and then all the anger and tension drained abruptly from me and I found, suddenly, that I could not stand. Afraid, I groped for a chair, bed-post, anything to support me: failed, and fell. And the first pains struck, and I knew that a crisis, a rush of emotion, would bring on the birth of this baby, just as that letter from my great-aunt had accelerated the birth of Kit.

But Kit's birth had been easy, an early child slipping swiftly into the world. This was not.

I had thought I could cope with any pain, mental or physical, but I was not prepared for this: the iron clawing fist within me, opening and closing, the contractions which seemed like to tear my slight body apart, the exhaustion which, after a night spent sleepless and pain-racked in labour, overwhelmed me so that I could no longer help my baby's struggles to be born. A terrible fear filled my heart and soul, that after all this, both I and the precious, so dearly wanted child would die, and Francis, all unknowing, would be doubly bereft.

And my consciousness narrowed to the sphere of my body and its pain, and I was barely aware of Mistress Gooch or Dr Wright as they tried to help me. But all the time Grainne was with me, holding my hands, encouraging, smiling, cool and calm, wiping away the tears of pain: but there was nothing any of them seemed able to do. I was vaguely aware that it was daylight again, that I must have been twelve hours and more in labour, I was beyond counting: but I could make the effort no longer. All I desired now was rest, and peace: the will to fight seemed to be slipping away into darkness. I closed my eyes, feeling my mind detached, floating. Grainne's hands shook me, slapped my face, urgently, insistent. 'Thomazine! Come on, you're nearly there, don't give up now, for God's sake – *fight!* You are *not* going to give up, do you hear me, you are *not* going to die, you're going to have Francis's baby, and you're going to live, because soon he'll come back for you. Now *fight!*'

I came back with reluctance from the warm comforting peaceful dark. Fighting meant pain, and effort, and struggle: after the night, it was too difficult. 'I can't,' I muttered. 'Grainne, I can't.'

But she did not give up, and in the end it was easier for me to do what she said, and fight for myself and the baby, because Francis would need us, than to resist her uncharacteristic bullying: a tactic in which the Widow joined with her usual gusto. 'Come on, lass, not long to go, now push!'

Just when it seemed as if I could go on no longer, and would have to surrender after all to the darkness, the baby was born. Gasping with pain and strife, totally exhausted, I closed my eyes, unable to make any kind of effort any more, and with a remote feeling of relief heard the necessary ritual slap, followed by an anguished wailing. 'Nothing wrong with her lungs,' said Mistress Gooch approvingly, and I felt her nudge. 'There you are, lass, take a look if you can – a lovely little girl.'

The sight of my daughter and Francis's, an unappealing slippery red creature screaming her heart out at this new cold limitless world, was the last thing I remembered with any clarity, that terrible day: or indeed for several days after that, for I became very ill from the strains and exhaustion of the birth, and for a while, so the Widow cheerfully told me later, my life was despaired of. But the weakness and fever lessened at last, and there came a day when I could think and speak again, and had control of myself, although as weak as the proverbial kitten, or weaker. And Mistress Gooch rose from her place by the bedside and went over to a corner of the chamber beyond my sight, and came back with a voluminously wrapped bundle that squirmed and gurgled in sleepy protest. 'Here she is, your little one, we've fed her for you and kept her safe. Dear little thing she is too, much prettier than the last time you saw her!'

I held my daughter in my arms, as I had once held Kit, and with the same feeling of wonder and awe. But this child was different, would always be different, for Kit's father I had hated and despised, and my daughter's father was the man I loved so dearly. Too early to see the print of Francis in her face, such as it was, but she was pale-skinned, mistily blue-eyed, and the few wisps of hair on her head were as fair as ash. I touched her mouth with my finger, and she sucked it automatically, and Mistress Gooch, smiling, unlaced my nightgown for me and held the baby to my breast.

I did not want to let her go when she had finished, but lay, propped on my pillows, studying my daughter – a love-child indeed, so dearly longed-for, and loved, child of delight and joy and truth.

'We didn't have her baptized till you was better, we didn't know what you wanted her called,' said Mistress Gooch. 'Got any thoughts on that yet? Or is it too soon?'

I had got thoughts, and I smiled up at her. 'Oh, yes, I have a name for her, and it's not one any of our family have borne before, but it's lovely all the same. I shall call her Alethea: for in Greek, it means "Truth".'

*

I had so many visitors that day, that in the end Mistress Gooch, stalwart as ever, had to turn them out and bar the door, for she feared I would relapse. But before she did, I learned from Grainne what had happened to Meraud.

'She's gone,' said the Irish girl, my dear friend. 'She went the day Alethea was born, John and Malise made sure of that. Mary was the only one who might have put in a good word for her, but she's been prostrate with grief over Richard – I didn't know she had so much love in her,' Grainne added drily: she and Mary had always enjoyed at best an armed neutrality between them. 'And all the fight had gone from Meraud, she seemed numb, uncaring almost, and just let herself be bullied by John. I could almost have found it in me to be sorry for her, for she's lost pretty well everything now.'

'She'll always survive, that one,' I said. 'She's a winner born – in the end she'll always come through, don't waste any of your pity on her. Where has she gone?'

'I hope you don't mind,' Grainne said slowly, 'but I suggested that Malise take her to Pennyfarthing Street. From there she may gather herself and make plans . . . And God help me, I also reminded her that there was still one person on this earth who cherished love and affection for her: and told her to make the best of him, for she would get no more of any Heron, or Sewell.'

'Poor Charles,' I said. 'He'll marry her, I don't doubt, and I pray she will prove as faithful and loving towards him as he doubtless will to her. If she is wise, she will be content with him and all his sisters and that little plain old manor-house he used to tell us about, and put up with his terrible jokes and his tobacco and his endless stories of the war . . . and be content for once with what she has. *If* she is wise.'

'I hope for Charles's sake that she has learned something of how to deal fairly with her fellow-mortals,' Grainne said. 'But one thing gives me leave to doubt that – for she's left Eleanor behind.'

That poor rejected baby, not six months old, had enjoyed the love of neither parent. 'We must bring her back to Goldhayes,' I said. 'Perhaps I can look after her here, as well as my own two . . . and then Alethea would have a sister, and Eleanor some love to make up for all she has never known . . . would Mary like that, do you think? Her first grandchild?'

'She's in no state to like or dislike,' said Grainne. 'Do what you think is right – only never look for Meraud in Eleanor, for too often that sort of thing fulfils its own prophecy. And may all your children, adopted or true, prove as dear and worthwhile as mine have been to me.' She smiled into my eyes, and took my hand in hers. 'Malise has gone with her, as I said, to escort her and the maid – I gave Betty into her service, they've always accorded well – and when he's left them safe at Pennyfarthing Street, he will go on to Ashcott, and if Francis is not there yet, I told him to travel to London and seek him out there. It should not be too difficult to find Dan, and Dan will know where Francis is, if he is not with him. So all you have to do is wait, and hope, and grow strong again . . . for at last, we are free of Trevelyans.'

The bees hummed soothingly as they went about their business in the walled garden, buzzing blunderingly, pollen-laden, in amongst the heavy-scented roses. Such a beautiful day as this was not one for skulking indoors, even though it was only three weeks since my daughter's birth: and so I had taken her, and Eleanor, and a book and some sewing, into the garden with me and sat now on the chamomile lawn, where once Richard Trevelyan had spoken of the rumours of war to us, eight years ago and more, dreaming in the dappled shade under the four ancient apple trees. My mind wandered drowsily over those eight years; of the deaths we had suffered, Henry Sewell, Edward, Jamie, Grainne's little daughter Hester, and of course Richard: of those who had come into our lives to influence their course, for good or for ill, Charles and the Widow, Malise and Dan Ashley, and those who had not died but left us, like Simon and Nan, or Tom Sewell, last heard of in Germany.

But above all, I thought of the children, the new generation who would people Goldhayes with fun and laughter, and weave their own loves and intrigues, when we, their elders, were middle-aged or in our graves. What would be the fate of Jasper, so intelligent and enthusiastic and full of bright promise? Or his sensible, practical, maternal little sister, rooted in generations of Suffolk yeomen, with no visible trace in her of her mother's fey Irish blood, prominent already in Jasper? What would become of Kit, whose childhood up until now had been a confusing nightmare of spoiling and loss, bewilderment and hatred and love? Or the cheerful, endearing Hugh, fatherless and landless, and Eleanor, whose father was also dead, and whose mother had rejected her? What would Alethea, child of love and truth, inherit from her parents, of good or ill?

I glanced at the two babies lying beside me in a nest of linen: Eleanor awake, gurgling and snuffling peacefully, her blue eyes staring fascinated at the flickering pattern of leaves weaving and dancing above her head in the soft breeze, a child who somehow did not give the promise of inheriting her mother's stunning, ethereal beauty. And Alethea asleep, as she usually was, already growing and thriving, her hair silky, ashen wisps and her eyes already starting to change their colour to her father's shadowy green. My feeling for her was something I had had to hide from Kit, whose capacity for jealousy had already been abundantly displayed: he must never know that this child inspired in me a love and devotion I gave to no one else, save to her father, must never realize the rushing strength of my emotions when I beheld her perfect, fragile smallness. Hard to hide such overwhelming affection: but for Kit's sake, and the baby's, it had be done. Already I could sense the ambiguity of his reaction to her: although fascinated by her tiny size, her miniature hands and face and feet, since her birth he had returned somewhat to his old clinging ways, and a peaceful moment like this, alone with the babies, was difficult to obtain without much firmness or cunning. Today the latter had sufficed, and Kit, Hugh and Jasper were out with their ponies under John Sewell's grandfatherly eye: and so for once I had some peace and quiet.

Not for long, though. Through my dreamy contentment I heard, distantly, feet on gravel, and voices. It took a little time for the significance of those voices to filter into my sun-dazed mind, and by then they had ceased, and there was only one set of footsteps, coming steadily nearer. The voices had been male, I realized suddenly: but save for John, and the servants, there were no men left at Goldhayes.

The footsteps ceased: a shadow lay across my lap. I looked up, creasing my eyes against the sun: and Francis knelt before me, smiling, with something in his hands which he laid in mine, and pulled the silken wrappings from around it.

It was long, and slender, and sweetly curved and twisted, and come from the forests of Muscovy, or the deserts of Africa, or the mountains of Hy Brasil: wherever there might be Unicorns. And it possessed for both of us its own light, its own beauty, and its own significance: not just a Unicorn's horn, proof against poison, but a symbol of love and hope and delight: a link with the children we had been, and the children we would make, and the dreams and imaginations that made us what we were, and joined us together, in a marriage of true minds that no longer, after eight years of hope and tragedy and parting, admitted any impediments. And there was no need of words, for we both knew that now our life was truly beginning.

'A surprise for you,' he said, when our lips at last had separated, and we knelt together, awkwardly, our arms around each other as if we were afraid to let go again. 'Did I not tell you, once, that I would buy you a Unicorn's horn, for your chamber when we are wed? Here is your bridal-gift, my dear, dear lady, and the marriage licence is in my saddle-bag: and nothing more will part us, ever again.'

'I have a marriage-gift for you, too,' I said. 'Did Malise not tell you?' I saw from his enquiring expression that he did not know: and I slipped gently from his arms, and brought him Alethea.

A man less reserved might have laughed, or wept, or shouted for joy: Francis only looked, but his soul stood naked in his eyes, and wondered. 'Her name is Alethea,' I said, seeing he could not trust himself to speak, 'and she is three weeks old, and a day, and two hours.'

'And yours, and mine: a child of dreams and truth and Unicorns, and a love-child in the best sense of the word: you named her well,' said Francis at last, very softly. 'And now we are complete and our future is here: what more can we ever ask for?'

Only a wedding: a double wedding, for Dan had come with Malise and Francis to Goldhayes, having at last managed to arrange for Francis's release from the prison where he had been incarcerated for some months, because of his Leveller activities in London: and asked Mary, with his grave, dry diffidence, for her daughter's hand in marriage. And Mary had roused, a little, from her torpor of grief, and made at least a show of gladness. So Lucy and I entered the church together, like sisters, and Kit, shining and proud, bearing the bowl before us, seemed to accept cheerfully the fact that his mother was to be married. And Dan and Francis, two very different and dearly loved figures, turned to greet us at the altar.

When our vows had been made, and promises spoken, we walked down the aisle of the little dim church, hand in hand, with all our friends around us, and out into the brilliant, blinding sunshine of a June morning, startling in light and heat and colour. And to salute us from above, invisible in the deep fathomless cloud-free blue of the summer sky, poured the joyous torrent of a skylark's song.

'Listen!' said Francis, pausing, tilting back his head

to search for the singer: and the shining sun touched all the fine, delicate outlines of his fallen-angel, ironic face with silver fire, and my heart caught in my throat for love of him. 'There is our wedding music: the trumpets of heaven are sounding in our honour, lady, for we are each other's at last, for all time to come.'

And smiling, he put his arm about me, and the other around his sister, and together we walked down the path through the churchyard, with all our dear friends behind us: and before us lay Goldhayes, and the life that we would make there, stretching out before us in joy and fulfilment at last: and Alethea.

Fiction

☐	**Castle Raven**	Laura Black	£1.75p
☐	**Options**	Freda Bright	£1.50p
☐	**Dupe**	Liza Cody	£1.25p
☐	**Chances**	Jackie Collins	£2.50p
☐	**Brain**	Robin Cook	£1.75p
☐	**The Entity**	Frank De Felitta	£1.95p
☐	**The Dead of Jericho**	Colin Dexter	£1.50p
☐	**Whip Hand**	Dick Francis	£1.75p
☐	**Secrets**	Unity Hall	£1.75p
☐	**Solo**	Jack Higgins	£1.75p
☐	**The Rich are Different**	Susan Howatch	£2.95p
☐	**The Master Sniper**	Stephen Hunter	£1.50p
☐	**Moviola**	Garson Kanin	£1.50p
☐	**Smiley's People**	John le Carré	£1.95p
☐	**The Master Mariner**		
	Book 1: Running Proud	Nicholas Montsarrat	£1.50p
☐	**Platinum Logic**	Tony Parsons	£1.75p
☐	**Fools Die**	Mario Puzo	£1.95p
☐	**The Boys in the Mailroom**	Iris Rainer	£1.50p
☐	**The Throwback**	Tom Sharpe	£1.75p
☐	**Wild Justice**	Wilbur Smith	£1.95p
☐	**That Old Gang of Mine**	Leslie Thomas	£1.50p
☐	**Caldo Largo**	Earl Thompson	£1.75p
☐	**Ben Retallick**	E. V. Thompson	£1.75p

All these books are available at your local bookshop or newsagent, or
can be ordered direct from the publisher. Indicate the number of copies
required and fill in the form below   10

....

Name..
(Block letters please)

Address..

_____

Send to CS Department, Pan Books Ltd, PO Box 40, Basingstoke, Hants
Please enclose remittance to the value of the cover price plus:
35p for the first book plus 15p per copy for each additional book ordered
to a maximum charge of £1.25 to cover postage and packing
Applicable only in the UK

While every effort is made to keep prices low, it is sometimes
necessary to increase prices at short notice. Pan Books reserve
the right to show on covers and charge new retail prices which
may differ from those advertised in the text or elsewhere